Kate Furnivall was born in Wales, has worked in publishing and TV advertising and now lives by the sea in Devon with her husband, with whom she has two sons. This is her sixth novel.

Visit Kate's website at www.katefurnivall.com

KATE FURNIVALL

Shadows on the Nile

Sphere
An imprint of
Little, Brown Book Group
100 Victoria Embankment
London EC4Y 0DY

An Hachette UK Company
www.hachette.co.uk

www.littlebrown.co.uk

SPHERE

First published in Great Britain in 2012 by Sphere
This paperback edition published in 2013 by Sphere

A CIP catalogue record for this book
is available from the British Library.

ISBN 978-0-7515-4337-7

Typeset in Baskerville by M Rules
Printed and bound in Great Britain by
Clays Ltd, St Ives plc

To Lilli
with all my love

Acknowledgements

A huge thank you to Catherine Burke and all at Little, Brown for their brilliance and for their enthusiasm for this book at every stage. They are a dazzling team. Particular thanks to Thalia Proctor for her sharp eyes on the copyedit.

To Teresa Chris for skilfully being my agent, a force of nature and my friend all at the same time – thank you.

Research trips are always fascinating, but I owe very special thanks to Richard and Anne Sharam for making my research journey through Egypt not only immensely valuable, but unforgettable fun.

My gratitude to Aml Demos for showing me her country and to Wendy Clark for delving into 1932.

Many thanks to Marian Churchward for deciphering my scribble and for lending me her name.

Warm thanks also to Anneli and Horst Menke for providing their beautiful garden for me to write in when I needed it.

Finally, my love and thanks to Norman for his help and support every sandy step of the way.

1

England 1912

Night noises are the worst. They are the ones that come at you out of the darkness and seize you by the throat. They are the ones that slither under the door of your bedroom.

Stop it. Don't do that. Jessica rapped her knuckles against her forehead.

Don't. You're too old to be frightened by nothing. Too grown up. Seven years and eight months. Not like little Georgie, her younger brother, who was tucked away by her parents in a tiny bedroom at the far end of the corridor. Like something dirty.

Still the noises came at her. Voices soft and secretive. A whisper cut short. Her mother's quick and urgent footsteps on the landing. Other sounds that didn't belong, that crept like thieves in the shadows. Jessica didn't like the dark, and she could never understand how the air could become so solid at night or why its weight was sometimes so heavy on her chest that she had to pummel her lungs to make them work. She drew her knees up to her chin and wrapped her arms around her shins, hugging her winceyette nightdress – the one with blue ribbons – tight against her skin. Even under her eiderdown she was cold.

Suddenly it came again, the sound that had woken her, a whimpering that made the blonde hairs rise on the back of her neck. She threw off the eiderdown and leapt out of bed. Her heart was juddering against her bony ribs as she pushed her way through the darkness, parting it with her hands like a curtain until she reached her bedroom door. She gripped its brass knob and quickly turned it. Nothing happened. Her fingers tried again. Nothing. It was locked. Jessica's skin crawled, the way it did when a spider dropped on her arm.

Why would her father lock her in?

Why would her mother agree?

Fear, sharp and brittle, poked at her chest. She crouched on the floor and wriggled onto her side on the cold linoleum until her eye was pressed to the ribbon of light between door and floor, but she could make out nothing except a blur of carpet on the other side. Again the whimper fluttered along the landing, followed by a high-pitched frightened squeal. Rage seized her and she leapt to her feet, pounding her fist on the door, shaking it on its hinges.

'Georgie!' she screamed.

Abruptly the light on the landing flicked off. Silence, thick and oily, flooded the house.

'Georgie!' Jessica shrieked. 'Georgie!'

She banged on the wooden panels of the door.

'Let me out!'

Nothing but silence.

'Mummy!'

Nothing but darkness.

She held her breath, listening so hard her ears hurt. Suddenly she heard a distant click. It was the front door closing.

Georgie liked the park. He liked to stand next to the big round pond, the one with the fountain and the stone lion in the centre. Around it the railing was a frill of knee-high metal loops to keep children and dogs from falling in. Water lily pads spread out like green stepping stones and, if they were lucky, a dragonfly would dart in and out of them, bright as a rainbow.

Georgie would gaze silently for hours at the big slippery shapes of the goldfish that moved like ghosts through the water. His favourite was Watson, the one with the silver stripe down its back, but there were Watson's friends as well: Farintosh, Armitage and Hatherley. The smallest one with the bite out of its dorsal fin was Mrs Hudson. Jessica had let Georgie name them all.

When he watched them, he calmed down. That's what had happened today. She had stood beside him, not holding his hand exactly, but her fingers close to his at his side, and he had started humming. She knew then that he was happy. Happy in a way he couldn't be in the house with people too close to him. But then Mummy had spoilt it.

'Come along, children, time to play ball.'

'Not today, thank you, Mummy,' Jessica said politely.

Her mother frowned and sat down on the bench to read her magazine but her lips were tight and her ankles kept crossing and uncrossing. When she could stand no more, she said, 'It's getting late, time to go home.'

Georgie shook his head, his blond curls defiant.

'For heaven's sake, George,' his mother snapped, exasperated. 'Enough staring like an idiot at fish all day. You're five years old and should know better.'

Jessica grew nervous. She murmured to Georgie that Watson wanted to be alone now. She tried to coax her brother away, gently, one step at a time, but as always Mummy lost patience and seized his wrist to drag him from the railing.

Don't touch him. He doesn't like to be t—

Georgie had started to scream. Not like other children scream. He screamed as if he was dying, as if someone had taken an axe to him and sliced him right down the middle.

Jessica thought about it now, as she lay jammed against the door, clutching the blue ribbon of her nightdress. She blinked fiercely on

3

the floor in the darkness of her room, remembering her mother's white lips. It was Georgie's scream in the park that had slithered under her door and was now writhing inside her head.

The morning sun prodded her awake. She lifted her head from the hard floor and regarded the door with hostility. She scrambled to her feet, cold and shaky, and there was a greyness inside her head, like dust behind her eyes. It was without much hope that she grasped the knob and turned it. To her surprise the door opened easily, just as the grandfather clock in the hall downstairs struck eight. For a moment she panicked, because every morning she always got to Georgie first, to wake him and persuade him to wash and dress. Before Mummy.

She ran on tiptoe down the corridor to the door at the end and held her breath as she gently eased it open. She didn't know what she expected to find, but her young mind was certain it would be something bad, something chaotic, something that would hurt her for the rest of her life. But a huge smile of relief nudged the fear from her face because everything was absolutely normal.

Her blue eyes grew round with pleasure as she inspected the small bedroom with its dark green curtains, its chest of drawers stacked high with books, the never-used cricket bat leaning against the wall. It was a gift from their father to push Georgie into a sport he hated. To be honest, Georgie hated all sports without exception, but to please her father Jessica had taught him to catch and throw a ball. It had taken infinite patience.

Nothing had changed. In the narrow bed lay Georgie. He was still asleep, his face buried in his pillow, but his glorious golden curls shone with life and one leg was thrown out from under his quilt. Jessica noticed he was wearing his red tartan pyjamas and she felt a tiny thorn of alarm prick at her throat. She knew that last night she had put him in his favourite blue ones. Georgie adored blue. Whenever he wore blue, he was better. Jessica had tried to explain this to her mother but she had said, 'What nonsense!' and bought him a red coat. Red was the worst, the very worst colour. He was impossible in red.

4

'Georgie,' she said softly. 'It's me.'

He murmured into the pillow.

She approached the bed. With a laugh she tugged at his quilt but was careful not to touch him. 'Wake up, sleepyhead.'

He turned to her and smiled.

It wasn't Georgie.

'Who are you?' Jessica demanded.

'I'm Timothy.'

'You're not Georgie! Get out! Get out of his bed.'

She took hold of the front of his pyjamas – of *Georgie*'s pyjamas – and yanked this impostor out of her brother's bed. She shook him hard, her face furious. What did she care if this small boy cried? Or if his stupid shoulders trembled? Still gripping the pyjamas in her fists, she thrust her face right down to his.

'Where . . .'

She shook him.

'Is . . .'

She almost lifted him off his bare feet.

' . . . Georgie? What have you done with my brother? Where have you come from?'

His blue eyes were swimming with tears but they glared at her defiantly. 'I am Timothy.' His small hand pointed at the bed. 'That's my bed. I live here.'

'No, you don't,' Jessica shouted in his face.

Her own hands were shaking, her mouth so dry that words stuck to her tongue. But he nodded, his teeth clamped on his trembling lip. He nodded and nodded at her.

'Who are you?' she yelled at him.

'I am your new brother.'

His words were merciless. They reverberated in Jessica's ears as she flew downstairs and burst into the kitchen. Her mother was seated at the table with a cup of tea in front of her, spooning sugar into it. She never took sugar in tea. Her face looked grey and slack, and she was wearing the same fawn dress as yesterday. Usually her appearance was elegant and crisp and she was always nagging her daughter to be tidier or to brush her hair more, but today she had the unkempt appearance of Mrs Rushton – their cleaning lady who came on Mondays – and it dawned on Jessica that maybe her mother hadn't been to bed.

She recalled the footsteps on the landing, the furtive whispers, and suddenly she knew what they'd done. The thought swelled, terrifying, in her head and she sucked in her breath.

'Where is he? What have you done with him?' she demanded.

Her mother looked at her oddly. There was anger around her mouth and Jessica felt the weight of her scrutiny.

'Jessica, don't make trouble.'

'Where have you sent him?'

Don't shout, don't shout at Mummy or . . . She didn't let herself think of what came after the *or*.

She made her voice small. 'Where is Georgie?'

'He's gone. You have a new brother now called Timothy. I want you to love him just as much as . . . ' A pause. Her mother's slender fingers wrapped around the cup for warmth. ' . . . as much as your father and I will.'

No, Jessica wanted to shout across the kitchen but she hid the word behind her lips. 'Where did you find him?'

'We didn't *find* him. We chose Timothy from among many other children in an orphanage.'

'Where is *my* Georgie?'

'He's not *your* Georgie. He's gone. We will never speak of him again.'

'No!' This time the word escaped. Jessica gripped the back of the wooden chair in front of her to stop her hands clawing at her mother's face. 'No, Mummy, please, please. Bring him back.' Tears were flowing down her cheeks and she was ashamed of them because she knew her mother despised what she called histrionics. 'I'll look after him better, Mummy. I'll teach him to behave, please, please, please . . . ' Her voice was beseeching.

She saw her mother look away.

'Mummy, I promise I can make Georgie stop annoying you so much and—'

'Stop it, Jessica.'

'But I love him. And he loves me. He needs me to . . .'

Her mother's beautiful blue eyes turned on her, flat and weary, dulled by sadness. 'Don't fool yourself, Jessica.' She shook her head. 'That boy is incapable of love.'

'No, no, when I read him stories, he loves me, I know he does.'

'He's sick. Sick in the head.'

'No!'

'Yes. He's gone to a place where he will be properly cared for by people who know what's best for him. He will be happier there, I assure you, and will forget about us before the week is over.'

'No!'

'Yes. He's selfish like that.' For a brief moment she leaned forward across the table, her gaze fixed on her daughter's face, and her tone became unexpectedly gentle. 'In your heart you know it's true. I'm sorry, very sorry, because I know you care for him even though he is impossible to live with, but now we must accept that he has gone from our lives for ever.' She sat upright once more, pulling back her shoulders and printing a smile on her mouth. 'From now on we will all love your new little brother.'

'Can I visit him?'

'Who?'

'Georgie.'

Her mother rose to her feet. 'No.' She expelled the word in a harsh gust. 'Forget that boy. He doesn't want you. He no longer exists for us.'

The silence stretched for ever. Jessica's breath was racing in and out of her throat. She wanted to howl Georgie's name but instead she stood rigid, fists clenched tight at her sides, in bleak isolation.

'Mummy,' she whispered, 'if I am good and love my new brother, will you let Georgie come home?'

Her mother sighed. 'Oh, Jessica, you're so stubborn. You're not listening to me.'

*

Jessica hid behind the door. The moment her father's key pushed into the lock she swung it open and stood in front of him.

'Papa, I must talk to you.'

He had not even stepped over the threshold. He took one look at her and his expression seemed to retreat from her, though his body didn't move. He was an average-looking man, of average build in an average grey suit, with light brown hair parted neatly on one side. He wore spectacles which he hated because he saw them as a weakness, and her father was not a man to tolerate weakness. Only his intense blue eyes gave any sign of the fierce intelligence that drove him to seek out perfection – in himself and in others. Jessica always found him daunting.

She moved back into the hall, took his hat and placed it carefully on the hall table. He shut the door behind him but didn't hurry to remove his overcoat.

'Well?' he asked. 'How is your mother?'

'She's in the drawing room. With my new brother.'

'How is Timothy?'

'Playing with Georgie's train set.'

Her father's eyes lit up. 'Is he, indeed?'

Georgie never played with it. He just took the engines apart.

'Papa, I have written a letter.' She pulled a small blue envelope from her skirt pocket. 'To say goodbye to Georgie.'

Her father jabbed his spectacles further up the bridge of his nose and quickly hung his coat on the coat-stand. She could tell he wanted to move away from her, but she placed herself between him and the drawing room door and smiled.

'I like my new brother.' She couldn't bring herself to say his name.

'Excellent.'

'But I need Georgie's new address to write on the envelope.' She kept smiling. 'Then I can forget about Georgie.'

He sighed. A long sour sound.

'Oh, Jessica, I know how clever you are.' He held his hand out for the letter. 'I will address and post it for you.'

8

She didn't argue. Just handed it over. Knowing it would burn on the fire.

'Papa, Georgie is clever too. He can read almost as well as I can. Ask Miss Miller.' Miss Miller was the most recent in a long line of nannies who had come and gone.

Her father lifted her chin, tilting her head back, and studied her keenly, examining the lines and contours of her face. She felt like one of the spaniels that her Uncle Gus judged at dog shows.

'Jessica, the ugly truth is that George is an extremely difficult human being who cannot live with normal people. Hush, don't start denying it. You know it is true and you have to accept it.'

'Papa, if I am bad will you send me to the same place?'

He released her chin. 'No. So don't try that.'

'Would you send me somewhere else?'

For a moment he didn't speak and a nerve twitched at the side of his mouth. She realised he was struggling not to shout at her, so she put her smile back on.

'Don't be foolish, Jessica,' he said briskly. 'The past is over and done with. It's finished. Forget about it. This is a brave new start for us all, including young Timothy.'

He stepped around her, avoiding her, and opened the drawing-room door with a wide smile spreading across his face as he looked inside. 'So how is my fine boy?' He vanished into the warmth.

Jessica remained in the empty hall, struck dumb with sorrow.

2

London, England 1932

Twenty years later

A fox barked. The eerie sound of a feral creature wandering the streets of London in the middle of the night made Jessie Kenton's hand pause as she checked that the window catch was securely closed. The animal barked again, its voice echoing as lonely as a lunatic's across the gardens of Putney.

Jessie backed away from the window. The flat was on the first floor and her bedroom looked out onto the street where a lamp-post further up the road stood patiently, watching out for her like a friend. Its yellow light pushed its way every night through the wide gap between her curtains, so that she could move from room to room without turning on the lights. It was better that way. She didn't want to give any sign that she couldn't sleep. That she might be nervous.

Anyway, she didn't want to disturb Tabitha.

She moved on silent feet into the living room. It was darker here, the curtains drawn fully closed, and she felt her heart-rate pick up a notch. But she could steer her way around each chair and table even with her eyes closed, so reached the broad bay window with no mishap. There were three catches. She slipped her hand behind the curtain and tested each one. All locked. Her heart rewarded her by climbing back down the scale, and she smiled, shaking her head at herself. She was tucking the curtains back into place when the yellow light outside wavered and her breath stalled in her throat. She made herself look again.

Nothing moved. The light had settled, but something – or someone – had crossed its path. From behind the swathe of curtain she examined the quiet residential road with care, inspected each solid pouch of darkness and scoured the black outlines of the shadows.

I can wait.

I can wait longer than you can.

'Oh, Jessie, what on earth are you doing up at this hour?'

Tabitha flipped the switch and Jessie blinked in the sudden flood of light that swept through the room. She stepped quickly away from the window.

'Just restless,' she shrugged. 'Can't sleep. Too much wine last night.'

'I love it when you come to the club to hear us. I always play better.'

Jessie laughed.

Tabitha Mornay had shared the flat with her for the past three years. She possessed straight black hair that hung halfway down her back, and very white skin. That may have been because she lived her life the wrong way round – she slept much of the day and emerged only when the sun went down, full of energy and passionate about her music. She was a saxophonist in a jazz band called The Jack Rabbits, which played a smoky London club every night. Though nearly thirty years old, she looked no more than nineteen.

Tabitha twined her hair into a sleek snake over one shoulder.

'Who was that good-looking man you were dancing with at the end of the evening?'

'No one particular.'

'Hah! I wish I had a "no one" like that.'

'I didn't like his skinny moustache. Like a bootlace.'

'His moustache was elegant. He had style. You're too picky for your own good, my girl.'

Jessie rolled her blue eyes. 'Next time I'll stick his head down your saxophone and you can play his moustache your tune.'

Tabitha chuckled, yawned, wrapped her horrible pink satin robe more tightly around her waist and slunk off into the kitchen. Immediately Jessie darted into Tabitha's bedroom and checked the window catch. This side of the house faced out onto the back garden and she peered closely but nothing was moving in the blackness, except the branches of the lilac tree. For the room of a smoke-hardened jazz player, it was eerily neat and tidy. She returned to her own bedroom but paced back and forth across the yellow slash of light until she heard Tabitha's door close, and only then did she emerge again. She quietly tested the window catch in the kitchen and although it was definitely locked, she tightened it further. Then in the dark she stood with her cheek pressed against the front door, listening.

I can wait.

I can wait longer than you.

Timothy Kenton inspected his companions at the round table with an interest that he kept carefully veiled. But his quick eyes spotted the small movements of their fingers where they lay splayed out on the gold cloth in front of them, tiny twitches of tension. He heard their breath, rising and falling in unison. He saw hope staring blatantly out of their eyes and he wondered if they saw the same in his. The room into which they had been ushered was high-ceilinged and ornate, with its tall windows covered in heavy purple drapes that failed miserably to keep out the piercing draughts. He wished he'd kept his overcoat on. It was as cold as a blasted sepulchre in here and it gave off a distinct odour of bad drains that the scented candles did little to disguise.

Timothy counted six clients at the table, including himself: four other men and a woman of about forty who had wisely chosen to wear a fur coat. Obviously she had been before. She wore heavy make-up but her lips were pale, almost bloodless, and she chewed on them incessantly. Six clients or sometimes nine – that was the usual number, always divisible by three. Only two of the men did he recognise: Fabian Rawlings and the Right Honourable Phillip Hyde-Mason. Like himself they were both in their twenties and both old hands at this game. He nodded a brief greeting to them across the table but no one spoke. You only spoke when Madame Anastasia invited you to do so.

She was seated on Timothy's right, magnificent in a purple and gold feathered headdress that made her dramatically taller than anyone else in the room. She was a middle-aged woman with strong hawkish features and tonight she was encased in a stiff purple gown, a figure as intimidating to her clients as she must be to her spirit guide. She sat now with her hands flat on the table in front of her, palms down, eyes closed, murmuring strange words under her breath while her clients waited. Timothy always found the waiting hard, impatient for the action to start. Spittle gathered in his mouth and each time he swallowed, it took an effort. He always had the odd sensation at these sessions that one of the spirits was hovering behind him, its fingers around his throat. But that was something he kept firmly to himself. Didn't want to sound a complete dunce. What would Rawlings and Hyde-Mason make of such nonsense?

Such nonsense?

Was the need to get in touch with those who have *passed over* nothing more than pathetic human frailty? Superstition? Just nonsense?

He frowned, irritated by his sceptical mood, and stared down at Madame Anastasia's hands. Her fingers were stretched out wide on the table next to his own. She had good hands, elegant and

13

expressive. Free of all rings and without that odd grasping hunch to them that afflicted many of the mediums he had encountered, as though they were readying themselves to snatch the spirits from the air around them, as well as the money from his pocket before either had time to blink.

A chill wind suddenly whistled through the gloom. It seemed to swirl around the ceiling cornices and made the hairs rise on the back of Timothy's neck. However many times it happened and however many times he told himself it was trickery, it still set his guts churning. The candles near the windows flickered and died, steeping much of the room into darkness, except for the three candles that formed a triangle at the centre of the table. They cast shadows on the eager faces, turning them into skulls.

'They are here,' Madame Anastasia intoned and opened her eyes.

Timothy felt the familiar tug in his chest. Always it was the same. Something seemed to shift position inside him, realigning itself, edging itself forward. Elbowing its slippery way to the surface. Something that cried out for a voice.

'We welcome you, Beloved Ones.'

Madame Anastasia spoke with a solemn voice that Timothy had come to expect of mediums, but there was a quality underlying it that made his nerve ends tingle, a sweetness as enticing as barley-sugar to a child. What spirit could resist such beguiling tones?

'We welcome you, Beloved Ones,' she declared again, 'with gifts from Life unto Death.'

All eyes focused on the simple offering of bread and soup that stood in the centre of the triangle of candles to attract spirits, who still yearned for physical nourishment and who still craved warmth and light.

'Come with us and move among us.'

The air grew thicker in Timothy's lungs. Madame Anastasia tipped her head back, the weight of the headdress resting on her chair, and closed her eyes once more, her purple-swathed bosom moving heavily. This was the moment when Timothy watched for any sleight of hand. A tug on a cord, the push of a button with the knee to create a moment of magic when the spirit makes its presence felt. It was what they were here for.

On the table her clients' hands lay flat, each person's last finger touching that of the person next to them, forming a symbolic circle, a necklace of hands. It intensified the energy in the room. Timothy could feel the tension rising in the older man on his left. He wore a calm benevolent expression above a neat goatee beard that gleamed white in the shadows, but his fingers were trembling. They sent ripples into Timothy's flesh. On the other side of the man, the fur-coat woman's eyes were open wide and fixed on a spot directly above the feathered headdress.

'I see them,' she whispered.

Timothy's gaze jumped to the blank space above Madame Anastasia's head, his heart thumping.

'Where?' He could see nothing.

Abruptly Madame Anastasia's chin dipped forward onto her chest and her voice became that of a child's, one who was clearly excited to be standing with one foot on each side of the divide between worlds.

'I am Daisy.' Her young voice was high and pure as a choir boy's. 'I have a man with me. He is a gentleman who is seeking his child. He is nervous of coming forward ... in case his child does not want contact.' The last words were added in a whisper, so that they all had to lean closer to hear.

'Father!' The fur-coat woman's voice quivered. 'Is that you? Stephen Howe?'

Instantly a strange anger seemed to flicker around the table. Timothy felt its heat rise through the cloth, penetrating his fingertips. His eyes darted from face to face in the shadows and saw the anguish on each one. How many here had lost their fathers? On the other side of Madame Anastasia a middle-aged man was seated, a small figure in an expensive suit and with a birthmark reaching across his neck. He was looking closely at the slumped medium, squeezing her fingers, but she didn't respond.

'Well?' he demanded. 'Tell us, little girl, is he the spirit of this woman's father?'

'Many of us have lost fathers,' the woman sobbed. 'The Great War robbed a whole generation of them.'

The little girl told them sharply to hush while she spoke further with the gentleman. In the silence that followed the tension in the room rose and all eyes focused in silence on the medium's lips. Finally the client with the goatee beard lost patience and asked, 'Daisy, my dear, can you tell us the name of the child that the spirit seeks?'

A knock on the table made them jump.

A trick, Timothy told himself, *a trick*. But his heart was racing. Suddenly he wanted to break the circle of darkness, to leap to his feet and walk away from whatever it was they had conjured into their midst. He was a fool to believe that the world this side of the veil could tinker with those on the other side with impunity. Seconds ticked past and foreboding bunched in his chest, still and cold as stone.

'Daisy,' the man tried again, 'we thank you for the sign. What name does your gentleman seek?'

'He is sad. He says his heart is heavy.' The girl's voice did not sound remotely like Madame Anastasia's own.

'Will it help him to speak with his child?' the man asked.

Again came the sharp knock on the table. Timothy saw the candles quiver and the air in the room grew heavier.

'Daisy,' the fur-coated woman spoke slowly, struggling for words, 'tell us, dear. We've all gathered here to speak to someone who has passed to spirit. I badly need to communicate with my mother, Audrey Howe, who passed over four years ago. I would like you to ask your gentleman if he is my father, Stephen?'

'No,' the girl answered immediately in a sing-song voice. 'He is not Stephen.'

'Oh.'

'Who is he?' Rawlings asked.

'His voice is fading.'

16

'Quickly, then,' Rawlings urged. 'Ask him now.'

'So many voices, all chattering in my ears. They are restless and they all want to speak out at once.'

Timothy's hands pressed down hard on the table. 'Is it the letter K? Tell me! Does the child's name start with K?'

A definite knock rapped on the table, louder than before, as he knew it would. *Yes.* 'It's Kingsley, isn't it?' he called out. 'The child is Kingsley. You always said you would communicate, you were always a missionary for the cause.' The words were tumbling out now. 'You promised and I never stopped believing you. Do you—'

Two sharp knocks. Curt. Dismissive.

'He says no,' the child's voice whispered. 'Not Kingsley. But he says yes, it is the letter K.'

'Kenton starts with the letter K,' Hyde-Mason pointed out. 'Maybe it's you – Timothy Kenton. You could be the one the spirit is seeking. It could be your father here tonight.'

Timothy's heart stopped. This wasn't what he'd come for. Not this. He snatched his hands from the table, breaking the circle, and stumbled to his feet. The goatee man shouted something but Timothy's ears seem to have disconnected from his brain because it didn't make sense of the words. He hurried across to the door, pulled it open and rushed outside into the hall, slamming the door behind him to block off the spirits that were calling to him. His brain buzzed, as if insects were trapped inside, fluttering their wings. He breathed deeply, dragging in the ice-cold air, but none of it seemed to clear his head.

The hall was huge, a great marble entrance area with an ancient coat of arms above a columned fireplace, half hidden in the gloom. It was a dim and sombre place. The only light came from a solitary candelabra on a window ledge and its flame swayed in and out of focus.

His coat. Where the hell was his coat? He was freezing.

He moved unsteadily towards an armoire table at the far end of the hall where a pile of garments lay, but when he bent over them to search for his navy overcoat, his mind seemed to stutter and forget why it was there. His hands rummaged aimlessly among the coats and clutched at a dark sleeve. He pulled. But instead of the sleeve coming towards him, he came towards the sleeve. It swayed and undulated in front of him. The darkness of it seemed to flow up into his head and he closed his eyes, thankful for the peace as he slid to the floor.

3

Jessie Kenton was walking up Putney Hill in the rain. It was a dank and soulless evening, and an ambulance raced past, its bell clanging. It sent a shudder through her, and made her walk faster, head ducked to fend off the wind that charged down from Putney Heath.

It was the end of October. Cold, wet and dark. Winter had sneaked in early this year. Jessie hated October with an intensity that even she recognised was out of all proportion, but there was no doubt in her mind that she functioned at her worst at this time of year. Her drawings became flat and unoriginal, reluctant to take shape. Pens and pencils lay sluggish in her fingers while she tried to cudgel her brain into activity. Bad things always happened to her in October. That was why her heart jumped prematurely at the noise of the ambulance and she lengthened her stride as she hurried to reach home.

Around her, London growled its nightly chorus. The engines of cars and cabs, trams and trucks belched out their black breath as the workforce of the city spilled out of offices and factories to fight their way onto trains, trams and buses. Jessie worked in a design studio in the Fulham area of west London and she usually cycled home the few miles along Fulham Palace Road and over Putney

Bridge, enjoying both the exercise and the sight of the River Thames. It slid under the bridge like a dark thread of history – King Henry VIII himself had skated on its surface four hundred years ago in the days when it used to freeze. Prime Minister Gladstone had escaped from under the eagle-eyed gaze of Queen Victoria to prowl its muddy banks in search of prostitutes to save. Sherlock Holmes had slunk through the foul mists that coiled from its polluted depths.

The last thought made Jessie smile and she reminded herself sternly that the inimitable Sherlock was nothing more than a figment of Arthur Conan Doyle's imagination. But today she had walked home. A furniture removal cart had clipped her front wheel and buckled it this morning. She had sat in the gutter nursing a grazed shin and cursed all carts. Cursed October. Cursed her luck. When a passing car had offered her a lift, she had glared at the driver, rejected his undoubted kindness and hobbled the last half mile to the studio pushing a wonky bicycle. She had deposited it in the oily but capable hands of a bicycle shop mechanic on the corner of Fielding Road and at the end of the day she'd headed home on foot.

She quickened her pace now. On each side of the road perched rows of discreetly respectable houses, the kind of houses where librarians and undertakers lived, curtains already drawn like armour against the outside world, the smoke of coal fires gusting down from the chimneys into Jessie's nostrils along with the rain. As she reached the turning to her street, she glanced over her shoulder. It was automatic. This need to check.

Behind her, Putney Hill fell away, gleaming wet and secretive in the dark, its pavements lit by an occasional street lamp or car headlight. There was no one in sight. Hardly surprising, as it wasn't a night for an evening stroll. A dog with long yellow ears and sodden flanks was mooching around dustbins, but otherwise the street lay lifeless. That suited Jessie just fine. She felt her heart steady to no more than a dull thump. All week this had been going on, this need to search behind her.

All right, tonight she was mistaken. Tonight there was no one. But other nights, footfalls echoed behind her so clearly that she would swing round to confront, face to face, whoever it was who was following her all over London. Yet there was never anyone she could pick out of the shadows by night, and by day there was only the usual flow of pedestrians going about their business, no one's eyes meeting hers, just the stolid indifference of city-dwellers to those around them. Some nights she hesitated to turn, afraid that she'd see behind her a lean and hungry figure with blue eyes.

'Jabez!'

No answer. Her flat felt cold as a tomb as she closed the curtains. October was seeping through the cracks in the plaster.

'Jabez!' she called again, switching on the overhead light, but there was no sign of activity.

She dropped her coat and scarf on the sofa and unwrapped a newspaper packet of sprats. Instantly the stink of raw fish permeated the air, thick and salty, and Jessie was thankful that Tabitha was out at work, so there would be no complaints. Jessie headed towards her bedroom, frowning slightly at the sight of the door ajar, because she distinctly recalled making a point of shutting it before leaving for work this morning. There was mud on her eiderdown.

'Jabez,' she said sternly.

No answer.

'Where are you hiding?'

She wafted a sprat by its tail through the air and her pillow trembled. A small heart-shaped face and two pointed ears emerged from under it. A pair of vivid green eyes blinked at her and a loud purr shook the bedding.

'Jabez, you are not allowed in here when I'm out. You know that.'

The cat stretched one coal-black front leg and pretended to ignore the silvery offering that dangled from her hand. Instead he rolled onto his back, wriggling all four feet in the air, inviting her to

21

admire his sleek black belly. But she wasn't fooled. She stepped forward quickly and whisked the pillow from her bed.

'Jabez! You are a *brute*.'

On the spot where her pillow had lain curled the corpse of a squirrel, its mottled fur as dull and flat as its eyes. She prodded it with the sprat. The animal was already cold and stiff. It saddened Jessie. It takes so little for life to be snatched from your grasp: scampering around Putney Heath and leaping from branches one moment but dead as a butcher's bone the next. She stroked the tiny creature with one finger, then picked it up and carried it out to the kitchen, ignoring Jabez's cries of protest. She wrapped the squirrel in an old tea towel, rummaged round for the small trowel that lived under the sink and went downstairs, out into the rain, where she buried the corpse in the back garden under the forsythia bush.

It was while she was standing invisible in the darkness, with hands all muddy and hair flattened by rain, that Jessie had an unsettling sense of doing this before. Burying something. But the memory wouldn't quite come to her, what it was she'd buried or where. She stared up at the window of her flat and saw the curtains move and Jabez's small face peer down at her with what she kidded herself was remorse. She had found him as a kitten shut in a Huntley & Palmers biscuit tin up on the heath on Christmas Eve, a tiny starving handful of fluff, and she had taken him with her, nursed him back to health and given him a home. Now he was family. No matter what his unseemly habits.

To have abandoned one member of her family was bad enough. To lose another would be unbearable.

The telephone jangled, startling Jessie. She let it ring unheeded. Jabez opened one eye, stretched out a paw from the stack of paper on top of which he was curled and sank his claws into the woolly sleeve of her jumper. *Don't move. Stay here.* She trailed a finger between his ears, matching him stare for stare, and let the telephone ring.

She was working. Spread around her on the table and littering the floor like discarded underwear, sheets of paper rustled against each other, creating that sound she loved. It meant that her drawing was going well. When the flow of ideas stopped, there was nothing but cold silence. It froze her, paralysed her pen. But this evening the designs were dancing into her fingers as she sketched images for a series of posters for a new soap product.

The telephone rang again.

With a sigh she walked over and picked it up. 'Hello, Alistair.'

'Hello, Jessie. How did you know it was me?'

'I'm psychic.'

He laughed, uncertain whether she was serious or not.

'It's a dismal night,' he commented cheerfully.

He was going to ask if he could come over.

'Can I come over?'

She released a convincing yawn. 'It's miserable out. How was your day?'

But he sidestepped her delaying tactic. 'I thought you might fancy some company?'

'Sorry, Alistair. I'm working.'

There was a brief, meaningful silence. Like drips of cold water in her ear.

'You're always working, Jessie.'

'That's not true.'

'True enough.'

She didn't argue. She had been seeing Alistair on and off for a few months on a casual basis, and at the start she had enjoyed his company. He ran his father's car-construction business which made delicious little open-topped two-seaters and had introduced her to the thrills of sports car racing at Brooklands. He was a considerate and amusing companion. So why did she do this? Push him away. It was always the same in every relationship she embarked on. *Don't crowd me. Don't come too close. Don't reach in and squeeze my heart. If you do, I might . . .* She shook her head. Might what? Might explode? Might turn into a frog? Might commit murder? She never stayed around long enough to find out.

She listened to Alistair's tight breathing at the other end of the line and relented.

'How about Sunday afternoon instead?' she offered. 'We could go to Kew Gardens. The hothouses will warm us up.'

'Or we could go for a meal after you've finished your work tonight.' Alistair was stubborn as granite. He inherited it from his Scottish father.

'No.' A pause. 'Sorry. Too tired.'

'I could bring over a steak and cook it for you?'

'Thanks, but no thanks. See you on Sunday afternoon.'

She hung up, irritated with herself for being cross with this man who so generously offered to cook a meal for her. She was damn sure nobody barged in on Beethoven with an *Apfelstrudel* when he was hard at work on his *Heroica* symphony.

Jabez yawned and treated her to a cool stare.

'I know, you greedy creature, you want steak instead of sprats.' She ran a hand along his sleek back, triggering a purr, aware that she could easily have done the same for Alistair. *Get it right, Jessie*, she told herself. *You are no Beethoven and this is no symphony.*

She inspected the sheet of sketches in front of her. With a sigh she drew a thick black line across the page and flicked it to join the others on the floor. It was never good enough. Was that what Beethoven said to himself? Was the music ever good enough? Always there was this chasm between what was in her head and what was on the page. She pulled a fresh sheet of paper towards her. She would go on all night, until she got it right.

The telephone leapt into life once more and this time she answered it with alacrity.

'Hello, Alistair,' she said. 'That steak sounds—'

'Hello, Jessica.'

'Pa!'

'I need you to come over straight away.' Her father was not a person who believed in small talk.

'I haven't finished the designs for you yet, so—'

'Right now, Jessica.'

24

Even for her father, this was abrupt. The evening was dark and wet outside and Beckenham was an hour's drive away.

'Can't it wait?' she asked.

'No.'

One word. That's all. But she heard the fear encased within it, and it set the hairs on her neck on end. Her father was afraid of nothing.

'What is it, Pa? What has happened?'

There was a silence. She had a sense of something growing under her ribs and felt a thump deep in her chest.

'Your brother has gone missing.'

4

There were some things Jessie wasn't willing to lie about. Not even to herself. But the whereabouts of her brother wasn't one of them. She had spent an absurd amount of her life lying through her teeth for Timothy. It was amazing that her tongue hadn't turned blue from all the cold-hearted lies that had slid off it. Her words were finely honed ice-picks to the soft centre of the girls and, later, of the young women who came knocking on the door in search of her brother with their sweet smiles and insistent pleas. Jessica possessed a whole arsenal of excuses.

'I'm sorry, Isabella, but Tim is playing cricket.'

'He's in bed with the 'flu.'

'He's caring for his aunt in Peterborough.'

'Thanks for the Sobranie cigarettes, Amanda. Tim will love them. But he's working late tonight.'

'No, absolutely no more cigarettes, Amanda. He's given up.'

As the years went by, the excuses became increasingly bizarre.

'Don't you know that he's in training to be a monk?' or, 'Sorry, but he's having dinner with Noel Coward.'

It wasn't Timothy's fault. The girls fussed over him like bees on a honeycomb, fluttering their pretty wings at him. All his life his golden good looks and his effortless charm had been his undoing. They thwarted the attempts of his first-class brain to be taken seriously and undermined his own resolve to make full use of it. Whenever he bewailed his harem-shadow, Jessie would narrow her eyes at him and say nothing. What was the point? Her brother knew his own weaknesses even better than she did. Nevertheless she carried on lying for him because even she was not as immune to his sunny smile as she liked to pretend.

Even though she was only seven when he first invaded her life, she had kept to her word. She had made herself love her new brother. In the first year it had felt like chewing on needles every time she smiled at him or touched her lips dutifully to his skin. But that was what did for her. The kissing of his cheek. Cuddling him on her lap, brushing his shining curls, and tickling his chubby little body until it was boneless in her embrace. His arms would wrap around her neck, imprisoning her, and his kisses landed on her face whether she wanted them or not.

To be able to hold her brother's hand was unheard of before. It captivated her young heart. His skin was peach-warm against hers. It made something inside her ache, and alone in her own bed she would cry with relief as it filled up a cold empty place hidden inside her chest. Sometimes she would creep into Timothy's bed at night, snuggle under the blankets and read Sherlock Holmes adventures to him by torchlight, just for the pleasure of feeling his head on her shoulder. She would sniff his hair and twirl a curl of it between her fingers and let herself imagine it was Georgie's.

Georgie. As she drove south of London through the rain to her parents' house in Kent, she allowed his name to enter her mind for once. She had learned eventually to lock it out. She had banned it. Refused to let it rampage through her thoughts and bring her to tears at all the wrong moments. She had never seen or heard of Georgie again after that terrible night, yet now echoes of his voice sounded in her head. The windscreen wipers of her Austin Swallow squeaked on the windshield glass and she peered out into the darkness ahead.

She had passed the cricket club of Dulwich Village on her left and was on the A234 when she felt her spirits sink, and her foot – with a mind all of its own – eased off the pedal. Her speed dropped to little more than a crawl, as if the car itself were reluctant to enter Beckenham. It was always the same when she drove to her parents' house.

Your brother has disappeared. Those were her father's words on the telephone tonight. *We must find him.*

Twenty years too late.

'Good evening, Jessica. You took your time.'

'It's raining, Pa.'

'Of course.'

Of course it's raining? Or of course she took her time? Which did he mean? It didn't matter. Either way, he would find fault. She had entered the house through a side door which led straight into her father's printing workshop because she'd seen light spilling from its barred window, painting the raindrops butter-yellow. She would prefer to speak to him first. Before facing her mother.

'I drove as fast as I could in this filthy weather,' she pointed out and could hear the annoyance she had meant to banish from her voice.

'Don't get snippy with me, my girl.'

He put down the container of black ink in his hand. He was wearing his brown work-apron to protect his clothes from splashes, but as usual his hair was immaculate, each dark thread Brylcreemed in place, and his beautiful brogue shoes gleamed like black ice. As he approached her, she regretted her words because his eyes were tense behind his spectacles and a telltale looseness at one side of his mouth betrayed that his emotions were bubbling only just beneath the surface.

'Tell me, Pa, what has happened?'

'Timothy has vanished.' He flicked a hand towards the window, as if her brother might have crawled out that way. 'We haven't heard from him.'

'How long?'

'Seven days.'

'Oh, Pa, only a week! He's a grown man,' she said with a gentle smile. 'He's twenty-five, not fifteen. He's probably off enjoying himself with friends somewhere.'

'Jessica, don't underestimate your brother. You know as well as I do that he always telephones your mother if he is going to be away from home overnight. So that she won't worry.'

'Yes, I know.'

Kind. Considerate. Thoughtful. A loving son. Timothy was all these things. She was not. She was wary of love because she knew it could damage you. That's what she'd learned one cold October night when she was seven. She had moved out of the family home the day that she reached eighteen, trying to outrun the long shadow cast by her childhood. She had worked her way through St Martin's School of Art and Design, drawing by day, waitressing by night in her black dress and dainty white cap in the Lyons Corner House on Tottenham Court Road. Each Saturday she had set up a stall to sell her paintings in the market in Portobello Road.

Only recently had she and her father managed to work together on occasional projects with her designs and his printing presses. In the last year they had begun to make allowance for each other. She glanced around the neat workroom and inhaled the familiar tang of ink and hot metal from the small printing press in the corner, a smell she always associated with her father. It followed him around like a dog. Just as she associated the perfume of freesias with her mother.

The substantial printing company, Kenton Print Works, which her father owned and ran with fierce dedication, had its main presses on the outskirts of Sydenham. But he liked to keep his hand in with small, private jobs here in his workshop. She was the same herself, doing much of her design work at home in her flat, away from the bustle of the studio. The difference was that her father's workshop was clean and orderly, everything rigidly in its place, whereas hers was a wanton mess. Here the books and files were arranged in alphabetical order. Disciplined stacks of pamphlets. Neat towers of brochures and leaflets.

A large pile of posters caught Jessica's eye. From the top one the face of a handsome man stared out at her, immensely pleased with himself, and she recognised it immediately. It was Oswald Mosley. The charismatic founder of the newly formed British Union of Fascists was a wealthy baronet who had tried his hand as a Member of Parliament in both the Conservative Party and the Labour Party. But he was an impatient and arrogant man, and he had parted from them acrimoniously. Instead he'd set up his own political party – the British Union of Fascists.

Jessie frowned. She felt a ripple of distaste and turned away. She walked over to her father's desk, perched on the high stool, folded her arms and said, 'Tell me exactly what happened.'

'Nothing.'

'What do you mean?'

'Nothing happened. That's what I can't understand.'

He started to pace. Back and forth across the centre of the room, his face creased in a scowl. Jessie noticed his hands fingering a pen as he talked, the same way hers did when her mind was fretting at something. But her father's hands were refined and elegant, the hands of a thinker, whereas hers were short and spatular.

'When did you last see Timothy?' she asked.

'Last Friday morning. He came home for a clean shirt before going to work. He spent Thursday night with you, remember?'

That was news to Jessie.

Something in her face must have raised doubts in his mind because he asked abruptly, 'He did, didn't he?'

'Of course.'

Lying about her brother's whereabouts came naturally.

'I thought he might have said something to you, Jessica. Especially as he has been spending so much time at your place in recent weeks.'

Jessie hadn't seen Timothy for at least a fortnight.

'No,' she said quickly. 'He said nothing. Have you contacted the museum to see if he's been to work?'

'Yes. They haven't seen him since last Friday.'

Jessie felt her stomach give a shaky lurch. Timothy loved his job at the British Museum, where he was employed to catalogue their Egyptian antiquitie   For him to be missing from work was a bad sign. Bad enough to make her rise to her feet.

'Have you contacted the police?' she asked suddenly.

'Yes.'

That surprised her.

'What did they say?'

'They didn't want to know.' Her father's shoulders lost their stiff line. 'They implied that I was making a fuss about nothing. They said, as you did, that Timothy is an adult and will turn up when he's ready.' He looked embarrassed for a moment and his grey eyes glanced away from her. 'The sergeant suggested he had taken off with a girl. Is that true? Is there a girl, do you think?'

'Not that I know of.'

She stood there feeling stupid. Timothy did stay at her flat sometimes but not often, and when he did he told her little about his life. They usually talked about each other's work and ended up going out to the cinema or dropping in on Tabitha at the jazz club. Timothy liked Tabitha almost as much as he liked a glass of scotch whisky in his hand.

'I'm relying on you, Jessica.'

'Oh, Pa.'

'Don't let me down.'

She looked at the stern expression on his face, so familiar that she could draw every line and crease of it. He had always spent hours analysing, interpreting and weighing up the world around him, earnest and critical. Self-absorbed. But she heard the desperation in his voice and saw the exhaustion seeping down the hollows of his cheeks from sleepless nights spent listening for Timothy's key in the lock. She knew she should go to this man whose beloved son had

31

vanished from his home and put her arms round him. But she couldn't. She would rather pluck her eyes out.

'I'll go and speak to Ma.'

She turned quickly, jerking herself away from the grip of his eyes. He said nothing more.

The drawing room felt chill. There was a fire in the elaborate Victorian marble grate but it was a reflection of her mother – bright and energetic but small. Jessie's mother believed in keeping the body warm by constant activity, not by lazing in front of a blazing coal fire with feet up and a book in hand. The blood must always pump hard, the heart beat fast. She was knitting blanket squares, but not as other people knit. Not only did her fingers and metal needles flash in and out with a speed that defied gravity, but she strode up and down the room while doing so, the ball of white wool chasing behind her on the carpet like a pet mouse.

'Jessica!'

Catherine Kenton's stride froze when her daughter walked into the room and for a brief moment Jessie could hear them both breathing heavily.

'Hello, Ma. What's all this I hear about Tim going missing? Are you all right?'

'Of course I'm all right.' Her mother's fine blonde hair was pinned into an elegant knot at the back of her head and she was wearing a blue wool dress, its colour just a shade too bright and its skirt a fraction too full, as if she had something to prove. She resumed her march across the room. 'It's your father who is worried. It's really too bad of the boy not to get in touch.'

There were flecks of scarlet high on her cheeks but otherwise her skin was pale and her lips pressed tight together. For a woman in her late forties her figure was still slight and lithe, forever in motion, as though running from its own shadow.

'I was supposed to be at a meeting this evening,' she added with a sigh. 'Not here.' She glared at the heavy stiff armchairs with their starched antimacassars, at the cabinet of antique snuffboxes that

32

Jessie loathed, at the huge ornate mirror that dominated the mantelpiece. 'Not here,' she repeated. 'Not waiting here like a . . .'

Her voice trailed away. *Waiting like a what, Ma? Like a proper mother?* Instead of one who has always spent all her time at meetings. Political meetings, charitable meetings, social meetings, community meetings. It didn't matter what they were for, as long as they had a cause she could espouse. As someone who had marched alongside Emmeline Pankhurst for female emancipation, the greatest sins in Catherine Kenton's world were idleness and indifference. As children, Jessie and Timothy had quickly learned that in order to read their favourite Sherlock Holmes stories in old copies of their father's *Strand* magazine, they had to polish their shoes at the same time. Hands had to be never still when their mother was around.

'I'm sure he's just with friends,' Jessie said easily. 'He probably got a bit drunk and is sleeping off a hangover. No real harm done.' She tried a laugh.

Her mother gave her a look.

Jessie sighed, unbuttoned her wet coat and sank into an armchair near the fire. As she held her hands out to the flames, steam rose from her sleeves.

'All right, Ma. Tell me what happened. Did he have a quarrel with Pa?'

'Of course not. Your brother and father never quarrel.'

That put her firmly in her place.

'Did Tim mention anywhere that he was going? How did he seem?'

'You should know. He'd been at your place for the night, hadn't he?'

Jessie didn't even hesitate. 'Yes.'

'Did the pair of you discuss anything he was planning to do?'

'No, nothing special.' Her eyes followed the imprint of her mother's footsteps on the Persian rug, small and neat, but the gaps between them were irregular, the pace uneven. 'Tell me,' she said softly, 'what happened when he came home that morning for a clean shirt.'

33

'Nothing.'

Her mother's tone was sharp. The tip of one smart patent shoe scuffed momentarily against the heel of the other. Jessie rose to her feet, scooped up the ball of white wool from the carpet and wound the soft thread around her own wrist, anchoring her mother to her. Slowly she reeled her in; forced her mother's hands to cease their activity. The overhead light shone down on her pale skin, leeching the life out of it.

'What happened, Ma? What did you say to Tim?'

'Nothing.'

But her fingers gave her away. They pushed the stitches along the needle, pressing them hard right down to the bottom, crushing whatever pictures had reared up in her head.

'Ma, how can I find Tim if you won't tell me the truth?'

The words deepened the chill in the room, the same words she had uttered to her mother a thousand times while she was growing up. Except for the name. That was different.

Ma, how can I find Georgie if you won't tell me the truth?

The answer never varied. *Don't ask me again.*

Don't ask.

Don't.

The unspoken name resonated in the small space between mother and daughter until Catherine Kenton's blue eyes faltered and her lips parted as she dragged in a deep breath. She turned her gaze to the photograph on the mantelpiece, the one in the silver frame, the one of the young man with the wide laughing mouth and the eagerness for life brimming in his eyes. The one that was Timothy Kenton.

'We had words.'

Words. So deceptive a syllable. It stuck like a moth in Jessie's mind. Tim never had *words* with his parents.

'What about?' she asked.

Silence.

'Ma?'

Her mother's eyes remained on the photograph, as though it too

34

might disappear if she stopped looking at it. The thread of wool between her fingers was tightening, cutting into Jessie's wrist.

'About his girlfriend,' Catherine Kenton said at last and straightened her back, rising to her full height. She was still shorter than Jessie, even in her patent heels.

'I didn't know he had a girlfriend,' Jessie said.

'She's a colleague at work. One of the staff at the museum, he told me. She came with him here to the house that morning and waited for him. On the doorstep.'

'On the doorstep? Why not in the drawing room?'

'She is Egyptian.'

That took Jessie by surprise. *Egyptian?* Her curiosity was instantly roused and she could not suppress a smile. *Good for Tim.* She didn't think he had it in him to be so unconventional.

'What's her name?' she asked.

'I have no idea.'

One look at her mother's face and Jessie became aware of a sick feeling tight under her ribcage. She could imagine only too well the *words* her mother had had with poor Tim.

'Does Pa know?'

'No.' Suddenly her mother's eyes abandoned the laughing face and swung back to Jessie. 'You mustn't tell him,' she said fiercely.

Jessie felt a flicker of anger but curbed it. 'I'll do what I can to find him,' she promised. She waited for a *thank you* or even a faint smile, but none came. 'I'll take a look in his room first.'

'What for? He's not there.'

'For clues.'

'For God's sake, Jessica, be serious! This isn't one of your silly Sherlock Holmes games. This is real. This is ... ' Her voice broke and she looked desperately back at the photograph. 'This is my son,' she whispered.

'I know, Ma.' Jessie muttered. 'I know.'

The bedroom felt chill and unloved. Jessie intended to give it a quick once-over, nothing more, because she didn't really expect to find clues, though something with the name of Tim's new girlfriend would be useful. A scribbled note or a telephone number.

She skimmed through the bedside drawer, rummaging cursorily. Handkerchiefs, cufflinks, a passport, a jumble of bus tickets and a secret stash of Fry's chocolate bars. Inside the wardrobe she checked his jacket pockets but found nothing more interesting than a pack of French letters. She felt like an intruder, uncomfortable and disloyal, spying on her brother like this. It was obvious that he had taken himself off in a huff – quite rightly in Jessie's opinion – after his mother's *words*. The thing that worried her most was the museum, the fact that he hadn't gone into work. That nagged at her.

It was when, as an afterthought, she knelt and peered under the bed that she felt the atmosphere change. Down here the air was warmer, thicker, and it brushed her cheek. Like the touch of a finger. Down here, lying on the bedside rug, Georgie came to her and made her cry.

'Georgie,' she whispered, and stretched out an arm into the dark empty space.

His breath seemed to trickle over her fingers, his humming caressed her ears, and her cheeks ached with a sudden rush of need for him. They used to hide under his bed or under hers, concealed from the critical eyes of their mother or one of the nannies. Jessie would make up stories about a dog called Toby who had wild and breathless adventures, and Georgie would lay out two whole packs of one hundred and four playing cards face down in a jumble and would proceed to tell her what each card was when she pointed to it. He never got it wrong. It was if he possessed X-ray eyes.

It's easy, Jessie. Why can't you do it?

Now, with her forehead pressed against the rug, breathing in the musty, dusty under-bed smell, she fought back the tears and made herself sit up, his chortle of delight still alive in her head. She became angry with herself because this wasn't even Georgie's old room – his room was the small one at the end of the corridor that was now relegated to a boxroom full of suitcases and unwanted furniture. She jumped to her feet

'This is stupid.' She snapped the words out loud for the space under the bed to hear. 'First you imagine he's following you around London, out for revenge. Now you think he's lying in wait under Tim's bed.' Colour rose to her cheeks. 'You're the one who is sick in the head, girl.'

She strode towards the door, eager to be out of this room and to sweep the cobwebs of the past from her mind, but as her hand seized the brass doorknob, her eyes settled on the long shelf of books on the end wall and she hesitated. She walked over to the shelf, inspecting the titles and the state of the books. Some of them were old, the edges of their pages mustard-yellow and their spines dog-eared and cracked.

'Oh, Tim. You kept them.'

It was years since she'd been inside Tim's bedroom. She put out a hand and brushed it along the books, relishing the brittle well-read feel of them, listening to their voices, remembering. Whispers in the darkness, the forbidden candle late into the night. The tremors of excitement as Sherlock tracked down his prey, a delicious fear of what the next page would bring.

'You kept them,' she smiled.

She wanted to leave but the memories coiled through her head, holding her there. The books were copies of the adventures of Sherlock Holmes by Sir Arthur Conan Doyle, though now she noticed that Tim had added several volumes to them – Conan Doyle's autobiography, *Memories and Adventures*, and right at the end of the shelf stood Conan Doyle's final books – *The History of Spiritualism* and *The Edge of the Unknown*, the ones he wrote after the death of his beloved son Kingsley during the Great War. The great writer had died two years earlier in 1930 but his stories were still immensely popular.

Her hand suddenly reached up and took down one of the early books. She studied its title: *The Hound of the Baskervilles*. She lifted it to her face and inhaled. Its well-remembered scent made her head spin and her hands were no longer steady as she turned the front cover. She stared down at what she knew she would find on the frontispiece.

This book belongs to George Ambrose Kenton. If you steal it from me, I will track you down.

Jessie turned abruptly and left the bedroom, the book thrust deep inside her coat pocket.

5

Georgie

England 1932

'Where are you?'

The words lie like dust in my room.

I shout them. Hot pokers in my chest. It's Saturday, I know it's Saturday, I know it is. I have counted back the days and ticked off each one with a pea-green pen on the calendar that I made and which lives under my mattress for safety.

Saturday. Unless I missed a day. Sometimes it happens if I have a bad week and the needles come for me. They seek out my thigh, my buttocks, my arm, the way hunting dogs sniff out badgers with their sharp vicious wet noses. Sinking in their teeth.

It's afternoon. I can tell by the sunlight outside the window, even though today they have drawn a blind across the glass to try to fool me into thinking there is no sun out there, just a gloomy soul-stealing twilight. But I know better. I flick the light switch on and off and on again, on and off and on again. Brightness, blackness, brightness. If you're outside, in the garden, striding over the finicky gardener's weed-free lawn, you'll know it's me. You'll come.

Nothing.

No footsteps outside my door. The rattle of a metal trolley further down the corridor makes me shout louder.

'Where is he? Where is he? What have you done with him?'

No answer. Not even a *Stop that noise, George*. I feel the straight lines inside my head starting to twist and buckle and I crash a fist against the door, against the panel that is already cracked in places because my fist and the wood are old friends. I press my head against the moulding around the panel, so hard it carves dents in my forehead, but still the straight lines are buckling. I whisper to the door. I feel my panic seep into the cracks.

'Please,' I beg. 'Please. It's Saturday. Let Timothy come and I promise I will eat that foul slop you call food.'

They give me paper. Clean white sheets of it, quarto size, no lines, just as I asked. Dr Churchward pushed it across his desk at me and did that odd thing with his mouth that I used to think was a snarl but you explained to me that it is what is called a nervous tic. What has he got to be nervous about? Does he still think I will jump on his desk and kick my bare foot in his face the way I did when I was twelve and he told me that none of my letters to Jessie had ever been allowed to reach her? I broke two toes but I broke his nose too. I didn't like his blood on my skin.

Sometimes during our interviews I stare hard at the bump on the bridge of Dr Churchward's nose where it is not straight even now, thirteen years later, and I watch the veins in his neck thicken and the colour of his cheeks change to plum red. He doesn't like me. That's all right, I don't like him. But I say 'thank you' when he gives me the paper I asked for, the way Jessie taught me and which for years I forgot until you reminded me.

I sit at my desk. It's not really a desk, it's a wobbly bentwood chair that I like and a small mahogany table, but to me it is a desk. The paper waits in front of me. Alongside it sits the ink, a squat fat bottle of Quink. Royal-washable blue, not permanent blue, I was adamant about that. Permanent blue is an ugly colour, neither blue nor black, like the colour of sin, but washable blue is the colour of your eyes. No. I won't think it. It will make the ache in my chest grow too fierce and I need to think clearly today. It is not always easy because of the drugs they put in my food. This morning I refused to eat breakfast, so I can think with precision, and I remember everything with perfect clarity.

I pick up my Swan fountain pen, dip its nib in the wishing-pool of blue ink and work the tiny metal lever to make the rubber tube inside fill with ink. I find it pleases me, this small simple action. I like the efficiency of it. The cleverness. I make a mental note to discover who invented the fountain pen.

I have decided to start at the beginning. It is the only way to discover why you have not come. At first I planned to start at the end and work my way backwards but no, that would be a mistake. During the night while I sat on my chair by the window, waiting to see if you would flash a signal from your torch in the garden, I realised that I was going about it the wrong way, that I need to study everything in the correct order. In a straight line. Logically. That way, I will not miss any clues.

Sherlock Holmes never missed any clues. If I follow his methods, I will, as Dr Watson says of his brilliant friend, 'see deeply into the manifold wickedness of the human heart'.

The first time. It was as sharp and unexpected as a stamp on the foot. Two fourteen-year-old boys taking bites out of each other with their words. It was July 25th 1921. I am eating breakfast, the same one I've eaten for the last twenty years. Two fried eggs on toast, three fried tomatoes and three fried mushrooms. I always eat my food in an anti-clockwise spiral around the plate leaving the bright yellow heart of the eggs till last.

There are twelve of us in the room – twelve people, I mean. I don't count the staff as people. Their faces are false. Behind their masks they are guard-dogs and their teeth are needle-sharp, spilling poison into my blood. The twelve of us look towards the doorway where you materialise unexpectedly, all windblown blond curls and legs too long for you and a way of holding yourself that has the scent of freedom about it. It makes me want to howl with fury.

The skin of my neck prickles, tiny spiky points of pain, which I know means the start of an episode. That's what they call them – when I lose control. *Episodes.* Like part of a story. Episodic. The story of my life. I look away and concentrate on my egg, adding salt and cutting the toast into small triangles. I sit alone at the small square table, it's how I like it, no one too close. When I hear you place a chair opposite me and see your blazer-clad elbows on my table, I have to fight back the words that charge onto my tongue and clamp my hands between my knees to stop them hitting you. If I have an episode in the dining room in front of everyone, it will be more than just the needles coming for me.

'Good morning, Georgie. I'm Timothy.'

Georgie. Georgie. Georgie. Only one person ever called me *Georgie.*

'Go away.' I don't look at you.

'I'd like to talk to you.'

'No.' I back away to the limits of my chair, as far from you as I can get.

'Please, Georgie. I have gone to a lot of trouble to find you.'

'You haven't found me. I wasn't lost.'

'You were to me.' You hesitate. 'And to Jessie.'

I take my handkerchief from my pocket, unfold it neatly and place it over my face, holding it there with the tips of my fingers. 'Go away. Go away.'

You reach out and snatch the handkerchief from my face, leaving me naked, but still I don't look at your face. I see that your sleeve is smeared with yellow from my egg yolk. I bite my tongue so hard it bleeds, coppery and slick inside my mouth, but I notice your hands. They are not the hands that belong to your glossy blond curls, or to your voice that says love-me each time you speak, they are hands that do things. Build things. Dig things. Make things. There is a long jagged scar down the thumb of your left hand, the skin of it silvery white. Where a saw slipped? Or a rock-edge tore it open? If I do not leave now I will put my fork through your wrist, so I push myself to my feet but you lean forward, too close but you do not touch. As though you know you mustn't touch me.

'Georgie,' you say softly in your love-me voice, 'talk to me. Please.'

6

The British Museum looms like a mighty fortress of antiquity in Bloomsbury, tucked deep in the heart of London. The building was designed by Sir Robert Smirke in 1823 to house the finest and largest collection of ancient artefacts in existence anywhere in the world. The original collection was established by Sir Hans Sloane and added to by avid collectors like the 7th Earl of Elgin who removed the marble statues from the Parthenon and Acropolis in Athens.

Pillaged was the word that always leapt to Jessie's mind. Not *removed*. Pillaged the statues.

She glanced at the grandiose neo-classical exterior of the museum, guarded by forty-four colossal ionic columns, each one forty-five feet high. Jessie's head was full of these facts. *Robert Smirke. Hans Sloane. 1823. Forty-four columns.* It was Tim's fault. He was always bombarding her with them.

She approached along Great Russell Street, a tree-lined thoroughfare, dodging a lumbering dray hauling beer barrels as she crossed the road from Bloomsbury Square. A massive pediment loomed over the museum's main entrance and immediately she heard Tim's voice chattering in her head, full of enthusiasm and brimming with knowledge.

'See the sculptures on it, sis?'

Jessie had scowled at the fifteen allegorical figures poised above the entrance.

'They're by Sir Richard Westmacott. Installed in 1852,' he informed her. 'Superb, aren't they? It's a shame they are so high up and people are—'

'People are thinking,' Jessie cut in with a shake of her head, 'what a monument to British hubris and greed they are.'

'Now, Jess, don't start on that.'

'How would you like it if the Egyptians or Italians or Greeks came over and stole all the remains of our history the way we stole theirs? You would be the first to shout, "Whoa, something is not right here!"'

He had turned solemn blue eyes on her. Reproachful eyes. Eyes that made her sigh and want to snatch back her words. He could do that to her.

'Jess,' he laid both his hands on her shoulders, pinning her to the pavement, 'if explorers and archaeologists hadn't devoted their lives to rescuing these exquisite moments of history from the sand and the sea and the dank cellars where they were languishing, they would have been lost to civilisation for ever. Look at Henry Salt! Look at Howard Carter!'

He released one of her shoulders and waved a hand towards the monolithic building in which he worked. Despite herself, Jessie was always impressed by it.

'We owe them so much,' Tim reminded her.

'Thieves,' she muttered.

'Caretakers of the world's creative instinct.'

'Robbers.'

'Just wait until you see Amenhotep's head.' Her brother's eyes were shining. His hair, worn longer than their father liked, gleamed honey-gold in the sunlight.

Jessie had slipped her hand in his with a sigh of resignation. 'Lead on, "my intimate friend and associate".'

He had thrown back his head and laughed, and it was impossible not to laugh with him. How many times had those words of Sherlock Holmes to his dear Dr Watson tightened the knot between Jessie and her brother when it threatened to fray?

She ran up the front steps now. Tim would be there, she was sure he would. Back at work today, caressing and numbering his ceramics and potsherds, talking to them. He couldn't keep away. An indulgent laugh escaped her, snatched away by the icy wind that skittered up from the trees that lined Great Russell Street. *Be there, Tim. Stop sulking. You've given Ma and Pa enough of a scare.*

She walked with quick steps through the cavernous entrance-hall, but the past came at her, not with a gentle touch and a sleepy murmur, but with claws unsheathed. The milky blind eyes of the towering statues from Rome and Greece scraped her nerve ends and made her indifferent to their beauty. Her footsteps hurried, heels tapping on the York stone flooring, the breath of history coming fast and cold on her neck. Yet she saw other visitors ambling slowly from exhibit to exhibit, taking time to admire the fold of a marble cloak or the sweet delicacy of a maiden's arm.

Why can't I do that? Just stand and stare.

Tim was enraptured by this place. Why couldn't she be? She forced herself to a halt in front of the next exhibit and gazed up at the ten-foot-high colossal head of red granite. She knew who it was without looking at its plaque. Amenhotep III. One of Tim's favourite pieces, vast and regal. A great Egyptian pharaoh whose fist once held power over life and death, and whose head bore a massive granite *pschent*, the towering double crown of Upper and Lower Egypt. Part of his face was missing, a frailty that pleased Jessie.

'It was Giovanni Belzoni who found him,' Tim had told her. 'He brought him from Luxor in 1817. It took eight days to transport the three-thousand-year-old head, plus its eighteen feet long left arm, just one mile from the Temple of Mut in Karnak to the river. From there it was shipped on the Nile to Alexandria and on to London. Just imagine it!'

Jessie didn't care to imagine it. Instead she marched off down a side corridor, away from the hypnotic grip of that vast red granite face. But as she raised a hand to knock on one of the doors, she couldn't help wondering what went on in a person's head when he worked every day with objects and people who were thousands of years old. Did death become more real to him than life?

Jessie didn't look back. She could never bear to look back.

'Mr Kenton?' The man in the small stuffy office ruffled his moustache in a friendly manner. 'You should ask Anippe Kalim. She works with him downstairs in the basement, but he's not in today.'

'Have you seen him recently?'

'Miss Kenton,' he said with a chesty chuckle, 'I see many things in this place, more than you'd ever imagine.' He pushed his peaked cap to the back of his head. 'But no, I ain't seen your brother these last few days. When you do find him, tell him from me, old Charlie, that the last tip he gave me was a beauty.'

'Tip?'

'Lightning Lad. Won a nice little packet, I did.' He looked at her blank expression and added, 'At White City.'

Realisation dawned. 'Greyhound racing?'

'That's right.'

Tim, a gambler? Jessie frowned. She had no idea.

She tried not to feel like an intruder as she entered the room where Timothy worked. It was long and high-ceilinged, the walls lined with glass-fronted cabinets containing historic artefacts. Ceramic pots and silver amulets stood alongside extraordinarily beautiful sets of bead jewellery, laid out with loving care on sheets of cotton wool. Alabaster figurines and bronze sculptures stared at Jessie with ancient eyes. Underneath the cabinets were dozens of mahogany drawers and she could imagine them tightly packed with items that would make her brother salivate with anticipation, the way he did over a box of dates when he was a child. The electric light was harsh and bounced off the large rectangular worktables that filled

47

the centre of the room, and the smell of gypsum hung in the air, as well as a chemical that tasted waxy on the back of her tongue.

One person stood alone in the room, bent over one of the tables. It was a young woman. Her thick black hair was braided into a loop at the back of her head and her skin was the colour of dusky eggshell. Jessie watched her at work for several moments before she spoke.

'Miss Anippe Kalim?' she asked.

Only then did the woman's eyes lift to her, though she must have heard her visitor enter the workroom. Her eyes were black. Not black like coal is black, but black like the night sky, black within black. Layer after layer of it, with strange lights shifting inside it.

'Yes, I am Anippe Kalim.'

This was the kind of woman who looked you straight in the eyes. *But she doesn't want me here.* Jessie could feel it in the room, the unexpected animosity, like ants crawling over her skin.

'I'm sorry to interrupt you when you're obviously busy,' Jessie said.

When she approached, Anippe Kalim's hands hovered protectively over the fragments of bone in front of her, as though to ward off inspection. She was wearing an old-fashioned brown dress that reached almost to her ankles under a crisp white buttoned overall, and she slid her hands into its pockets as she turned to face Jessie.

'What is it you want?' she asked.

'My name is—'

'I know who you are.'

Jessie stared at her. How could this woman know who she was?

'You are Jessica Kenton.'

There was a flicker in the large black eyes. Something like amusement. The rest of her features were too strong to be called beautiful, though her mouth was well-shaped and her lips a full deep red, but her face was one that would always draw attention. There was an intensity to it that made it hard to look away. She was tall and slender like one of her Egyptian papyrus reeds and her movements

48

were precise and considered. Jessie felt at a disadvantage but didn't know why.

'He told me about you,' Anippe said. 'Described you.'

'Who? Old Charlie?'

'No. Timothy. He showed me a photograph.'

'A photograph of me?'

'Yes.' Suddenly a smile softened the lines of her face, and her thick black eyelashes fluttered. 'Timothy ...' she said his name with the emphasis on the last syllable, turning it into something exotic, '... told me that you are his *uraeus*.'

'His what?'

'His *uraeus*.'

'What is that?'

Jessie wasn't sure she liked the idea of her brother discussing her with his girlfriend, who now swung around to face the framed photograph on the wall behind her. She pointed to the impressive statue in the picture.

'Ramses the Second,' she told Jessie. 'The greatest pharaoh of ancient Egypt. Three thousand years ago he ruled the New Kingdom for sixty-seven years during the time of the 19th Dynasty. This statue stands in the Temple of Karnak, a temple so magnificent and so vast that I fell to my knees in the sand, pierced by awe and dread, the first time I laid eyes on it.'

Jessie couldn't imagine this proud creature on her knees to anyone. 'Where is Timothy?' she asked.

Anippe ignored the question. 'You see the headdress that King Ramses is wearing?'

'Yes.'

It flared stiffly at each side of his head, a bit like a nun's, and reached to his shoulders.

'That is called a *nemes*,' the young woman told her. 'Can you see what is on the front of the *nemes* on his forehead?'

Jessie frowned at the picture. 'A snake's head.'

'It is a cobra. Only the pharaoh was permitted to wear the cobra on his *nemes*. It was a sign of royalty and it was there to protect him from harm, a cobra spitting poison at any attacker.' Anippe's full lips stretched into a wider smile, but her cheekbones remained taut and hard-edged. 'It is called the *uraeus*.'

'The cobra's head?'

'Yes. Timothy regarded you as his *uraeus*.' She studied Jessie's face in silence for a moment, then said in a low respectful voice, 'It is an honour to be so regarded.'

'But it also means that the young blighter saw himself as a pharaoh!' Jessie pointed out crossly. How much did this person know about her?

Anippe laughed, a crystal clear sound that circled the glass cases and settled in Jessie's ears. She wanted to pluck it out but couldn't. She noticed that the Egyptian woman was wearing a chiffon scarf of blue and gold tied around her neck, to which her hands now crept. Tim had once told her that blue and gold were the colours of eternal life in Ancient Egypt, the colours of King Tutankhamen's death-mask, the one Howard Carter unearthed, glistening with gold and lapis lazuli. Now Anippe wore them.

'I'm looking for Timothy. Have you seen him, Miss Kalim?'

'No. He has not come into work this week.'

'Do you know where he is?'

'No. Do you?'

'I wouldn't be here if I did.'

A silence, as solid as the bones on the table, settled between them and Jessie felt her mouth turn dry. She was convinced that Tim was not just sulking.

'I need to find my brother,' she said firmly. 'I am worried about him.'

She stepped back and let her gaze rest on one of the cabinets, giving the young woman time to think. She leaned close to the cabinet and was dimly aware of a blur of rich turquoise within it, but her mind was struggling to think clearly.

'You came with Tim to our parents' house, I believe, on the morning of the day he disappeared.'

'I did.'

'Why did you come with him?'

'He wanted me to meet your mother.'

'I'm sorry. I apologise for my mother's . . .'

'No need. I am used to it.'

Jessie swung around to look at her. An outsider. Always judged by the colour of her skin. The young woman's expression possessed a stillness that gave no hint of what was in her mind. Or in her heart.

'Do you love him?' Jessie murmured.

Anippe Kalim lowered her eyelids until no more than a slit of darkness showed beneath them. Suddenly she stepped forward, so close that Jessie could feel her hot breath and see the raw hairline crack in the carefully constructed façade. She felt a strong grip on her wrist.

'Jessie, you are his *uraeus*.' The words came in a low hiss. 'Protect your brother.'

'From what? From whom?'

From you? Is that what you mean?

Anippe Kalim swept back to her table of broken bones where her fingers started to shift them around, zigzagging them back and forth like the pieces of a jigsaw.

'Women!' she said contemptuously, as if she were a different species herself. She didn't look at Jessie again. The conversation was over.

Jessie stood stiffly without speaking for two full minutes. Only the click-clack of the bones made holes in the dusty silence. When she had control of the words in her head, she straightened a smile on her face and approached the table once more. She picked up a nodule of bone and weighed it in her hand.

'Now,' Jessie said softly, 'enough of this. Please tell me what you know about what Timothy was doing and what you think might have happened to him.'

The stillness vanished from the dark eyes.

'Miss Kalim?'

Dusky fingers twisted at the blue and gold scarf. 'I have neither seen him nor heard from Timothy since that Friday.'

'What happened after you left my parents' house?'

'Nothing.' Her slender shoulders shrugged. 'We came here to work.'

'Was Tim annoyed with my mother?'

'Yes.'

'And after work?'

There was a moment. A blank spot. As if Anippe Kalim's intelligent mind had just hit a brick wall.

'We said goodnight.'

'Did you quarrel that evening? Did he walk away? Angry for the second time that day. Is that what happened?'

Jessie saw a mask fall into place, as rigid as Tutankhamen's, as the Egyptian woman answered, 'We were going to a lecture by Professor Bascombe about the exciting new finds on the Giza plateau near Cairo, but . . . ' she blinked, just once, 'but he told me he had somewhere else to go.'

'Where?'

'I don't know.'

'Did you ask?'

'No.'

Jessie could imagine it. This young woman too proud to ask, and Tim too absorbed in his own turmoil to notice. Did he come to Putney? To seek out his big sister. But she had been out that Friday night at the jazz club with Tabitha. A kick like a mule's hit her stomach but she didn't even flinch. It was guilt. Her old friend.

'If you hear from him – or hear anything that might give a clue as to where Tim is – please telephone me.' Jessie placed her business card on the mahogany surface of the table beside the ancient bones. It looked out of place. As if a segment of 1932 had accidentally slid down a fissure into the wrong millennium.

Anippe did not even glance at it.

'Goodbye, Miss Kalim.'

A faint nod was the only response, nothing more. Frustrated, Jessie walked away but as she did so, she felt a fierce sense of groping in the dark. Her footsteps echoed across the floor, like the footsteps on the landing that echoed in her mind.

7

Feed me. Please. Feed me.

The words were silent. Locked inside the eyes that stared dully up at Jessie from the gutter. A little girl, sooty as a chimney sweep, was sitting on the kerb, hugging her bony knees to her chest. Her thin coat was belted with string and her feet were bare in her shoes, the tips of which had been cut off to allow for growth. Her hand stretched out limply towards Jessie as she passed, but it transformed itself instantly into a sharp little mousetrap when Jessie placed coins in it. With a scrabble of limbs, the child scuttled away down a narrow alleyway under lines of washing.

Jessie watched the skinny legs vanish and she felt a surge of anger. The National Government was a sham. It was doing nowhere near enough to sort out the economic disaster in Britain right now and Prime Minister Ramsey MacDonald was a fool. A fool who had betrayed his own socialist cause. Each day the newspaper headlines grew worse and each day her stomach turned at the sight of despairing queues outside soup kitchens. The Great Depression they were calling it. The Slump. Though one MP had the gall to call it no more than a *set-back*. It didn't matter what name the politicians pinned on it, it all meant the same to the men and women in the street. Factories closed. No jobs. No bread on the table. Hardest hit were the workers of Scotland, Wales and the north of England where mass unemployment was rife, but even here in the East End of London conditions were appalling.

And now Sir John Gilmour, the Home Secretary, was going to snatch the roof from over their heads by cutting unemployment benefit and imposing a means test. The savagery of it had created unrest throughout the country, and here in these helpless, hopeless streets where people huddled, raw-faced in the wind, Jessie could sense the tension as thick as the yellow fog in the air. It made the hairs on her arms rise and the thickness of her winter coat feel like a disgrace.

'Archie, open this blasted door!'

Jessie's hand banged against the wood. Its paint was peeling and the smell of damp-rot sent sour spikes up into her nostrils. The dilapidated building was one of the many back-to-back terraced houses in a maze of narrow mean streets. It had outside steps leading down to a basement, and it was down this flight of crumbling stone stairs that she had descended to Archie Dashington's basement flat. In the gloomy stairwell, set ten feet below street level, rubbish had accumulated: discarded Woodbine cigarette packets, fish and chip papers, a sodden *Sunday Pictorial* and a broken clothes-mangle. Jessie knew it was no good expecting Archie to clean up the mess. He wasn't that type.

With one eye alert for rats, she rapped on the door once more and heard the soft pad of feet on the other side. It opened halfway to reveal a mole-eyed young man of about her own age with rumpled ginger hair, wearing a collarless flannelette shirt tucked into shapeless trousers. He looked – mistakenly – like a workman. Jessie had known Archie since he was thirteen, when he had given Timothy a black eye at school.

'Gosh, Jessie! Jolly early in the morning to come calling.'

'For heaven's sake, Archie, it's almost eleven o'clock. Hardly early.'

His small eyes blinked at her uneasily. He might have hidden his breeding behind second-hand clothes, but he betrayed himself in his upper-class vowels and a vocabulary straight out of a boarding school tuck-box.

'I need to talk to you, Archie. About Tim.'

'Oh?' He didn't open the door any wider.

'May I come in? It's filthy cold out here.'

He made no move to admit her, so she stepped forward, forcing him to retreat into the dank hallway.

'It's not frightfully convenient just now,' he muttered, belatedly standing his ground. 'Next week would suit . . .'

Jessie smiled. 'Come on, Archie. Whatever or whoever you're hiding in there, I won't tell, I promise.' She kissed his freckled cheek. 'Unless it's Tim, of course.'

'It's not Tim.'

'Then let's go in and talk.'

She slipped an arm purposefully through his and steered him towards the door to the living room. It was always the same with men of Archie's class, born to privilege and wealth. They might rule the British Empire but they had no idea how to stand up to a woman. She put it down to a childhood spent dominated by a nanny in starched white uniform who wielded the back of a spoon with enthusiasm over bare young knuckles. Why Archie Dashington had chosen to exist in this dismal working-class hovel while still drawing a generous monthly allowance from his father who was a minister in the Ramsay MacDonald's coalition government, Jessie had no idea. Archie certainly didn't appear to do any work, had in fact never held a job in his life, as far as she knew, not since leaving Harrow School along with Tim. She swung open the door, a tight grip on her host's arm to stop him bolting.

The smell struck her first. Unwashed socks and the sour breath from empty bellies. There must have been twenty men crammed in the small room. No sound. Just suspicious eyes fixed on her and a grey pall of cigarette smoke blurring the edges of scowls. Thin as ferrets, all of them, and dressed in work clothes. Some stood in huddles, others sprawled on the bare linoleum, a few propped up the damp walls. Jessie could sense their hostility.

'Good morning, gentlemen,' she said brightly.

'Who's this?' a voice demanded. It came from a man who wore a stained flat cap and was chewing on a crust of bread. In fact, Jessie noticed that all the men had something to eat in their hands.

'She's the sister of a friend of mine,' Archie explained with a dismissive shrug. 'Just fussing over something. Nothing for you to worry about.' He barged a pathway through the men, pushing her towards the tiny kitchenette at the far end of the room, and shut the door behind them, but not before someone's hand had touched her calf as she stepped over him. Tiny was too big a word for the kitchenette. It was barely larger than a telephone booth.

'Archie! What on earth is going on out there?'

'Just some men.'

'I can see that. Who are they?'

'They're marchers. Union men.' He pushed his face towards her, worried. 'Don't say a word about them to anyone, will you?'

'Marchers?'

'The Means Test march.'

'Oh, for heaven's sake, Archie, are you crazy?'

'No.'

An organisation called the National Unemployed Workers' Movement had rallied thousands of unemployed from all over the country to set off on a march on London to present a petition to Parliament. Against the Means Test. A million signatures. The snaking column of thousands of marching boots and banners was due to arrive for a mass gathering in Hyde Park the following Tuesday, 27th October. But rumours were spreading already. That it was Communist-led. That they intended to smash the government. That London was in danger. Panic was seeping under the closed doors of government offices throughout London. Here in the slums of the East End the mood was sour, and this close to Archie, Jessie could see the anger in his eyes. But there was something else there, too. Shame. That was it, a dark grey wing of shame.

'The police will be waiting for them,' she warned in a voice too quiet for the men in the next room to hear.

'That's why you must tell no one. Promise me, Jess.'

She nodded. 'Of course I won't. But you know you are taking a risk.'

He leaned his back against the door, and kicked a cigarette butt that lay squashed on the floor. 'Someone has to. Poor bastards. I am ashamed of this government.' He raised his eyes to hers. 'Ashamed of my father's part in it.'

For a moment in the miniscule kitchen with its greasy walls, they exchanged a look, as a thread of understanding stretched between them. It was what had always bound them together as friends, their mutual disconnection from their fathers. Never mentioned. Never discussed. As if words would inflict too much damage, spill too much blood.

'I'm sorry, Archie.' Jessie lightly touched her fingers to his sleeve. 'But don't get yourself into trouble. Those men are spoiling for a fight.'

'Wouldn't you be?'

'I don't want that pretty nose of yours to get into an argument with a policeman's truncheon.'

The muscles of his face relaxed, making him suddenly younger, turning him into the boy who used to be the conker king at school. He reached out for the dented tin kettle, ran water into it and placed it on a gas ring, all without moving more than a foot.

'So,' he rumpled his fiery hair and gave Jessie his full attention, 'what has that bally idiot brother of yours done now?'

'He has disappeared.'

'What?'

'Vanished.'

He laughed, a burst of sound that stirred up the chill air.

'Don't laugh,' she told him seriously. 'He's been gone a week. Nobody has seen him since Friday of last week.'

'Last Friday?'

'Yes. Do you know where he is?'

'Damn me! Vanished, you say.'

'Do you know where he went on that Friday night?'

'Yes, actually I do.' He held his hand out to the blue flame of the

57

gas burner for warmth. 'The same as he did most weekends. He was obsessed with it.'

'Tim? Obsessed? He never mentioned anything to me – except the museum's Egyptian collection, of course.'

'That's because he knew you would disapprove. You know what he's like, always desperate for big sister's approval.'

Jessie frowned. *Is he?* He had hidden that from her too.

'So where did he go?' she urged.

Archie hesitated.

'Where?' She shook his arm. 'Where?'

He looked away, suddenly awkward. 'To a séance.'

'What kind of idiot would do that?'

'For heaven's sake, Jess, it was only a stupid séance. Don't look like that.'

She snatched her car key from her coat pocket. 'Just tell me where.'

Séance.

A word that hissed and slithered. It crawled up her back and made her shiver. *Timothy, what were you thinking of?* She felt a tightness grip her chest. She wanted to sit down with her brother and talk to him calmly about this extraordinary secret obsession of his, but instead she was hurtling along the A40 at breakneck speed, knuckles white on the steering-wheel. Her little Austin Swallow swooped around a Saturday morning charabanc and a sign to Denham Village flashed past.

Who was it he was reaching out to? Who was he so keen to contact?

She shook her head, exasperated.

It was all the fashion, this idea of seeking out the spirits of the dead, a nation in chaos trying to find guidance in the past. As if the previous generation hadn't made enough of a mess of things without dabbling their interfering fingers in the present. Everyone was doing it. Biddy Bradshaw, a girl who worked alongside Jessie at the studio, was always threatening to bring in her ouija board for a session during their lunch break. It was society's latest craze, drawing in the hard-nosed intellectuals as readily as the fragile young widows bereaved in the Great War. It worried Jessie. That a nation could be so gullible, so eager to hear the voices of the dead when it should be listening to the voices of those starving on the streets.

How could she have missed it in Tim? Shouldn't she have spotted something so huge sitting on his shoulders and something so opaque clouding his mind?

She stamped on the brake as a cyclist with his dog trotting alongside came around a blind corner as if he owned the road. She sounded the horn.

Slow down. Think straight. She cast her mind back to the last time she'd seen her brother. They had gone to the cinema to see Johnny Weissmuller in *Tarzan the Ape Man* and she had cooked Tim liver and bacon, his favourite. She could picture him now, grinning at her across the table, his eyes a clear innocent blue. No clouds. No veil. No obsession.

She felt betrayed. Tim was the only person in her life with whom she could let her guard down, the one she could dare trust. The one she could dare love. Because she had learned at a young age that love was too dangerous, like a time-bomb in your chest waiting to go off. And yet again it had proved itself unreliable. It could not be depended on. Recently her life had been going well, so – stupidly – she had relaxed and forgotten to be watchful. She had looked away. Just for a moment.

So what did it mean?

'Timothy!'

It was the tone she always used to him when he was young and had pinched one of her carefully sharpened drawing pencils or when he bounced a tennis ball against her wardrobe while she was trying to read. She was never any good at reprimanding him, yet now she wanted to shake him till his eyes fell out – just as she did the very first time she found him in Georgie's bed.

Had death become more real to him than life?

As she turned left into a rural lane edged with thinning hedgerows, signposted Lower Lampton, she fought off a ferocious urge to jam her fist on the horn. To blast the quiet smug country air into pieces.

8

Georgie

England 1921

In the early days of your visits, you grow impatient easily. You do not know me yet, do not understand that my brain works in a different way from yours and takes twisted paths. You suggest that we sit and talk in the public room downstairs.

'Why?' I ask.

'Because it's more acceptable than sitting here in your bedroom.'

'I hate downstairs.'

'Why? What's wrong with it?'

'It's full of ...' I try to explain. 'Full of Others. I laugh when someone spills a drink or trips over. Dr Churchward tells me that my responses are "inappropriate" and that I have no social skills. He says I cause trouble downstairs.'

You sit in my desk chair and study me, until I feel my cheeks burn and my head is filling up with rage, though I don't know why. I stare hard at my blank white wall.

'You don't like being looked at, do you?' you whisper.

'No.'

'You don't like being touched.'

'No.'

'You don't like loud sounds.'

'No.'

'You don't like people.'

'I like you.'

'Really?'

'Yes.'

'But you don't ever look me in the eye.'

I say nothing. The wall is flat and cooling. I try to squeeze some of the rage out of my head and onto the wall instead. I do like you but I have never said those words before to anyone except my sister and I am frightened that you might disappear now that I have said them to you. I stand up without looking at you and take off all my clothes.

'Wait a minute,' you say quickly, 'what the hell are you doing?'

'I want you to see me truly, without the bits that are hidden, because I know parts of me are ugly but I want you to know that they are there, so that you won't run away when you see them at some point in the future.'

I tear off my socks and stand naked.

'Christ, you're crazy.'

It feels bad when you say that to me. It feels the same as when the boy downstairs with the droopy eye – one of the Others – stabbed me in the cheek with his fork and the prongs went right through to my tongue. I chased him up the stairs with the fork hanging out of my cheek, my blood dripping on the carpet. When I caught him, I—

'All right, Georgie,' you interrupt my thoughts. 'I've seen you now, so you can put your clothes back on, thank you.'

'Did you see the bad parts?'

'You look perfectly normal to me.'

I feel sick. I pull on my vest. 'Didn't you see the bad bits, the bits inside that are ugly and deformed?'

61

'Oh, Georgie, let me tell you a secret.' You lean forward, making me leap back towards the window in a panic, one leg in my trousers, one out, and I fall flat on my back. My head hits the skirting board. You stare at me, shocked. But you sit back down on your chair, wait for me to stand up and continue talking as though nothing has happened. I think that is the moment I start to love you.

'My secret,' you say, 'is that I also have bad bits inside that are ugly and deformed. But I hide them better.'

I listen to your voice, your soft sad voice, and I rub the back of my head.

'Show me one,' I say.

You think for a long moment. You run a hand through your thick curls and tug at them so hard it must hurt.

'I hated you, Georgie, when I was a child, even though I didn't know you. I hated you because Jessie loved you so much, and I wanted her to love me instead. I blamed you for making me miserable when I wanted to be so happy in my new family. I slept in your bed and each night in the dark I plunged one of Ma's hatpins – one I had stolen – into your pillow. And do you know what I imagined it to be?'

I shake my head. My heart is so cold it barely moves.

'I imagined it,' you continue in a tone that I have never heard in your mouth before, 'to be your eye. I wanted to do the worst thing I could think of to you, to blind you.'

'It was only a pillow.'

'Yes. Only a pillow.'

'Why do you come here?' You are surprised by the question, yet it is an obvious one. 'Why shut yourself in this prison for half a day each week when you have the whole of freedom waiting out there for you?'

You shrug, careless. 'Because you interest me.'

'Why? You think I am crazy.'

'We are all a bit crazy in this life.'

I don't know when you lie to me. I can't tell. So I don't know whether you are speaking the truth or doing what you call *teasing*.

I want to lie down on my bed and pull the blanket over my head but I know that if I do that, you will leave. So I stand there in front of you, watching the way you tap your fingers on the leg of the chair. I don't know why you do it. Is it a tune? Or is it a signal that I cannot understand?

'You never lie, do you, Georgie?'

'No. I say what is in my head.'

You smile. 'I've noticed.'

'Why do you come here?' I ask again.

You take out a cigarette and light it with a match. I am shocked but excited by the action, surprised by the smell. I have never smelled tobacco before and it is not pleasant, but it doesn't worry me and I hold out my hand. You give me the cigarette and I put it between my lips, inhale the way you did and cough till my eyes water. But I like it. You laugh and I laugh with you. We pass the cigarette back and forth between us until it is a tiny stub which I stamp out with the heel of my foot. I smile at the dead white stub, when really I want to smile at you.

'That was fun,' you say, giggling.

'The attendant will be angry. It smells in here.'

'So what? What can they do to you? Nothing much.'

I nod. It is my first ever lie to you. I do not tell you how much they can do to me with their needles.

'Why do you come here?'

'Christ, Georgie, you don't give up, do you?'

'Why should I?'

You laugh. 'You have a point. No wonder you're good at learning things. Not lazy like me. All right, I'll tell you why I come here.'

You are suddenly so intense, you frighten me. I stare at the white wall and say nothing.

'I come because you and I are two halves of the same person.'

'That is a lie. How can we be . . . ?'

'Not literally, Georgie. It's just a way of saying that you and I need each other.'

I nod. 'That is true.'

'I grew up wanting to be you. Wanting my sister to love me the way she loved you, but always knowing I was second best. I could never do the things you did, the clever stuff of remembering lists and patterns and reciting pages of Sherlock Holmes stories by heart. Jessie admired you more than she will ever admire me.'

I feel a heat in my chest, in my cheeks, in the palms of my hands. Jessie admired me. I didn't know. 'I thought she wanted me to be sent away,' I say and you shake your head.

'No. It was because of me that they got rid of you. I was responsible.' You tug at your hair too hard, much too hard. 'If our parents had not found me, you might have stayed there with Jessie and she would have taught you to behave properly. She can teach anything. She taught me to be you in many ways, to like the things you liked, to do the things you did, but I wasn't much good at it.'

My mind feels as if somebody's hands are inside it, taking it apart.

'Tim, did she talk about me?'

'Yes. But our parents never did. They would not let your name be spoken in the house, so I knew I had to make them love me or they would send me away as well. But Jessie told me how you used to stand up to them, how you defied them, and I envied you your courage.' You smile at me and I long to give you whatever it is you need.

'You have courage,' I say. 'You come to this place every Saturday. I would run away.'

You laugh and I am happy. I made you laugh. You stand up but you know better than to come close.

'So you see, Georgie, I could never allow myself just to be me. For Jessie I tried to be you and for our parents I tried to be the perfect son. And I'm still doing it.' You point a finger at me and then at my room. 'Only here can I be myself, no pretending, no lies. Just me. Just you. With all our ugly and deformed bits on view.'

I raise my eyes and make myself fix them on your face.

'Understand?' you ask.

'Let's have another cigarette.'

9

Chamford Court was not what Jessie expected. Some sort of pretentious Victorian pile built by a local merchant who had made his fortune out of wool or tin mining in the last century. A dreary home built to impress the local gentry. Solid and dull. That's what Jessie had expected and she had no patience with bad architecture. It grated on her nerves worse than sandpaper on teeth. But bad architecture wasn't what she found.

She drove into the village of Lower Lampton, a tired cluster of red-brick cottages with a last few roses losing their petals to the cold October wind. She enquired at the pub and was directed down a winding lane, past a sleepy church and up an incline. 'About a mile out of town,' the landlord told her.

Town? He called this dead-in-a-hole place a *town?*

'Can't miss it,' he added with a chuckle. 'It's got gates.'

It did indeed have gates. Twenty feet high. Wrought iron. Massive stone pillars on either side, with an arch spanning the gap between them and a magnificent stone stag rampant on top of it, but the whole gateway was in ruins. Rust and weeds had claimed it as their own, so that the stag was choked by ivy and the open gates hung by a thread on one hinge. Behind them a long potholed drive cut a line as straight as a poker through rough pastureland and disappeared behind a grove of beech trees that whispered and complained in the wind. She imagined Tim arriving here, listening to the whispers, to the voices of the dead. His heart thumping.

She pressed her foot on the accelerator and shot up the driveway.

The house stood on a low hill on the far side of the beech trees, hidden from the road, a vast and gracious Georgian mansion with elegant columns, an intricate pediment and perfect proportions. It was the kind of building that even on a grey day like today acted like sunshine on Jessie – the beauty of its lines made her skin glow and her heartbeat slow with contentment.

But like the gates it was swathed in a pall of neglect and dilapidation, weeds colonising along its roofline and sprouting from its gutters, paint peeling, upstairs windows boarded, a green skin of moss and ivy clinging to north-facing walls. Worse, far worse, was the east wing of the house. It had been gutted by fire and what was left of its blackened bricks pushed up from the ground like rotten teeth. Nettles and elder had taken a stranglehold, so the fire could not have been recent. Jessie had a sense of time suspended, of breath held, of the trees and the fields waiting to creep up to reclaim the hill.

Yet as she neared the house, freshly mown lawns spread out with billiard-table precision on either side of the drive and a gardener in a leather apron was tending an immaculate rose-bed. He lifted his head as she drove past. She parked her car in front of the columned portico and walked up the wide front steps, glancing over her shoulder at the view behind her. The Chamford estate stretched away in the distance in a shimmer of russet and amber shadows. She reached up, rang the big brass doorbell and waited. She inspected the heavy panelled door and felt the wind nip at her neck. She heard no noise inside. Presumably the bell sounded somewhere deep in the belly of the house, but just in case, she banged a fist on the door.

'Can I help you?'

The man's voice behind her startled Jessie. She swung round and saw it was the gardener, spade in hand.

'I'm looking for Sir Montague Chamford,' she said.

'That's me.'

'You?'

'Yes. But don't call me Sir Montague or I shall have to go and don a wing collar and a gold pocket-watch.' He laughed, amused by the notion, and she had a sense of someone who was accustomed to hiding behind laughter.

He, like his house, was not what she expected. No portly paunch or cigar-speckled waistcoat. No whiskers. He was thirty-five years old at most, with nondescript brown hair and sharp-boned features that bore the stamp of generations of carefully selected breeding. He was tall, with strikingly long arms as if he'd borrowed them from someone else, but even in his shaggy sweater and leather apron he looked undernourished.

'What can I do for you?' he asked with courtesy.

'I came here to ask about a séance that I believe was conducted here last week. On Friday the fifteenth.'

He had been standing two steps below her, leaning on his spade in a relaxed manner and looking up at her as though hoping she might perform a cartwheel or produce a rabbit from her pocket for his amusement. But the word *séance* shattered his cut-glass politeness. Abruptly, a hard energy stiffened his limbs. He leapt up the steps and pushed open the door without a word, just a curt nod of the head to indicate that she should enter.

She walked warily through the doorway and found herself in a high-ceilinged reception hall that reeked of mice and drains. Heavy oak furniture of much earlier ancestry than the house made the room gloomy, but Jessie barely noticed. She was too busy following Don't-call-me-Sir-Montague down a maze of cold corridors, tight on his heels, and through empty echoing rooms with exquisite ceilings and bold statuary, past good and bad oil paintings, faces hanging like ghosts on the walls, and into a large comfortable kitchen. It was clearly the only warm room in the house.

An ancient refectory table extended down the centre towards a fireplace where logs were burning inside an iron fire-basket, scenting the air with applewood. As they entered, a border-collie dog scrambled out of its basket beside the fire and leaned its shoulder against its master's leg, regarding Jessie with intelligent brown eyes that were a darn sight friendlier than Sir Montague Chamford's. He had folded his arms firmly across his chest and was studying her with suspicion.

'So,' he said curtly, 'I assume you are another of the journalists, sniffing around here again trying to dig up a story. Well, I'm telling you now that there's nothing to find. Yes, notable people have occasion to call in here sometimes, but these are private matters which have nothing—'

'I'm looking for my brother.'

'What?'

'Timothy Kenton.'

He frowned. The dog uttered a low rumble in its throat.

'My brother is Timothy Kenton. He came here on Friday of last week.'

It was subtle, the relaxation. But Jessie spotted it, the way his limbs grew less rigid, the threat of a smile arriving on one side of his mouth.

'Well, Miss Kenton, it seems I may have wronged you.'

'Yes, Sir Montague, it seems you may.'

For the slightest of moments there was a stand-off between them, both assessing the other's position, before he stuck out his hand.

'Please do excuse me,' he said with an engaging smile.

She inclined her head, shook his hand and accepted the hard-back chair that he offered her at the table. He took the seat opposite her.

'Tell me about your brother.'

'He came here on Friday the fifteenth. To a séance.'

She half-expected him to deny it. *A séance? Here? What nonsense!* But he didn't. He nodded.

'That's possible,' he said.

'So you know him?'

'No, I've never met your brother in my life. It's true that a séance is occasionally held here, but I don't meet the participants.' He said it casually, as if it were the most normal thing in the world to have a séance take place in your house, and ruffled his dog's ear, earning himself a flash of tongue across his wrist. 'You have to understand that seekers after spirits like to come here. The house is apparently bursting at the seams with ectoplasm,' he waved a hand through the air, 'and spirits drift in and out like Charing Cross Station. More ghosts than rats in a sewer, it seems.'

He laughed and suggested a sherry. Jessie declined.

'I don't believe in ghosts,' she told him. 'I believe in people you can touch, ones you can hold on to.'

'Like your brother, you mean?'

'Timothy is flesh and blood. He can't vanish. Yet ever since he came to your séance, he has been missing.'

He leaned forward, intrigued. 'Vanished into thin air along with one of my spectres?'

'No.' Jessie slapped the flat of her hand down on the table, making the dog jump. 'Nothing like your spectres. So will you please tell me what happened here that Friday night?'

He showed no sign of taking offence. He was an aristocrat to his fingertips; high prominent cheekbones and an air of benign tolerance, as if well accustomed to the boorish antics of peasants. He looked at her hard, his lazy brown eyes assessing her in a way that was not remotely lazy. His long limbs remained relaxed in an off-hand manner, and his mouth remained set in its amused curve. But Jessie wasn't taken in. There was no amusement in those eyes.

'In a bit of a flap, aren't you?' he said nonchalantly.

'I told you, I'm here to find my brother.'

'So I see.'

For a moment a silence funnelled into the room. They looked at each other while a soundless tussle took place and it was the owner of the house who backed off first by lifting his sherry in its antique cut-glass to his lips.

'Let's see what we can do, shall we?' he suggested.

'Do you know what happened at the séance?'

'I have no idea. Sorry to disappoint you, but I told you, I wasn't there. No, don't look so glum, it doesn't mean I can't find out.'

'Who else was here that night? The other people attending the séance, I mean.'

'There's only one person who can tell us that.'

'Who?'

'Madame Anastasia.'

'She is . . . ?

'The medium who conducted the proceedings.'

He said it formally, as if talking about a law court instead of a needy group of ghost-hunters. Jessie stood up. 'She's the person I need to speak to. Do you have her address? Her telephone number?'

To her irritation, Sir Montague tipped his chair back on two legs with an indolent air and regarded her over his glass.

'Slow down, Miss Kenton, slow down. Madame Anastasia is not an easy person to track down. She is an extremely private creature.'

'Sir Montague, listen to me. My brother, Timothy, has disappeared. That may mean nothing to you, but it does to me. I need to speak to this Madame Anastasia, and I need to speak to her now. Please tell me where I can find her.'

She could feel his reluctance, and it annoyed her. She wanted to pluck the languid expression from his face and make him sense the darkness that stalked the charred corners of his house.

'Her address?' she asked.

Slowly he rose to his feet. 'Madame Anastasia is always busy conducting séances on a Saturday,' he told her. 'So you won't find her at home today. She could be in Manchester or Maidenhead or she may have travelled all the way down to Cornwall, for all I know.'

'And Sundays? Will she be at home tomorrow?'

'Indeed she will.'

It struck Jessie that he knew a lot about the medium's habits. How close, she wondered, was his association with this woman?

'Then I shall drive over to question her tomorrow,' she said. 'I just need you to give me her—'

'No.'

'Pardon?'

'I said no. I will take you to her myself.'

'That's not necessary.'

'I think you'll find it is.'

Again that odd silence funnelled into the room and built a wall, brick by brick, between them. Jessie didn't waste her breath on arguing this time.

'Ten o'clock tomorrow morning, then,' she said. 'I'll be here.'

His hand rumpled his dog's glossy black ears, as comfortably as if they were his own. 'Make it two o'clock. Madame Anastasia doesn't put a foot out of bed before noon. Don't forget that she'll have spent a frantic Saturday wrestling with her spirits and her importunate clients. Let the poor woman have her rest before you plague her with questions.'

Jessie didn't like it. The way he'd turned her, Jessie, into the wicked witch in this situation.

'Two o'clock,' she nodded and headed for the kitchen door, but he reached it before her and swung it open with a courteous bow. 'May I see the room where the séance was held, please?' she asked.

'There's nothing to see,' he said, but shrugged and led her back to the main reception hall with its coat of arms and sweeping staircase.

He pushed open a heavy oak door to reveal a beautiful room with a gilded ceiling that resonated with light and brilliance. The tall windows that overlooked the front drive were hung with weighty purple drapes and two circular tables stood in the centre of the floor, one large, one smaller, each one surrounded by elegant Queen Anne chairs.

'This is where the deed is done. Like I said, nothing to see.'

She could picture Timothy here in one of the chairs – which

71

one? – his heart yearning for something he couldn't have. What was it? Who was he seeking with such single-mindedness?

'Sir Montague, why do you do this?'

'Do what?'

'The séances.'

He smiled at her with genuine amusement this time. 'Why do you think? For money, of course. People pay highly to share a spirit or two with the ancestors of an ancient stately pile like this one.'

'Are things so bad?'

'Pretty dire, to be honest.'

She continued to stare at one of the chairs, searching for her brother's imprint in the faded green silk of its seat.

'Is that why the rooms are so empty?' she asked. No furniture. No ornaments. No fine china or Georgian silver.

He shrugged eloquently and she felt a tug of sorrow for him, for the leanness of his limbs and the emptiness of his casual gesture. 'Sold to fix the roof,' he told her. 'I'm starting on the paintings now. Just shifted a Watteau at Sotheby's. Got a rotten price for it.'

She turned to study him. 'You are a lucky man to have them.' She thought of the men in Archie's flat, the ones with the flat caps and the flatter bellies. 'Most people have never even seen a Watteau, never mind owned one.'

He treated her to a polite nod. 'Lucky. That's me all right. In my lucky house. As lucky as a four-leafed clover wrapped around a rabbit's foot.'

Jessie didn't linger in the room, not with his words just asking to be ripped out of the air.

They emerged onto the front driveway, gravel crunching under their feet. All around them the estate spread out in soft rolling pastures and shadowy patches of woodland, through which Jessie could make out the silvery metallic surface of a lake. What, she wondered, did it do to you to be raised in a place like this? Where you were lord and master of all you survey. Did it make you believe you were the centre of the universe? She rather thought it might. At the very least the centre of your own universe.

'What disaster happened here?' Jessie asked.

For no more than a flash, her companion's brown eyes darkened and she caught a glimpse of inner turmoil. Then it was gone and in its place slid his usual ironic smile as he gestured in the direction of the east wing of the house.

'Ah, you mean our . . . structural restyling.'

They both gazed at the blackened remains on their left, at the charred shoulders of stone doorways and brick walls, sprawled with ivy and strings of bindweed. She stared sadly at the ruined section. In the fading light of the October afternoon, ropes of mist were creeping up from the distant lake with the stealth of a burglar.

'How long ago was the fire?' Jessie asked.

'Three years.'

'What happened?'

He dragged his eyes from the degrading sight of beauty gone bad, and gave a light-hearted laugh. It was out of place but she recognised that it was part of this man's armoury, an attempt to distract her from his words.

'My father – the previous and woefully extravagant Sir Montague Chamford – decided to incinerate himself. Bit drastic, don't you think? Admittedly the debts on the estate had grown so horrendous that he thought it was time to call it a day. The thing was,' his smile took on a fixed quality as though nailed to his face, 'he believed that if he burned down the whole lot, I – as his heir – would at least inherit the insurance money. Daft old blighter. They were onto him like a shot. Arson doesn't pay out, don't you know.'

'It must have been terrible for your mother.'

'She tried to save him. Died in flames, her hair a fiery halo around her head.' His smile didn't alter, but something in his eyes did, something he couldn't quite control.

'I'm so sorry,' Jessie murmured.

'Don't be. It's not your business.'

It was not said rudely, just a statement of fact. He walked over to her muddy Austin Swallow and opened its door for her. His manners were impeccable. He still wore his heavy jumper but had discarded the leather apron, so that he looked leaner than ever, his legs as long and fleshless as ladders.

'Two o'clock tomorrow,' she reminded him.

She climbed in the car but just when she was about to drive off, he leaned down and spoke through the window. 'Splendid. I look forward to it. Don't forget to bring your ouija board.'

'Very funny.'

As she drove off, she could hear his laugh trailing behind her in the bruised afternoon light.

So. That was over. Lies and all.

Montague Charles Gaylord Chamford drew a deep breath into his lungs as he stood on the front steps of his home and watched the little car scoot down the drive. Smoke was whooshing out of its skinny exhaust pipe. It didn't surprise him, the way she drove. It was the same way she walked – full of energy and a sense of purpose. For a moment he allowed himself to imagine what it would be like to jump into her tiny back seat and drive away for ever from this scorched albatross that hung around his neck.

He had enjoyed talking to Miss Kenton. She had brought a burst of life into Chamford, though her appearance here had scared the daylights out of him at first. She had popped up from nowhere like a bad conscience. Something close to a smile passed over his face. He watched the mist crawling on its belly out of the woods and up towards the house while he considered the way Miss Kenton held his gaze, eyes rock steady, navy flecks embedded in the blue of her irises. He recalled how her face grew intent when she was listening, how when she was really concentrating she forgot to blink and lifted the weight of her hair off the back of her neck.

Yet she had believed him. Of that he was certain. She was a young woman who seemed – unwisely – to possess so little guile in her own heart that she was slow to recognise it in others. Tomorrow may not be as bad as he'd feared, especially if Nell kept her turban screwed on straight.

'Coriolanus!' he shouted sternly into the damp air.

The dog was streaking across the lawn towards a rabbit foolish enough to venture out of the shadows to a patch of clover, but the collie veered back at the sound of its master's voice.

'No rabbit pie tonight,' Montague scolded.

One defenceless victim per day was enough.

10

Georgie

England 1922

You arrive in what you call your cricket whites. They don't look white to me. They are the colour of the pearls that I remember used to hang around my mother's neck, but your whites are streaked with green grass stains and there are what look like lipstick smears on your thigh. You tell me it is where you rub the red ball when bowling.

'Why do you rub the ball?'

'To help the bounce.'

I leave it there, though it makes no sense. I leave it because it brings back to my mind the feel of my father's hands on mine as he tried to adjust my small fingers on the handle of my cricket bat. The warmth of his skin burning mine. The strength of him. All powerful. When I think of that moment something starts to judder and shake inside me and I have to bend down to take off my shoes, so that you will not see my face. My father wanted something from me. He wanted a proper son. I look sideways at you with your bright blue eyes and your cricket whites that aren't white and it dawns on me abruptly that they must love you very much. You are a proper son. A proper brother.

When I think of Jessie loving you, waking you, laughing with you, reading to you, I feel cold inside and words tumble from my mouth before I can chain them to my tongue.

'Does Jessie know you come here?' I ask.

'Do you want her to?'

Your question sweeps into my mind, tearing something loose. 'No.'

'Are you sure?'

'Yes.'

We sit on the floor after that, across the room from each other, throwing a cricket ball back and forth. It is oddly satisfying. I drop it often but you laugh and so I laugh. You show me how to close my fingers over it as it thuds into my palm. I am getting better, but I do not like touching the ball because it is red.

'Why don't you want Jessie to know that I have found you?'

'It is obvious,' I tell you. 'You are too intelligent to need to ask.'

'Tell me anyway.'

'I don't want her to see me. Not like this.'

You are silent. You won't look at me. You look down at the ball in your hand. I wait for a time and when eventually you speak, your words sound tired, as though they have been on a long long journey.

'Georgie, I think she would love to see you. Whatever you are like.'

'No. You don't know her. Don't tell Jessie.' My voice is rising.

'It's not fair on her. I'm sure she still misses you.'

The burning in my chest is so fierce that I expect to see flames melting my flesh.

'No, Tim. She let me go.'

'No, that's not true. She tried to find you but—'

'Hush! Throw the ball. I never want us to speak of her again.'

'But, Georgie, she—'

'Shut up!'

You throw the ball and I throw it back. I count one thousand and ninety-two throws before I ask the question again.

'Does Jessie know you come here?'

'No.'

'Good.'

I never want us to speak of her again.

Those nine words haunt me all week. I pour them out onto sheets of paper, covering the blankness with my tiny writing that looks like black ants scurrying across the pages. Hundreds of pages. Drilling them into my mind. When you knock at my door the next Saturday, I open it and open my mouth at the same time to say those nine words to you again. So you will know that I am serious about it. That I mean it.

'Hello, old thing,' you say with your warm smile. 'Had a decent week? Mine was hellish. Old stinky Benton kept me in detention for—'

'Tim,' I interrupt. I shut the door behind him. My mouth is open. The nine words are ready. 'Tim, tell me about Jessie.'

No! The wrong words come out. We stare at each other, shocked. Jessie is one subject we have tiptoed around, afraid that if we unwrap it we will find a cobra inside. It will spit poison at our eyes, so that you and I will never be able to see each other clearly again, we will be blind. I know it. But still I ask.

'Tell me about Jessie. Didn't she ever wonder about me? Didn't she care about me? What has she told you?'

'Sit down,' you say in a voice so gentle I put my hands over my ears to trap the gentleness inside my head. 'Stop crying.'

'Crying?' I touch my face. It is wet. How long have I been crying? Hours? Days?

I sit on the bed and you drape my blue bedcover around me to stop my shivers. You take my desk chair, turn it so that its back is towards me and you sit on it facing me, legs astride the seat. I have never seen anyone sit on a chair like that before, and it strikes me as debonair. That's how a prince or a pirate would sit. I like it. Until

78

I realise that the curves of the chair-back are dividing us, covering your heart, keeping it safe from me.

You start to talk, quietly and for a long time, your blue eyes never leaving my face. I hide my eyes from you, but I can feel the warmth of your gaze, like sunshine on my skin. I listen intently. Memorizing each word. You tell me how angry and upset Jessie was in the early months after I was sent away, how she tried to find out where I was, using all her strength and cunning to extract the truth from our parents. Sometimes she would shout, sometimes cry, sometimes beg on her knees. She tried not eating, not talking, not walking. She tried being the perfect daughter, all smiles and good school grades, and just when Pa and Ma thought she had forgotten, she would suddenly slip in the question, 'Where is Georgie living?' Then everything would catapult back to square one and it would all start again.

Because always their answers were the same.

We will not talk about him.

He is gone. He is sick in the head.

You have a new brother. Forget George.

Silence! George is an aberration who is being properly cared for among his own kind.

Don't mention that name any more!

You pause, but you do not spare me the truth. They are ashamed of me and fear that I will contaminate their daughter if she sees me. I am not a human. I hug my knees to my chest and taste the word in my mouth: *an aberration*.

'Every Christmas and every birthday,' your quiet voice vibrates, as if someone is shaking you, 'she gave them a present to send to you, but after a while they didn't even pretend. They refused to take it and when she insisted, stamping her young feet, they put it in the rubbish bin in front of her. To make her stop.'

You describe to me how, whenever our parents were out of the house, she would rummage through their cupboards, prise open their desk drawers with scissors, tear open their letters, and she would take the cane marks on her palms without flinching when they came home and discovered what she had been up to.

I stare hard at my hands. Are they the same shape as hers? I picture them with red weals crossing them like tyre tracks. My teeth chatter uncontrollably but I am not crying. I am far past that. I force my eyes to yours and see that they have changed from blue to a dirty colourless grey, the same non-colour as the balls of fluff under my bed. I am frightened by the alteration and want to ask you to stop talking, to stop dragging the past into my room, to stop plunging your words into my head. But I don't. I can't. My tongue is paralysed.

'Sometimes she would get *me* to ask them,' you say, and I can hear a smile in your voice. 'That drove them mad. The cane came out for both of us then and those were the only times I heard her sob, "I'm sorry, I'm sorry."'

'To you? Or to our parents?' I whisper.

'Who knows? Maybe it was to you.'

I ache. All over. 'Jessie!' I bellow at the top of my voice. 'Jessie!'

'Shut up, Georgie. You're not wounded.'

'I am.' I wrap my arms around my bony body. 'I am, I am.' I start to rock back and forth.

You leap from your chair and you throw your arms around me, squeezing me to your chest so hard I can't breathe.

I scream, 'Don't touch me!'

But you are immensely strong. Fifteen years old and yet strong as a man. You are crushing me to death. I scream and beat your face with my fist but when your nose gushes blood over my hand I am sick over you. Blackness erupts in acrid patches in my mind, lights and bells flash and jangle behind my eyes, so that when the whitecoats suddenly seize you and force you to the floor, I do not know if it is real or in my head. I call your name.

'Tim!'

'Georgie, fuck off, you stupid old thing.'

I beg them to let you stay. They come at me with needles but you beat them off, and somehow we are suddenly again sitting down, me on the bed and you on the desk chair, alone in the room. I am trembling violently and fear that the whole eruption has been one of my *episodes*, another war zone that exists only in my mind, except that I can smell the vomit on myself and I can see the dried blood and bruising on your nose and upper lip. But now we are quiet once more, sipping water like civilised people.

'Go on,' I say. It takes a huge effort of self control.

'You're sure?'

'Yes.'

'Well, the strange thing was that when she reached ten years old, it all stopped. She no longer asked the question. She gave up.'

My heart folds up and dies in my chest.

'I've never heard her mention your name again, not since that time,' you continue, and thoughtfully you finger the damage to your swollen nose.

'Why?' I murmur, frightened.

'I don't know, Georgie boy. Maybe she decided to think of you as dead instead of shut away, maybe it was easier that way.'

Dead? Anger churns the acid in my gut.

'Of course she still had arguments behind closed doors with Pa and Ma over the years, but I rarely knew that they were about, and anyway that's normal for someone growing up.'

'Is it?' I ask.

'Yes. She's seventeen now.' You pick off a scab of clotted blood. 'I'm sure she will leave home very soon. I'll hate that. Being there . . . without Jessie.'

It had not occurred to me before, how vast the gap is between your life and mine. Mine goes in a straight line, like a short piece of string. Only the *episodes* leave it frayed and broken in places. Yours is a whole ball of string, all wound up and criss-crossing on itself, complicated and confusing, disappearing in different directions. Just the thought of it makes me short of breath.

'How did you find me?' I ask. I want you to say that my father gave the address to you on a slip of paper and told you to be my brother, but I know you won't.

You laugh. It is your happy laugh, not your sad one. I am better at voices than I am at faces. I understand you better when I close my eyes and block out the pictures, because pictures confuse me. I

81

listen now with eyes shut tight and can hear that you are pleased with yourself.

'It wasn't so hard,' you chuckle. 'I am more devious than your sister. I waited year after year, until Pa trusted me completely.'

Your voice comes closer. You must be stretching towards me. I shuffle backwards a fraction on the bed.

'I showed no interest in you, Georgie, or in your whereabouts. *Georgie who?* That was my attitude. Your name never passed my lips with our parents, even though when I was little I was sleeping in your bed, wearing your clothes, and reading your books.'

My books. That hurt. Why should that hurt so much?

'So,' I ask, 'how did you find me?'

'You sure you want to talk about this?'

I nod.

'Well,' you continue, 'Pa was on the telephone in the hall. He called me over and gave me – for the first time ever – the bunch of keys that lives in his pocket. He wanted me to fetch a document from his desk drawer in his study. Instead I shot straight to the safe that I knew was hidden behind the mirror in there, found the right key, unlocked it and . . . ' You laugh. 'Hey presto, here I am!'

'Hey presto, here you are. What does that mean?'

'It means I found a letter from Dr Churchward from this address. But don't look so depressed, Georgie.'

I flop on my back on the bed and stare up at the grey ceiling. A spider is busy in one corner and I know from experience that busy is good. I start to count to one thousand out loud. Numbers are stable. They never change.

'Oh, Georgie! My brother. Don't blame them. You were impossible to live with. Honestly you were. I've heard from Jessie all about your tantrums and screaming, your disobedience and your violent attacks on people.'

I shut my eyes but you lean over me, so close I can smell your chocolatey breath.

'It was hard on our parents, as well as on you and Jessie,' you say.

I push you away from me and roll off the bed. I stand facing the window with its bars, my back to you, and I rub my chest hard with both hands because the pain inside is so sharp.

'Georgie,' you say softly, 'what can I do to help?'

I think about it for a long time. 'Nothing. Nothing can help. Dr Churchward thinks his needles do. But numbers help more.'

'Numbers?'

'I count.'

'What do you count?'

'I count Jessie's heartbeats.'

'Oh hell, Georgie, sometimes you scare me.'

'Sometimes I scare myself.'

Like now. The pain is choking me, squeezing my throat in its grip. My lungs are starved of air, clawing at me, and my vision grows blurred, and I know an *episode* is coming. It rolls down from my brain, black and suffocating. I am frightened. My hands are shaking and I try to shout to you but no sound emerges. Death dances with heavy feet in my ears. I panic. Panic. Panic . . .

My hand seizes one of the heavy *Encyclopaedia Britannica* volumes piled up on the floor and rams it against the glass pane. The window shatters. Explodes in my face. Fresh clean air slams against my skin but still I can't breathe, my lungs are collapsing, dark and lifeless, a coal mine inside me. Lights flash and fade. Silence roars into my head.

I am dying.

I fall to my knees and feel a whisper of pain. Dimly I am aware of glass snapping like brittle bones under me and I grope blindly for a piece of it, annoyed when it bites my fingers and gouges into my kneecap. I lift a long icicle of glass and start to rake my chest with it. To let in the air. To make a hole for life to crawl back in.

Your hands are on me. I try to fight them off but my limbs are heavy and slow. I hoist up my eyelids and see you at the end of a long long tunnel. I am shocked to see your cricket whites are covered in blood and your mouth is moving but I hear nothing.

Nothing.

Just Jessie's heartbeat.

11

The music throbbed through Jessie's veins. It took her to new places that set her pulse racing. Up to cliffs she could leap off and all the way down to velvety whirlpools she could dive into. She took a swig of the whisky on the table in front of her and felt it burn away the day's images that were imprinted on the underside of her eyelids. She started to relax. Stretched out her legs in the small booth, elbows on the table, chin settled on her hand as she listened.

Something by Duke Ellington, she reckoned, something nice and low. Something to break your heart. The nightclub enveloped her in its twilit world, and she narrowed her eyes with pleasure as a sudden swoop of discordant notes chased each other around the crowded room. It sent a shiver down her spine. Shook her up. Dislodged her thoughts with its strange startling rhythms and sharp spiky edges. She liked it. Liked jazz. Liked the club with its smoke and its laughter and its salty hidden tears.

And she liked watching Tabitha play. Her flatmate knew how to handle a saxophone: as if it were her lover, caressing it, swaying her slender body close to it, her fingers darting over its silvery skin, her lips pressed to its mouth. Jessie often came to see her friend perform, to admire the way she laid out her soul for all to see, unafraid that it would be trampled on. Tabitha was the only girl on stage, the only white face in the band. The other musicians – on double bass, piano and trumpet – boasted varying shades of dark gleaming skin, as did many of the audience at the tables and tucked into the booths.

'My black brothers,' Tabitha always called them, flashing her small white teeth.

'Brothers,' Jessie told her whisky glass, 'are a commodity worth holding on to.' She took another stiff swig of the drink. Why was Tabitha clearly a whole lot better at holding on to them than she was?

'Can I bring you a drink?'

Jessie glanced up. A face hovered close. Too close. Male, with a loose self-indulgent mouth and blue eyes. She was always a sucker for blue eyes.

'No, thanks.'

'I don't like to see a lovely young lady on her own.' The blue eyes sparkled at her.

'I'm not on my own.'

He looked pointedly at the empty bench opposite her in the booth.

'I'm with a friend,' she told him and tapped her glass. 'My whisky.'

This struck her as so funny she started to laugh and once she'd started she couldn't stop. Everything seemed to break loose inside her and got all jumbled up. She laughed until fat tears were sliding down her cheeks and her hands flapped the man away from her booth. An elderly waiter waddled over and grinned at her, his curly hair stark white against his black skin.

'You okay, Jessie girl?'

'I'm just fine, Gideon.' But she accepted the napkin he gave her to mop her face and she hiccupped into it while he went off to fetch her a glass of water. 'Make it a beer,' she called after him but he shook his finger at her and chuckled to himself.

Jessie closed her eyes and let her mind drift on the tide of the music. But however hard she listened, however many times she ran with the notes in an escalating wail of longing, nothing was going to fill the brother-shaped hole inside her. It was too deep. Too turbulent. Too blood-stained. How long she remained like that she had no idea, but when she opened her eyes again a beer stood in front of her and Tabitha was seated on the opposite bench. Someone was playing 'It Don't Mean a Thing'. Jessie picked up the beer.

'You got style,' she told Tabitha. 'Real classy finger-work.'

In the near darkness, Tabitha's pale face seemed to swim above her slinky black gown as if disconnected. The thought brought Jessie up sharp. Is that perhaps what Tim saw at the séance, ghosts in the room, disembodied faces that twisted in and out of his conscious mind? She downed some beer to drown that thought.

Tabitha stretched out a hand and patted Jessie's cheek affectionately. 'You don't look so good tonight, honey.'

'I'm fine.' She balanced the words carefully on her tongue. 'Just fine. It's Saturday night and I'm out with my good friend.' She looked for her whisky glass but it had gone, so she offered her beer to Tabitha instead.

'Yeah, thanks.' Tabitha flicked back her thick plait of black hair, sipped the beer and pulled out an enamelled cigarette case packed with hand-rolled cigarettes. She lit one and dragged the smoke into her lungs with a sigh of pleasure.

'Still up in the castle, are you?' she laughed.

'It wasn't a castle,' Jessie insisted. 'It was a very magnificent but decrepit mansion.'

'You're crazy, you know that? Chasing after ghosts.'

'Timothy is not a ghost.'

'Oh, for heaven's sake, honey, he's just gone off for a wild week or two, I bet you. Let him enjoy himself.'

'It's not like him. Honestly, Tabitha, he's not like that.'

'People change.'

Jessie wanted to say, *No. No, they don't. Not really*. But she was beginning to doubt how well she knew her brother after today. *Who are you, Timothy? How much of yourself have you been hiding from me?* She reached for the beer.

'Tell me, Tabitha, do you think Tim has changed?'

'Let it go, Jess. For tonight, just let it go.'

Jessie leaned back in the booth. 'You're right. People do change. Look at you. When I first knew you three years ago, you were struggling.' She raised the beer in warm salute to her friend. 'Now look at you. The toast of clubland.'

'Hah! Don't remind me of those bad days. I couldn't even afford a decent instrument back then.'

It was true. The golden sound she coaxed from her sax now was a whole different animal and they both knew how much Jessie had helped her out. Fed her. Dressed her. Driven her to auditions. She had dried her tears and hidden her blasted cigarettes that wiped whole days from her life, even though Tabitha begged and cursed.

'Those bad days are gone,' Jessie echoed. 'You've changed.'

'We both have. You're much ...' Tabitha's mouth suddenly dropped open. 'Oh, Christ. Alistair.'

Jessie shot upright on the bench and her head swivelled sharply. 'Where?'

Tabitha burst out laughing. 'You should see your face! No, he's not here now. He came in earlier. I've only just remembered.'

'Looking for me?'

''Fraid so, honey. He left a message. Said he'd pick you up at two o'clock tomorrow. Something about an arrangement to go to Kew Gardens.'

Jessie rolled her eyes. 'Oh, damn. I have to telephone him to cancel. I'll be chasing after a medium tomorrow.' She rose to her feet and picked up her purse. 'Order me a scotch, will you?' she said as she clambered out of the booth. 'I'll need it after this.'

As she wove a path through the tables, she heard Tabitha's laugh behind her.

'I'm sorry, Alistair.'

Jessie counted to ten in her head, then added, 'I have to do this tomorrow if I'm going to find my brother. It's important to me, Alistair. But I promise we'll go to Kew Gardens another weekend.'

The silence expanded, trying to unsettle her with short stubby fingers of guilt. She pushed them away and gave a chuckle. 'Come on, Alistair, don't fall asleep.'

The silence burst. 'Where are you?' he demanded.

She looked around her quickly, checking on the dimly lit foyer and the greasy stains on the wallpaper. She thought about saying *At home*.

'You're at the Shoes and Blues club, aren't you?'

'Yes.'

'I knew it.'

'You don't like jazz,' she reminded him.

'You could have asked me, anyway.'

'Next time,' she said. 'I'll give you a call during the week.'

'I miss you, Jessie.'

'I know,' she said gently and blew him a kiss. 'Goodnight.'

On impulse – hell, why not? – Jessie picked up the telephone again, pushed more pennies into the slot and dialled. It rang for some time.

'Hello?' The voice on the other end didn't sound pleased.

'Hello, Pa.'

'Jessica! What's the matter?'

'Nothing.'

'Have you found him?'

'No.'

She heard his sharp intake of breath. Imagined him in his striped pyjamas and striped dressing gown, standing at the hall table, pushing his spectacles up his nose with annoyance.

'So why are you calling?'

'I thought you'd want to know that I have traced Tim to somewhere on Friday night where he went to a . . . ' She hesitated. The word *séance* felt like a huge balloon in her mouth. It wouldn't come out.

'Where he went to a what?' her father urged with impatience.

'To . . . a meeting.'

'Then what?'

'I don't know yet.'

Another silence, as prickly as a fistful of thistles, nudged against her ear.

'Jessica, do you know what time it is now?'

'Er . . . not exactly.' She squinted at her wrist-watch but the foyer was too dark. 'It's . . . ' she stumbled on her words, ' . . . lateish.' She fell silent.

'It's nearly one o'clock in the morning.'

Damn! It couldn't be.

'Oh. Sorry, Pa. Did I get you out of bed?'

'Jessica, are you drunk?'

'Of course not, I'm tired. I've been running around after Tim all—'

'Go to bed, Jessica,' her father said tightly. 'Go home and sleep it off.'

Without a goodbye, he hung up on her.

She stared at the piece of black Bakelite in her hand, as if it were responsible for the pain that felt like an axe was carving the back of her head off.

'Goodnight, Pa,' she whispered into it. 'Sweet dreams to you too.'

12

Jessie knew. The moment she opened the door to her flat, she knew.

'Who's there?' she called out.

The room lay in darkness. She listened intently for movement, the hairs rising at the back of her neck, then flicked the switch, flooding the spaces with light, forcing the shadows into the corners. Her heart hammered in her chest.

'Who's there?' she called again.

As if a burglar would say, *Hello, don't mind me, I'm just rummaging through your cupboards.*

Something touched her ankle, making her jump.

'Jabez!' she hissed as the cat rubbed its cheek against her shin. The animal seemed unconcerned, uttering a purr of welcome. That was a good sign, unlike the open drawers in the sideboard and the wanton scattering of papers and books on the floor.

Someone had been here. She searched each room in the flat. They had broken in through the kitchen window which now stood wide open, letting in the dank night air. The cupboards in the kitchen, in the bathroom and in Tabitha's room were untouched, but in her own bedroom and in the living room every drawer and every cabinet hung open with its contents disturbed.

Oddly, Jessie wasn't frightened. She should be. Alone at two o'clock in the morning in an empty flat that had been burgled – she knew she should be scared witless. But she wasn't. She was angry. Angry and sad. She strode over to the telephone and started to dial the emergency number for the police but she stopped after only the second number. She stood there for a long moment, earpiece in one hand, its cord swaying, thoughts charging through her mind, and then she hung up.

She couldn't do it to him.

Instead she walked into Tabitha's room, a space he hadn't violated, and sat down on the bed. Jabez was on her lap in a flash, green eyes half-closed with contentment, his claws kneading through the material of her dress to her skin underneath. A mixture of pleasure and pain. That's what she felt whenever she let Georgie into her head – pleasure and pain, in unpredictable combinations that she couldn't control. It could be an ordinary burglar who had done this, of course it could, most probably was. She knew that. But what if it wasn't? Could she take that risk?

Because in a hard immutable place in the centre of her brain she was convinced it was Georgie who had tracked her here and broken into her flat. Examined her belongings. Thrown them around. Brought disorder into her life, the same way she had brought chaos into his by not looking after him better when he was a child. By not locking her arms around him and refusing to let him go. Where was she when he cried out for her that night twenty years ago? Sobbing on her carpet. What use was that to a frightened little boy?

Her breathing came fast and shallow. She did not know how she would feel if she had walked in while Georgie was still here, seeing one of her drawings or even her pillow in his hands. She would want to hold him, to hug him close, to press him back into that precious Georgie-shaped hole that bled inside her, and he would hate that. She tried to imagine his adult face and his adult hands, but couldn't. They would be a stranger's face and a stranger's hands.

She leaned forward and brushed her cheek against her cat's silken fur. 'Did you see him?' she whispered into the pointed black ear. 'Did he touch you?'

Jabez purred and closed his eyes on his secrets.

Do you have a cat, Georgie? Can you tolerate such contact now?

Not for a minute did Jessie think there would be pink clouds of happiness if they met now. He must hate her. She had abandoned him. And sometimes she hated him. Because . . . the words struggled to form in her head . . . because if he had acted just a bit more like a normal brother and done the small things she had told him to do, like let Ma touch his hair once in a while or not tell Pa his breath stank like a cowpat after a cigarette, they would have let her keep him. None of this need have happened. That's why – sometimes – she hated Georgie.

It took her over an hour to tidy up the mess and there was nothing missing that she could see, but by the time Tabitha arrived home with her yawns and tousled black hair released from its plait, the flat was back to its usual state.

'What are you doing up at this hour?' Tabitha asked as she flopped down on the sofa, kicking off her shoes and stretching her feet up on the cushion.

Outside, the night had turned raw and the air hung black and matted with fog. The flames of the gas fire murmured quietly to themselves as though drifting off to sleep.

'Not in the mood to sleep,' Jessie said cheerfully and vanished into the kitchen. She returned a few minutes later with a cup of milky cocoa for them both and a ginger biscuit for Tabitha.

'Thanks,' Tabitha said and dunked the biscuit in her drink, her eyes on Jessie. 'What's the matter?'

'Nothing.'

'Huh!' Tabitha sipped her cocoa. 'Tell me, Jess, what's got your eyes so bright all of a sudden? Met someone special on the way home, did you?'

'Don't be foolish,' Jessie laughed. It sounded almost convincing.

'I'm just on edge about tomorrow. Each day that goes by, Tim could be in worse trouble, needing my help.'

With a lazy grin Tabitha rolled her eyes and pointed her biscuit at Jessie. 'You're crazy, you know that?'

'That's not the way to talk to someone who has just brought you a life-sustaining cocoa.'

Steam from their cups drifted between them, warm and sweet-smelling.

'It's not your job, this seeking for Timothy. He may be your brother, but you're not his keeper.'

You're not his keeper. How wrong could she be?

'Of course it's my job.'

'It's not. It's your father's and your mother's. Or it's the job of the police. Not yours.' Abruptly Tabitha swung her feet to the floor and leaned forward, the tips of her elbows balanced on her knees. 'I don't want to see you get your fingers burnt, honey. Honestly I don't. Stay out of it.'

The sudden severity of her friend's tone and the sharpness in her dark eyes startled Jessie.

'Do you know something, Tabitha? That I don't? Did Tim tell you he was involved in something?'

Tabitha looked away. Jessie felt her heart pitch sideways and she waited. After a long silence during which she watched her friend's face, Tabitha turned back to her and her expression had changed. Jessie didn't like it. It was caring and tender.

'Look, Jess,' she said softly, 'you're getting too obsessed. I hate to see you like this. Even at the club tonight you couldn't relax.'

But Jessie would not be sidetracked. 'Do you know something?'

Tabitha sighed. 'Not really.'

'What exactly does that mean?'

'It means just that. Not really. Tim told me last time he came to the club that he was . . . ' she hesitated.

'Was what?' Jessie pressed.

'Was involved in something with your father.'

'Involved in what with my father?'

93

'He didn't say.'

'Did he give any hints?'

'No. But I'm sure it's nothing much or your father would have mentioned it.' Tabitha paused, a frown creasing her pale forehead. 'Wouldn't he?'

Jessie placed her cup of cocoa firmly on a side table and stood up. 'Excuse me while I go to my room and kick something.'

'It's eight o'clock in the morning and it's Sunday. This had better be good, Jessica.'

There was a light drizzle, enough to dampen her father's dressing gown and spatter his spectacles as he stood in the doorway. He opened the door wider and stepped back into the hallway. It smelled strongly of flowers, the same musty floral scent as at a funeral, and Jessie saw a huge bouquet of bronze-tinged chrysanthemums in a vase on the hall table. She wondered who had sent them.

'Pa, I have to talk to you about something.'

They remained in the hall, making no move towards the drawing room. As if she were a stranger who had barged in off the street. Whenever she entered this house, the moment her foot touched the Afghan rug in the hall, it sent her tumbling back into her childhood. This was where the past lived. Trapped here. She rubbed shoulders with it each time she stepped over the threshold, aware that it was a solid presence that walked up and down the stairs, its heart beating, its breath smelling of rhubarb and custard. Its voice murmuring Georgie's name.

Her father stood stiff and sombre, his grey eyes examining her face, a distance of far more than a few feet of woven carpet stretching between his paisley slippers and her wet shoes.

'What is it now, Jessica?' he asked in a quiet voice. 'What has got you all riled up this time?'

She ignored the barb, just added it to the nest of barbs that lay hidden away inside her where no one could see. She kept her tone neutral. 'I heard that you and Tim are involved in something together.' She saw something flicker. So it was true. 'Wouldn't it have been better to tell me? Before sending me off into the bull-ring?'

'You exaggerate,' he said.

'Do I?'

He removed his spectacles and wiped them clean on a folded handkerchief from his dressing-gown pocket. He was gaining thinking time for himself. What was it he had to think about? What were her father and his blue-eyed boy engaged in that was not meant for her ears? She waited, keeping her words inside her head, knowing that her father had never been able to abide a silence. As a child, it had been her only weapon against him, but now the hallway started to fill up with it until they were drowning in it.

'It has nothing to do with his disappearance, Jessica, I assure you.'

'Can you be certain?'

'Yes, I can.' His words carried conviction. He would have made a good politician.

'So tell me, what is it that you have involved him in?'

Light footsteps sounded on the stairs and they both looked up to see Jessie's mother descending. She was fully dressed in a pleated skirt and white embroidered blouse, her fair hair arranged in an elegant twist at the back of her head – clearly what she'd been doing since the doorbell rang. Her face was powdered, her lashes heavy with mascara. Catherine Kenton was not one to enter the fray of life without her armour on, but at the sight of her daughter a crack appeared in it. Her blue eyes widened with alarm and her feet hurried down the last stairs.

'Any news?' she asked urgently. 'Is Timothy . . . ?'

'No, nothing. Not yet.'

'Oh.'

'I just came to ask Pa a few questions.'

'At this hour?'

'I have other things to do today – like searching for Tim.'

There was a slight pause. Her words sounded melodramatic on

95

a quiet Sunday morning in a leafy suburb of England, not at all what she intended. She turned back to her father and he realised that she was not going to go away until he told her what he'd been doing with Tim. He tightened the belt of his dressing gown.

'Timothy was helping me set up meetings and arrange publicity for the BUF, that's all.'

'The British Union of Fascists?'

'That's right.'

'Oswald Mosley's new party?'

'Yes.'

She recalled the pamphlets in his workshop. 'No,' she said softly, shaking her head. 'Please don't drag Tim into . . .'

'Timothy makes his own choices, young lady. He recognises the party's worth and the strength of its aims to put this country back on its feet.'

'Jessica,' her mother interrupted sharply, 'will you join us for breakfast?'

Jessie caught the look her father gave her mother.

'No, thank you, Ma. I have to get back.'

They walked her to the door faster than she expected. 'What does Tim do for the BUF?' she asked her father.

'Oh, anything really. Just lends a hand.'

That was it. No more.

She smiled at her mother and for once, because she looked so tight with worry, Jessie kissed her powdered cheek. It smelt of freesias.

'I'll let you know as soon as I learn anything definite,' she promised. She glanced back around the hall, remembering waiting behind the door for her father all those years ago, a letter in her pocket. Her gaze fell on the chrysanthemums. 'Nice flowers,' she commented.

Her mother nodded. 'From Sir Oswald, actually. And his wife, Lady Cynthia, of course.'

So correct. Yet the whole world knew that Mosley was having a blatant affair with Diana Mitford, who was married to one of the Guinness family. As Jessie walked to her car through the drizzle, she wondered what had prompted Oswald Mosley to send her mother flowers.

Jessie swung into the drive at exactly two o'clock and parked next to Sir Montague Chamford's elegant cream automobile. His tall figure was standing beside it, polishing the high arch of its front mudguard with his handkerchief till it gleamed in the thin afternoon sunshine. She recognised it as a Rolls-Royce by the Spirit of Ecstasy mascot that was poised on the tip of its long bonnet. He informed her it was a 1922 Silver Ghost and had belonged to his father.

The present Sir Montague, dressed in tweeds, spent the first part of the journey through the country lanes chatting with animation about the car, expanding on its charms. Discussing its silent engine, its huge reserves of power which were delivered in what he termed 'an unruffled manner', his enthusiasm was infectious. His long-boned face softened as if he were talking about a lover who set his pulse racing.

'She has a magnificent seven and a half litre engine, with two spark plugs fitted to each of the six cylinders.' His fingers ran around the steering wheel, stroking it fondly. His nails were spotless today. 'Phosphor bronze and nickel steel are used in the construction of the timing gears,' he informed Jessie, 'which are all ground and polished by hand. They are a thing of beauty, I assure you.'

'I'll take your word for it.'

He raised a dark eyebrow. 'Am I boring you?'

'Not at all.'

He concentrated on manoeuvring the long gear stick as they bowled through the streets of High Wycombe, a town of furniture manufacturers north-west of London, where heads turned to admire the Rolls-Royce as it passed.

'Do you hear that, Coriolanus?' Sir Montague called out to the sheepdog on the rear seat. 'We have a sceptic in our midst, I do believe.'

The dog pushed its wet nose against its master's ear from behind, as though whispering something private. Sir Montague laughed, but when Jessie didn't join in he glanced across at her, his eyes checking her face and then her hands tight on her lap.

'Are you all right?' he asked quietly.

'Of course. I'm fine.'

'Not frightened? Of mediums?'

'No.'

But it wasn't true. Jessie *was* nervous. Not of the medium herself but of what she might say, of what revelations might tumble out of Pandora's box.

After a moment's awkwardness, Sir Montague shifted easily to stories of picnics in the car with his parents and outings to Oxford for punting. 'Never could get the hang of the dratted pole,' he grimaced, 'and always ended up in the bally river.'

He paused for her to laugh, but she didn't. She didn't want this man beside her to try to amuse her, to entertain her with unlikely stories of getting dunked in the Isis, to think she was so easily blinded by charm and chatter. She held him responsible. Firmly and unforgivably responsible. She blamed him for Tim's disappearance. It might be unfair of her, it might be grossly unjust, but if it hadn't been for Sir Montague and that burnt mansion of his, Tim would be walking on Putney Heath with her on this Sunday afternoon, teasing her and throwing bread at the ducks. That cold certainty had lain with her on her pillow all night, and now sat like a fist in her throat, blocking her words.

So, no. She couldn't laugh at his stories or pin a smile on her face to please him. Nor did she want to be riding in a car called a Silver Ghost. The irony of it surely had not escaped him. Travelling to a medium . . . in a Ghost.

Oh, Tim, where on earth are you?

Give me a clue, like in the old days when we would hide from each other in the park. Don't leave me like this.

Sir Montague blasted the horn and overtook a coal wagon with a wave. His hands were strong and capable, at odds with his beanpole figure which seemed as if it might blow over in the wind. On either side of them as they drove along the A40, the fields lay brown and barren, ploughed into ridges.

'Heading for Oxford, are we?' she queried.

Just a simple question. But it caused him to stare ahead blankly through the windscreen for a moment, as though it meant more than she intended.

'Not far now,' he said vaguely and she was glad when he drifted into silence.

13

Georgie

England 1922

'I envy you, Georgie.'

We are playing chess. I am winning. I always win.

'Why?' I ask.

'Because you don't have to do maths homework.'

'What is wrong with maths homework?'

'It's like chewing on broken bottles.'

'What?'

'Just an expression. Ignore me.'

'You are lazy today.' But I never ignore you. 'Show me how to do your maths.'

I take your queen's bishop and you groan.

'It's hard,' you warn me.

I grin. 'Good.'

I stop delaying your king's demise and put an end to the game.

After that day, I do your maths homework every Saturday while you read *The Maltese Falcon* and smoke cigarettes.

You don't want to work today. You are tetchy – a word I know because you say it to me. *Don't be tetchy*, you complain when I sit on the bed with my back to you and watch the rain with my ears closed to your words.

Today it is you who are tetchy.

It makes me nervous. I am seated at my desk and write out the Greek alphabet in long smooth columns. It is very beautiful, though nowhere near as beautiful as the hieroglyphs of the Egyptian alphabet that I have taught you. That's what you are fiddling with half-heartedly. I want to snatch the pencil from your inept hand.

'You are lazy today,' I say.

You make a noise and jump to your feet. It startles me. You stand with your back to me.

'What colour are my eyes?' you ask.

'The colour of their iris pigment.'

'And what colour is that?'

I panic. I put my hands over my ears.

'I don't know,' I say.

'You should know. I've told you before that you should look at me when I speak to you.'

'Why?'

You sigh. 'For heaven's sake, Georgie, this damn place is making you worse.'

Silence.

I stand and stalk over to the door. I open it and stare at your shoes. They are brown and handsome. 'Get out.'

'Georgie, don't . . .'

'Get out!' I know I am shouting.

You go.

'I killed a bird,' I tell you.

You put down your book. You are reading Shakespeare and finding it hard.

'What?'

'I killed a bird when I was five.'

I don't know why I tell you. Why now? I think it is because the sun is on your hair, burnishing it the colour of a finch's gold crest. Or is it because after all these years I cannot keep my crime inside me any more, shut away in the dark?

'How did it happen?'

You are interested. I hear it in your voice, that catch in your throat when you are really interested. You can never disguise it.

'Does our mother still keep songbirds?' I ask.

'Gosh, no. I've never known her to keep birds.'

'She used to. She must have got rid of them all after I was ...'

We leave the end of the sentence unsaid. But I play with possi-bilities in my head. After I was ... *abandoned? Locked away? Incarcerated?* Take your pick.

'So how did it happen?' you ask again.

'Jessie and I were left with the nanny. I forget which one, they were all ...' I search for the right word, '... despicable.'

You grunt. That means you are not sure what I say is correct, but you were not there. I was.

'Ma had left us with her while she had lunch with a friend. The birdcage was in the morning room and I used to watch the birds sing by the hour. I was fascinated by the way their throats vibrated and I longed to see how such a tiny creature could make all that noise. So I fetched a penknife Pa had given me for Christmas, caught the little finch and slit it open.'

'Christ, Georgie! You were a little monster.'

'Was I?'

'What did Ma say?'

'She never knew. When I saw the tiny innards of the creature, its miniature heart and lungs, the bones of its throat no thicker than pins, I started to cry. Jessie found me under my bed with the bird slit open in my hand. She put me to bed, closed the curtains and told everyone I was sick.'

My throat grows tight at the memory. The air won't go through it.

102

'Didn't Ma miss the bird?'

I swallow. I can hear the finch's song, needle-sharp in my ears.

'I didn't find out until later that Jessie told Ma that she had accidentally let the bird out of the cage and it had flown out of the open window. She was punished.'

'The cane?'

'Yes. Six of the best.'

Six of the best on her soft young palm.

'What did you do with the dead bird?'

'Jessie buried it in the garden.' I am shaking uncontrollably.

You come over and you put me to bed and read me the story of Cleopatra.

Today is a bad day. My head is crammed full of darkness. I have closed the curtains in my room because the sunlight hurts my skin and makes my hands twitch. I sit on the floor in the gloomiest corner beside the wardrobe and I place a blanket over my head. It is better this way. Alone in my world of darkness.

I am not like other people. I know that. They are all out there playing a game they call life but I do not understand the rules. I get it wrong. Again and again. It is better this way.

'Georgie?'

I hear your voice. I have a feeling I have been hearing it for some time but without being aware it was there.

'Georgie? Come on out from under that blanket.'

You start to sing to me. Old nursery rhymes. 'Three Blind Mice' and 'Hey Diddle Diddle'. Only one person has ever sung to me before and she has nothing to do with me now. *Wants* nothing to do with me. My hands are wet and I realise I am crying silently. I wipe my face on the rough wool and jerk the blanket away, I am so eager to see you. The light hits my eyes with the force of a cricket bat.

'Hello, Tim.'

You are there. In the chair. Seen from down here at this angle your legs are longer than the door. That amuses me. I am interested in angles, how they change things, alter the way we see things. You once said to me that the only thing wrong with me is that I am looking at the world from a different angle. I want it to be true, so that if I move my feet, the angle will change and I will see the world like everyone else. But it doesn't happen. I have tried. I can tell from the way you are sitting, slumped in the chair, that you have been here a long time. It is not a comfortable chair. You are wearing a bright green jumper. I rise to my feet and sit in my usual place on the edge of the bed, smoothing the cover flat all around me.

'Your hair needs washing,' I say.

It's true. It curls in dusty blond clumps on your head but I hear you utter a sigh that gallops up from your lungs.

'I've been busy, Georgie.'

You speak very quietly. To protect my ears. You have explained to me in the past that kindness is doing things like that for people. Making them happy. I remember now that you say I must not make what you call 'personal remarks' unless they will make someone happy. I try again. I want you to be happy.

'Your legs are long.'

You smile. 'Better.'

I risk a quick look at your eyes and am startled by their greyness. Where has the blue gone? What does it mean? I want to crawl under your skin and find out all the things I cannot understand about you.

'Georgie, I've been thinking.'

'I think all day, every day.'

'I know, of course you do. But I want you to show me your arm. Push up your sleeve.'

'My right or my left?'

'Your right.'

I undo the cuff button on my shirt sleeve and roll the material back in neat folds up to my elbow.

'Look at your arm,' you say.

I look. Nothing strange. Just my arm. I quite like it.

'Now look at this.' You push back your own sleeve all bunched up in a green hummock, and hold out your arm towards me. 'See the difference?'

'Yours is ugly.'

It is true. Mine is pale, with a pattern of blue veins beneath its translucent skin; it is smooth and elegant like marble. Yours is the colour of honey, with tiny golden hairs over it and several small craters which I know are chicken pox scars. Yours is twice as thick as mine with crudely fitting big bones at the wrist, but I suddenly remember to put a hand over my mouth, as you have taught me, to stop my thoughts leaking out. You lean closer, and I try not to push you away.

'So why do you think there is such a difference?' you ask me.

'Mine is prettier.'

'Yours is like a girl's arm, Georgie.'

'Is that bad?'

'Yes.' You flex your muscles under your skin, making the flesh move. It looks horrible. 'Mine is the arm of someone who does things. I have been digging troughs in the earth all week at the remains of a Roman villa near Cheltenham and I'm exhausted, but I was working outdoors every day, and getting good exercise.' You pause and inspect me slowly from head to toe. 'I think you need more exercise, Georgie.'

'I exercise every day,' I explain. 'We all do. Half an hour every afternoon and an hour on Sunday.'

You snort. I don't know what it means, but you add a smile. Not a nice smile. 'They herd you all out into the garden and make you shuffle round in a circle for a while, no running in case you fall, no jumping or kicking a ball. Nothing to get the heart beating.'

'How do you know?'

'I have watched you.'

'In the garden?'

'Yes.'

I stare at your dirty hair. I feel naked. You have spied on me.

'So.' You jump to your feet. 'We are going to start an exercise regime. You are nothing but skin and bone, pale as a ghost.'

'Nothing but skin and bone? That is not true, Tim. I have a heart and lungs and kidneys and ...'

'It's just an expression. Don't take it literally.'

'But it is a lie.'

You sigh again. 'Let's concentrate on the exercises. Don't look so miserable. Look what I've brought you.'

You lift up your coat from the floor. Under it lie two beautiful Indian clubs. About the length of my arm, bulbous at one end, smooth rich wood. You hand one to me. It is heavier than I expected but when I see you start to swing yours in a wide figure of eight in front of you I copy you, careful not to bang into anything.

My blood grows hot in my veins and my arm takes on a force of its own. I feel powerful for the first time in my life.

14

Monty Chamford could not stand uncertainty. It put him on edge. He liked things clean-cut. But here he was turning into a quiet cul-de-sac of terraced houses without the faintest idea who Nell would be today. She and her spirit friends dealt in uncertainty on a daily basis, relished it with a gusto that drove him mad. And it amused Nell – he was sure of it – to keep him guessing. On the telephone he had laid down the rules for today, *Keep it low key*, but with Nell, blast her satin turbans, he could never be sure. Madame Anastasia liked to play games.

Monty parked the Rolls outside Nell's tiny front garden, which was choked with weeds that his fingers itched to uproot. He jumped out of the car, aware of net curtains twitching, but before he could whisk the door open for his passenger, Miss Kenton had emerged and was heading for the front gate. He liked the way she was dressed today, a bit arty with a loose flowing cape and strong colours. She wore her hat at an angle and it looked slightly mannish in style, almost a trilby, hiding the soft waves of her fair hair. She meant business, he had no doubt of that.

'My dear young lady, how lovely to meet you,' a woman's voice floated out in greeting.

Monty blinked, and turned his bark of laughter into a cough.

Nell had taken him at his word – *low key*. This was a Nell that was new to him. She had emerged from the front door kitted out in a long tweed skirt, a brown hand-knitted cardigan that did nothing for her full figure, and heavy brogues. Only the weighty pearls at her throat possessed a milky gleam, a hint of hidden secrets and better times. Her hair was rolled up into sausage curls and she was wearing tortoiseshell spectacles. Spectacles? Monty knew she was forty-nine but she could have passed for sixty today. She looked like everybody's spinster aunt, trustworthy and honest, but rather dull and bookish. *Oh Nell, my wicked Nell, you have surpassed yourself. She is going to believe every word you say.*

He stepped forward. 'Miss Kenton, let me introduce you to Madame Anastasia.'

The two women eyed each other speculatively and shook hands.

'Come inside, my dear, into the warm,' Nell invited and led the way indoors, stomping along in her thick shoes that seemed a touch too large for her.

Monty could not suppress a smile as he entered the living room. Banished were the dramatic purple swathes of material that usually smothered the settee and chairs, gone were the strings of tinkling bells and scattering of crystals. Instead there were lacy doilies frothing on every surface, an aspidistra, a sullen canary in a cage and in a corner a vile stuffed stag's head with moth-eaten ears. Where had it all come from? For a fleeting second he made eye-contact with Nell and mouthed, 'Perfect', behind Miss Kenton's back.

The two women sat down opposite each other, the younger woman's eyes trained on Nell's face with all the intensity of a portrait painter. Monty wondered what she did for a living. Could be something in medicine. Or even connected to the police. That thought made him shudder. But it was in the way her blue eyes dissected things with such precision, as if she could see under the skin to the colour of the blood in a person's veins or the exact shape of a person's thoughts in their head. Monty propped himself against the piano, unwilling to take a seat.

Miss Kenton sat still and attentive, her hands in her lap. The afternoon sun was slanting through the net curtains, turning her hair to gilded threads while she waited for Nell to stop fussing, then she asked her question outright.

'Can you help me? Madame Anastasia, my brother disappeared ten days ago after he attended one of your séances.'

'Did he indeed?'

'Do you know my brother, Timothy Kenton?'

Nell tilted her head to one side, her dark moody eyes assuming a motherly expression. She patted one of her sausage curls. 'No, not exactly, my dear. I don't know the boy, but I believe our paths did cross this side of the veil as we sought to—'

'So you know him? He was definitely one of your clients?'

'I prefer to think of them as fellow seekers rather than clients. Together we try to penetrate the darkness, to give voice to those spirits who have passed over but who have a message to convey to a loved one still on this fragile earth.'

Nell spoke in a Sunday-school teacher's voice, gentle but with a conviction that shone through. *Nicely done, little Nell.*

'Please tell me what happened on that evening? Was Timothy upset? What time did he leave? And was he alone or with someone else?'

'My dear, we are all with someone else at all times, the spirits hovering close, but too often people are unaware of them.'

Miss Kenton made a tight little sound under her breath. 'I mean with another person.'

Don't goad her, Nell. Give her something.

Unnervingly, Nell seemed to pick the thought out of his head.

'Your brother came alone,' she told her visitor. 'But he did seem to know a couple of the seekers who were present at the circle, two other young men.'

'What were their names?'

Nell gave an unladylike snort. A sign of disapproval that was her habit when irritated. 'Ah now, young lady, I couldn't tell you that.' Nell managed a beatific smile. 'Everyone who enters into one of my séances does so with the assurance of complete confidentiality. I cannot break that. I give my word to those needy souls who come to me.'

109

'Madame Anastasia, my brother is missing. I need to know where he is. I'm asking you to help me.'

She said the words with such need that even Nell faltered, startled out of her kindly smile. The small room suddenly grew smaller and there was a sense of movement in the crowded space. *Damn Nell and her spirit friends.* He swatted the air with a hand, just in case one had sneaked too close. Nell thought she knew all there was to know about death and no one could tell her different, but Monty was a believer in life and he didn't care for mumbo-jumbo.

He stepped forward, on the edge of annoyance. 'Tell her.'

Nell cast a ferocious look in his direction. 'One name,' she conceded sulkily. 'Dr Scott was present.'

'Dr Scott,' Miss Kenton repeated, but her face was turned towards him, not to Nell. 'Who is he?'

Monty ignored the question. 'Tell her what happened at the séance.'

Miss Kenton's blue eyes widened for a second, then narrowed warily. He realised she didn't trust him. Why should she? But she switched her attention to Nell now and he could feel the full force of her determination to extract the truth from the medium. But the truth was always a variable feast and Nell was an expert at cooking up her own version of it, spiced with the whisperings in her ears that pestered her all day.

'Tell me what happened at the séance,' Miss Kenton said, her hands spread on the low table in front of her as though ready to snatch up Nell's words the moment they emerged.

Nell closed her eyes and drew in a deep rattling breath. Then silence. No tick of the clock on the mantelpiece. No creak of the old timbers. No sniff of the wind at the glass panes. A silence as empty as his bank account. Monty waited patiently, accustomed to Nell's antics, but the younger woman flashed a quick glance at him, brimming with restlessness. She would thrust a hand down Nell's throat and yank out the words herself if they didn't come soon.

He coughed a warning.

'An elderly man came to me through my spirit guide,' Nell murmured immediately. Her voice sounded different, younger and kinder. 'He wanted to speak with your brother, Timothy Kenton, but . . . ' she popped open her eyes and glared at the young woman opposite, ' . . . he would not have it. Your brother shunned the contact. I felt the old man's pain, sharp as a serpent's tooth, and heard the trickle of his tears.'

Miss Kenton had not moved a muscle. 'Tell me. What happened?'

'It's veiled in mist, my dear.'

Get on with it, Nell.

'Your brother became annoyed. Agitated. He broke the circle – destroyed the contact – and staggered to the door.'

'Was he ill?'

'No. I believe he was frightened.'

A gasp. 'Frightened of what?'

'Of what was in his head, of what the spirits were telling him.'

The silence elbowed its way back into the room. Brittle this time. Unyielding.

So. What next, Nell?

The older woman reached forward, planting her hands over Miss Kenton's on the table, trapping them there.

'Do you want me to search for your brother beyond the veil?'

'No!' Fierce. Angry. 'Timothy is not dead.'

'Do you have something of his? Something I could hold while I . . . ?'

'No!' She snatched away her hands.

Nell shrugged. She was getting under the young woman's skin, rattling her. *Enough!* Monty prowled back and forth in front of the piano.

'Tell Miss Kenton what happened afterwards,' he prompted. 'Did you see anything more of her brother?'

Nell's cheeks were flushed. She shook her head. 'But I heard him. Out in the hall, complaining in a loud voice that it was not what he expected, that . . . ' she hesitated. For a moment Monty feared she had forgotten her lines, but she continued with a sadness that was convincing. 'He called out that he was going home.'

111

'Did you hear Timothy, Sir Montague? In the hall?'

'No, I did not. I had the sense to be tucked away in the warmth of the kitchen. Ask Coriolanus.'

Her eyelids fluttered for a second, uncertain.

'Then I heard a car start up on the drive,' Nell insisted, 'and he drove away. I was glad to see the back of him, to be honest, young lady. He had wrecked the séance. Done my reputation no good.'

Better, Nell. Much better.

'Didn't you check on him?' Miss Kenton demanded. 'To see that he was all right?'

'No. I had my other seekers to pacify. And the spirits were wailing through the house, screeching in my ears until I couldn't stand it. I had to end the session.' She said it with regret, as if it pained her physically to do so.

'They all left?'

'Yes.'

'How long after my brother?'

'About half an hour, I suppose around ten-thirty.'

'And this Dr Scott? He left too?'

'Yes, of course.'

'Where can I find him?'

Nell closed her eyes and refused to answer. Monty watched Miss Kenton's expression change into one of quiet obstinacy. She was going nowhere. He released a silent sigh of annoyance but walked over and sat down on the settee next to Nell.

'Miss Kenton, I know this Dr Scott.' He saw hope brighten her face and for a moment she forgot to mistrust him. 'He's always up in Northumberland for the weekend at this time of year, bagging his tally of grouse, but he'll be back here at his club on Monday night.'

'You'll give me the address?'

'I'll do better than that. I'll take you there for breakfast on Tuesday and introduce you.'

The smile of gratitude she gave him didn't loosen the knots in his stomach. It tightened them.

*

'That was quite a show you and your Madame Anastasia put on for me.'

'Pardon?' Monty jerked his head round to look at her. She was staring straight ahead through the windscreen at the road.

'You and Madame Anastasia.'

'What do you mean?'

'What is she like usually? More dramatic and unpredictable, I suspect. Was it her idea to act the dependable mother-figure or yours? To reassure me, I presume.'

Monty felt something sharp slide under a rib and he recognised it as failure. Not a sensation he cared for.

'Listen to me, Miss Kenton. We just wanted you to know that your brother left my house of his own accord and that he is probably at this very minute drinking coffee in a London hotel with a charming female companion. That's the usual reason young men go missing.' He paused, glancing across at her profile but it revealed nothing. 'How did you know it was an act? She was damn good.'

'Small things.' She shrugged. 'The shoes were too big. The skirt – someone else's – covered in dog hairs. The fawn material of the sofas too new-looking, as if they were usually covered up by some other rug or fabric. I imagine something more colourful. And she kept touching her hair, so I suspect it was not her usual style. And, of course, the spectacles.'

'What about the spectacles?'

'Plain glass.'

Monty released a burst of laughter. 'Sherlock Holmes himself could not have done better. How observant you are, Miss Kenton. I am impressed.'

For the first time since leaving the house, she smiled. Not much of a smile, small and private, but it was a sign that she was human. Not just a hound on the scent of blood.

Monty swung the wheel and turned into the drive of Chamford Court. As always, his heart gave a thump of pleasure. The day had turned grey and a band of surly clouds threatened rain but still the sight of the old house hit him squarely in the chest.

Damn the place. Damn it to hell. Its grip on him was like a vice.

He dragged his gaze away from it as he accelerated up the hill, and instead studied the solemn face at his side. They had not spoken for most of the journey back and, as he drove, his mind had wrestled instead with the problem of what to do with the lower east field. Mr Grainger, his estate manager, swore it would be flooded again this winter if they didn't sink some pipes pretty fast. But now he noticed that Miss Kenton's cheeks were pale, her fingers clenched into tight balls on her lap.

'You must love him very much,' Monty said suddenly, 'this brother of yours.'

She turned, her blue eyes full of some dark emotion he couldn't read, but her voice when it came was calm and controlled.

'You must love it very much,' she echoed, 'this house of yours. To do what you do.'

To do what you do. He had a brief flash of Timothy Kenton's limp body heavy on his shoulder as he carted it through the rain, the golden curls matted into dark patches.

'Yes,' Monty answered in a light tone. 'Yes, I love this place of mine far too much.'

The light was fading. The day was yielding its last fragments before being swallowed by the night. Jessie was seated at the window, drawing, letting her pencil do her thinking, but the dead weight of disappointment lay in her chest.

Who are you?

The face half-formed on the paper stared back at her but gave few answers. With each touch of her pencil it became more of a presence in the room.

I like the way you dip your head courteously when you speak to me. I like the way your large hands hold the steering-wheel, as if you are friends with it.

She sketched an ear, tucked back neatly against his head, and a lick of hair springing across his high forehead.

I don't like the way you lie to me. I don't like the way you connive to deceive me.

Her pencil roughed out a patch of cross-hatch shading in the hollow of his cheek and under his eyes. Bruising them. It was his eyes she was having most trouble with. Inquisitive, yet cautious. Guarded, but friendly. Two people in one. Hiding secrets from her.

Who are you? What is your involvement?

'Who is that?'

Her flatmate's voice caught Jessie by surprise and dragged her back to the world around her. It was always the same when she was drawing; she tumbled into a different life, an altered reality, and it took a moment and a deep breath for her to settle back into her flat in Putney.

'It's supposed to be Sir Montague Chamford.'

'Ah! I like his smile.' Tabitha bent over the drawing and ran a finger along his wide mouth, along the full curve of his lips that invited you to laugh at the world with him.

'He is a man of many smiles,' Jessie muttered.

Tabitha nudged her, jogging her drawing-arm. 'You are reading too much into it, Jess. He's just a nice person being nice.'

'Is he?'

'Yes. He's probably just wanting to be helpful. His sort is bred like that, to rescue a damsel in distress. Knights in shining armour and all that kind of tosh, generations of riding white chargers.'

Is it true? Is that what you're doing?

Tabitha moved off and sank into an armchair with a decisive grunt. 'That's what I think anyway.'

She lapsed into silence as the room gathered the twilight into its corners. Jessie hovered over the drawing, trying to discover more of the man in the unruly disorder of his heavy eyebrows or the controlled set of his long jaw, but she heard her friend sigh. Instantly she put aside the pad and pencil, poured a glass of red wine in the kitchen and brought it to Tabitha, who knocked back a good mouthful with a murmur of pleasure. She closed her eyes, but said nothing.

Jessie perched on the arm of the armchair. 'What is it, angel? What's getting to you?'

Tabitha's free hand rummaged through her dense black hair, as if she could untangle her thoughts.

Jessie drew closer. 'Trouble with Nathan?'

Nathan was a member of the band. He and Tabitha regularly had a spat about one thing or another.

'No.' She shrugged unhappily. 'Oh, Jess, it's just that sometimes I don't like myself. I get sick of being inside my own skin.'

'Well, just for the record,' Jessie said firmly, 'I like you, Tabitha Mornay.'

It took a full minute before her friend's eyes opened a crack. 'Draw me?' she whispered.

'I was hoping you'd ask,' Jessie lied with a smile. It had been a tiring day.

She fetched her pad, discarding her previous sketch while the young musician draped herself decoratively in the chair, her robe pushed off one bare shoulder, a leg stretched out over the arm, her long hair swept to one side like a river of ink. Jessie started to draw. Under Tabitha's bed there already lay a heap of pencil and charcoal portraits of her that Jessie had done during the past years and this would be another to add to the dusty pile. It was as if Tabitha feared that without the pictures, she might not exist. That she might forget who she was.

Is that what happened to Tim? Did he really go off – of his own free will – forgetting who he was and ignoring how much others would worry? *Are you free, Tim? Free of us. Is that what you want?*

Jessie glanced across at the sketch of the man who had been 'nice' to her today and she had a sudden thought that made her shudder. It was a dangerous thought. What if ... she let it expand in her head ... what if she took her pencil and scribbled all over that sketch of him, covered it in a thick layer of grey graphite until none of the drawing could breathe, would Sir Montague then cease to exist? Like Georgie did?

15

Jessie was early. She liked it that way. Not one for unpunctuality. She had inherited that from her father, not one of his most endearing traits, she was willing to admit, but not one she could root out of herself either. She paced the pavement outside the Cockington Club waiting for Montague Chamford to put in an appearance, and she imagined him dashing up to town by car, not leaving enough time, caught in a snarl of traffic at Hammersmith and blithely indifferent to the ticking of his gold pocket watch. Probably it had belonged to his father, too.

This part of London just off the Mall was quiet at such an early hour, residents still scoffing their kedgeree and digesting *The Times*. It was an avenue of graceful cream-coloured buildings and mottled plane trees, their leaves turning gold and carpeting the paving stones, muting the sound of her footsteps. A Harrods delivery van trundled past and a man with top hat and whiskers strode down the steps of the Cockington Club, swinging his cane. A maid attached to a dog on a lead scurried along the pavement opposite.

The sky couldn't decide whether to be pink or grey, so played with streaks of both, and the morning air tasted of the usual soot, gritty between Jessie's teeth. She scrutinized the street in both directions, willing her escort to materialise. She had been informed patronisingly by the doorman that ladies were only allowed to enter the club's hallowed portals when accompanied by a man, so she was cooling her heels on the pavement, her attempt to outflank Sir Montague thwarted. But all the time a clock was ticking inside Jessie's head. She was aware that every minute wasted was a minute that could be vital to Tim.

Somewhere a church clock struck eight.

'Ready for breakfast? Ravenous, I hope.'

Jessie spun around. On the top step of the club's entrance stood Sir Montague Chamford, having just emerged from its interior. Impeccable in an elegant pin-striped suit and waistcoat, his brown hair sleek and trimmed, his watch-chain visible across his chest, his black shoes polished like glass, he was not the Sir Montague she had brushed sleeves with in the car yesterday, or the one she had found ankle-deep in spadework the day before. Today even his smile was sleek and polished. Jessie felt a lurch of dismay. This man was not one to be backed into a corner so easily.

She stretched out her hand. 'Good morning.'

He gave it a firm shake but held onto it for a moment too long, as if quietly assessing the strength of it. She had a horrible feeling that he had been standing on that step watching her for longer than she realised, and by doing so that he had stolen a march on her in some obscure way.

'Is Dr Scott here?' she asked immediately.

'Indeed he is. Come and join us for breakfast.'

Us? Dr Scott and Sir Montague already swapping stories over toast and coffee?

Jessie followed him into the club through a landscape of dark oak-panelled walls and leather armchairs, the scent of beeswax failing to obliterate the musty fumes of tobacco that seeped from the fabric of the building. But Jessie liked the quietness, the sense of calm that lingered in each room, just the murmur of men's voices pitched low and the chink of fine china as she walked into the large breakfast room. She could understand why they came here, with their waistcoats and cigars and rules of engagement.

'Miss Kenton, let me introduce you to Dr Scott.'

A plump man at one of the tables rose to his feet, plucked off the napkin that was tucked into his starched wing collar, and inclined his head courteously. Medium height. A neatness about him that inspired instant trust. She could easily imagine him as a doctor, dispelling a patient's fears. His fine silvery hair was parted in a ruler-straight line, showing a pink scalp, and he wore a white goatee beard that made his bland features more memorable. His cheeks were ruddy, as if there had been a keen wind on the grouse moor at the weekend. Or maybe it was one brandy too many last night. He shook hands and waved her to a seat next to his with a welcoming smile.

'So you are the young lady who has lost her brother. He has vanished,' he announced with a shake of his head. 'How extraordinary.'

Jessie felt a sense of relief bubble unexpectedly in her chest. To have someone think it 'extraordinary', instead of regarding it as what a young man might naturally do if the mood happened to take him.

She smiled at Dr Scott. 'Yes. It is extraordinary.'

'You must be worried.'

'I am. That's why I need to talk to you.'

He pushed aside his plate with its remnants of scrambled egg and immediately a waiter materialised at his side, but Jessie declined the offer of full breakfast.

'Just coffee, please.' She turned back to Dr Scott. 'You were with my brother at the séance at Chamford Court, weren't you?'

'I was.'

He didn't blink or look away. He was not embarrassed by being one of Madame Anastasia's seekers.

'Can you tell me what happened?'

'Of course.' He tapped a finger on the pristine white linen tablecloth, jogging his thoughts. 'We all sat in a circle, hands touching, and Madame Anastasia was approached through her young spirit guide by an elderly gentleman who wanted to contact his son. There was the usual paraphernalia of flickering candles and knocking, and it turned out that the son's name began with the letter K.'

'Kenton?' Jessie felt a cold finger on her spine.

'Well, that was the odd thing. Your brother seemed convinced the K stood for someone called Kingsley.'

'Kingsley?'

'Do you know a Kingsley?'

Jessie sat back in her chair, shaken. Was this what Tim's obsession with séances was about? A crazy search for Kingsley's father?

'Are you all right, Miss Kenton?'

The words had come quietly from Sir Montague, seated opposite her. He was sipping Earl Grey tea and smoking a cigarette, watching her through the smoke. She had not seen him with a cigarette before, so maybe it was a London habit.

'Yes, I'm fine.' But she wasn't. 'Kingsley was the son of Sir Arthur Conan Doyle,' she told them. 'He died during the Great War, after which Sir Arthur claimed to be in constant touch with his spirit.'

'Didn't Conan Doyle write a book on spiritualism?' Sir Montague queried.

'Yes. He was a fervent believer in it and always swore that he would make contact with the living after he had "passed over" himself. He died almost three years ago and now lots of people are claiming to commune with him regularly.'

'But not Madame Anastasia,' Sir Montague pointed out.

Jessie made no comment. Instead she glanced around. She was the only female in the room. The tables were full of men in suits and ties, robbing the room of colour. Over by the window she recognised one of the government ministers from Ramsay MacDonald's coalition cabinet deep in conversation with a portly man who had a world-weary stoop to his shoulders and a fat cigar in his hand even at this hour of the morning. A banker, perhaps. Or a newspaper editor. She could imagine men like these in rooms all over London, making the decisions that would later be rubber-stamped by Parliament. But where were the women?

'Did Timothy speak to you?' she asked, turning back to Dr Scott.

'Yes, my dear, he did.' He threw wide his arms in an expansive gesture, almost toppling the milk jug on the table. 'When we were all attached in the circle of power I could feel the tension in the boy. His hands were shaking.'

Jessie tried to imagine it. To feel what Tim felt. But she failed miserably. How could Tim be so gullible?

'What did he say?'

'He said an odd thing. He muttered under his breath that it was harder than climbing.'

'Climbing!'

Dr Scott looked uncomfortable at her outburst in the muted atmosphere of the room. 'Your brother's exact words were, "This is a damn sight worse than the climbing I'll be doing tomorrow."'

'Climbing? It doesn't make sense. Why would he do that?' Jessie picked up her cup and sipped her coffee with a hand that could pass for steady. 'I've already telephoned every hospital in London,' she informed them quietly. 'No record of him.'

'That's good, anyway,' the younger man said and stubbed out his cigarette.

'Have you spoken to the police?' Dr Scott asked. His fingers took to his goatee beard, stroking it thoughtfully.

'My father did. They weren't interested.'

'Maybe they're right,' Sir Montague said.

'And maybe they're wrong,' Jessie snapped.

He raised an eyebrow at her.

'I'm sorry, but I think the police should show greater concern than they do,' she told him more politely.

'Of course, it's understandable that you think that. But try to see it as a good sign that the police, from experience, believe your brother will turn up safe and sound.'

'I hope you're right.'

He put down his teacup and turned to Dr Scott. 'Did he say where he was going climbing, by any chance?'

'No, he didn't. Rotten luck, this whole business – don't you think, old boy?'

With one of those disconcerting flashes of insight, Jessie realised this meeting was not going right for any of them.

'Did you hear any noise from my brother after he left the room?'

Dr Scott frowned. 'I think I heard a car drive away, but that's all.'

'Nothing in the hall outside?'

'No.'

'What happened in the séance room afterwards?'

'People were upset. The medium was clearly and understandably annoyed. She tried to resume but it didn't work.'

'Did the "seekers" think his behaviour odd?'

'Of course. One of the young men said he'd seen your brother at other séances and he had never behaved remotely like this before.'

'Do you know the name of that young man?'

'No, I've never met him before or since.'

It struck Jessie how helpful this stranger was being, how patient with her.

'My dear young lady, if you keep staring at me like that, I shall turn into a pumpkin or something equally obscene.'

Jessie blinked. She had been sitting in silence, staring like an idiot. Colour rushed into her cheeks.

'I apologise, Dr Scott. I was thinking about what you have told me.'

'I'm sorry I can't help more. Now,' he shook out his napkin, 'let me tempt you to some excellent orange marmalade. The club makes its own, you know.'

There was a pause. Sir Montague leaned forward, alert and watchful. 'I think Miss Kenton is disappointed in us, I'm sorry to say.'

Enough of this.

Jessie rose abruptly to her feet and both men looked startled.

'Not leaving us, surely, Miss Kenton,' Dr Scott said.

'I have to get to work, I'm afraid. Thank you for your time and your help. I'll leave you to enjoy the rest of your breakfast in peace.' She smiled at him and held out her hand.

To her surprise, Dr Scott wrapped both his hands around hers, gripping hard. Anchoring her to him. His gaze scoured her face, her hair, her frock of pale grey wool with its silvery pearl buttons and bright orange collar.

'My turn to ask a question,' he said, 'if I may.'

She nodded, aware of the strength in his fingers.

'Is your father dead?'

'No. No, he's alive and well, living in Kent.'

'So why would your brother think the dead father at the séance might be his?'

That had not occurred to her. 'Tim is adopted.' It felt like a small betrayal, revealing so much to a stranger.

'So is he wanting to find his natural father?'

Jessie shivered at the thought. 'No,' she said. 'He has never mentioned him.'

There was another awkward pause and the small sounds of the room seemed to grow louder.

'One more thing,' Dr Scott said softly, 'something that puzzles me. Just before the splendid Madame Anastasia made her grand entrance that night, your brother sat with his eyes closed, murmuring four names under his breath.'

He stopped.

'What were they?' she asked.

'McPherson. Hatherley. Hosmer. And Phelps. Do they mean anything to you?' Still he gripped her hands between his.

'No.' She kept her eyes innocently on his. 'No, nothing. But I must leave now. Thank you for your help, Dr Scott.'

He stood there, ill-at-ease for a moment, before collecting himself, and he smiled courteously at her, releasing her hands. 'I wish you success in finding this Tim of yours, Miss Kenton. Do let me know what happens. You can always drop me a note here at the club.'

'Thank you, I will.'

She turned to take her leave of Sir Montague but he was already on his feet and moving away from the table.

'I'll walk you to the underground station,' he said.

Outside, leaves were scuttling along the pavements of St James's Square like damp hands clutching at her ankles. Jessie walked fast, head down, thoughts in a helter-skelter.

Somebody was lying.

It was all wrong. Why would Tim think Sir Arthur Conan Doyle would want to contact his son on earth when he knew perfectly well that Kingsley was long dead? Why would he decide to go climbing? Why would he murmur aloud the names of four characters from Sherlock Homes stories? McPherson, Hatherley, Hosmer and Phelps. Like an incantation. To summon Conan Doyle's spirit to him? But then he staggered off in apparent distress and drove away.

None of it made sense to her whichever way she turned it.

'Miss Kenton?'

She lifted her head. They were descending the broad steps down to the Mall, the clouds grey and clammy. They seemed to press down on her, locking her thoughts inside her skull, and it was with a jolt that she became aware once more of the tall figure at her side. She stopped abruptly and he had to back-track a couple of steps to be on a level with her. She was again struck by the change in him in London, the sense of quality that hung on him as elegantly as his suit.

'Sir Montague . . . '

'Please call me Monty. The *Sir* just gets in the way.' He gave a gentle smile. 'Like umbrellas.'

She turned her gaze away from him towards the relentless traffic on the Mall, as though the sight of the taxis for hire and the bus with the Bovril advertisement on its side could drag her mind back to the normal life she seemed to have lost touch with in the last five days.

'Monty, what went on in there?'

'What do you mean?'

She looked at him hard and he had the grace to let his understanding show.

'Miss Kenton, we are trying to help you. Not to deceive you. I assure you Dr Scott is trustworthy. He was honest with you about what happened with your brother.' His voice was low and she had to listen carefully above the clamour of the harsh rhythms of the city. 'Why wouldn't he be? He has nothing to gain.'

She stepped closer than good manners allowed. 'And you, Monty, are you being honest with me?' she asked steadily. 'Do you have anything to gain?'

Instead of a reply he took hold of her hand and drew it through his arm, setting off once more down the steps, so that she was obliged to move with him. She lengthened her stride to match his.

'I can see how much your brother means to you,' he said.

You have no idea what my brother means to me. You have no idea that losing Timothy is like losing part of myself.

They strode towards the archway that led into Trafalgar Square and she let him keep her hand captive.

'I am being honest with you, Miss Kenton, please don't doubt that. If I seem at all ... ' he flicked his fingers towards the sky, ' ... dubious, it is because I feel the weight of responsibility for the séance heavy on my shoulders. Hence the antics with Madame Anastasia. I regret ... ' His voice trailed away.

Jessie turned her head, fixing her eyes on his thin face with its cliff-edge cheekbones, sensing that something more solid was about to come from him. But she noticed his frown, alert as a gundog as his attention was drawn by some movement beyond the grandiose stone of Admiralty Arch ahead. Noises filtered through. Loud voices. Shouts. From somewhere came a sudden brittle crack, like the sound of bones snapping, and it sent Jessie's heart racing to her throat.

16

Monty could smell blood. Could sense fear. Thick as lard. On the wind and in the shouts that gusted out of the square ahead. His fingers tightened their grip on her.

'We should perhaps retreat,' he suggested, keeping it casual. 'Caution being the better part of valour, and all that rot? Don't you think?'

He saw it, the sharp flash of disappointment in her eyes, and he knew what she was thinking. Is this the man whose ancestors have ridden into battle with fearless leadership, flinging caution to the ground under their horses' charging hooves? *Retreat?* A word not in their vocabulary.

But he said it again. 'We should retreat.' More firmly this time.

It was obvious that there could only be one reason today of all days for blood and fear to be found outside the sedate pillars of the National Gallery in Trafalgar Square. He had more sense than to get involved. And yet he felt her flicker of scorn like the thinnest tip of a whip stinging his skin, bringing blood to his cheeks.

She kept walking.

'What is it?' she asked. 'What's going on?'

'A demonstration of some kind, by the sound of it.'

'Of course! It's the marchers. They are arriving in London today to protest against the Means Test. You must have heard about it, thousands of them have come from up north and from Wales to vent their anger. They're presenting a petition with a million signatures to—'

'I know. Poor devils don't stand a chance.'

She started to hurry forward, dragging him with her. 'All the more reason to cheer them on. To give them support as they march past. Heaven knows, they need it.'

'No, Miss Kenton.' He pulled her to a halt.

She tried to break free but he held her arm through his. He could feel the heat in her, rising.

'They will have come from their rally in Hyde Park,' he told her calmly, 'and feelings will be running high. It could be unwise. The police will . . . '

'Come on, even you should be willing to show the police that what Ramsay MacDonald's government is doing to the unemployed is wrong. He has to repeal . . . '

She stopped, as a noise hit them. It sounded like waves dragging across a pebble beach, harsh and out of place in this leafy thoroughfare from Buckingham Palace. The noise issued from beyond the archway.

'Horses' hooves! They're charging,' Monty shouted.

Instantly they both broke into a run, racing into Trafalgar Square, but they were brought to a halt by the scene in front of them. It was carnage. A battlefield. Dear God, the heart of London had cracked open. The Metropolitan Police Commissioner must have lost his mind.

Hundreds of men were running, men in heavy boots and thin jackets, men with panic in their eyes and anger in their voices. They were hurtling across the open spaces, flattening themselves against the plinths of the four stone lions that stood guard over Nelson's Column. Monty could hear their shouts and pitiful cries reverberating through the square, while grey waves of pigeons swirled above their heads as the birds took fright. Metal bars slammed against anything within reach that could be smashed and used as a weapon. Kerbstones and bottles ploughed through the air, while full-grown men were abandoning their protest placards and throwing themselves in the fountain.

All trying to escape. Desperate to flee the dark menacing wall of police uniforms that drove them from one end of the square to the other. Monty's heart pounded with rage as the police horses charged the men on foot again and again, their hooves skidding and sparking. Truncheons flashed back and forth, solid wood seeking bone, lashing out at heads and backs, crashing down on shoulders and chests. Men screamed like pigs in panic as their elbows shattered.

It was obscene.

How could Sir John Gilmour as Home Secretary condone such a response? Seventy thousand police in London deployed to control the marchers. It sickened Monty's stomach and made him ashamed. Ashamed of Britain. Of its damn government. Of its brutal laws. He spotted a man in a long raincoat make a stand and launch an attack on one of the constables on foot, knocking his helmet to the ground, calling for other protesters to back him up, his face twisted with hatred. But blue uniforms swamped him, battering him to the ground and dragging him off towards the Black Maria vans parked outside the church of St Martin-in-the-Fields.

Another man raced up to where Monty and his companion were standing, backs wedged against the stone upright of the arch. The man's hands were clutching a placard on a wooden pole, and words daubed on the board were painted in red: DEFEND SOVIET RUSSIA! He took one look at Monty's suit and shoes, swung back his placard and aimed it straight at Monty's head. Monty ducked effortlessly – years of being school boxing champ – taking Miss Kenton with him, and wrenched the pole from the man's hands. It was slick with blood. *Whose blood?* Its owner vanished into the crowd.

'Damn communist!' Monty shouted after him but it was swallowed by the noise around them.

He was worried about Miss Kenton at his side, her eyes dark with distress, her hand trembling on his arm, her body rigid. From shock or fury or terror – he didn't know. Now was definitely not the time to stop to find out.

He threw the placard on the ground, face down in the dirt.

'Out of here! Back up the Mall,' he urged. 'Run!'

But at that moment a hand came out of the mêlée of figures streaking past and seized hold of Miss Kenton's shoulder. Monty wrenched it off.

'Jessie. What the hell are you doing here?'

Jessie. So that was her name. Like the glamorous Jessica Mitford with whom he had dined last month.

'Archie!'

She threw an arm around the scarecrow frame of the young man in front of her and peered closely at his face. He was dressed in workman's garb with a cloth cap clinging precariously to his ginger curls, and despite the cool wind he was sweating. The bones of his face were almost visible beneath his taut skin. He looked like a workman and smelled like a workman, but Monty knew at a glance that it was all a pretence and it was that knowledge, rather than the adrenaline pumping through his veins, that set Monty's heart hammering in his chest. He could feel Jessie's affection for this man.

'Archie, what went wrong? Come with us, quickly.' She pulled hard at the young man's sleeve but he didn't move.

'It's bloody Trenchard. The bastard has set his fucking dogs on us.' Lord Trenchard was the Metropolitan Police Commissioner, a man with a tough implacable mind. Monty could see that Archie's eyes were wild, his pupils huge holes in his head. 'As if we are rats to be exterminated.'

A livid bruise pulsed on his jaw and a thread of scarlet snaked down from his scalp. In his hand he clutched half a brick. There was blood on its jagged edge.

'I must get Miss Kenton away from here,' Monty said urgently, but Archie remained rooted to the spot. He wasn't leaving the square. Monty recognised the anguished reckless thirst for battle that he had once possessed himself. Until it tore his life apart.

'It wasn't us.' Archie shook his head. 'We just wanted a peaceful march.'

'What about the petition? The million signatures,' Jessie asked quickly. She was holding her friend close, as though frightened to let him go.

'Stolen from us!' Archie spat on the ground, a pink gob of spittle. 'The bloody police seized it at Charing Cross station and confiscated it.' He stuck out an arm, pointing at the demonstrators still pouring into the square, still brandishing their NUWM banners. It had become a riot. 'A hundred thousand of London's workers turned out to cheer us on, but look at them now. That traitor to socialism, MacDonald, has sold his soul to the Tory devil, he . . .'

Ten yards away a white-haired man wearing spectacles and an expression of outrage was trying to argue with an officer who was twisting the arm of a gangling youth up behind his back. But it was far too late for words; they fell to the pavement unheeded. The air throbbed and crackled with violence. It had become the only currency in the square. The policeman struck the older man across the throat with his truncheon with so much force that he collapsed to his knees, clawing at his collar.

'Davies!' Archie bellowed. He launched himself into the crowd and barged a path to the man's side.

Monty saw him slam a fist full into the policeman's face but his timing was all wrong, because at that moment a phalanx of fresh reinforcements in uniform entered Trafalgar Square. Three of them caught sight of Archie's action and fell on him, unleashing a barrage of blows from their truncheons, driving him into a broken huddle on the ground.

'No! No!' The scream came from Jessie.

To hell with it. Monty kicked away a crushed helmet at his feet. This wasn't his fight. These weren't his estate workers or his villagers. These men were nothing to him, definitely not his responsibility. He carried more than enough of that on his shoulders already, and now this . . . He glanced at Jessie's white face as she started forward in a direct line towards Archie.

Monty seized her and jammed her back against the wall. 'Stay! Here!' he grimaced, and against everything he knew to be sensible, he launched himself into the seething stampede. He pushed and shoved and elbowed his way to where Archie lay curled up tight on the ground, hands clamped over his face. Blood had turned his shirt and his hair into a clown's costume. Monty bent over and swung the limp figure onto his shoulder like one of the unwieldy sacks of potatoes on his farm, swearing under his breath. Berating the stupidity of Archie and of Ramsay MacDonald, but most of all of himself. Curses poured from his lips, so ferocious that they kept him on his feet even when a truncheon smashed down on his arm, numbing it. He kept moving.

It was the horse that finished him. It loomed close, then panicked and reared up. Its metal shoe clipped the back of Monty's head, sending him crashing to the ground. *Fuck.* All he could see were feet and lightning flashes of what looked like red cricket balls but couldn't be. His brain felt like a foreign creature growing bigger inside his head, but he managed to ease his human passenger into a bundle on the ground beneath him. It was time to get out of here. He had just clambered up onto his knees when the first blow landed on his back. He grunted. Something between his shoulder blades seemed to explode. When he pushed himself onto his unsteady feet, he felt his knees vanish, to be replaced by something like porridge. He swayed. Lord Nelson's Column seemed to be falling on him.

Suddenly a small shoulder hitched up under his arm, halting the spinning world. He blinked and saw a bone-white face, a mass of golden hair. Fierce blue eyes glared into his.

'Don't you fall down!' Jessie ordered. 'Hold onto me.'

He nodded. A mistake. It took another ten long seconds to find his eyes again. Together they hoisted Archie's senseless form onto Monty's good shoulder and staggered towards the archway, but a police constable got there first. Red-faced and breathing hard, his small eyes were bright with excitement. He was young and out of control. He ignored Monty, ignored the slumped body of Archie, but he had greedy eyes for Jessie.

'Out of our way, officer,' Monty commanded in his best Sir Montague Chamford voice and the constable automatically yielded to the tone of authority and stepped aside.

But as they hurried past, the hand clutching the truncheon could not resist. It flicked out. Monty saw the wood connect with Jessie's temple, heard the dull reverberation of pain and her intake of breath. Her knees buckled. He wrapped his free arm around her to keep her on her feet, but his right foot shot out and nailed the constable's shinbone just below the kneecap. The policeman screeched and bent over, clutching his leg, his chin perfectly placed as Monty's knee rocketed up to crack open his jaw. He toppled sideways onto the road.

Monty tightened his grip on his two companions. 'Let's get out of here before he wakes up.'

Jessie raised her head to look at him, her shoulders trembling, her eyes out of focus but struggling for a smile of some sort. He liked her for it.

'Thank you,' she mumbled. 'What are you? St George fighting the dragon?'

He uttered a grim laugh and started to carve a path for them back up the Mall. 'Something like that.'

17

Georgie

England 1928

You knock. I open the door and you are there with a wide smile on your face, your blond hair trimmed shorter than usual. My blood flows faster at the sight of you, as if it is your energetic heart that is pumping for both of us. That's what it feels like, that I am a pale translucent ghost for six days a week, but on a Saturday I become a person. I notice how tall you are now.

'Happy birthday, Georgie.'

'Is it my birthday?'

'Yes. Today's the day.'

'We have never celebrated it before.'

'But today you are twenty-one.'

You are full of movement, your hands, your shoulders, your golden eyebrows, and I am frightened you will touch me, but you don't. You know me. You know me well.

'Today,' you say, 'you must come out of your bubble.'

'I don't know what you mean.'

You smile at me and say – with that something in your eyes and

133

in your face that makes me feel like warm toffee inside – 'I know, dear Georgie. Let's just enjoy today. No lessons for you or me on your birthday, all right?'

I nod. You have taught me that it is the correct response to a statement ending in 'all right?'

'Look at the present I've brought you.'

I expect a small box with a pink bow like in the books I've read. But you open the door again and push two armchairs into my room, though they only just squeeze through the doorway. I have never seen chairs like this. They are curved like the end of a bath-tub, made of silky pale wood the colour of milky tea and have seats of ivory leather. I touch it. Soft as my tongue. They are the most beautiful objects I have ever seen in my life.

'They're the latest style,' you tell me. 'The wood is maple. Do you like them?'

'Yes.'

'Then smile.'

I make a smile. But it is not real. What I want to do is cry because they are so beautiful. I can feel the tears creeping up behind my eyes. You wave a hand at the seat of one of the chairs.

'Try it out.'

I sit in one, my heart beating fast, and stroke the butter-smooth veneer where my hand lies, my fingers tingling with excitement. I am touched to the core.

'Like it?' you ask.

'It is the most uncomfortable chair I have ever sat in. The back is too straight and the seat too long.'

But I do not mind. I sit there in silence, wrapped in beauty. It is several minutes before I realise something is wrong. I don't know what. I don't know why. But you are not speaking. I just sit. Waiting.

'For heaven's sake, Georgie, you needn't have said that. It took me a lot of time and trouble, not to mention hard-earned vacation money, to get you these. You could at least ... ' You stop yourself and take a concentrated breath. 'If you are ever going to get out of here, you must learn to filter the words that come out of your mouth. Like I use a sieve in my excavations of old ruins to get rid of sand and earth and all the rubbish I don't want. I keep only the valuable bits. You must discard your rubbish thoughts. You must filter them out. Now try again.'

I go through the list you have taught me. It is written out in the big booming silence in my head.

1. I'm fine, thank you. How are you?
2. Won't you sit down?
3. Thank you.
4. No, thank you.
5. How nice to see you.
6. What fine weather we are having today.
7. What can I do to help you?
8. Would you like a cup of tea?
9. You look very smart today.
10. I'm sorry, I don't understand. I didn't mean to offend you.

I panic. Because you are angry. I don't know which to choose. I look at you. I look at the chairs.

'Won't you sit down?' I say.

You sit. You wait for more.

I perch on the edge of the bed. 'What fine weather we are having today.'

You look out of the window. It is raining.

The list of sentences blurs inside my head, like the rain on the window-pane. They run into each other, they melt into the words you spoke: *If you are ever going to get out of here.* It is a prospect as distant as the sun from the earth, ninety-three million miles, and as terrifying, yet you have placed it in my lap. It burns right through my flesh, and I feel my heart expand in my chest until it is hard for me to breathe. I struggle to find the correct words to give in return.

'Won't you sit down?' I offer.

No, no. It's not right. You are sitting.

You frown.

I am running out of air.

'Georgie, for God's sake, can't you ... ?'

I gabble out another from the list. 'I'm fine, thank you. How are you?'

Your mouth is a tight line. I remember at last, your instruction, over and over you tell me, *Don't panic. Breathe. If in doubt, go for Number Ten.* It is underlined in blue ink in my head. *And for heaven's sake, SMILE.*

I can't breathe but I can smile. 'I'm sorry, I don't understand. I didn't mean to offend you.'

You become very still. I don't know what is the matter. I am no good at faces. I see a face change from wide eyes to narrow eyes, from mouth turned up to mouth turned down, I see lines creep across a forehead and I don't know what they mean. I can read ancient Greek and Latin and ancient Egyptian but I cannot read a face. I cannot tell whether it is surprise or annoyance. You once brought me twenty photographs of faces and you wrote on each one what the expression meant – happy or unhappy, angry or confused, surprised or disappointed, bored or interested. You tested me on them for weeks until I could get them right every time. You taught me that the size of a person's iris changes when they lie.

But it is much harder to do with real people. I want to hold the photographs next to your face. To compare. I go to the drawer and take them out but you start to shout at me. Harsh cruel words that I have never heard from you before. I cover my ears with my hands because the pain in my head is so bad. This is wrong, wrong. You are wrong. My mind is filling up with red mist, my chest is drowning in scarlet. But still the dirty gutter-black words spill from your mouth at me.

'Filter!' I scream at you. 'Filter your rubbish words, Timothy.'

You stop. You stare at me, eyes wide as oranges. Mouth open. I remember the photograph: it means *shocked*. A noise starts to escape from your lips, a growl at first, then it turns into a laugh, and you laugh so hard you fall off the beautiful uncomfortable chair onto the floor. You laugh and laugh.

I walk over to the window and stare out at the lawn. I do not understand.

136

18

Jessie woke with a jolt. Her heart was going crazy inside her chest, her skin hot and tight. She had been dreaming. In the dream she had been fleeing naked down Piccadilly pursued by a pack of baying foxhounds, while ahead of her Dr Scott stood with a shotgun in his hands. She knew that her only escape was to fly over the roofs but she couldn't unstick her feet from the ground.

She blinked hard and realised she was lying fully clothed on a settee. In her own flat, wrapped in a blanket. That was odd, as she had no recall of how she got here. But she dragged in a deep shuddering breath of relief and let her mind untie its knots. She sat up. Huge mistake. The whole room cartwheeled and a thousand hammers got to work on the underside of her skull.

And then she remembered.

The brutality of Trafalgar Square, horses with huge frantic eyes, shouts and screams drumming in her ears. Archie! Poor Archie! Where was he? She threw aside the blanket and was about to fight her way to her feet when she caught sight of a figure in an armchair by the window. The room was gloomy. It was dark outside and only a dim table-lamp burned in one corner, casting deep navy shadows over the silent figure.

'Archie?' she breathed.

But even as she said it she realised her mistake. His legs were too long and his shoulders too broad. Doubting her own thought processes, she stared hard at Sir Montague Chamford and as she did so, she felt something open up inside her, something sore and battered, and in its place flooded gratitude to this man she barely knew. He had saved Archie. He had saved her. And taken a beating in exchange. It was no wonder he had broken that constable's kneecap. Now she thought about it, the surprise was that he hadn't snatched up the constable's truncheon and broken his other kneecap too.

Jessie rose slowly to her feet, waited for the walls to stop dancing a can-can, and walked on stockinged feet over to the armchair for a closer look. He was asleep. His head tilted slightly to one side, a lock of brown hair had fallen over his eyes, and his large hands were clasped together on his lap as if he had been twiddling his thumbs, waiting patiently for her to wake up. She glanced at the clock on the mantelpiece. Two fifteen. *Two fifteen?* In the morning? Where had the day gone?

Why was he here?

Oddly Jessie felt in no way threatened by his presence, alone with this man in her flat, though she knew Tabitha would be home soon. Was there something in him she sensed, something decent, something of St George? As she turned to look down at him again, disjointed scenes slotted in and out of her vision but not in any order. Nurses in a hospital, Archie on a trolley, a doctor shining a light in her eyes, blood in a taxi-cab, vomiting over Monty's trousers; the images flashed in and out.

Vomiting over Monty's trousers?

She could smell it on him now, the sickly sweet stench of vomit. Her cheeks burned at the memory. His legs were stretched out and crossed at the ankle and she wanted to take off his beautiful suit trousers and dunk them in the bath. Not really feasible without waking him. He had removed his jacket and was wearing just a shirt, waistcoat and silver tie, the elegance of which was spoiled by the dark stains on them. Dried blood, long streaks of it.

He uncrossed his ankles and murmured something in his sleep, frowning, but didn't wake. In the shadows she studied the firm lines of his face, the thick sweep of his eyelashes, the resolute set of his mouth even in sleep. What kind of man was he? What lies slid off his tongue, hidden by the silky charm of his class? How far could she trust this quiet controlled face?

A shape moved in the room. It was Jabez. But as she stroked his black fur, nausea hit her. She dived for the bathroom, flicked on the light, squinting in the sudden brightness, and flinched when she saw the face in the mirror above the washbasin.

It was ugly. She barely recognised it as Jessica Kenton. The face in the mirror was pale as chalk-dust except for a nasty swelling on her left temple which was sprawling up to her forehead with black and purple streaks. As though someone had painted it on while she slept. Her hair was a mess. The thick blonde waves were sticking out in all directions, as if trying to escape. She didn't blame them. She would escape if she could. Worse were the eyes. They were big and round, and looked wary. Eyes that didn't know how to trust people, today or any other day. They scared her. Guilty eyes. What we remember of ourselves from our childhood is never forgotten and never forgiven.

Quickly she ran the cold tap. Splashed water over her skin, her mouth, her eyes, eager to wash away the face in the mirror, to find a new one underneath. She dragged a brush through her hair and cleaned her teeth. Her teeth were the only part of herself she liked, white and straight and happy-looking.

He woke almost imperceptibly. Jessie watched him. One moment he was asleep, the next he was awake, with barely a ripple between them.

'Hello,' he said softly from his chair. He didn't move.

'Hello, Monty. Feeling sore?'

'No worse than you, I dare say.'

There was a pause while they smiled at each other, a small acknowledgement of something they shared. The smile felt alien on her face, at odds with the images in her head.

139

'What time is it?' he asked.

'Four-thirty in the morning.'

'I've been asleep too long.'

'I'm sure you needed it . . . and more. Go back to sleep.'

He noted the blanket she had tucked around him and nodded his gratitude, but gave no indication of returning to his slumbers.

'What about you?' he asked. 'How are you feeling?'

'Headachey. But I'll live. More important, where is Archie?'

'At St George's Hospital on Hyde Park Corner.'

'How is he?'

'Not great, to be honest. But he'll live, too. You rang his parents.'

'I did?'

'Yes, you did.'

'It took courage to do what he did.' She let her gaze rest on his features. 'And to do what you did. Thank you.'

He put a hand up, like a wall between them, fending off her gratitude. 'What happened today in Trafalgar Square is a national disgrace. It has to be investigated at once and someone's head must roll, preferably Gilmour's. It was—' He abruptly brought his words to a halt. 'Let's not discuss it further. Not now.' His eyes shone hard and angry. 'There's enough horror in our heads for tonight. Let's not add more.' His voice was sad and it stirred something within Jessie. He was right. If she talked about it she would be sick again.

'What are you doing?' he asked.

Jessie was seated at the table, the lamp at her side. She had changed out of the blighted blue dress of this morning and was wearing a woollen dressing-gown, belted at the waist.

'Reading,' she said.

He rose awkwardly to his feet, supporting his weight on the arm of the chair and straightening up slowly before moving across the room to stand at her side. This close to her, the flesh of his face looked grey and exhausted but his eyes were still quick. Jessie felt an urge to put her arm across the page of notes in front of her to hide it from him.

'What are you reading?'

She said nothing as he picked up the open book at her elbow and gave a wry smile when he saw the title.

'Sherlock Holmes stories, I see.'

Did he see? She doubted it.

'Would you like an aspirin?' she asked to divert attention from the sheet of paper on the table.

'A whisky would help more.'

'There's a bottle in the kitchen cupboard next to the sink. Glasses above the bread bin.' She wasn't leaving him alone at the table.

He hesitated and she could feel his resistance, but in the end he went quietly.

'I'll help myself, then,' he said.

'Please do.' She added a small smile.

'Explain it to me again.' He was sipping his whisky.

Jessie sighed. He didn't really want her to explain her theory again. What he wanted was for her to speak it out loud one more time, so that she would hear how ridiculous it sounded.

Her hands kept fidgeting with the sheets of paper in front of her, shuffling them, tweaking their corners, planting a row of ticks along the bottom. It was obvious now, clear as day. But it had taken her hours to find it. She made an effort to appear calm, and regarded Monty with a steady gaze.

'I told you. The four names that Dr Scott said my brother muttered at the séance – McPherson, Hatherley, Hosmer and Phelps. I recognised them immediately.'

'You told Scott they meant nothing to you.'

'All right, so I was lying.' She shrugged impatiently. 'They are from the Sherlock Holmes stories that we used to read as children.'

'Read obsessively, by the sound of it.'

Jessie ignored him. 'So I've been sitting here working it out while you slept, going through the four stories again in which the names occur. But I could find no connection between them and Tim. McPherson is the science master in *The Adventure of the Lion's Mane*. Victor Hatherley is the unfortunate victim in *The Adventure of the*

141

Engineer's Thumb and Hosmer Angel is the elusive fiancé in *A Case of Identity*. While Phelps is . . . '

' . . . in *The Adventure of the Naval Treaty*. Yes, yes, I accept that is true. You certainly know your Conan Doyle.' He shifted restlessly in his chair. 'But that doesn't mean your huge jump of mental tightrope-walking has any logic to it at all.' He was studying her, concern in his eyes.

Her head throbbed painfully. Was she wrong to trust him with this? What had possessed her to blurt it out? But it had come to her in a blinding flash just as he placed a tumbler at her elbow, a generous splash of whisky at the bottom of it, and offered her a tea-towel wrapped around a bundle of ice cubes from the refrigerator.

'For your head.' He'd pressed it against her temple, touching her hair, sending welcome icebergs to the heart of the pain. It cleared her mind.

At that moment it had come to her. The connection to Tim. And she had blurted it out.

'It's the Nile.'

'What?'

She flicked a hand over the sheets of paper with the lists of every character in each of the four stories, of every plot line and every possible cross-reference between them. 'This case is a three-pipe problem,' she muttered in a deep voice.

Monty stared at her as if she had lost her senses, but passed no comment. She had noticed that he had a knack of leaving gaps for other people to fill. She took the ice-pack from his hand and knocked back her whisky. Adrenaline was making her careless.

'That means it was a tough case for Holmes,' she explained. 'He needed to smoke three pipes of tobacco to think a particularly difficult problem through to the end.'

'I can offer you a cigarette instead.'

She shook her head and instantly regretted the movement. 'The solution is not in the names of the characters, it's in the names of the stories.'

His eyes gleamed darkly in the shadowy light. 'Tell me.'

So she told him. 'If you drop the *The Adventure of* and *A Case of* from the beginning of the title of each one, you are left with *Lion's Mane, Engineer's Thumb, Identity* and *Naval Treaty.*'

'So?'

'Now take the first letter of each.'

'L.E.I.N. That spells nothing.'

'Rearrange them.'

'N.I.L.E.'

'Exactly!'

He had gone silent on her and thrown himself back into his armchair with an air of exasperation. But none of his huffs and puffs could shake her conviction. Now, as he sat there sipping his whisky, the shadows seized him and turned him into a stranger, a different person from the one who had clasped an arm around her on the Mall and who had draped a blanket over her on the settee. This person she didn't know.

'It makes sense,' she urged. 'Tim is an archaeologist who works with Egyptian artefacts. I am convinced he has gone to the Nile.'

Her words fell into the absolute silence of the room and became small unlikely things. Inert and laughable. But he wasn't laughing. He was angry and she didn't know why. For a long moment neither spoke and the sense of disconnection was only broken when Jabez abruptly popped up out of the shadows and with feline persistence leapt onto Monty's lap with a demand for attention. The tension in the room slid down a notch as he ran a hand along the cat's back.

'The letters also spell LINE,' he pointed out mildly.

'What is that supposed to mean?'

'I have no idea. But it's equally possible.'

Another silence trickled between them, but this time Jessie had no patience with it.

'I believe Tim was sending me a message.'

'You weren't even there!'

'He must have known something was going to happen and I would come looking for him.'

'My dear Miss Kenton, with the greatest respect I think the blow to your head has scrambled your brain.' His breath came out sharp. 'The whole Sherlock Holmes idea has led you astray and the line between fact and fiction has become blurred in your mind.'

His voice was like slivers of glass buried in soap. Scented on the outside, razor sharp on the inside. Jessie rose to her feet to ask him to leave, but the sudden movement set her head spinning and it felt as though a steamroller had landed on top of it. She stumbled. The room retreated to a tiny circle of light in the centre of a swarm of darkness.

Hands held her on her feet. A voice murmured words but they blew away like autumn leaves, rustling as she walked over them. She wondered why dead leaves were scattered on her carpet. *Jabez*, she told herself. *He must have brought them in, silly cat.* She put out a hand and stroked him lovingly. She could tell him anything without receiving a sceptical grunt in return. She gave him another caress and wrapped her hand around his warm head, dimly wondering where his fur had gone.

Jessie woke. On the settee again. Still dark. Through slitted eyes and moving her head no more than an inch, she inspected the room. No figure in the armchair this time. She released a sigh of relief but at the same time realised that she felt oddly empty, which annoyed her, especially when she recalled the barb about fact and fiction being blurred in her mind. She felt colour rush to her cheeks and was glad he was gone. Very glad.

Carefully she moved her head, experimenting with the steamroller, and nearly fell off the settee when she found a shadowy face right beside her. She blinked to remove it but it didn't go away.

She groaned.

'Hush,' he murmured, 'just rest.'

She felt stupid. He was sitting on the floor beside the settee, smiling gently at her. How long had he been there, watching her sleep? Worse – far worse – she was clutching his hand. Clutching it for dear life.

She groaned again and closed her eyes.

*

When she woke this time, she heard voices. Low and secretive, coming from the kitchen. She recognised her flatmate's smoky tones, which meant Tabitha was home from the club.

What was Monty saying to her? Spreading his theory – that Jessie's brain was scrambled – to all who would listen? Damn the man! She already regretted telling him of her discovery of the meaning of Tim's coded words and questioned now why she had done it. Maybe he was right; maybe her thoughts *had* become scrambled and she had foolishly thought she could trust him.

Too late to take it back.

All she could do now was get rid of him. Muscle by muscle, bone by bone, she eased herself off the settee. So far, so good. It was still dark outside, the blackness edging sideways into the room around ill-drawn curtains and Jessie had to curb the urge to fiddle with them. Instead she aimed for the closed kitchen door. Weird sparkles like Christmas lights reflecting on water kept getting in the way, but she made it and opened the door.

The light was bright. It spiked right into her temple. Standing on one side of the narrow strip of flooring were Monty and Tabitha, their eyes wide with astonishment at the sight of her. Opposite them stood another man, leaning his bulk against the sink. Even through the racket that the steamroller was making in her head, she recognised his voice, and his face. Dr Easby. Her father's doctor. In Kent. What the hell was he doing here in Putney?

'Good morning, everyone,' she said in a bright voice. 'I assume it's still early morning, anyway.'

Tabitha was the first to move. 'Jessie, honey, thank God!' She threw her arms around Jessie, squeezing her tight, making the room rock.

Over her friend's shoulder Jessie saw Monty watching her intently. He thrust his hands in his pockets and shifted from foot to foot. Did he think she was going to throw him out? Something about him had changed. As if a thin layer of his skin had peeled away while she slept, leaving him slightly raw at the edges. He looked drained, but he made a sound that she recognised as a low

145

laugh, a sound of welcome. She was too tense to laugh. She extricated herself from Tabitha's embrace and turned to the other occupant of the small space.

'Dr Easby, what are you doing here?'

She held out a hand for him to shake but instead he placed his fingers on the pulse of her wrist and studied her eyes in a professional manner. He looked immensely serious – unusual for this jolly bon viveur, who was wearing a crumpled suit with the Fair Isle waistcoat his mother knitted for him before she died of meningitis last year. He had soft warm hands and a soft warm smile that he dispensed along with his medicines. Jessie's father thought the world of him.

'What brings you to London?' she asked.

'You do.'

Not good. Not good at all.

'I asked Tabitha to telephone your parents,' Monty told her.

'We thought it was for the best,' Tabitha added.

Jessie wasn't aware of her expression changing but it must have because Monty reacted immediately.

'You were asleep too long, Miss Kenton. You had us worried.'

Jessie withdrew her hand. 'It is morning, isn't it?' She directed her gaze to the black square of window. Just a flicker of daylight out there in the east.

'Yes, my dear, it is morning,' Easby soothed, 'but it is *Thursday* morning. You've been asleep over twenty-four hours and your father thought it best that I should come up to town and check you over. You remember receiving the bump on your head?'

She started to back towards the door. 'I'm fine.' The thought of people man-handling her while she was asleep was too ghastly to contemplate. 'I'll just go to my room and ...'

'Now, now, my dear girl,' Dr Easby said with his soft treacly voice, 'you need to relax. I've given you something to calm you down, something to get you over the shock of ...'

'I'm perfectly calm.'

She stopped herself wiping her palms on her dressing gown.

'I'm glad to hear it.' He smiled his warm smile. Paused a moment. Everyone knew there was more to come. He held out his hand, palm up, the way he would offer an apple to a nervous horse. 'Take these. Just in case.' There was a small white tablet-box. 'For your nerves.'

He took a step towards her, so she snatched the box quickly and slipped it into her dressing-gown pocket to stop him coming closer.

'Your parents are worried.'

'Not worried enough to come and see me themselves, it would seem,' she said and walked out of the room before he could reply.

By the time she reached her own room, her head was foggy and she could feel sweat beading on her forehead. She leaned her back against the closed door and slithered slowly to the floor, gathering her knees to her, clasping her hands around them to hold everything together. She was overreacting, she was aware of that. But she didn't want some doctor reporting on her to her father, whatever his motives. The gap between her father and herself was too precipitous, altogether too barren to allow such flimsy seeds to grow. She wanted her father to believe she was in the best of health. *Nothing wrong with me. I'm not Georgie. You can't shut me up in a home for the sick in the head. You can't.*

She was shivering. The pain sent fingers down from her temple to her jaw, making her teeth ache, but that was low on her list of concerns. After a long moment's thought she yanked up both sleeves of her dressing gown and inspected her arms. She found what she was looking for. Two puncture marks. Her heart lurched. What had he injected into her? While Tabitha and Monty stood by in docile agreement because a doctor was a god of sorts. The power of life and death lay in his hands.

She removed the tablets from her pocket, examined them for a name, but found none. Her hand was trembling.

Was she stupid? Was Dr Easby right? Did she need help?

Jessie threw the tablet box across the room and heard it collide with her artwork portfolio that was propped against the wall. In the black portfolio lay her pictures, the ones she had drawn for herself,

147

the ones that mattered to her, and their images reared up uninvited in her head. She rubbed her arms vigorously, feeling suddenly chill, because she knew those images were all about belonging: a child's fingers in a parent's hand, a cat on a lap, a pair of lovers asleep, a girl plaiting her mother's silken hair, a pearl hanging from a woman's ear . . . She could go on and on. It's what her hand drew, she couldn't help it. Belonging together. Not alone. Not disjointed. Not a child left to cry helplessly on a bedroom floor.

She rested her head on her knees. 'Tim,' she whispered. 'Come home.'

19

Georgie

England 1929

'Do you know what this is?' You unfold a white five-pound note. You crackle it between your fingers.

'Of course.'

'What is it?'

'I know what it is.'

'So tell me.'

'I am not a performing dog.'

'It's money.'

I look away.

'Do you know what money is?' you ask.

I want to hit you. Instead I jerk myself over to my desk and start drawing, small neat images in graphite that crowd the blank sightless sheet of paper in front of me. An owl. An eagle. A hand. I repeat the pictures. An owl, an eagle, a hand. Over and over until the page is full. At the bottom I squeeze in one more picture of an owl and then a single feather. I put down my pencil. Over and over it spells out an M and an A and a D in ancient Egyptian hiero-glyphs.

'Pleased with yourself?' you say.

'Yes.'

'Now can we continue our conversation?'

'It was your conversation, not mine.'

'All right, I will assume that you know what money is and what it is for.'

The five-pound note is still in your hand but I try not to look at it. *Money is the root of all evil.* But I think not. How can money be a root? Mankind has evil growing within itself as big and fat as hydrangea flowers in summer, but money is lifeless. Life less. It is only paper and metal, but it has the scent of hatred all over it. I can smell it from my desk. Sour and brown.

'What good is money to you in here, Georgie?'

You waft the banknote through the air like a piece of cheese, as if you know how much I want to touch it. I have never even seen money before, let alone touched it, but I do not tell you that. I don't want to be a Nobody-Know-Nothing. Not like the man in the next room who thinks that voices are beamed from the stars into his head at night, voices and violent pictures. He has cat-shit for brains and cannot understand that dreams come from your own subcon-scious. I have read Sigmund Freud's *The Interpretation of Dreams.* I am not a Nobody-Know-Nothing.

I want to snatch the money, to crumple it in my palm and feel its evil power.

'Your room here in this Domicile of Doom costs money, you know, Georgie.'

I blink. I blink because I am a Nobody-Know-Nothing after all. Disgust, like a white-hot poker, burns my skin. I stand up from the desk and throw myself onto my bed where I lie down, curled up with my back to you. Your voice is soft and full of feathers, but it won't go away.

'To feed you and clothe you and keep you here with doctors and nurses year after year takes lots of money, have you never thought of that?'

'Who pays?' I whisper.

'Your father.'

I howl. It goes on and on, as dark and slippery as diarrhoea in my mouth.

You try to make me stop but cannot. You read to me but I don't hear the words and the howling grows louder until you leave. I howl for three days and then they take me to the Treatment Room. When you come again next Saturday, I am a zombie on the bed.

'Don't talk,' I mumble. 'Just read.'

You read *The Adventure of the Speckled Band*.

20

Jessie rang the doorbell. The door was opened immediately, as though her mother lurked behind the door. She saw that both her parents were standing in the hall with their coats on.

'Jessica! You should have telephoned to say you were coming. We're just on our way out.'

It was her father who spoke. Her mother stood holding onto the door, staring at Jessie's battered face.

'Oh, Jessica,' she murmured so softly that it barely brushed her lips.

'It's all right,' Jessie told them. 'Just bruising.' It wasn't what she had come to talk about. 'Can you spare a few minutes?'

'What were you doing in Trafalgar Square, Jessica?' her father asked reproachfully. 'What possessed you? You're not like young Dashington, I hope – in league with the damn communists who organised the march. They are the ones who started all the trouble. The damn young fool is a disgrace to his father.'

'No, Pa. Don't worry, I'm not a communist. But don't be hard on poor Archie. He was trying to help the workers to make their point after their leader, Harrington, was arrested.'

'He brought shame on his father's fine name! Lord Trenchard

did what he had to do in sending the police to deal with it by force. To protect this country's law and order.'

Jessie sighed. She didn't want this argument now. After a long day at work, a visit to Archie in hospital, and then the fraught drive down to Kent in the dark, the steamroller was back.

'I just wanted a quick word,' she said.

Her father nodded. He looked restless, eager to be off. The folds of his face were stiffly controlled, and as always Jessie had the feeling that he had more important things to do than talk to her. She turned to her mother.

'I have news.'

'You've found Timothy!'

'No, nothing definite, Ma, but I have an idea where he might have gone.'

'Where? Tell me. Where?'

'To Egypt.'

'What? He wouldn't go all that way . . . not without telling us. When he went on that archaeology trip to Egypt two years ago, he told us in advance. Why not this time?'

'You must be mistaken,' her father stated flatly, adjusting his bowler hat and doing up the buttons of his coat. The material was a very dark grey, almost black, a good thick wool. Jessie had never realised before how dark the hall of the house was with its oak panelling, and tonight the darkness seemed to centre on the coat, creating a soft thrumming in her head.

Or was that the vibration of her mother's distress? Because Catherine Kenton's eyes were frozen with fear. Her slender face looked smaller, as if it had been chiselled back to the bone, and dun-coloured smudges were painted under her eyes. The energy that was her trademark had vanished and in its place lay a bright foolish smile that convinced no one. Even so, her small frame was elegantly garbed in a stylish camel coat, tan leather gloves and a chocolate-brown hat with a single black feather at an angle. A tiny discreet veil obscured the creases of tension on her forehead. Jessie felt a rush of concern for her.

But she turned to her father. 'Pa, I came to ask you if Timothy's passport is still in his room, or has it been removed? If he's gone to Egypt, he'd need it.'

Ernest Kenton considered the question and considered his daughter. He removed his hat and placed it on the hall table in such a way as to make Jessie aware that he was showing patience with this small gesture.

'Of course it's in his room. I'll go and fetch it,' he said and started up the stairs.

His back was straight, his movements brisk.

'Pa?'

He turned, expectant.

'Pa, thank you for sending Dr Easby to me in Putney.'

A faint trace of a smile crossed his face. 'I knew you wouldn't go to a doctor in London.' He nodded at her, just a brief dip of his head, then continued upstairs.

She didn't ask why he hadn't come himself. Alone in the hall with her mother, the air was quieter. Stiller and more muted.

'Ma, are you all right?'

'How can I be all right, Jessica?' her mother said softly. 'How?' She held up one gloved hand. It was shaking. 'Look at me.'

Jessie took the small hand in her own and drew her mother to her, wrapping her arm around the small frame, holding it close. They stood there in the gloomy hall, not speaking.

When she heard her father's footsteps on the landing, Jessie murmured, 'I'll find him. I will.'

'I'll hold you to that.' A faint whisper in her ear.

They stepped apart as Ernest Kenton descended the stairs, and Jessie had to push down the tears that rose in her throat. He handed her the dark blue British passport and she made no comment at the sight of her brother's flamboyant signature on the front of it, nor when she flicked it open and saw the photograph of his handsome face inside. She shut it quickly.

'Thank you, Pa.' She took a deep breath. 'I intend to travel to Egypt to see if—'

'No!' Her father's voice boomed in the confines of the hall. 'I forbid it.'

Jessie allowed no flicker of annoyance to show. 'But Pa, I really think he seems to have left some kind of coded message to indicate that it is to Egypt that he's gone.'

'That's preposterous.'

'Today in my lunch hour I went to the British Museum again. Still they have heard nothing from him, but there's worse . . . ' She heard her mother take a ragged breath. 'Worse,' she continued, 'is that his girlfriend,' she almost said the words *Egyptian girlfriend* but remembered in time that her father was unaware of her existence, 'has given in her notice and also disappeared. It might be that they are together somewhere.'

'What girlfriend is this?' her father demanded.

'Someone he worked with,' Catherine Kenton said quickly.

'You never mentioned her.'

'No.'

A lull. Brimming with unsaid words.

Her mother suddenly pointed at the blue document in Jessie's hand. 'His passport is here.' The bright smile widened. 'He can't have travelled abroad without it.'

'He may have travelled on a false passport.' Jessie had thought about this. 'I'm told they are not difficult to acquire. Though why he would do so is . . . '

Her father gave a snort of annoyance. 'Now you are in fantasyland, my girl.' His patience was running out. 'You must give up this childish idea and face reality.'

Both Catherine Kenton and Jessie fixed their gaze on him and a faint tightening of the mouth was the only sign that maybe he regretted his outburst.

'What,' Catherine Kenton asked, 'do you mean by "reality", Ernest? What is it that you think has happened to Timothy that you are not telling me?'

Ernest Kenton switched his eyes to his daughter. 'I believe,' he said, 'that while he was staying with you the night before he disappeared, you said something to him, Jessica, not something intentionally hurtful, I dare say, but it was something that distressed him. Something that made him decide to abandon his family.' His grey eyes were as flat and unyielding as slate. He touched a finger to his moustache, weighing his words. 'Something about George, I suspect.'

'No! That's not true.'

Jessie turned to her mother but already Catherine Kenton had stepped away from her, as if she were unclean.

'No,' Jessie said again. 'I swear it's not true.'

Her mother reached for the front door. She swung it open. Activity, always activity. If you keep active, life will never catch up with you. Stay one step ahead of it at all times.

'We really must be going,' she said brusquely. 'We have a meeting to attend.' Cold air jumped through the doorway and wove around their legs.

'What meeting?' Jessie asked dully. Shock had left her numb.

'We're going to listen to Oswald Mosley,' her father announced. 'He's giving a speech over in Bromley. There is a huge swell of new members in his British Union of Fascists party after the riots. People are angry.' He was back on familiar territory now and the tightness around his lips was sliding away. 'Jessica, I want you to abandon this foolish notion of going to Egypt. Why don't you join us at this meeting? It will do you good to listen to what Mosley has to say.'

Jessie could think of nothing worse. 'No, thank you. I am tired.'

'Of course.'

She walked out of her parents' house, hands balled into fists in her coat pocket. 'Enjoy your evening,' she said as she headed for her car.

'We will.'

Her mother hovered in the doorway. 'I'm sorry about your face,' she muttered.

It wasn't much. But it was something.

*

The night was black as peat by the time Jessie turned into her road. The London street lamps threw out nets of amber but it was the blackness that won. The blackness always won. Even up here on Putney Hill, far away from the belching factories of Bermondsey and Bethnal Green, the fog had slunk up from the river and merged with the industrial filth suspended in the air.

Knowing your own darkness is the best method for dealing with the darknesses of other people.

Jessie had read those words by Carl Jung and they had lodged in a coil of her brain. On the drive home along the streets, busy even at this late hour, she examined the dark corners within herself before allowing herself to think about the accusation her father had made. That she was the one who had said something to Tim that – wittingly or unwittingly – had driven him away from his family, a family that was held together by threads more fragile than her mother's ball of baby-wool. One flick of the fingers and they snapped.

I swear it's not true. Her words to her father.

But no one disappears without a reason. All the way home she replayed in her head the conversations she'd had with her brother during the last weeks, tearing them apart, seeking out a word or phrase that might have—

A car blasted its horn behind her, making her jump. It flashed its lights at her and she realised she had stupidly slowed to a hedgehog's pace. As if she could decelerate the world, dislodge time, turn the clock back and start the last fortnight all over again. She parked outside her house, climbed out of the Swallow and automatically checked the street in both directions, but nothing moved in the shadows cast by the street lamps. She opened the gate and hurried down the tiny front path, her key ready in her hand. The figure that emerged from the darkest patch right next to her front door made her heart leap to her throat. Her hand shot out to ward him off as she thrust the key into the door-lock and she opened her mouth to scream like a skinned cat to scare him away.

'Miss Kenton.' Fingers closed around her wrist and lowered it from in front of his face. 'I'm sorry if I startled you.'

'Monty! Didn't your mother teach you not to lurk in dark corners? You could get your head knocked off.'

His fingers were still attached to her wrist and he laughed softly, making her aware of how small her bones were next to his.

'How's your head feeling?' he asked.

'Much better.' Jessie reclaimed her wrist. 'What about you?'

He flexed his shoulders and winced with an exaggerated groan. 'Like my father's chauffeur used to say, I feel as old as two old horses.'

She laughed, the easy sound of it astonishing her. 'Come on in and I'll make you a cup of coffee to warm you up, but then I warn you I'm chucking you out.' She opened the door and turned on the hallway light, and its beam bounced off his pale face. She noticed he was looking at her slightly oddly. She must look as rough as she felt. 'I've had enough of today,' she said.

She just wanted to close her eyes and vacate her life for a few hours before launching herself on the next step, the thought of which excited and terrified her in equal measure. But right now, she needed sleep.

*

It was hard, up in her flat, to stop herself standing in front of her guest, hands on hips, and asking him straight out why he had come, what did he want? But she didn't. To do so might drive him away, and she realised with surprise that she wasn't ready to do that yet, despite her tiredness and the drumbeat in her head. This man had chosen to help her – whatever his reasons for doing so – and she found herself swinging erratically between gratitude and suspicion. Tonight, gratitude won.

She fussed about in the kitchen, making two cups of cocoa rather than coffee and added two shots of whisky to the tray. Medicinal purposes, of course. When she carried it into the living room she felt a flutter of irritation to see that he had abandoned his place on the settee where she had sat him down. He was on his feet, inspecting her bookcase and a copy of *The Good Earth* by Pearl Buck lay in his hand. He replaced it quickly, as if aware that he had overstepped the mark. A person's books are private, not to be poked around by others at will. They say so much. What conclusions was he drawing about her?

He nodded approval when he noticed the whisky. 'Good thinking,' he said and returned to the settee.

She noted that despite the obvious soreness of his shoulders, he moved with the easy confidence of his class, with a conviction that he was welcome in whatever situation he found himself in. His bones settled against her cushions as if they belonged there, and his brown eyes observed her over the rim of his cocoa in a way that made her feel like the visitor rather than the host. She slumped down in an armchair and knocked back her whisky. Better. Definitely better.

For a full minute they sat quietly, sipping their hot drinks, and through the steam Jessie examined his face. It had an austerity to it that was belied by the upward curve of his mouth and the readiness of his brown eyes to smile. But he was a good actor, that much she had already registered. So how much of this was a mask? How many masks did he possess? Yet she liked the stillness of him and the fact that he didn't always feel the need for talk. The silence in the room was companionable, the hiss of the gas fire relaxing.

'So.' Jessie put down her cup and saucer. 'I went to see Archie in hospital today. He's very annoyed at being out of action. Missing everything. He told me that you had been in to visit. That was kind of you.'

He frowned and shrugged dismissively. A man who did not appreciate thanks.

'The National Unemployed Workers' Movement is making the most of their moment of glory,' he commented. 'Still locked in running battles with the police all over London and splashed over every front page of the newspapers.'

'My father believes that Sir Oswald Mosley is the man to take control now, a strong leader in time of crisis.'

'Mosley is the one who said, "The art of life is to be in the rhythm of your age." He's good at sensing the mood of the people in this horrific Depression and knowing what they want.'

'Yet he's a baronet, isn't he? Related to the royal family. Do you know him?'

The frown deepened and he drank his whisky. 'We've met.' He put down his glass and abruptly leaned forward. 'Tell me, Miss Kenton ... '

'Call me Jessie.'

One corner of his mouth tipped upwards. 'A charming name.'

'I can do without the gallantry, thank you.'

He chuckled and seemed to unwind another notch. 'Now tell me, Jessie, what do you believe has happened to your brother?'

The change of subject and the directness of the question threw her. How much was she prepared to tell him?

'I don't know, but it seems to me that there are two obvious possibilities.' She spoke carefully, giving herself time. 'Either he has left the country to avoid some unpleasantness that he has become involved in here ... ' She paused, her heart pumping harder.

'Or?'

'Or he has left England specifically to take part in some activity in Egypt – hence the *NILE* code. The fact that it all seems to be secret doesn't look good, and could involve Egypt's antiquities.'

She didn't mention the passport.

'No innocent reason? Like a few weeks away with his girlfriend?'

'What do you know about his girlfriend?' It came out sharp. A quick bite at him.

He held up his hands, palms towards her. 'Nothing,' he said, 'Nothing at all. I was just pointing out the obvious, that's all, and wondering why you are choosing to ignore it.'

She didn't need the obvious pointed out to her. Too many had done so already. Even Archie. 'I asked around Tim's other friends,' he'd told her, his head heavily bandaged on his hospital pillow, his eye swollen and his cheek like a split plum. 'No one has heard from him.' Archie's attempt at a smile drew blood from his bruised lips. 'You know Tim, he'll be wining and dining a girl somewhere, the old scallywag.'

That was the point. Jessie did know Tim. This wasn't about a girl, not even the lovely Anippe. This ran deeper.

'Do you have a sister, Monty? Or a brother?'

'No.'

'Then maybe you don't understand. That the *obvious* is not always the path to choose when it comes to brothers and sisters.'

No words. No smiles. No kink of an expressive eyebrow. Not this time. He stared at her, a direct gaze that didn't waver as he murmured, 'So much conviction and such blind loyalty.' The words were separated, giving each one room to breathe, as if it were a foreign language to him.

Jabez stopped washing his ears in front of the fire and stalked across the patch of rug that divided them, his tail upright like a lightning rod. As if he felt a shift in the air, the threat of a storm looming.

'I intend to set off immediately for Egypt,' she announced. 'The journey is a combination of aeroplane and train, apparently. So first thing tomorrow morning I will buy tickets for ...'

He stood up and offered her a cigarette from his silver cigarette case. She shook her head, annoyed by the deliberate interruption.

'A good smoke clears the thought processes,' he urged.

After a moment's hesitation she accepted one and he lit the cigarette for her before returning to his seat. It was only then that his eyes grew bright with suppressed energy, and Jessie was in no doubt that whatever he was about to say was the real reason he had come here tonight. She drew on her cigarette and waited.

'I have a chum,' he said, 'who has a girlfriend in Paris, a dainty French dancer, Giselle, all feathers and garters. Anyway, Jack is so besotted by this exotic filly that he flies over in his small plane to see her every weekend, just as soon as he sheds the daily shackles of his father's bank. He flits across the Channel to Le Bourget airport on a Saturday and quaffs grand quantities of absinthe and French ooh-la-la!' He gave a boisterous laugh, but the sound of it did not quite match the expression in his brown eyes. 'He'd be more than happy to help out. A quick hop to Paris. Then it's the train to Brindisi and a flying boat across the Med.'

Jessie released the smoke and studied her companion through its flimsy curtain. 'Why would he do that?'

'Because I asked him.'

So he was already certain she would go.

'Thank you,' she said. 'But no, thank you.'

He ran a hand through his hair, pushing it off his face, and she could sense his frustration. 'Why not, Jessie? It would make a quicker start for us.'

'Us?'

'Yes, you and me.'

Jessie stood up, looking down on his upturned face. 'There is no *us*. I shall be travelling alone.'

She walked out of the room into the kitchen, returned with the whisky bottle and poured them both another drink.

'I'll see you when I get back and tell you all about it,' she smiled.

He stretched his legs in a good imitation of relaxing, and shrugged with studied nonchalance.

'Don't be foolish, Jessie. It's over two thousand miles. You can't travel all that way alone. And anyway, I have your brother's disappearance on my conscience – I'm not having yours on it too.'

'Your conscience is your own business, not mine. I am quite capable of making the journey to Egypt on my own.'

'Of course you are, I don't doubt that for a moment. But that's not the point. It's too dangerous for a woman alone in that part of the world.'

'Have you been there?'

'Once, when I was eighteen. I idled a summer away before I went up to Cambridge, sailing around the Mediterranean. Morocco was where I spent most of my time.' His eyes changed, the lines of his face softened, and Jessie could not help wondering what memory he had tapped into. He roused himself with a vague wave of his hand around the dimly lit room as if it were a wide open blue sky. 'But I did mooch around Alexandria for a while, up on Egypt's north coast. It's a beautiful city, very British and astonishingly elegant. You'll love it. Unfortunately I didn't get down as far as Cairo, nor all the way south to Luxor, though I'd like to have seen some of the pharaohs' tombs and the great Karnak temple there.'

162

His words were forming a barrier. A wall across the room.

'No,' she said firmly. But it bounced back at her. 'No,' she repeated and this time he listened. 'Thank you for the offer, but I intend to travel alone.'

He gave her a long look, then pressed the heels of his hands into his eye-sockets. Whatever he was thinking was masked from view.

'Tired?' she asked.

He removed his hands. His gaze was no longer that of someone offering assistance to a damsel in distress. He was looking at her with desolate need. She felt her heart lurch. She wished suddenly that he wasn't there. That he hadn't come. He was muddying the decision inside her that had been clear and straightforward just moments ago.

'Jessie, listen to me,' he said gently. 'It is a man's world in Egypt, a country where women are relegated to the kitchen and the bedroom. You will be far more successful in your enquiries for your brother if you have a man at your side.'

'But . . .'

'Yes, I know it goes against the grain,' he gave her a rueful smile, 'for a modern young woman like yourself to accept it in 1932, but it's true.' He sighed softly. 'I promise you it's true. So let me come with you. I meant what I said about my conscience. I feel responsible because the séance that seemed to trigger Tim's disappearance was held at my house. I'm sorry. Truly sorry. I don't want to see you injured too.'

'Injured? What do you mean? What makes you think Tim is injured?'

'It's only that surely he would have contacted you if he were well?'

She shuddered. What if he was right? There were too many what ifs. What if she needed this man as much as he needed her?

She knocked back her whisky and welcomed its heat inside her.

'Very well, Monty, we shall make up a travelling party of two.'

He smiled at her. It was settled.

'Where do we start looking?' he asked.

163

'Cairo.'

He raised his glass. 'To Cairo,' he said. 'And to Tim.'

Tim. Her brother's name reverberated in her head. Was she already too late?

21

Georgie

England 1929

It is snowing. I like the snow. I open the window and thrust a bare arm out through the metal bars to feel the icy flakes settling on my skin. I know how snow is made – I have read how water vapour in the atmosphere condenses into ice crystals, and ice crystals aggregate into snowflakes that fall to the ground.

But my mind frightens me because I start to wonder if they are miniature space ships from Mars, engineered to vanish into a droplet of liquid at the touch of a human. It is possible. Everything is possible. But I think about the needles that Dr Churchward sticks in my arm and I know I have lost count this week. I hate to lose count. Hate, hate, hate it.

I feel my mind escaping from me, slimy and treacherous, and out of my mouth spill the words, 'Tell me what Jessie is doing, tell me what she looks like now.'

You blink, like the blue-eyed cat that I watch stalking the birds in the garden. 'She looks like you,' you say.

That's when you take the photograph of my sister from the breast pocket of your jacket and show it to me.

I start to cry and I don't stop.

I have a secret.

I have to train myself not to tell it to you, just like I train my muscles with the Indian clubs every Saturday. I am not allowed to keep the wooden clubs because *they* say I would be dangerous with them, but you smuggle them in each week. Like you smuggle in newspapers. I have to wear gloves to read them because I cannot stand the black ink blurring onto my skin and you only let me read certain pages because you say they will shock me. Even so, I am shocked. At the violence. At the murders. But I like to read about them because they make me realise I am not alone.

I would murder Dr Churchward if I could.

My arms and my chest are a man's, you tell me, not a girl's any more. They were never a girl's, they were mine, but I don't point that out. I am learning.

I have a secret. It concerns the roof of this residence. Sometimes it takes all my strength not to share it with you. But it is too dangerous.

22

Croydon Airport had style. The terminal building was constructed only four years earlier in 1928. It oozed confidence and calmed nerves with its distinctive aroma of cedarwood polish. Monty stood under the central glass dome in its vast booking hall and looked up at the blue sky above. A good day for flying.

He watched Jessie walk towards him across the acres of parquet, weaving her way smoothly through the crowds and past the towering square pillars where motes of dust in a beam of sunlight flickered around her head like fireflies. He felt the familiar clench in his chest at the sight of her, the not altogether unpleasant sensation of a stranger's hand pushing between his ribs and ripping his lungs out. An unwieldy mixture of pain and pleasure. Right now he concentrated on the pleasure. He smiled and waved his panama hat at her and headed towards her to relieve her of the small leather suitcase. He liked that. The way she travelled light.

She was wearing a jaunty cloche hat and a fitted navy jacket that came down low over a cream skirt of a soft floaty material. It swayed from her hips as she strode up to him in her practical flat shoes. He greeted her with a kiss on each cheek.

'The French way,' he laughed, 'as we're heading for Paris.'

She nodded, looking around, her interest caught by the wooden column on which clocks were displayed showing the time at all the major airports in the world. 'I like this place.'

'It's the pride and joy of Purley Way. People flock here just to watch the planes. Come on, let's book you in at the Imperial Airways desk, then let me show you the observation deck upstairs.'

He picked up her case and drew her hand through his arm. To his surprise, she didn't resist.

The thing about being up high is that it alters perception. Ask Amy Johnson in her Gipsy Moth. It removes you from scurrying around in the dirt alongside all the other ground-dwellers and lets the wind rush in to rearrange your thoughts. Monty leaned on the railing of the observation deck on the roof of the terminal building, smoking a quiet cigarette, and for the first time in a long while asked himself why the hell he was fighting so hard to maintain the Chamford Court Estate. It would be so much easier to let Dr Septon Scott build his filthy factory and tenements on it and be damned.

'What did you say?' Jessie was waiting for a reply.

'I didn't say anything,' he answered and wondered which words had made it from his mind to his mouth without his noticing.

She was standing beside him, strangely quiet. Totally free from the sense of tense activity that bustled around the other passengers who were waiting for the 12.30 flight to Paris. She was focusing on the planes swooping down onto the grass airfield like great grey birds coming home to roost. As each one landed and taxied towards the concrete apron, he named it for her: an Imperial Airways three-motor Argosy or a KLM Fokker monoplane, and parked over by the hangers were a veteran De Havilland 50, a Nimbus and a couple of French LeO 21s.

'You know your aircraft,' she commented.

'Too many misspent hours reading *The Aeroplane* magazine under the blankets, I'm afraid, when I should have been acquainting myself with Herodotus,' he laughed. 'I was always a lazy blighter.'

She gave him a sideways glance. 'Really?'

He pointed to the throng of spectators down in the enclosure who had paid their penny to gain a good viewing position. It cost threepence to access the roof.

'Do you know,' he murmured, 'over seventy thousand people have paid to watch the aeroplanes here so far this year?'

'I don't blame them. It's like sitting on the edge of the world, waiting to launch yourself off into ... ' She stopped. The wind snatched at her hat and she held onto it tightly, her profile to him, her skin like warm cream in the sunshine.

'Into what?' he asked.

'Into a piece of the future.'

A small three-seater Puss Moth side-slipped down out of the sun and purred to a halt on the grass below.

'Is that what you hope to find in Egypt ... a piece of your future?'

She swung to face him, her eyes full of the wide blue sky. 'No. I want to find my past. To cut it loose.'

They sat side by side. She didn't speak much. Monty appreciated the way she left him to his silences without trying to fill them with chatter. In his experience, that was rare in a woman. But at times when she thought no one was observing her, she touched the small curtained window at her side with the flat of her hand, as if trying to hold on to a slice of the sky.

'"Luxury aloft",' Monty commented. 'Imperial Airways certainly live up to their claim for their Silver Wing service.' Jessie had insisted stubbornly on sticking to her plan of travelling without help from him, so Jack and his plane had been politely rejected.

She smiled at him. 'It's smarter than my flat.'

'And warmer than my kitchen. Better food too.'

She laughed. 'A bit noisier though.' In the background the four Bristol Jupiter engines hummed incessantly. She was showing no sign of nerves at flying for the first time. Quite the contrary, in fact. If anything, her eyes kept flicking forward to the door of the pilot's cockpit, as though impatient for the aircraft to increase speed.

The Handley Page 42 biplane was impressive. It carried thirty-eight passengers in a level of comfort that reminded Monty more of one of the great ocean liners than an aeroplane, all plush cushioned seats and varnished woodwork, white damask table cloths and fine bone china. Even an electric bell to summon a steward from the buffet. What it was not known for was speed.

'This plane is as steady as the Rock of Gibraltar,' Monty commented, as coffee was placed in front of them by a uniformed steward, 'and about as fast.'

'Three and a half days to get there,' Jessie muttered under her breath. 'How much can happen to him in three and a half days?'

'It will pass quickly.'

'Will it?' A lock of her hair fell forward, a slender shimmer of gold, but it didn't prevent him seeing the tension in the muscles along her neckline.

He thought about putting his hand over hers.

'We'll be in Cairo before you know it,' he assured her.

'Eighty hours to Cairo.'

'And then what?'

'Simple. Then we find Tim.' She did not let him look at her eyes.

In Paris it was raining. They landed at Le Bourget airport and Monty took Jessie sight-seeing, as they had time to kill. The train that would whisk them all the way across France and down to Brindisi in southern Italy was not due to leave the Gare de Lyon until 9.30 that evening, so Monty took Jessie to his favourite Parisian landmark, the Sacré Coeur Basilica. He kept her interested with stories of the insurrection by the Commune of Montmartre in 1871 that led to the commissioning of the great white church on the hill.

'It was built here as a memorial to expiate the rebels' crime,' Monty explained.

She turned from the church to look at him. 'Expiation. How very appropriate.'

To his surprise she pulled out a drawing pad and stood sketching the church with a few deft pencil lines. He held an umbrella over her while she did so, but he was certain that she was unaware of it, lost to the world, so totally absorbed was she in what she was doing. When she had finished depicting its Byzantine domes, she snapped her notepad shut before he could see it, and tossed it in her shoulder-bag as if it were worthless. She slipped her wet arm through his and said, 'Let's eat.'

He took her to Fouquet's, its red and gold awning offering a haven from the rain on the Champs Elysées. In its elegant panelled dining room she insisted she wasn't hungry but he looked at the paleness of her cheeks and ordered for them both: escargots, trout meunière, followed by pigeon rôti and grapefruit sorbet. Her fork chased her food around her place but she ate little. Only the coffee and the liqueur seemed to bring her pleasure.

'How does the Sacré Coeur stay so white?' she asked suddenly. 'Why isn't it black with city soot and pollution, like the Houses of Parliament are in London?'

'Because it's constructed from Château-Landon stone. When it rains, the stone reacts with the water to secrete calcite which acts as a bleach.'

She rested her elbows on the table and slowly smiled at him across it. 'You know a lot of odd things, don't you?'

'Nothing of use, it seems. Nothing like . . . ' he lit her cigarette, ' . . . like why your brother is in Egypt or where he is in hiding. Have you considered the possibility that he doesn't want to be found?'

'You think that hasn't occurred to me? Of course it has. It keeps me awake at night. But why would he leave me clues if he didn't want me to find him? Why?'

'Are you sure they're clues? Not just something you are reading into a few random names?'

'Of course they're clues.' She exhaled impatiently. 'But they are clues that no one else would recognise, which means he wants to keep secret the fact that I am following him. I am worried it might endanger him in some way. So you must be discreet too.' She watched his reaction.

He was impressed by that quality in her, her directness. Her honesty. Now he was under no illusions. If any poor blighter – and that included himself – was fool enough to step in the way of her finding her brother, dismembering limb from limb would be just the first course.

'Jessie,' he said softly. Because she had to be told. 'This adventure is splendid, but it's utterly madcap. You do know that, don't you? We haven't a cat in hell's chance of finding Tim. You must be prepared for . . . disappointment in Egypt.'

Her eyes widened, and he saw a flash of anger in their depths before they suddenly grew foggy and oddly blurred, and it dawned on him with horror that she was fighting back tears. *Christ, Monty, you blithering idiot.* This wasn't an adventure for her, this was a gruelling ordeal. He looked away, his eyes roaming the room, inspecting the other diners, giving Jessie time. He picked up his brandy and swirled the amber liquid around the glass.

'So,' he said quietly after a moment, 'very well, Jessie, we will not discuss that possibility again.'

When he glanced up, she was still sitting there, but now she was grinning at him. 'Hah! A weak spot revealed at last. A damsel's tears.'

'I'm a Chamford! We have no weak spots.'

She laughed and he summoned the bill. When it arrived he tossed a hefty fistful of franc-notes on the silver platter, brushing aside her attempt to add her own to the pile, and she sat back in her chair, lips in a tight line.

'Thank you. But I thought you were skint,' she muttered. 'Strapped for cash in your big empty mausoleum.'

'I hocked another painting.' He tapped his pocket cheerfully. 'Rolling in the stuff now.'

'I thought it was meant for the roof.'

'The bally house can wait.' He whisked her into her coat and out onto the glistening pavement. It was dark outside and still raining, so he put up the umbrella and she tucked her arm through his, raindrops lodged between her eyelashes. The Paris traffic was heavy, headlamps dissecting the Champs Elysées, but Monty was in no hurry to reach the Gare de Lyon where the train and their travelling companions would be letting off steam. Just for this moment he could forget Egypt, forget séances and leaking roofs and chasing nebulous phantoms across the sands. Instead they sauntered along the street like any other normal couple in Paris and he could feel the warmth of her snaking from her slender arm into his ribs.

'And you?' he asked. 'Are you rolling in the stuff too?'

She leaned close into his shoulder to make herself heard above the barrel-organ on the street corner that was grinding out 'Frère Jacques' for the tourists. 'I've saved my money all my life,' she confessed. 'Even as a child with my piggybank. Tim was always sticking a knife into it to slide out a few coins because he was forever broke. I always felt . . .'

He waited but no more words came.

'Felt what?'

'That I had to be prepared.'

'For what?'

'For . . .' Her breath plumed in the damp air between them. 'For a disaster that was coming my way.'

He stopped in his tracks and turned to face her under the umbrella. 'In heaven's name, Jessie, what kind of person are you?'

She rolled her eyes at him, teasing. 'An unpredictable one.'

They laughed together in the rain.

At the station it was different. She seemed to shut down, to withdraw into herself and vanish from his reach. Yet Monty felt his blood stirred by the noise and bustle, with porters shouting, whistles blowing, the wave of handkerchiefs and the glisten of fur coats. Shoe-shine boys touted for business and newspaper stalls rattled in the wind, while a hot coffee counter was doing good business, its aroma drawing in last-minute customers. A violent argument flared up between two travellers and had to be settled by a railway official. There was no such thing as silence here. Just voices, and voices and more voices.

But over them all breathed the massive steam engines like creatures from another world. Monty possessed a schoolboy's passion for these beings of iron and steel, oil and fire, that were waiting patiently to be unleashed. Clouds of steam billowed along the low platform, spitting flecks of soot into his eyes and nostrils, leaving its fingerprint on his cheeks, and he felt his pulse accelerate at the prospect of the journey ahead. The air bloomed grey and thick inside his lungs. Pigeons fluttered to the ground, seeking scraps of baguette from under his feet, and a child with a tray around his neck was selling shoelaces, chattering away at them in some alien patois.

It was all a world away from Chamford Court.

Monty stood on the platform with Jessie, waiting while fellow passengers clambered up the steep steps onto the train. Coats damp, faces eager. A thousand miles lay ahead of them: by rail to Brindisi in Italy, where they would transfer to the aeroplane that would carry them to Athens, and then across the Mediterranean to the port of Alexandria in Egypt. A thousand miles. *That's a lot of miles.* A lot of time. He imagined the minutes ticking away. Imagined sitting next to her. Today was Wednesday evening and they wouldn't arrive in Brindisi until Friday morning. Thirty-six hours.

As he handed Jessie up the steps into the train carriage, her gloved fingers curled around his for a brief moment and he caught the sweet smell of rain in her hair. Her face was tense now, quite unlike in the plane. On the ground it was as though she knew she was vulnerable. No wings to fly away. And she was right. Like the shimmering pheasants on his estate, the ones he regularly blasted out of the air as they struggled to escape, she didn't know what was coming. Any more that he did. The thought made him tighten his grip on her fingers, and her eyes flicked to his face with unspoken questions.

'Chocks away,' he said and she smiled at him.

He accompanied her straight to her sleeping compartment in the wagon-lits. The corridor lamps were muted, creating a soft somnolent world. In the doorway she turned to him, preventing him from crossing the threshold. He placed her case at her feet.

'I think I'll rest,' she said. 'But thank you for today.'

'You won't join me for a nightcap?'

She shook her head. 'You go off and shine your armour.' Her hand landed lightly on the exact centre of his chest and lay there. 'You might need it tomorrow. Goodnight.'

And then the door was shut and he was staring at its fine-grained wood. Slowly he rubbed a hand back and forth over the front of his waistcoat, buffing it to a shine fit for a white knight, even for one riding only an iron horse. He touched the spot where her fingers had lain.

It burned as though he'd been branded.

He could stand guard outside her door all night. Arms folded, repelling all boarders. But damn it, she would bite his ear off. The reason he had suggested that they travel first class was not just for added comfort on the rough European trains, as he had told her. It was really to keep her safe. There were fewer passengers milling around the first-class coaches, nowhere near as many strangers strolling up the aisles who might have other things on their minds than a trip to the Parthenon or the pyramids.

He stood there outside her door for half an hour according to his pocket watch, until everyone had settled down in their couchettes or in their seats and the corridor was empty except for the lingering smell of Gauloises. He'd heard no sound from behind her door. He imagined her stretched out on the brocade cover of the bunk, shoes kicked off, reading a book, probably another of her piffling Conan Doyle tales that she set such store by. Keeping her mind from escaping down dark alleys. He didn't like to think of her stumbling around in those alleys, real or imagined.

At the end of half an hour he moved silently along the corridor, threw his own case into his sleeping compartment and headed for the dining car. Under him the great wheels kept turning, sending him swaying from side to side as the flat landscape of northern

175

France rippled past, wreathed in the sleep of an autumn night. An occasional cluster of lights blinked at him out of the darkness and the thought of Jessie Kenton's hand on his chest hung around in his head.

Monty was well down his second scotch and soda, fending off scenarios as to the whereabouts of Timothy Kenton. Jessie had shown him a photograph before they boarded the plane at Croydon and it had skewered him right through his throat, so that for a moment he couldn't speak. The photograph was curled at the edges and warm from her pocket. It showed the two of them, Timothy and Jessie, brother and sister. They were sitting on the floor in her flat, playing a game of bagatelle, and they were both laughing. Looking at each other and laughing. Not like most people do when amused which is with an easy release of delight. This was different. They were looking at each other with such joy, such love, such intensity, his hand on her shoulder, her fingers buried in the Father Christmas beard he was wearing. As if they couldn't bear to let go in case . . .

In case . . . what?

One vanished? Like now. Confronted by her worst nightmare.

He would like to know who took the picture. Tabitha, her flatmate, presumably. He wondered if she reacted as he did, with an envy that tasted vile in the mouth. To be loved like that. To love like that. It took something – and someone – special.

He had studied the image of Timothy carefully, but without comment. A mass of blond curls, an interesting face because it was so well-shaped and perfectly proportioned. Straight nose and good chin. It might have been bland, if it weren't for the eyes. They were bursting with laughter and loaded with energy. This was a person it would be easy to love – except for the mouth. It was full and generous, like his sister's but around the edges there lay a weakness, a kind of neediness that leaked from the wide smile like whisky from a cracked glass. As though he were living a life that wasn't quite his. No wonder he was holding onto Jessie for dear life.

'May we sit here, young man? Do you mind?'

Monty dragged himself out of his scotch and soda. He glanced up at the couple hovering at the side of his table in the dining car, and registered a retired military type with an ebullient moustache and a wife who looked as if she were chiselled out of chalk, so white were her hair and skin.

'Do you mind?' she echoed. 'Everywhere else is taken.'

She was right. Each table was occupied. Late night brandies and coffee for the passengers. He rose courteously to his feet and waved a hand at the two vacant seats opposite him across the pristine expanse of white napery.

'Please do, delighted to oblige.'

It wasn't true. He wanted to be alone. But neither was it true when he greeted someone with 'Good morning' when it was pouring with rain and the stock market had plunged. They were just words. The sticking plaster of society.

The couple eased into the chairs and beamed at him. 'The name's Lieutenant-Colonel Forester. My wife, Mrs Forester.'

Monty shook hands across the table. 'Montague Chamford.'

They ordered two vodka martinis, and Monty summoned another scotch for himself as they proceeded to inform him that they were travelling to Alexandria – their daughter had married a diplomat out there – and to criticize the Egyptian nation for demanding a degree of autonomy from the guiding hand of His Majesty's government, their British overlords.

'We granted the Egyptians the right to have their own parliament last year,' the chalky woman declared, 'and you'd think that was enough, but no, they always want more, always more. After all we've done for the Egyptian people – look at the Suez Canal, at the cotton trade we've developed for them throughout our Empire – you'd think they'd be grateful to the British. But no.'

'Really?' The single word from Monty was curt. 'You surprise me.'

She pinned him with a steely gaze. 'Mr Chamford, we were stationed for many years in India and it was exactly the same out there, I assure you. No gratitude whatever.'

'Is that so?'

It was the woman's husband who was more alert to the edge in Monty's voice.

'We don't want to tar them all with the same brush, my dear,' he urged his wife. 'Remember old Rajat Singh. He was a real card and loved the British.' He ruffled his moustache in an attempt to lighten the mood and chuckled.

The woman picked up her martini the moment it arrived and flared her nostrils over it. 'Not capable of ruling themselves,' she insisted. 'You have to treat them like children, you know.'

'Mrs Forester,' Monty leaned forward across the table, closer to the layers of white face powder that sought to eradicate decades of sun-ravage in the sub-tropics. 'If I came into your home and told you how to run your household, would you like it? Would you be grateful? Would you thank me for making your life miserable?'

For a full ten seconds no one spoke. On the woman's cheeks a flush of colour bled into the white powder. Monty remained leaning forward, waiting for an answer.

'Sir!' It was the Lieutenant-Colonel who found his tongue first. 'I expected better of you! A man of your breeding should know more about the world and – more to the point, young man – should know how to treat a lady.' The veins on each side of his nose pulsated with fresh blood.

Monty wanted to hit it. To make this woman see what it felt like when someone assumed they had a right to physical violence to make their point.

'Apologise!' Forster barked.

'For what?'

'For your rudeness to my wife.'

'No, sir. I will not.'

'I insist.'

His voice was rising. Heads turned. Monty knocked back his scotch, and somewhere dimly in the soft ticking of his mind he knew that this was about Jessie, not about Egypt or India or about the baloney spouted by these two arrogant colonials. This was

178

about punishing himself. He switched his gaze back to Mrs Forester's not-so-white face. If he scraped off the powder with a trowel, what kind of human being would he find underneath?

'Madam,' he said in a tone cold enough to freeze her bloody martini, 'if I were a native working for you and you treated me like a child, I would—'

'Well, well, boys and girls, what's the point of fisticuffs over a few native jigaboos who don't give a tinker's cuss about you?'

All three looked round, startled. The voice possessed an East London accent you could hack with a knife and belonged to a middle-aged woman who had risen from her seat across the aisle. She smacked a hand down on their table so hard that the glasses hiccupped. Monty had noticed her earlier on the platform. She wasn't the kind of woman you could miss in a crowd because she was easily as tall as he was, sticking up like a flagpole. Her spectacles hung on a bright blue cord around her neck, resting on her sparse bosom like a spare pair of eyes.

'Madam,' Lieutenant-Colonel Forester snapped back, 'this is a private conversation.'

'Private, my arse! If you want private, don't yell so much.'

'Kindly leave us alone, madam.' Forester swung round to Monty, seeking support for his umbrage.

But Monty did not oblige. Instead he tipped his head with deference to the woman and indicated the vacant seat beside him. 'I'm sorry we disturbed you. Won't you join us? You can be umpire.'

Without hesitation the tall figure slid into the seat and beamed at Forester opposite. 'Now this is right cosy, isn't it, duckie?'

'It certainly is,' Monty said warmly, to goad the Lieutenant-Colonel further. 'We must have some champagne to celebrate the start of our journey. Mrs Forester, can I tempt you?'

The newcomer's laugh swooped through the carriage but Forester rose speedily to his feet and addressed his wife. 'Come, Amelia, let us retire for the night.' He directed a scowl at Monty. 'You, sir, are no gentleman.'

'And you, sir, are a bigot.'

His wife finished off her martini with a well-practised hand and joined her husband in the aisle. After much adjusting of garments and twitching of gloves, she gave Monty a cold stare.

'My husband fought for his country and watched his friends die for their country. What did you ever do?'

'Ah, there you have me, madam.' Monty spread his hands in surrender.

Satisfied, the Foresters marched off to their sleeping quarters and the newcomer nipped around to their side of the table, so that she was now facing Monty. He could study her more thoroughly. At least fifty, judging by her eyes, but no more than forty, judging by her good skin, so probably somewhere in between. Not wearing a hat or headscarf of any sort, as most of the ladies did, but her mousey-blonde hair was pulled back in a bun so tight that it lifted her eyebrows. Her face was narrow with a pointed chin and of all things she put Monty in mind of a heron. Especially with her habit of shrugging her bony shoulders within the folds of her long grey coat, the way a heron ruffles its feathers before diving into the water once more.

'Thank you,' he said with a smile.

'What for?'

'For removing unwanted guests.'

'Any time, young man.'

'Champagne?'

'If you're paying.' She rested her elbows on the table. 'She got to you, didn't she, that snooty mare? With her parting shot.'

'Right through the heart,' he said lightly and raised his glass to her.

'I dare say you deserve it. You toffs don't actually do much, do you?'

'I polish my monocle now and again. My butler will vouch for that.'

She laughed good-naturedly, jiggling her shoulders with amusement. 'My name's Maisie Randall. I'm from London. Headed for Egypt. What about you?'

'I'm Montague Chamford. From Chamford Court. Headed for hell, I suspect.'

'Not a Lord Someone-or-other? You look like you'd wear one of them top hats in bed.' She chuckled at the idea.

'How did you guess?'

'You talk like you got mothballs in your mouth, that's why. No offence or nothin'.'

'None taken, dear lady.' He spoke quietly in a conspiratorial manner that drew her towards him. There was a shrewd alertness underlying the laughter in her pale moth-grey eyes. He'd seen the same look on a fox on his front lawn, the look of a creature who knows how to survive when times are harsh. In a low voice he admitted, 'To be honest, it's *Sir* Montague. But I keep it quiet because ...'

Too late.

'*Sir* Montague,' she crowed. '*Sir* Montague!'

Heads swivelled in the carriage, curious glances skipping in their direction.

'I knew it!' She stuck out a hand. 'Pleased to meet you, *Sir* Montague. It's *such* an honour.'

Monty sighed. 'Enough,' he murmured as he gave her hand a no-nonsense shake. 'You've had your fun. Or I shall start talking cockney to you – with comments on your *barnet* and asking where your *titfa* is, as well as demanding to eat jellied eels.'

'Jolly good show, my lord.'

He relaxed back in his seat with a smile. The oddest thing about travelling was the people you rub shoulders with while rattling along in a train and this Maisie Randall was the last one he'd expect to find in a first-class dining car en route to Egypt. It brightened his day no end. He took out his cigarette case.

'Would you care for a smoke?'

'Nope. Filthy habit.'

Instead she dived into a cornflower-blue handbag that matched her gloves, clearly brand new, and drew out a narrow Bakelite box. She popped it open to reveal a row of skinny black cheroots.

181

'Now that's what I call a smoke.' She offered him one.

'I'll stick to my own, thanks.'

He lit both and the split second of intimacy when she leaned over his flame gave him an unexpected sense of well-being. There was something so alight in this woman that you could warm your hands on it.

'Travel much?' he asked.

'First time abroad.'

'On your own?'

'That's right.'

'Nervous?'

'Scared bloody witless.' She exhaled a string of foul-smelling smoke. 'Excusing my French, my lord.'

'I have a feeling it's the Egyptians who will be scared when they see you coming.'

'Get away with you!'

'Why Egypt?'

'Why not? Everyone has made such a bloody fuss of this digger-fellow, Howard Carter, that I thought I'd take myself off to get a butchers at this King Tutamen.'

'Tutankhamen.'

'That's the chappie.' She narrowed her eyes and paused, thoughtfully inspecting Monty. 'And you? Why Egypt?'

He glanced out of the window, at the night thundering past, solid and impenetrable. What he saw was his own face looking back at him, black holes for eyes and cheekbones about to push through the skin. He looked away.

'I felt like some fun,' he answered with a smile.

'I'll drink to that.'

He laughed and waved a hand at the waiter. 'Splendid. Now where's that damn champagne?'

'Tell me more about Tim, Jessie. What kind of person is he?'

They were eating breakfast. Or, to be more exact, Jessie was scoffing breakfast while he poured a pot of coffee down his parched throat. His head felt as if a donkey was kicking around inside it and chewing the back of his eyeballs. Opposite him Jessie looked up from her breakfast plate, surprised.

She looked young and fresh this morning, her hair gleaming, its corn-coloured waves loosely nudging her shoulders as she lifted her head. There was a special morning shine to her.

'What kind of person is he?' he repeated.

She thought for a moment. 'He's the kind of person you'd want watching your back if you were in trouble.'

Such a statement. Such an open declaration of sisterly love. It simply took his breath away. To cover the moment he sipped his black coffee though it tasted like tar. 'I know Tim is familiar with ancient Egypt, but . . . '

'He and the pharaohs are like that.' Jessie twisted two fingers together. Teasing him.

'But how much does he know about modern Egypt?'

'What exactly do you mean?'

He was careful to buff the sharp edges from his words. 'Just that there is some unrest over there.'

A forkful of scrambled eggs was halfway to her lips. She returned it to her plate and pushed it aside.

'Tell me,' she said.

'Oh, you know, it's the usual hot-under-the-collar stuff. It will probably blow over.'

The smile slid from her eyes. 'But they have their own king in Egypt, King Fuad. And their own democratically elected parliament now. I thought everything was quiet out there.'

'It is. More or less.'

'But?'

'But would you be quiet if you had another country's military jackboots strutting up and down your streets?'

'Don't.' She shuddered.

He tasted more of the tar and shut up. He didn't want her to lose her shine because of him.

'I realise,' she said, 'that as a colonial power we are bound to be unpopular at times, but ... ' Her fingers moved to the centre of the table and waited there.

'You have to keep in mind the country's history,' he pointed out. 'We invaded Egypt in 1886 and have been the masters there ever since. It is a territory regarded as vital for us because of where it lies geographically, a strategic point halfway between Britain and the jewel of our colonial crown, India. So of course we are ruthless in keeping our stranglehold on the Suez Canal and our military might on show in the streets.'

'I know. Tim was always regaling me with lurid stories of the great battles that have been fought over Egypt. I can't tell you how many times I've lived through Lord Nelson's Battle of the Nile victory over the French.'

She tried to laugh, a small self-deprecating sound, but it didn't quite come off. It was the mention of Tim. Monty felt a sadness spilling out of her and quietly he started to fill her mind with Egypt instead. 'Egyptians have suffered foreign occupation for the last two thousand years. It if wasn't the Persians, it was the greedy Greeks and Romans. And they only left because the cunning Turkish Mamelukes seized power and had their wicked way with Egypt for centuries before Napoleon and the Ottomans got in on the act. I tell you, we British are newcomers to the game in the Middle East.'

Gradually he became aware that she was watching him instead of listening to him. He stopped speaking.

'You know a lot of things,' she said.

'All totally useless to me when I'm digging out ditches on the estate.'

She smiled, the kind of smile that reaches the eyes and keeps on going. 'Maybe you should abandon your ditches to the weeds and try your luck at something else – and I don't mean séances.' Her hand slid forward, easing into his half of the table, and he picked it up. It wasn't a delicate hand. It was broad and square with short flat fingernails and no jewellery. His fingers closed around it.

'Thank you for coming,' she said quietly. 'I am grateful. It would

184

be harder without you.' The smile on her face gained a twitch of amusement. 'You look rough this morning,' she told him.

He tore his gaze from her face and looked down at her hand nestled in his. 'I feel rough.'

The human heart is wreathed in darkness. That's how it seemed to Monty, that mankind has an infinite capacity to inflict pain on its fellow members. He had witnessed it before and had his illusions ripped apart by man's ingenuity at the task, but still he harboured hopes that he was wrong. Ridiculous, pathetic hopes that Timothy Kenton was playing a game of some sort, one designed to goad and test his sister for some piffling reason known only to himself.

It was possible.

It was unlikely, but it was possible.

Monty was seated on his narrow wagon-lits bed, listening to the great iron wheels turning beneath him. It would be so damn simple if everything were pre-ordained, if life rolled along on a pair of silvery rails with just a few undulations along the way. He lit a cigarette and shook his head. The image of Jessie's hand encircled by his own was still in there. Unsettling him. No, he didn't believe in destiny, well, not that kind anyway. Not the kind that laid down the rules for you all straight and narrow. That would suit politicians, of course, everything tied up neat and dandy, like the way that fellow Adolf Hitler was imposing a new regime on Germany with his Nazi party right now or that poppycock Mussolini who was strutting over Italy with his Fascist party. And let's not forget the bastard Mosley who saw himself as the saviour of Britain, bringing Fascism to our green shores. God forbid!

No. You create your own destiny. You make your own choices, right or wrong. They pre-ordain the mess you get yourself into. He gave a grim smile. Hell, that was what made life thrilling – that you could at any time make new choices, new decisions to haul yourself out of those damn bottomless wells that in your infinite wisdom you decided to jump into. This train was his rope and he was hauling himself up hand over fist, towards that small circle of light at the top.

It was almost dark outside now; that moment in time when the day holds its breath before it exhales a last whisper and draws the shadows of night over itself. The mountains of Switzerland hung blue and bruised-looking around them, leaning so close at times it was as though they were trying to peer inside the carriage. As they thundered past one snug village of steep-roofed houses, the church-bells were ringing and a herd of goats stopped what they were doing to watch the train, round-eyed as children.

This was the time to make new decisions. To alter destiny. Before it was too late.

23

Georgie

England 1929

Facts circle inside my head. You laugh at me and my facts but I learn not to mind.

The *Encyclopaedia Britannica* has been my Bible for so many years that I have read each volume until their embossed covers are tattered and hold the imprint of my hands. I cannot help it if I remember facts.

We sit in the beautiful uncomfortable chairs and I tell you facts.

'Knapping is what they call the process of shaping a flint. Or it could be a piece of chert or obsidian or any other conchoidal fracturing stone used to manufacture stone tools. Lithic reduction is the term used for chipping away segments of stone to create a sharpened edge.'

'Thank you for that piece of information,' you say.

I am pleased. Today you are interested in my facts, which is not always the case. Sometimes you tell me to shut up. I have learned from you that I must not bore people, so I swap subjects to entertain you.

'Do you know that using trigonometric parallaxes is the way to find out the distance of stars?' I lean forward, excited. 'This is the good part ... that by using the earth's orbit as the base-line, the distance can be found in parsecs from the angular size of the parallax. Hence $d = 1/p$, assuming of course that both the sun and the star are not moving with a transverse velocity.'

'Utterly fascinating, Georgie.'

I feel so good that I bang my hand on the maple arm of my birthday chair, the way you do when you're pleased. I expect you to do the same but you don't. Instead your foot starts to tap on the floor. I study it in its brown leather brogue, uncertain how to interpret the movement. I feel my right eye twitch. It has taken to doing that recently. Dr Churchward pointed it out to me and made me take a yellow tablet instead of a blue one. As long as it isn't red, I don't fight it.

I recite Frege's mathematical Theory of Aggregates but this time you say nothing. I try to understand your body movements without looking at your face but you have not yawned yet, so I have to rely on your hands. They are fiddling with your shirt buttons. Not a good sign. Fiddling equals bored. You told me that.

I shift from science to the arts.

'Today is December the seventh,' I point out.

'So?'

'So on this day in 1783 Emperor Joseph the Second engaged Amadeus Mozart as chamber composer at court.'

'How nice for him.'

'Yes, it was. He was paid eight hundred gulden a year. But when he died on the fifth December 1791 he was penniless and was buried the next day with only the gravedigger in attendance.'

'That's sad.'

'Why?'

You shake your head slowly like you do when your cricket team loses and I know you are not going to try to explain. All you say is, 'He was a great composer.'

'I know. But I've never heard his work.'

Suddenly you beam at me. 'Next week I will bring you music. Yes! We shall have music and you will dance.'

I try. For you I try my hardest. But my feet and the music and my counting out loud all get jumbled up together and I step all over your shoes.

'You are an uncoordinated dunce!' you say but you laugh, really laugh, as you say it, so I know you're not cross.

This is what I do not understand. You call me *an uncoordinated dunce*, when we both know I am not a dunce. So it is rude, yet you are laughing. So you mean it kindly. Yet downstairs one of the whitecoats, the one who arranges the pathetic group quiz on a Friday, is always saying 'You're a right clever dick, aren't you?' and you tell me it is an insult. Even though he calls me clever. I do not understand. Words have so many meanings that don't make sense.

You arrive with a dark blue box in your arms, the size of a child's suitcase, and you ask permission to place it on my desk. I want to say no. My papers are all lined up in a special order on my desk, with my pens and pencils neat as a row of soldiers on the right, my stack of spiral-bound scrapbooks on the left. They are full of photographs that I have cut out from the newspapers and magazines you bring me. You call it *Georgie-land*, my version of the world out there. I worry that I might have got it wrong, so I am protective of my spiral-bound scrapbooks. If anyone touches them, I . . . *say it, say it* . . . I have an *episode*.

But I lift the scrapbooks and place them in a corner of the room. Then I cover them. With my striped dressing gown. You place the dark blue box on my desk and open it. I am fascinated. It is a gramophone. I stroke the chrome arm, feel goosebumps up my wrist when I finger the velvet turntable and squeal with joy when you let me wind up the spring motor using the handle at the side. You take a record out of its brown paper sleeve and hand it to me.

It is the most beautiful object on earth, even more beautiful than the chairs. I tell you this.

'You haven't seen enough objects,' you say in an odd voice. 'Or touched enough things, my dear brother.'

But I scarcely hear. I am holding the record and I know I will never want to let it go. It is perfect. A perfect twelve-inch circle with another perfect circle at its heart, black and shiny, flat but ridged. It is the ridges, the grooves, that bring a strange peace to my mind. A blankness sweeps through me and my limbs lose the muscle spasms that afflict them when I am excited. I imagine that this is what Bernadette felt when she saw her religious visions in Lourdes in 1858.

But it is not God I worship. It is the grooves. They turn in a tight-fitting spiral until they reach the outer edge. A spiral is a plane or curve that extends in length and width, but not in height as it winds around a fixed centre point at a continuously increasing form. I touch it with awe.

'Don't touch,' you say. 'Grease and sweat from your fingers can block the grooves and then it doesn't play properly. It's a 78.'

'78 what?'

'78 rpm. Revolutions per minute.'

I stare at it.

You take it from me and wipe it carefully with a yellow duster. I want to snatch it back. But I don't.

'It's Mozart,' you say. 'Waltz Number One.'

I cannot believe such perfection of sound can come from such a small blue box. The rhythms soften the raw edges inside me and when I close my eyes I am carried elsewhere, somewhere blue and sparkling where I am flying alongside a flock of gaudy blue kingfishers. I look down at a stream below me and see Dr Churchward lying on his back under the clear water. His eyes are open. He is trapped there. My heart rejoices, soaring out of my chest and . . .

'You like Mozart?' you ask.

I open my eyes. 'Yes.'

It is all I can say. The music's mathematical complexity enslaves me.

'Shall we dance?' you ask.

I nod.

You hold out your hands to me. A quiver of panic ripples through me because we never hold hands. I have never held hands with anybody, not even Jessie, and certainly never with Dr Churchward. But you have given me something huge and I want to give you something in return. So. I take your hand. My mind grows jerky. My teeth chatter. But I hold you.

'All right,' you say, 'we dance to the beat of three. One, two, together, one two together . . . just copy me but you must move forward and I'll move backward.'

The skin of your fingers is touching mine. How can I count when all I can think is that your skin is against mine? Sloughing off your dead cells onto me. Your body's oil oozing onto me. Your sweat. Your heat. My feet stumble.

'Let's start again,' you say and you rewind the gramophone.

We face each other, at arm's length you take my hands once more and we dance. In a straight line across the room. Again. Again. And again. I am getting better. I am smiling. I flick a glance at your face and see that you are smiling, a big broad clown's grin, and then we start to laugh. We are dancing and laughing, laughing so hard my sides hurt but I keep holding onto your fingers, and now we are humming the music together, humming and laughing and dancing to Mozart. My feet are disobedient. My head knows the moves but my feet flounder after yours and you tell me I am an uncoordinated dunce which makes us laugh even louder. A massive bubble of happiness floats inside my chest and makes it hard to breathe.

'Cut it out! Stop that bloody racket!'

It is a whitecoat. He has barged into my room with a face all screwed up like a used handkerchief, and is banging his fist against the doorpost. You drop my hands and lift the needle off the gramophone record, so that Mozart is cut off and the room is suddenly bursting with silence.

'I was showing Georgie how to . . .'

I start screaming. I go right up to the whitecoat and scream into his handkerchief face, 'Get. Out. Of. My. Room.'

'Georgie, don't get upset,' you say, 'don't . . .'

'He . . .' I gasp, pointing a finger like a gun at the whitecoat's head, '. . . just ruined . . .' I am clutching my chest, short of air, waves of blood charging through the blood-vessels of my ears, so that I am almost deaf, '. . . ruined the happiest moment of my life.' I am shaking. So badly that my knees start to buckle.

Oddly, the whitecoat backs out. He leaves the room in a hurry with a narrow-eyed expression that I cannot translate, but he is staring fixedly at you. I swing round. I look you straight in the eye and my feet try helplessly to dance, but your face is all twisted. Your blue eyes are drowning. Tears are pouring down your cheeks.

24

The Short Calcutta flying-boat smacked down on the glittering water of Alexandria's harbour with a roar and a judder that sent Jessie's heart skittering. She turned to Monty in the seat beside her.

'My dear Watson,' she declared, 'the game is afoot.'

He laughed. 'Any more words of wisdom to speed us on our way, Sherlock?'

Jessie leaned close to the window of the aeroplane, her heart thumping as she studied her first glimpse of an Egyptian city shimmering in the sunlight. Alexandria, one of the pearls of the colonial crown, had wrapped itself possessively around the curve of its iridescent blue bay, as though hugging it close, jealous of intruders. The Qaitbey citadel stood forlornly on guard at one end and the Corniche like a ribbon of pale silk stretched along the water's edge.

'Life is infinitely stranger,' she quoted from *A Case of Identity*, 'than anything which the mind of man could invent.'

Monty bent forward to peer over her shoulder. She could feel his breath on her cheek and sense it speeding up, though he made no comment. Together they watched the minarets of Alexandria drift closer.

*

Tim, I'm here.

Help me.

The first thing she noticed was the smells ... and then, a heart-beat later, the heat. What is it about the warmth of the sun that alters the component parts not only of the skin, but also of the brain? As Jessie stepped off the plane her mind seemed to shed the London fog that had been swirling through it, clinging damp and cold to her thoughts ever since she'd heard her that brother was missing.

Here her mind gained a clarity that increased with each lungful of Egypt's air that she drew in. At this time of year it was as balmy as an English summer's day but that's where the similarity ended abruptly. This air was as bright as if it had been polished, so bright that it felt like fireworks going off around her, making her blink. And each breath was impregnated with the scent of sea and shell-fish, heavy with invisible grains of sand and unknown spices. She could taste them on her tongue.

Oddly, she wanted to laugh. To shout. To send her voice boom-ing down the valley of the Nile ahead of her to let Tim know she was coming.

Tim, I'm here.

Help me.

It was as the passengers were steered towards the customs build-ing – it sat squat and official ahead of them – that a tall woman fell into step alongside Jessie.

'Holy Moses,' the woman exclaimed, making Jessie smile. 'Just look at this place. I've fallen down a rabbit hole straight into the Bible, I swear.'

It was Mrs Maisie Randall. Monty had introduced them on the train and Jessie had instantly taken a liking to her fellow passenger's ready laugh and frank manner. It made a change from the stiff demeanour and poker-faces of many of the other British travellers. Yet the woman had kept herself to herself for much of the time, a lone female adventurer who liked it that way, it seemed.

Her tall shadow pushed ahead of Jessie's, eager to get wherever it was going, as she strode out in a loose flowered dress and gigantic straw hat with scarlet silk peonies on it. She was staring at the throng of workmen who bustled around the harbour in their long flowing robes which gave them a grace of movement that was immensely pleasing to the eye. Out on the dazzling blue water a mix of large ships and small pleasure craft rode at anchor, and in the quayside a string of dusty camels was being loaded up with bricks, turning each of the animals into a long-legged pyramid of sorts. Jessie was tempted to duck over there with her sketchpad, but Monty had this morning delivered two stern instructions with his brown eyes fixed on hers, as if he would drill his words into her head.

'Rule number one: Don't wander off.'

She had sighed at him, but he hadn't finished.

'Rule number two: Don't wander off – for *any* reason.'

She didn't sigh a second time or shake her head at him. She could sense the urgency behind his words and she was touched by the concern that was stamped in every line of his face. As she looked around her now at the crowds of Egyptians, she saw no women, just men wearing the long *galabaya*s with a turban or round cloth cap and open sandals. Many had beards obscuring their faces. At first glance she would be hard pushed to pick out one if she had to.

'This is just the beginning,' she commented, more to herself than to Maisie Randall.

The woman gave Jessie a quick interested glance. 'Stopping here in Alexandria, are you?'

'No. We go straight on to Cairo by train.'

'For the pyramids?'

Jessie nodded. 'Of course. Aren't they what everyone comes to Egypt to see?'

'Me too. Off to Cairo. I wonder what the native trains are like. I bet a pound to a penny that it'll be a right old bone-shaker.'

'If you ask me, I reckon that the whole of Egypt is going to shake up our bones. It will change us. I am expecting . . .'

Jessie let her eyes travel inland, skimming the tops of palm trees that swayed their long silky leaves in the breeze off the sea. She could feel the land drawing her, pulling at something within her so strongly that she wanted to break into a run.

'Expecting what?'

Jessie blinked and brought her gaze back to Maisie Randall. The grey eyes were bright with curiosity. 'Expecting to be amazed by Egypt's wonders,' Jessie finished.

She quickened her pace and saw out of the corner of her eye one of the camels lash out a hind leg with such a force that a couple of porters collapsed yelping to their knees. Just at that moment the haunting call to prayer of the muezzin drifted like the wings of birds over the rooftops.

This land had laid down its marker. She must walk with care.

The train ground to a halt. Grey steam belched from its heaving engine and the ten carriages behind bucked and rattled as they lurched to a standstill in Cairo's busy Misr station. It was evening. A darkness so solid that Jessie could touch it.

'We're here,' Monty announced when she didn't rise from her seat on the train.

He lifted down her small case from the luggage net above their heads and then helped Maisie Randall and an elderly German couple with theirs, ever courteous. When he turned back to Jessie she saw the surprise on his face that she was still seated, her hands tucked between her knees.

'Ready?' he asked.

She nodded. She was ready. More than ready. But she waited while the other passengers tumbled down onto the crowded platform outside, leaving only herself and Monty inside for a moment before the crush of new passengers barged their way on board the train. Just one brief moment. In her head she imagined Tim here. On this train. Arriving in Cairo, his whole body aching from a hundred and twenty-five miles of being shaken and jostled all the way from Alexandria. His hair as dusty as hers was now, his shirt sticking to his back with sweat because of the heat from the bodies crammed into the compartment.

She closed her eyes. Pictured him. *What did you feel that day?* The same dry throat, the wide-eyed excitement, the heart jittery in the chest? Or was someone beside you in your stuffy compartment, someone who was dictating your moves? Someone you care for or someone you hate?

A hand was under her elbow, drawing her to her feet, and Monty's arm encircled her shoulder. For no more than it took her to draw a deep breath, she leaned against him, feeling the steadiness of him, absorbing the calm strength of him. He positioned himself in the doorway of the carriage, barring the incoming tide of humanity, and smiled at her.

'If you don't come now,' he said in mock alarm, 'I shall be torn to pieces and fed to the chickens.'

A bearded man was trying to push a crate of poultry through one of the windows and the birds were squawking in panic. The shouts from outside broke like a tidal wave of sound as Jessie stepped forward and jumped down onto the platform, case in hand.

'Now,' she called out to Monty above the noisy stampede for seats, 'a taxi is what we need.'

Vendors swarmed around her the moment her feet touched down.

'Pretty lady, you buy postcards?'

'*Shai*, drink *shai*, tea, you like?'

'I carry suitcase?'

'*Baksheesh?*'

'Necklaces, lovely necklaces.'

'You want *bastet*? Fine price! No rubbish.'

'*Min fadlik?*' Cupped hands pushed against hers. 'Pleese? *Baksheesh*? You give?' The ancient plea of beggars.

For a moment, Jessie was overwhelmed. She stood immobile while they surged about her, faces lined by generations of sun and poverty, hands thickened by a life of hard labour. Yet their dark eyes were good-humoured and hopeful, and the child with the postcards smiled at her shyly.

She opened her purse, aware that she had no small coins, just notes of large denomination, but before she could settle her dilemma, Monty came wading through the crowd to her side. From somewhere he had acquired an ebony walking cane and he prodded them with it, cutting a swathe for her to pass through. He tossed a handful of piastres at them and gathered Jessie to him, linking her arm through his.

'Don't,' she said, 'ever let me do that again.'

'Do what?'

'Have no coins in my purse.'

He laughed. 'My dear Jessie, you will go home a pauper if you give to every beggar who wriggles into your heart. The children are especially adept at it.'

He bounced his cane lightly on the head of a young boy who was walking backwards in front of them, hand extended, hoping for more.

'*Imshi*!' Monty bellowed but without rancour. 'Go away!'

'Mrs Randall,' Jessie called out to their travelling companion further down the platform. 'Would you care to share a taxi?'

'No thanks, dearie. I'm all fixed up.'

The tall woman was ploughing her way towards the long row of taxis and horse-drawn cabs outside under the yellow glare of the street lamps. Behind her, two grinning porters were touting her suitcase and holding her big black umbrella over her, though it was neither raining nor even daylight. A silvery gleam of moonlight robbed everything of colour.

Jessie hesitated a moment, amused, and called out again, 'Mrs Randall! Where are you staying?'

'At Shepheard's.'

Jessie nodded approval. Even she had heard of Shepheard's Hotel, the finest in Cairo. Built by an Englishman in the nineteenth century, its elegant terrace on Ibrahim Pasha Street became world renowned as the place to see and be seen. Yet it surprised her. Shepheard's was where the celebrated and elite of society chose to stay, and the wealthy with time on their hands. Mrs Maisie Randall didn't strike Jessie as fitting into either of the first two categories, but maybe she slotted comfortably into the third one. You never could tell.

'Nice work if you can get it,' Monty muttered at her side, and sauntered over to a battered old Chevrolet whose taxi-driver salaamed, and opened the dented rear door for Jessie with a torrent of Arabic and English in an incomprehensible mix.

'Where you go?'

Jessie looked at the man. In his long *galabaya*, khaki green in colour, a dark scarf wound around his head, his bottom front teeth missing from his wiry face and a smile ready and waiting on his wide mouth, he was exactly as Tim had described Egyptian workers to her. On his first dig in Egypt two years ago at Medinet Habu, the mortuary temple of Ramses III, the men had impressed him. Eager and obliging, working long hours, skin the colour of the evening desert sand and a look in their eye as old as the pharaohs themselves. They had seen it all. Masters come and masters go. When you live in a land as ancient as this, everything is ephemeral. Even life itself.

'Where you go?' he asked again politely.

'Mena House Hotel.'

25

Mena House Hotel was a bizarre concoction. An impressive mix of Moorish and English architecture that sprawled in all directions and sprang up at Jessie out of the utter blackness of a desert night. The taxi-cab had ground its way out of the city of Cairo and up onto the Giza plateau, and now was rattling down the drive along the hotel's dusty avenue of palm trees that loomed in the headlamps.

The car sighed to a halt outside the hotel's grand entrance.

'Jessie,' Monty murmured beside her, his hand pinning hers for a second to her seat, 'don't expect too much.'

She looked out of the side window at the hotel's Arabian arches and elaborate latticework, at its curved balconies and its army of sparkling lights that obliterated the stars.

'I expect,' she said quietly. 'to find *something*. I don't know what . . . but *something* that will point the way.'

His hand cradled hers. 'How can you be so damn sure that this is where Tim would come?'

She turned to him and for a moment in the patched back seat of the tumbledown car, the gap between them seemed to narrow. She felt a connection to this man. Not just because he had travelled so far across the world at her side, but because she could feel a part of herself linked to him. From the start it had been there, this sense of something more between them. Something unsaid. She didn't understand why or where it came from. She had constantly pushed it away, refusing to acknowledge its presence, but now, in the darkness of an Egyptian night – suddenly it was here between them on the seat of a taxi-cab, as insubstantial as the starlight in the black sky.

'He is my brother,' she said. 'He may not have stayed here at this hotel, but he knows this is where I would come to start looking.'

'Why here?' he asked.

But at that moment the doorman opened Jessie's door with a flourish and a rush of chill desert air brushed her cheek. She tried to move, but Monty tightened his grip on her hand.

'Take care.' He leaned forward and kissed her forehead. 'Take good care of yourself now we're here. I'll always be watching your back.'

He released her hand and climbed out of the car.

But who will be watching yours?

How do you put a value on a word?

Sir.

Such a small word, yet worth its weight in gold, it seemed, in this world of sultans and princes.

Sir Montague.

It opened doors. Jessie understood now that he was right. Men's eyes skipped over her and came to rest with respect on the tall Englishman in the pale linen suit and crisp panama, on whose shoulders the right of entitlement sat like a second skin. Her value depended solely on his, and his was high. She could see it in the bowing and scraping and the deep salaams as he strode across the wide reception hall, and in the bright eyes of the man behind the desk. They recognised the breed of man who had stamped his foot all over the British Empire and painted almost half the world pink on the map.

'Did you have a good journey, Miss Kenton?' the man on the desk asked politely. He had smooth shiny skin and an attentive manner, but she wasn't fooled.

'Yes, thank you. Very interesting.'

There was no point in letting it irritate her. Here in Egypt she may be a third-class citizen just because she was female, but it meant attention would not be on her. She was nothing more than a pale shimmer of moonlight next to the sun that was *Sir* Montague Chamford. It would suit her purpose perfectly. She smiled at him and looked around her with interest.

They had walked into a magnificent Arabian palace, complete with mashrabiya windows of exquisitely carved latticework and elegant horseshoe archways. The whole place was luminous. It dazzled with its gold decorations and polished brass, and lavished on its visitors the reflected light from embossed brass doors, blue tiles and mosaics of marble and mother-of-pearl. Like the *Sir* of Sir Montague, it was there to impress.

And Jessie *was* impressed.

No wonder Sir Arthur Conan Doyle had brought his wife, Touie, here to Mena House Hotel in the winter of 1895 when she was dying from tuberculosis. Did he place her on one of these richly coloured sofas? Did he weave for her a thousand and one tales of Sherlock Holmes to keep her alive, the way Scheherazade did for her Persian king? Did Touie lie here looking out at the pyramids, envisaging her own tomb?

Jessie knew it was time to act before they left the desk. She turned quickly to find Monty signing the hotel register.

'I think this place will do us nicely, Sir Montague,' she smiled.

But for once he didn't respond with his usual laugh. 'Yes, I rather think it will.' He addressed the desk-clerk. 'We believe Miss Kenton's brother stayed here recently, so could you look and see when he was here?'

The man's face took on a pained expression as he handed back their passports. 'I am sorry, Sir Montague, so very sorry, but we cannot give out any information about guests.'

'Please, make an exception in this case,' Monty said, turning the full force of his aristocratic charm on the Egyptian clerk. 'I would be very grateful.'

He slid an English five-pound note onto the counter. It took three seconds for the man to make his decision. His black eyes flitted around the hall to check for observers, while his hand crept forward. The note vanished. He straightened his tie.

'The name?' he asked.

'Timothy Kenton. Some time during the last month.'

The clerk popped a pair of rimless spectacles on his nose and with a casual air started to flick through past pages of the register, running his thick thumbnail down the list of names.

'There's no Mr Timothy Kenton.' He looked unhappy to be the bearer of bad news.

'Oh, come now. Check again, there's a good chap.'

He checked again.

'Still no Timothy Kenton, sir.'

'He may have been with others.' From his breast pocket, Monty drew a photograph that Jessie had given him. This one was of Timothy wielding a croquet mallet at the All England club. 'Maybe you recognise him. Fair-haired and a very amiable young fellow.'

The clerk looked miserable. 'No, sir, no. I don't.' He shook his head balefully.

'Ah. That's a bally nuisance.'

'May I take a look at the register?' Jessie asked. 'There might be the name of one of his friends I recognise.'

'*La*! No!' He pulled the register to his side of the desk. 'It's not permitted.'

Monty took his time lighting a cigarette, and puffed a stream of smoke straight at the offending register. 'Not even if I am *extremely* grateful?'

The man shuddered and shook his head regretfully. 'No, sir. I cannot. I lose my job. The manager is just here.' He glanced over his shoulder at the closed door behind him.

'Is he, indeed?'

Time was running out. They had the keys to their rooms and a porter was hovering over their luggage. Jessie wanted to snatch the register and run.

'The esteemed Sir Montague Chamford, I believe?'

Monty raised a smile for the smart young stranger approaching them, as if he received such greetings wherever he went. The stranger was dressed in a dark frockcoat over a white tunic and was wearing the traditional red tarboosh hat with a black tassel. 'I am Mohammed Sawalha.' He salaamed respectfully, but did not even glance at Jessie. 'I come from Prince Abdul al-Hakim. My prince sends greeting to our esteemed visitor to Cairo and extends the hand of friendship.'

Jessie watched Monty salaam gracefully to the young man and wave a hand at herself. 'May I introduce my travelling companion, Miss Kenton.'

'Good evening, Miss Kenton. I am honoured to meet you.'

He didn't look honoured, not one bit. She nodded stiffly.

'To what do we owe this pleasure?' Monty asked.

'Prince Abdul heard of your arrival in our favoured city today. He is holding a reception at his palace this evening and wishes to invite you to join him. He would be honoured. The British High Commissioner and his wife will be attending, as well as most of the British and French "top brass", I think you call it.'

He extended a beautifully groomed hand that held out what was clearly an official invitation on a thick embossed card edged with ornate gold. Monty took it, inspected it, and looked expectantly across at Jessie.

No, Monty. She felt a swoop of disappointment that he was so easily distracted from their purpose here. She gave a quick shake of her head.

'You go,' she said quietly. She started to turn away, uneasy at the sudden change in their situation. Who were these people who knew they were here? How did they find out?

'Please convey my thanks to Prince Abdul,' Monty said courteously to Mohammed Sawalha. 'I shall be delighted to attend.'

'We shall send a car for you. In one hour.'

The messenger bowed and, pleased with himself, he strutted towards the door of the hotel. Monty stared thoughtfully after the departing figure and stubbed out his cigarette in the brass ashtray on the desk.

'Interesting,' he muttered. 'Don't you think?'

'I think it has been a long day,' she said.

He frowned. 'It's not over yet.'

'I hope you enjoy your evening.'

'Pardon?'

'I'll see you in the morning,' she said.

She heard his intake of breath. Abruptly he drew her further from the desk and lowered his voice. 'Did you think I would go without you?'

'You are a free agent, Monty. You do as you wish.'

She started to move away but he immediately stepped close to her and laid a hand on her shoulder, anchoring her.

'Don't do this, Jessie. Don't push me away. Not now.'

His voice was different. The light, lazily bantering tone that was so much a part of him had vanished. This was the Monty Chamford from Trafalgar Square, the one who had fought his way to her side when she was in danger. For a heartbeat the moment hung suspended on a thread, then she smiled.

'I haven't come all this way to go gallivanting round blasted palaces,' she told him.

'On the contrary, this could be exactly what we need.' He wafted the invitation through the air, releasing her shoulder. 'Think about it. There will be many from Cairo's European clan there, I'm certain. They may have crossed paths with your brother or heard of his arrival. Someone may know something.'

'You're right. I hadn't thought of that. Of course we must go.' Jessie felt a rush of sudden excitement. 'Tim might even be there.'

'Don't get your hopes up too high.'

She was grateful. He didn't call her a fool, though the idea that Tim would be at this evening's reception was utterly foolish. Jessie knew that. But she also knew that nothing about this trip was predictable. Anything was possible.

'Silly me,' she said, tapping a hand to her forehead in mock despair. 'I forgot to pack my ballgown.'

'You look lovely in any frock.'

'But seriously, I do need evening gloves, long white ones, or they won't even let me in!'

'No need for such . . .' He stopped, frozen in mid-thought, eyes wide. 'Come,' he whispered.

He whirled round and strode back to the reception desk. He waved the embossed invitation under the nose of the startled clerk who snatched off his spectacles and jumped back a foot. Monty placed a guinea on the counter.

'My travelling companion, Miss Kenton, requires a pair of ladies' white evening gloves,' he declared in his best and loudest Sir Montague voice. 'I'm certain you have spares lying around here. You chaps always do.' He rapped the counter with the ivory head of his cane. 'Ties, gloves and umbrellas. Must have cupboard-loads of the things. Go!' He pointed at the door behind the clerk. 'Go and inform your manager. White gloves.'

'But, sir, I mustn't leave this . . .'

'Go, man! Gloves!'

'Please, I . . .'

'Now!'

'But . . .'

'Go!'

The man went. Jessie didn't hesitate. Before he had even closed the door behind him, she had seized the register, twirled it to face her and was scouring the lists of guests.

Less than one minute later the clerk emerged with a wide grin on his face and a delicate bundle of tissue paper held across his hands like a votive offering.

'White evening gloves,' he announced.

'Good man,' Monty praised him.

The register was back in place. Jessie's heart was hammering in her chest.

'So?' Monty asked.

Jessie waited until she had shut the bedroom door. The porter, in his white belted tunic, had insisted on padding around the ornate room, prodding the bed to prove its softness, throwing open the carved wardrobe to reveal its spaciousness, pointing out the alabaster bowl loaded with peaches and dates for her refreshment. He pulled the heavy wine-coloured curtains closed.

'No open window,' he chattered happily. 'Night full, bad mosquitoes.' He pinched at his own brown arm to demonstrate their viciousness. 'My name Youssif. Anything to you, I get. I good.'

'Thank you, Youssif.' She dropped a few of Monty's Egyptian piastres into his waiting hand and shooed him out the door.

'So?' Monty repeated.

'I have it.'

He rolled his eyes impatiently. 'Who?'

'Reginald Musgrave.'

His eyebrows drew down into a sceptical line. 'Who the hell is Reginald Musgrave?'

She threw off her jacket and opened her mouth to speak, to say why the name had jumped out at her from the register at once. But all that was in her head suddenly seemed to crash together and instead of words, a strange gasping sound escaped. Immediately he came to her. His arms gathered her to him, gently stroking her back. The shakes lasted no more than a minute, but her cheeks burned with embarrassment.

'I'm sorry,' she muttered and attempted to pull away.

But he held her.

'Hush,' he whispered. 'Relax. Breathe gently.'

She closed her eyes and felt something inside herself hitch loose, something that had been stretched too tight. She let the murmur of his voice wrap around her and felt the weight of his jaw against her head. Slowly the hard knot in her throat untied.

'I'm sorry,' she said and lifted her head from his shoulder, surprised at a small damp patch on his pale jacket. Had she been crying?

'Don't be.'

He released his hold on her and tousled the thick blonde waves of her hair with his fingers. The gesture was so unexpected, so intimate that it took Jessie by surprise.

'Thank you,' she said.

'My pleasure. A mere ripple on the smooth surface of our plans.'

And that was that.

'What are these *plans*?' she queried. 'Other than snatching hotel registers, I wasn't aware that we'd formed any plans.'

He chuckled and lit a cigarette for each of them. 'It sounds better,' he said, 'to talk of plans. As if we know what we're doing. Not just flying by the seat of our bally pants.'

'Does that scare you?'

'No, quite the reverse. But I'm worried you'll go streaking off somewhere when my back is turned.' He exhaled a narrow string of smoke. 'That does scare me.'

'Don't you trust me?'

He considered her carefully, as if counting every hair. 'No,' he answered, 'no, I don't think I do.'

'I'm offended.'

'Don't be. I am no more trusting of people than you are.'

'What makes you think I don't trust people?'

He moved closer and tapped both his forefingers on her eyelids, gentle butterfly nudges. 'These. The way they look at people.'

'I trust you,' she insisted.

'No, you don't.' He shook his head. 'But I don't blame you in the slightest. I wouldn't trust a blithering idiot like me either.'

'Monty!' she said sternly.

'Yes?'

'Stop it.'

He looked startled, as though caught with his fingers in the honey jar, but then he laughed.

'Now,' she said, sitting down on the bed, 'let's talk about Sir Reginald Musgrave.'

'Ah! The mystery name in the hotel register. A baronet, I assume.'

'The twelfth baronet, no less. His ancestral home is in Hurlstone.'

'Not heard of the blighter.'

'You should be ashamed of yourself, Sir Montague.'

'Enlighten me.' He stubbed out his cigarette.

208

She reached forward, picked up a peach, warm and soft in her hand, and tossed it across the room to him. He caught it smoothly, washed it in water from the bottle on the table and bit into it with relish. She watched him.

'Well?' he prompted, juice on his lips.

'Sir Reginald Musgrave is a character in the Sherlock Holmes story *The Adventure of the Musgrave Ritual*.'

Monty's mouth dropped open. 'Pardon?'

'Tim signed the register as Musgrave because he knew I'd recognise it.'

'Really? Are you sure about this Musgrave business? It seems to be carrying the Conan Doyle theme a bit too far, if you ask me.'

'There's no such thing as too far. Not for Tim.' Colour crept into her cheeks as she added, 'Not for me.'

Monty put down the peach-stone. 'You do realise,' he pointed out, 'that it means Tim must be travelling on a false passport. If this hotel has him registered as Reginald Musgrave, that's the name that must be in his passport.'

'I know.' She rose to her feet and went over to Monty's chair, stepping over the reach of his long spidery legs to stand in front of him. 'How does Prince Abdul al-Hakim know you are here?'

There was something in her voice. She didn't mean it to be there, but she heard it. So did he. Something not quite right.

His eyes fixed on her. 'Are you accusing me of . . . ?'

'No!'

'The sultans and princes of this country are bound to have a network of watchers, men spying on people who enter or leave the country. King Fuad himself will let nothing slip by unnoticed. It is a land of bitter rivalries and great wealth in high places.'

She thought about it and nodded. It made sense.

'I recall Tim telling me that the British High Commissioner was accused of allowing King Fuad too much control of the government. Not a policy to go down well back home in Westminster. Tim thinks that Sir Percy's days are numbered.'

'Is that what you did together? Discuss Egypt?'

'Sometimes, yes. We talked about his work or my work – you know, like brothers and sisters do.'

He said nothing and she remembered that he had no siblings. He was the only heir, with all that entails, and she was aware of a sense of isolation within him. On impulse she squatted down on her heels in front of him. 'You were good with that desk clerk,' she smiled, 'very bossy. I can't decide whether to be impressed or frightened.' She tapped his knee. 'Thank you.'

He took hold of a lock of her hair and threaded it through his fingers, staring at it as though he had never touched hair before.

She didn't move. She didn't want him to stop.

Instead she spoke in a voice loud enough to replace the silence, but soft enough to leave the thoughts in his head undisturbed.

'This place, the Mena House Hotel, is where Sir Arthur Conan Doyle came to stay when his wife, Louise – whom he called Touie – was ill with TB. For the dry air. It's supposed to be good for the lungs, though I'd have thought the sand that is carried in the wind might be a problem for lungs.'

Her eyes were fixed on the rhythmic rippling of the blonde strand through his fingers. She could feel the slight tug of it on her scalp, as if it were deciding which one of them it belonged to.

'Tim knew that I was aware of this visit of Sir Arthur's. He knew that if he directed me to Egypt with his first Nile clue that I would come here. It's the obvious place to start.' She paused.

'I understand.'

'Now this second clue. Sir Reginald Musgrave.'

His eyes flicked to hers. 'What is the story about?'

'It's not one of his best, to be honest. Written in his twenties for *The Strand* when he was still a practising doctor.' She smiled. 'But good old Sherlock is as impressive as ever. The story is about Sir Reginald who comes to him and tells him that the butler and housemaid have gone missing from his ancestral pile – a bit like yours, I suspect. He calls it a labyrinth.'

He smiled.

'Listen to me, Monty. This is important.'

210

He released her hair. It swung back into place and for a second Jessie felt bereft.

'In the story,' she told him, 'the butler is found dead in a cellar beside an empty chest. He has been shut in there to die. Like a tomb.'

Monty sat forward.

'Sherlock works it out in his usual brilliant fashion from a riddle,' Jessie continued, 'that in the chest had lain the ancient gold crown of King Charles I, but it was stolen by the missing maid.' Jessie tapped his knee once more. 'So you see . . . ' She spread her hands. 'It's blindingly obvious.'

Monty nodded slowly, but it was a reluctant movement. His expression did not strike Jessie as one of joy.

'Come on, Monty, It's easy,' she said quickly. 'It's either the King's crown . . . '

'Which means Cairo museum, the Museum of Egyptian Antiquities. That's where the golden trappings of King Tutankhamen are kept.'

'Or . . . ?'

'The tombs. In Luxor.'

'Exactly. We'll find Tim in one or the other, I'm sure.' She was breathing fast. 'We're so close now.'

Monty stood up abruptly. 'We'd better get changed for this evening's reception.'

Jessie was baffled by his sudden change of mood. Uncertain what to say.

'Aren't you pleased?' she asked, as he headed for the door. 'Can't you be pleased? For me? For Tim?'

He stopped as he approached the door and looked back at her.

'No, Jessie, I find I'm not pleased.'

The bluntness of it hurt.

'Why?' she whispered.

'Because . . . ' he said, 'I do not ever want to find you next to an empty chest. Shut in there to die.'

26

Georgie

England 1930

Some days we just sit and read. And then we talk about what we've read. These are the easy days. I like the days when you are not trying to change me.

We talk of astronomy and the French Revolution and the Eye of Horus. We read together the Viking sagas and long to own a blue dun stallion like Hrafnkell's Freyfaxi and to string up Dr Churchward from the roof beams by his Achilles tendons, a routine punishment in the Iceland of legend.

But most of all we read about Ancient Egypt. I love Ancient Egypt. I can recite the names and dates of all the pharaohs and list all the gods. You call it obsessed. I call it focused. I teach myself to read the Ancient Egyptian alphabet and some of their hieroglyphs and then I teach you.

When Howard Carter – a brilliant Egyptologist and archae-ologist, though an artist by training – in 1922 discovers and opens the tomb of King Tutankhamen, you bring me all the newspaper reports on the wonders he's found and you tell me that the world has gone Egypt-crazy. Together we read Carter's own account of the excavation in his book, *The Discovery of the Tomb of King Tutankhamen*. I read it twenty-one times.

You bring me a magnifying glass, so that I can study the photographs of the artefacts in greater detail – the lion-headed couch, the golden throne with the king's cartouches and winged serpents, the corslet of inlaid gold with the Kheper beetle supporting the solar disk. Kheper is one of my favourite gods. Imagine the power he must possess. To roll the sun across the sky. It makes the hairs on my neck stand on end each time I take a look at that photograph. The Egyptians were a highly intelligent and skilled people. I admire that. But they were also highly creative. I admire that even more because I am not.

They watched the scarab beetle – *scarabaeus sacer* – rolling a ball of dung to its burrow, the ball held between its antenna, and they made a huge jump of imagination. The ball became the sun, and each day without fail in the hot climes of Egypt the god Kheper – in the form of a scarab – pushes it across the sky.

That is what I do not possess. An imagination. It is why I like a sunny day, so that I can sit at my window and *try to imagine* Kheper at work.

But the Kheper corslet is not the best artefact in the book. Oh no. Howard Carter has more in store for me. The best object is one I would cut off one of my fingers for. Just to hold. It is a royal staff. Listed as A in Plate LXXI. This staff, it says, is decorated with ornamental barks and is inlaid with elytra of iridescent beetles.

Elytra. Of iridescent beetles.

My pulse bangs wildly at the thought.

An elytron – elytra is the plural – is the tiny hardened forewing of a beetle. Its function is to act as a protective wing-case for the hindwings underneath which are the ones used for flying. If Howard Carter did not state it as true, I could not believe it. I peer at them on the staff through the magnifying glass for hours and

213

resent the black-and-whiteness of the photograph when they should be *iridescent* colour.

But the whitecoats take the magnifying glass from me. When they find it, they say I might use the glass to hurt myself. When I tell you this, you are so angry your cheeks go red and you start shouting at the whitecoats. I do not like it. I ask you to stop but you rage downstairs to Dr Churchward's office and I go inside my wardrobe.

I know that Dr Churchward will tell you.

I sit in the darkness and hear you return. You throw open the door of the wardrobe and I hide my face against my knees.

'Why didn't you tell me?'

I press my eyeballs so hard against my knees that I see flashing lights. I concentrate on the colours of the lights and wonder if this is what the aurora borealis is like.

'Why didn't you tell me, Georgie? That you have cut yourself before.'

Your voice is big. Big enough for both of us, so I say nothing. You stand there for a long time, so still. I cannot see you, but I can hear your breathing. It sounds the way I think a train must sound. I hear another sound, a kind of strangled wailing and I hate it because I know it is coming from my own throat. You close the wardrobe door, leaving me to the comfort of my own darkness. It is a long time before I come out but when I do, you are still there.

'Well,' you say as if we are in the middle of a conversation, 'I'll bring the magnifying glass each time I come.'

And you do.

27

I am he who crosses the sky, I am the Lion of Ra.
I am the Slayer.

Not exactly the welcome Monty expected. The words were carved
a foot high into the huge marble archway into the great hall of the
palace. Prince Abdul was clearly no slouch when it came to getting
his message across, reinforced by the two life-size bronze lions
standing on each side of it.

'From the *Book of the Dead*,' Jessie whispered at Monty's side.
'That's the list of spells used in Ancient Egypt to help the dead survive the dangerous journey through the underworld and into the
afterlife. Very important to them.'

Monty regarded her, surprised. 'So I'm not the only one who
hoards useless knowledge, I see.'

'It comes of having an Egyptologist for a brother. Some of it rubs
off.'

He found it hard to look at her. And hard not to. There was no
sign of fatigue about her, despite the long journey of the past three
days. She was dressed in a plain white summer frock, a simple
effortless design that showed off her slender waist and made her
look young and fresh. Around her bare shoulders she had draped
a shawl of exquisite antique lace that caused other women to turn
and look. The men turned and looked anyway, but not because of
the lace.

'The lion-god Aker guards the gateway to the netherworld, *Duat*,' she elaborated for him. 'The sun must pass through it each day. It's all about death and rebirth.'

He raised an eyebrow at her. 'Let's hope this evening is just about rebirth, shall we? Frightfully gruesome, those Ancient Egyptians.'

He watched her smile. Watched the way she held her head, her throat poised and almost as pale as the lace. He watched her hair, pinned up on one side by a mother-of-pearl clip. The way it moved, as though each strand possessed a life and an energy of its own. They were standing in a line of guests shuffling forward to be presented to their host, Prince Abdul al-Hakim, so Monty took time to gaze around. To drag his eyes from her.

There is not one single word in existence that can describe an Arabian palace, he realised. Sumptuous. Resplendent. Gilded. Luminous. Yet when mixed together these words might just suffice, but only if combined with 'unrestrained', 'ostentatious' and 'downright idiosyncratic.' Thirty-four massive columns encased in intricate gold filigree towered over the guests, while the marble walls around them were draped in luxurious cloth of gold. On the floor stretched swathes of Persian rugs, and covering the wide sofas were rich materials edged with blood-red jewels and brilliant peacock-blue beads. Brass cobras raised their heads in corners and the skins of cheetahs lay unheeded underfoot.

It was a world etched in vibrant colour. As if to beat back the relentless desolation of the arid desert that was only a breath away. Was that it? Did the people of Cairo, prowling the streets of their city at night like jackals, hear the hiss and the sigh of the sand as it shifted restlessly in the wind?

Around the edges of the grand room stood a hundred chairs of carved ebony, with sphinx armrests and heavy lion's paw feet that made Monty think of Coriolanus at home in front of his estate manager's fire. But it was the throng of guests in the room that drew his attention. He gave a wry grimace. So this was it, the cream of Cairo. The colonial grandees had turned up, all togged out in their Sunday best: elegant gowns, Savile Row dinner jackets and military dress-uniforms of every hue and from every nation. The scent of hair oil and cigars, of fine perfume and false smiles drifted aimlessly towards the archway, bringing with it the sound of lies and laughter.

'I stand out,' Jessie nudged him. 'In my mufti.'

'They'll park you in a corner and throw rotten dates at you, I expect.'

She laughed, and they moved forward behind a man in Italian military uniform who smiled at Jessie in a way Monty didn't like and said, '*Buona sera.*' She did stand out, she was right about that, but not because she was in mufti. Suddenly he was drawn forward and found himself shaking hands with Prince Abdul, a western custom obviously adopted out of courtesy to the country's masters.

'Welcome, Sir Montague,' the prince said warmly in an impeccable English accent. 'It is an honour for the whole of Cairo to receive such a distinguished visitor.'

'Thank you, Your Highness. This is my first visit to Cairo and I appreciate the invitation tonight.'

The prince was a well-fed man in his forties, magnificent in flowing white robes and *kufiya* that were intricately embroidered along the hem with the traditional patterns of Ancient Egypt. He waved a hand, his knuckles weighted with nuggets of gold, at the crowded room, sending his robe swirling through the air like a startled flock of egrets over the Nile.

'Take your pleasure here,' he boomed through the profusion of his beard. 'May Allah bless your first evening in the beautiful heart of Egypt, Sir Montague.'

'Thank you, you are generous. May I introduce my travelling companion, Miss Jessica Kenton?'

He was glad to see that Jessie knew better than to offer her hand to a Muslim male. Instead she touched her hand to her heart.

'I am honoured to meet you, Your Highness.'

The prince bared his splendid teeth at her. 'The pleasure is all mine, Miss Kenton.'

They were supposed to move on. The next guest was waiting, but Jessie stayed rooted to the spot. Monty touched her elbow.

'Your Highness,' she said, her wide blue eyes fixed on her host, her lips curved in a respectful smile as she leaned just a fraction closer than was wise, 'you have great knowledge of your country. You know its ways and its troubles. You are well informed.' She paused.

Monty felt his heart scramble up to somewhere behind his teeth. *No, Jessie!* His grip tightened on her elbow.

The prince inclined his royal head.

'You know its secrets,' Jessie added softly.

The prince's black eyes narrowed. 'Your meaning?'

'You knew Sir Montague was here almost before he arrived.'

'My dear Miss Kenton,' the teeth gleamed in a practised smile but the eyes didn't change, 'you overestimate my prescience, I assure you.'

'I doubt that very much,' she smiled at him, and swung back her thick blonde hair. Instantly his desert wolf eyes sank to her throat. 'I am looking for someone.'

Don't, Jessie. We don't know this man.

'I'm looking for a dear friend of mine, Sir Reginald Musgrave. He came to Cairo recently.'

'I hope you find your friend, Miss Kenton, *inshallah*. What makes you think I know anything about this Musgrave?'

'I thought you might have invited him to one of your receptions. Such a distinguished young gentleman would be deeply honoured to meet the renowned and respected Prince Abdul al-Hakim.'

The teeth chuckled. 'Nothing would give me greater pleasure, Miss Kenton, than to be of assistance to you. But almighty Allah in his everlasting wisdom has not granted me the eyes to witness all that occurs in this great city, so I am sorry but I cannot help you.'

She touched her hand to her heart again. 'I am grateful for your time.' She dipped her chin in respect to him and finally allowed Monty to steer her away.

'What the hell was that about?' he asked in a low voice as they entered the crowded room. 'I thought the whole idea was to keep the search undetected.'

'He knows who does or doesn't enter this country.'

'My sweet Jessie, we can't be certain of that.'

'A twelfth baronet? The famous Sir Reginald? Of course he knows, just like he knew you were here.'

'Even if that is true, it doesn't mean he has any idea of Tim's whereabouts now, does it?'

'No.'

But he knew this was not the end of it. 'He will make enquiries.'

She nodded.

Monty recalled the way Prince Abdul had looked at his enchanting young visitor from England. It set his teeth on edge and made him scrutinise her fine-boned face with cautious eyes. How far was Jessie prepared to go to find Brother Tim? With a muttered curse he snatched two champagne glasses from a passing tray.

'So,' he asked grim-faced, 'what are you expecting?'

She accepted the drink, her eyes bright. 'To learn under which rock the snakes are hiding.'

'Snakes,' he reminded her, 'bite.'

Monty was careful to be gracious to all who came seeking out the newcomer with the title attached to his name, and the striking girl attached to his arm.

While Egyptian music played softly in the background, he smiled at army generals and captains, he nodded serenely at tedious British government diplomats and listened with attention to a passionate young man, Herr Zimmermann, from the German delegation who advocated the imminent seizure of power in Germany by Herr Adolf Hitler to replace the senile Field Marshal Hindenburg. But it was the Egyptians that Monty sought out. Most had adopted the western dress of suits and high collars, but some came decked out in traditional Egyptian robes that made the Europeans look like drab sparrows by comparison.

He moved smoothly between the different groups, casually inserting the name of Musgrave into the conversation at intervals but each time drew a blank. That struck Monty as odd. Informers should have picked him up, whether for the British or the Egyptian authorities, yet somehow he seemed to have slid through their nets. It sent a shot of cold lead down his spine. On the excuse of tracking down a brandy, he broke free from the chatter around him. Enough was enough, damn it. He headed over to a bald man who was standing near one of the many arched windows, eyeing the gathering balefully over the rim of a whisky glass. To Monty's annoyance, Jessie had already been spirited away from his side by a couple of the more glamorous evening gowns and now she was barely visible to him, firmly secured behind a phalanx of attentive white evening jackets. A flash of lace, a shimmer of pearl hair-clip, that was all he had of her for himself.

'Good evening, ambassador,' he said, extending his hand. 'We met in London last spring.'

'Remind me, young man.' The American accent was smooth as honey, and he tapped his temple with his glass. 'My mind is too full of names.'

Monty smiled easily. 'I'm not surprised. Mine is Montague Chamford.'

'Ah, yes, you're that new guy causing the women to flutter their silly fans. A lord or knight of the realm, aren't you? Some darn title.'

'Something like that. Tell me, sir, how are things out here at the moment?'

Ambassador William Jardine was a rare breed of man: one who was immensely practical, as well as immensely academic. A farm boy from Idaho made good. His passions were agriculture and education, and he had served both well as Secretary of Agriculture under President Calvin Coolidge. But politics is always a dirty game and two years ago in the Herbert Hoover administration he had been elbowed out to the post of American ambassador to Egypt, where his expertise in agriculture could be put to good use.

Monty had respect for his judgement.

Jardine scratched one of his large ears. 'We're looking at a very

fragile stability of the triangle of power, I can tell you, Montague.'
He held up three fingers. 'The British Residency, King Fuad and
the Wafd Nationalist Party.' He clashed his fingers together. 'You
Brits had better keep your wits about you. I keep saying the same
to old Pompous Percy over there, but does he listen . . . bah!'

'Pompous Percy?'

Jardine tossed back the last of his bourbon and growled, 'Hell,
boy, that's what we call your High Commissioner, lord of all he sur-
veys. Sir Percy Loraine himself.'

He nodded in the direction of a distinguished gentleman standing centre stage in the room, with his hair oiled straight back and
a cleft in his jutting chin. To Monty's surprise, a slender figure in a
white frock and a mother-of-pearl hair-clip was at the man's side,
talking earnestly.

'But I heard he was working closely with King Fuad, handing
him more control over the government. Giving Egypt to the
Egyptians,' Monty pointed out.

'To the *rich* Egyptians, you mean. The man's a jackass. And don't
think I'm telling tales out of school because I tell him the same to
his face. He's asking for trouble back home and, more vitally for all
of us, asking for trouble with the Nationalists.'

'The Wafd Party?'

'Yep.'

A silent servant in brilliant red robes with a white sash and cap
glided to Jardine's elbow with a tray of whisky. Clearly the ambassador's tastes were well known.

'Bourbon?' Jardine checked.

'Of course, *effendi.*'

'Take one, young man,' Jardine said to Monty. 'You'll need it out
here, I warn you. It lubricates the throat in this sand-blasted country.'

Monty accepted the drink. As he took a swig, he wondered how
close to the ground the Americans had their ears. 'Have you crossed
paths, by any chance, with a young English chum of mine? Sir
Reginald Musgrave is his name.'

'Another English toff! God knows, Cairo fills up with them at this time of year when you all flock over for a break from your miserable weather.' He inspected Monty more closely. 'What does this fellow of yours look like?'

'Fair-haired, blue-eyed, an archaeologist.'

'Ah, one of those guys. Nope, can't help you there. Well, he has probably shifted up-river to Luxor. That's where most of the digs take place. Not a man for mucking around in the past myself.' He took a generous swig of his drink. 'The future, that's what counts.'

Monty raised his glass. 'I'll drink to that.'

'Excuse me now, if you don't mind. Time for me to go and bend the wealthy ear of our illustrious host. I'm trying to get him to fund an irrigation scheme for local farmers.'

'Of course. It was a pleasure to meet you again.'

As Jardine was about to walk away, he clapped a hand on Monty's shoulder, his eyes suddenly serious and whisky-free. 'You strike me as an intelligent young man, so I'm giving you a word of advice if you stay in Egypt. The Wafd are not the ones to worry about. Unrest is growing on the streets. Not yet at the riot stage like it was in 1919 when an anti-colonial frenzy got eight hundred of the poor bastards killed. But it's getting there.'

Monty listened attentively. 'If not the Wafd, who is to blame?'

'The *Ikhwan*. That's the Muslim Brotherhood. New on the scene, but deadly. Hassan al-Banna, he's inciting them. He's the one to watch. A darn schoolteacher, of all things. That's the guy who is the real threat to you Brits and to your inflated imperial egos.'

'Thank you for the warning, sir.'

'You're welcome. Just a friendly word.' He tapped the side of his nose. 'I hear whispers that they're even in league with the Nazis. They're distributing Arabic translations of *Mein Kampf*, Adolf Hitler's cheerful little treatise.'

'To stir up trouble with the Jews?'

'You got it in one.'

'Another nail in the colonial coffin.'

'May the good Lord preserve us. Here, have a cigar. We need to make the most of the good things in life while we can still enjoy them.'

He thrust a fat cigar into Monty's breast pocket and rumbled away into the crowd.

Monty took his cigar out into the night on the terrace. Flanked by gigantic black and gold sphinxes and by awesome statues of blank-eyed pharaohs – all with their distinctive high forehead and almond eyes – he felt Egypt reaching out to him. It set his pulse racing. He'd only been here a few hours, for Christ's sake, but already he found himself slipping into the grip of its overpowering sense of time-lessness. As though nothing had changed for thousands of years. Its ancient dynasties had fought and killed to possess this country, just as fiercely as this Hassan al-Banna and his followers were planning to do now.

As he leaned his elbows on the parapet overlooking the fragrant garden below, the darkness rose up to greet him like the breath of its ancient gods. He drew it deep into his lungs, aware of its power to play tricks on the mind. Instantly it swept into his head the image of Timothy Kenton, a trickle of blood seeping from one nostril onto the flagstones, his hand limp and unresponsive between Monty's fingers.

'Timothy!' he had called out, his heart trampling on his ribs. 'Can you hear me?'

The eyelids lay still as the gateway to a tomb.

'We'll take care of him,' Scott had announced. 'Let's get him into his car. Go and deal with the rest.'

And Monty had dealt with it.

The memory gave him a jolt and he drew hard on the plump cigar, relished the aromatic smoke clogging the pathways to his brain. He'd made the wrong choice, but it wasn't too late. Please God it wasn't too late. He would have to tell Jessie. He knew that. He exhaled a thick trail of smoke into the darkness, as if it could spiral its way into the past. He'd have to tell her. Soon.

28

'Hello, stranger. You deserted me.'

It was Jessie. He had meandered down into the black shadows and paced restlessly between the shrubs and palm trees away from the lights of the palace. He had just seated himself on a stone bench carved in the shape of a scarab when she found him. She sat down beside him and her arm immediately encircled his waist, warm and secure. She leaned her shoulder against his.

'Not enjoying it?' she asked softly.

'I just needed to clear my head. It's been extremely interesting, in fact. How about you?'

'Yes. I am entranced.'

'How was the High Commissioner,' he asked. 'Sir Percy?'

He felt a small tremor skip through her and wondered why.

'He was fine.'

'But?'

'But it seems new arrivals from abroad are often checked out by the police.'

'Oh.' He tilted back his head and gazed up through a web of palm leaves at a sky filled to the brim with stars. 'Not good news.'

'No. Tim's travelling on a false passport. But at least we know he got as far as Mena House.'

'Yes, that's something, I suppose. But where next?'

She followed his gaze upwards, rolling her cheekbone across the curve of his shoulder. The night sky arced over them in a layer of velvet. It seemed solid and touchable, just like Egypt's history slowly delivering up its secrets to man's probing fingers.

'Why does the sky look so much bigger in Egypt?' Jessie murmured.

He smiled in the darkness and felt her body relax against his. 'Maybe because it's older.'

She touched the back of his hand with the tips of her borrowed evening glove. They felt warm on his skin.

'Thank you, Monty. For coming with me.' She lifted her head and with one hand she gently turned his face to hers. In the deep shadows her eyes were masked from his view but he could see the outline of her cheekbones and the glint of her hair in the starlight. 'Why,' she asked, 'did you come?'

It was easier. Having this conversation in the dark.

'I told you.' He spoke slowly. Letting her think about the words. 'I am responsible for the séance and it was the séance that was responsible for Tim's disappearance, it seems to me. I'm trying to make amends.'

'You think he's dead, don't you?'

No words came. They sat knees touching, looking at each other's eyes in the scented darkness, unable to peel back the shadows to see the truth in them. Monty heard her breath, caught the sound of her swallow, and instead of answering her question he leaned forward and kissed her mouth. A firm decisive kiss. The taste of her lips was like none he'd ever known. It stopped all thought in his head. She tasted of sky and the fresh breeze off the Nile, of peaches and spiced wine, of unknown secrets that lingered on her soft lips. With a shock he realised she already tasted of Egypt.

He drew back.

She took a long breath and he could feel her thigh pressed against the length of his own.

'Jessie,' he murmured.

He took her hand and undid the pearl buttons of her glove, peeling it back to expose her bare skin. Slowly he lowered his head and buried his lips in her palm. Instantly her other hand found his hair, trailed fingers through the short bristles of the back of it and down the muscles of his neck. He took her in his arms and she felt small and slight but she fitted perfectly against his chest as if handmade for it. Her response was strong and needy. Her hands cradled his face at first as he kissed her mouth, but then her thumbs dug into the skin of his temples. Her fingers twisted themselves into his hair, into his jacket, twined around his neck. She was fierce with her kisses. He caressed the long line of her back and when his lips found the soft slope of her throat and the delicate dip inside her collarbone, she uttered a low aching moan.

He breathed in the scent of her, found himself consumed by it as it scored deep channels through him. He could feel the frantic pounding at the base of his throat and it was with a huge effort that he pulled away from her. Gently he held her by her bare shoulders, the shawl discarded on the ground, her breath hot on his lips.

'Jessie, we must go in.'

'Must we?'

Even in the blackness he could see that her eyes were huge. She made a sighing sound and he felt his heart lurch, but he forced himself to his feet, retrieved her lace shawl from the dirt and held it open for her. She took a long breath, then stood in front of him, but instead of turning her back to him so he could wrap the shawl around her shoulders, she remained facing him and lifted her hand to smooth down his hair and straighten his tie, soft tender touches.

It was no good. To be so close. He could not prevent himself reaching for her once more, his arms curling around her waist and drawing her against him.

'You smell of Egypt,' he whispered into her hair.

'What? Of donkeys and camels and bad drains? Thank you.'

They laughed and the tension flowed out of them with the laughter. He kissed her one last time and released his hold on her. After he had replaced the shawl around her, he took her hand in his and together they walked back towards the lights. But now nothing looked the same.

Monty was fetching her a long cool drink of pomegranate juice.

'I won't be a minute,' he'd said.

Her face was changed. A soft fullness drenched her mouth that had not been there before.

'I'll wait,' she said as she stared at the mosaic floor and smiled.

After the cool of the garden, the air inside was slick with heat despite the huge brass ceiling-fans stirring the mix of tobacco smoke and perfume. As he strode back with the drinks he was accosted by an elegant Egyptian wearing an Eton tie, eager to discuss the recent riots of the Unemployed Workers' hunger march in London. Monty brushed him off lightly, but by the time he reached the spot where he'd left Jessie, she had vanished. Where? He looked around, eyes quick, and he spotted her over by an indoor fountain with a bronze lion in the centre.

Her eyes were half closed and her head swayed gently to the music. She was watching golden carp gliding through the pool of water at the base of the fountain, mesmerised. He opened his mouth to call her name as he approached, but a plump man in a white dinner jacket and carrying a briar pipe in his hand hailed her first.

'Miss Kenton, I do believe. What a surprise! What are you doing all the way out here in the Land of the Pharaohs?'

Monty saw Jessie turn.

'Dr Scott!' she exclaimed.

Monty was there in an instant. 'Scott, good evening, I wasn't aware that you were in Cairo.'

'Dear boy, I come every year, don't you know?' He smiled with pleasure at Jessie. 'Dicky lungs, I'm afraid. Touch of mustard gas in the war.'

Jessie looked delighted to see him. 'What a coincidence to meet you here.'

'Isn't it?' Monty said drily.

Dr Septon Scott winked roguishly at her, and Monty's stomach sank as he realised the man was flushed with drink. 'If you're not careful,' Scott joked, 'I'll get the idea that you are following me, Miss Kenton. When did you arrive?'

'Just today.'

'There you are, then.' He waved his pipe expansively. 'I came a few days ago. That proves my point,' he chuckled. 'A wonderful country, Egypt is. You'll love the pyramids. It's like stepping back into history, eh, Monty?'

'Indeed it is,' Monty said coolly. 'Do you know this Prince Abdul well?'

'Oh, our paths have crossed every now and again. He gads about Europe often enough. And talking of paths crossing, Miss Kenton,' he observed her amiably as he drew on his pipe, 'any news of that brother of yours?'

She moved to stand beside Monty and shook her head mutely. Monty thought about hitting him. Knocking his pipe right down his throat. Instead he handed Jessie her glass of juice, aware of her fingers brushing his and the quick intimate glance she gave him, and said in a neutral tone, 'Jessie, the High Commissioner's wife mentioned that she would like a word with you.'

He saw the dismissal register. She didn't blink. Just a brief tightening of her mouth before she nodded pleasantly enough.

'Of course. I'll go and find her.'

After she left, he didn't move. For a heartbeat of time he watched her, then he rounded on Dr Scott.

'What the hell are you doing here?'

Scott looked surprised. 'I told you, Monty, I always come out for the dry air. Does my old lungs a power of good.'

'Scott, we both know you go nowhere unless you can turn a profit.'

'Ah, now, now, dear boy, no need to be—'

'Timothy Kenton hasn't turned up.'

'So I gather. Bit of a mystery.' He stared thoughtfully into the

228

bowl of his pipe. 'Can't imagine why. We left the fellow in good fettle.'

'That's what you told me in London. I am beginning to doubt it.' Monty watched Septon Scott closely. 'You took him back to London, you said, and he recovered fully from his "accident", enough to drive himself off in his car. What then?'

A little of Scott's good humour was wearing away. 'There you've got me. Not heard from him since, exactly as I told his sister in London.' He glanced around for a passing drink but none was in retrieving distance. 'By the way, what on earth are you doing bringing the pretty young filly out here? Not a place for women right now, not with all the political disturbances going on. Damn foolish, if you ask me.'

'I'm not asking you.'

A silence settled between them. Neither looked at the other. If Monty looked at this man too long, he would be tempted to put an abrupt end to the strained civility between them that passed for politeness.

'Give me your word,' Monty said with a grim expression, 'that Timothy Kenton has not been in touch with you since.'

Scott removed his pipe from his mouth. 'Suspicious bastard, aren't you?'

'Your word?'

Scott drew himself up to his full height, his already ruddy cheeks growing a shade darker. 'You have my word.'

For what it's worth.

'Thank you.'

Monty turned away, unwilling to remain any longer breathing this man's smoke. He moved off to find Jessie.

'Made a decision yet, have you, Monty?' Scott called after him. Monty looked back. 'No.'

'Well, I'm not waiting for ever. If you don't sell me that land, I will have to foreclose on the loan.'

Wisely, Monty walked off without a word.

*

In the centre of the palace lay a courtyard. The word 'courtyard' was far too scant for the lavishly appointed arena crammed with entertainers of all kinds. Monty paused for a moment at the edge to watch. It was the sort of spectacle that made the boy in him cheer boisterously: fire-eaters and snake charmers, acrobats and whirling Tanoura men, all in a kaleidoscope of colours and noise that made Monty think of the circuses of his youth. Belly-dancers with bold eyes and scarlet skirts swirled their veils at him and rippled their stomachs as they swept past. He tossed one a coin and watched her spin on one foot in return at a speed that made his eyes water. The crowd was thickest across the far side of the arena where a man with black Nubian skin and black robes was giving a display of horsemanship on the back of a magnificent white Arab stallion.

Monty's heart tightened at the sight of the horse and its proud white mane. He was drawn across the arena by a sharp need to touch the animal. His own horses were all gone, even his beloved Jezebel. He approached close enough to admire the animal's fine lines and powerful hind quarters, joining in the rapturous applause for its beauty as it dipped its forelegs to allow its rider to sweep a gold coin from the ground with his sword. That was when the explosion came.

A dull thump. It vibrated his eardrums, punched his ribs. For a second, white lights sparked behind his eyelids. A bomb. God knows, he'd heard enough of the evil devices to recognise the sound at once. But the explosion was not in the courtyard. His pulse pounded, while around him people screamed, though none was hurt. He turned and ran.

Only one thought crashed through his mind: Jessie.

People were in a panic, uncertain in which direction to seek safety. No music playing now, just shouts and cries and a French woman having hysterics. He bellowed Jessie's name as he elbowed a path through the crush of guests, but instantly he realised that the bomb must have exploded in the garden because all along that side the windows had blown in. Thank God for the wooden latticework. It had taken the worst of the blast, but still he saw traces of blood on faces and a woman picking glass from her hair.

'Jessie!'

He couldn't see her. Frantically he searched. The garden? Had she gone back out there? Back on their scarab bench when the blast went off? Images of her golden hair streaked with blood shackled his brain.

'Jessie! Jessie!'

And then he heard her voice.

'Monty! Over here!'

He swung round in the direction of the sound. He saw her at once.

On the lion. She had scrambled up the fountain onto the back of the bronze lion to reach a vantage point from which to search for him.

'Monty!'

She waved both arms and he raised a hand to her. He pushed forward, but his path was barred by servants rushing towards the garden, arms piled with blankets. He saw Jessie slither off the lion's back and splash through the water, so fast that she slipped and disappeared from view.

Oh Christ, Jessie.

He dived around a cluster of white robes where heads were locked together in heated discussion and forced a gap in front of him. Where was she? Where the hell had she . . . ?

She slipped into the gap. He reached out to take hold of her but something about her made his hand pause in mid-air. She was standing there, eyes huge, with her shoulders hunched over, her chest shuddering, her body looking like a doll that has had its stuffing torn out. Her white dress was sodden up to her thighs, clinging to her legs like seaweed, and she seemed so vulnerable that it felt indecent to be looking at her at all. Worst were her hands. They hung at her sides, shaking.

'Jessie,' he whispered softly and opened his arms to her.

For a split second she didn't move. Then she flew to him and he folded his arms around her so tight that she uttered a moan. She

231

clung to him, hands locked behind his neck, her body jammed against his, as though she were trying to climb inside him. He buried his face in her neck and inhaled the sweet knowledge that she was alive.

'Come,' he said quickly. 'We must leave.'

But she didn't release her grip on him. She pulled back just enough to look up into his face. With shock he realised her eyes were no longer blue. They were choked with flecks of black, like soot from a steam train, but this soot had risen from somewhere within her.

'Monty, I thought you were dead.' Her eyes filled with tears but she blinked them back. 'I thought I had lost you too.'

They didn't talk. On the taxi ride back to their hotel there were too many words in their heads to let them out. They sat on the rear seat with a gap yawning between them, their hands resting in it, their fingers scarcely touching.

The route out of the city was convoluted on account of the chaos around the palace, but the car skirted the black chasm that was the Nile, and once out on the rough road up to Giza, the desert air tumbled in through the open window and Monty felt his mind clear. He was able to pull together the fragments of the evening and think carefully about what they meant. What happened back there had changed things.

The moon had risen and its flat light skated over the black landscape, creating startling shapes and hollows that weren't there. As they approached Mena House, the hotel complex stood out alone in the darkness, a bright oasis where they could draw breath. The car passed through the gates and entered the avenue of palms, the sound of their leaves fretting in the breeze. He hated this awkwardness between Jessie and himself, as though this evening they had gone too far too fast and seen too deeply into each other. She seemed now to have withdrawn inside her shell. He wanted to make her laugh and have her treat him to one of her teasing stares, eyelids half lowered.

Instead he rolled down the window further and said, 'Jessie, we should count ourselves lucky. Not many were hurt. It was clearly intended more to scare than to kill.'

'But why would they bomb the prince at all? Surely he's an Egyptian, one of their own. It doesn't make sense. It's the British who are regarded as the oppressors.'

'Yes, but the Nationalists would see Prince Abdul as a collaborator. Just look at all the top brass there tonight, bristling with military medals and knighthoods. Like a red rag to a bull.'

He felt, rather than saw, the movement of her head in the dusty air as she turned to look at him.

'Don't you think it's a strange coincidence that Dr Scott is here too?' she asked.

'No.'

They were talking. That was something.

He said goodnight to her outside her door.

'You'll be all right?' he asked. Her skin was white with exhaustion.

'Of course. I hope you sleep well.'

'Thank you.'

All so formal. He leaned forward and placed a brief kiss on her forehead. She gave him a half-smile and before he did anything stupid, he walked away.

'The museum tomorrow,' she called after him.

'Yes. The secrets of the king's treasure.' He waved goodnight without looking back.

He had learned to be an expert at never looking back.

When the soft tap came on the door of his room, it startled him. He had been thinking about Scott and his thoughts had turned sour. He padded in bare feet to the door, expecting a servant to be there, though why one of the servants would be tapping on his door at midnight, he had no idea. But when he opened the door, it wasn't a servant standing there. He'd got that all wrong.

'Jessie!'

'I forgot to say something to you.'

She was standing in the half-light of the corridor, her hair loose and entangled with shadows, an oriental robe of dragonfly-blue silk wrapped around her.

'May I come in?'

He stepped back. 'Of course.'

After a moment's hesitation, she did so. She glanced around the room, at his white shirts hung neatly in the open wardrobe, at the half-glass of whisky by the bed. But she passed no comment.

'Can't sleep?' he asked.

'As I said, there's something I forgot to say earlier and I saw the light under your door, so . . .'

He spread his hands. 'As you see, I'm not exactly busy.'

'I'm sorry that I . . .' she swallowed, as though the words had formed a ball in her throat, '. . . over-reacted earlier. It was foolish.' He saw a flush rise to her cheeks and it struck him that she might be talking about what happened in the garden, rather than after the explosion.

'Jessie,' he said softly, and he moved towards her, as careful not to startle her as he was when tending a young doe on his estate, 'please don't apologise. There is no need. All it takes is a spot of blood and gore on the scene, and we all "over-react".'

She nodded, but still the sooty flecks were there.

'Would you care for a drink?' He waved a hand at the bottle on the chest of drawers.

'That wasn't what I came to say.'

'Ah.' There was more.

She looked him full in the face. 'I want to say thank you. For before.'

Before? Before what?

'No need for thanks,' he assured her. 'No need for apologies. I'm here to watch your back, remember?'

'But who is watching yours?'

'It's all right. I have eyes in the back of my head.' He touched a spot at the back of her skull. 'Just there,' he assured her.

A small chuckle escaped her lips. He saw the tension in her slide down a notch. He walked over to his drink, knocked the last of it back and poured a fresh one from the bottle.

'Here,' he said. 'Get this down you. Now we're here in Egypt, let's talk seriously about what the hell that brother of yours might be up to.'

She took the drink and set it down on a table. Outside, the wind swept across the arid wastes of sand and scree, hurling a fistful of it at the window. Automatically Monty glanced towards the sound, and when he looked back Jessie was so close to him that he could smell the perfume of the soap she'd used on her skin.

He couldn't not touch. It was beyond him.

The back of his hand gently stroked her long throat and she raised her chin a fraction, like a cat wanting more.

'Jessie, let's talk about Tim. I've asked at the reception desk here and no one can recall whether he was alone or with others. It's the possibility of *others* that we have to consider. If he is . . .'

Two of her fingers stole onto his lips, silencing them. Her eyes were huge.

'Tonight,' she murmured, 'Tim is not here. We are.'

Her arms encircled his neck and drew his head to hers. He wrapped an arm around her, aware of how easily these delicate bones could have shattered tonight. He felt the heat of her body under its skin of Chinese silk and the rise of her hip-bone, the fall of her slender ribs beneath his fingers. He pulled her close.

Her body seemed to melt against him as his lips found hers, small animal sounds whispering out of her. He kissed her softly at first, light easy brushes of his lips over the corners of her mouth, but the ache for her made the kisses grow fierce and hungry. Her mouth opened eagerly to his. He tasted the ripeness of her tongue, the delicate insides of her cheeks, softer than honey and twice as sweet.

She was opening up to him, letting him explore the convoluted twists and turns of her. Not just physically. It was more than that. Far more. He could sense the closed doors of her mind letting him in, exactly as her soft lips were doing, and it touched him deeply.

235

How was it that she could create such a storm of emotion within him, such a rush of tenderness for this unpredictable creature who possessed an endless capacity for loyalty?

His hands caressed her, swept over the tight curve of her buttocks and up again to the sharp angles of her hip. He heard her suck in her breath when his palm circled her breast and she uttered a raw sigh when his kisses descended into the valley between the folds of her robe. When he drew back his head to look at her, to scrutinise this different Jessie, she was no longer regarding him from behind a safe wall, as if expecting to get bitten. Her eyes glittered and her cheeks were flushed. He kissed her nose. It was a gently curved nose with flared nostrils that gave her a look of arrogance that was misleading. The one thing Jessie was not was arrogant. A tremor rippled through her.

'We're alive,' he said quietly. 'That's what counts. The rest we can deal with.'

Her eyes widened. 'It's not shock, if that's what you think.' Her lips looked fuller, softer, as though the string that held them tight together had come untied. 'I'm not deranged by the terrible events of tonight.' She said it with an attempt at a laugh, but the sound of it hooked into the flesh of his throat.

He pressed his lips to her forehead and kept them there, conscious of her thoughts crouched on the other side of her skin and bone. 'Let's breathe in this moment, no other.'

She tipped her head to one side and gave him her slow teasing grin. 'I thought that you Chamfords, like the pharaohs, only care for your grand dynasty. For the past and for the future of your name. The present is merely a blink in time.'

He frowned. 'I shall have to prove you wrong, won't I?' he said and whisked her up into his arms. She laughed and slid a hand under his shirt as he carried her to his bed.

29

Georgie

England 1930

The thing is, we have a problem. The problem is Flinders Petrie.

You sit sideways in one of the chairs with your long legs over the arm and kick the back of your heel against the beautiful maple wood. It makes the same noise as rain on the roof. I tell you to stop. You grunt. You are not happy about Flinders Petrie.

W.M. Flinders Petrie is the greatest archaeologist who ever lived. That's what I think. That's what you think. You call him a force of nature, though that doesn't make sense to me. This is what he is: the founding father of modern methods of excavation. He introduced new standards.

He strides out across the sands of Egypt with his bushy beard, trowel in hand, his young wife Hilda at his side, and conducts the most painstaking digs anyone has ever done, recording, photographing and studying every aspect of a site and its artefacts. He is the one who trained Howard Carter, and he has had some amazing

237

finds – like the origin of the Merenptah temple and the discovery of the Israel stele. He has supplied the museums of Cairo and London with many historical objects, including mummies.

When in England, rather than in Jerusalem where he now spends most of his time, Sir Flinders Petrie lectures at University College, London. He is a professor.

This is the problem: you are studying archaeology at University College. Sometimes you let me write your assignments for you – the last one I did was on preservation techniques when on location in Egypt. The Egyptians were profligate in their use of fine layers of gesso on woodwork, before they painted scenes on it or applied an overlay of gold leaf. But over centuries the wood shrinks and so the gesso buckles. The answer – surprisingly – is initially hot paraffin wax to fix everything in place, and a spray with a solution of celluloid in amyacetate. Beads are another nightmare for excavators. Egyptians were passionate about them. Everything had to have brightly coloured beads. A single mummy might wear so many necklaces, collars, bracelets and girdles that there are thousands and thousands of beads to recover whose threads have all rotted away. Answer? A thin layer of soft plasticine to hold them in the correct arrangement before being rethreaded in a museum laboratory. Papyrus must be wrapped in a damp cloth for hours before straightening, limestone objects must have the salt washed out of them, whereas faience needs . . .

'Come with me,' you say. 'To Petrie's lecture next week.'

There is the problem.

My heart stops. Literally. I feel it stop.

'I am not allowed out of here,' I say.

As if you don't know already.

'I could try to smuggle you out.'

We have been here before. You should know better.

'Do come with me, Georgie. You will love it.'

I will hate it. We both know that. But you are bursting with so much enthusiasm, you look like a balloon that is about to pop.

'I cannot,' I say.

'You mean you will not.'

'There will be too many people. Too close to me.'

'I'll keep them away from you.'

'How?'

'I will pick you up in a taxi. The lecture is in the evening, so it will be dark. No one will see you.'

'But I will see them.'

'Not if you wear a blindfold.'

'A blindfold?'

'Yes.'

'No.'

'It's the same as being inside your wardrobe.'

'It's not a bit the same. It doesn't rain inside my wardrobe. There aren't other people in my wardrobe.'

'I want you to try, Georgie. To try the outside world.'

'I go in the garden.'

'That's not the outside world,' you say firmly.

'Why? Why do you want me to go?'

'Because I know you will enjoy it and because ... ' You swing around in the chair and I can feel your gaze fixed on me, though I am staring at your shoes, 'because I want you to see the world outside.'

I almost tell you then. My secret. The one about the roof. I want you to know, but I am scared of what you might say. I clamp a hand over my mouth.

'Please, Georgie,' you say so warmly that the words melt between us. 'Do it for me.'

For me.

I want to hate you for this. But I can't. I pull my sweater over my head, so that I can see nothing.

'Georgie?'

'Yes.'

'Yes, you'll come?'

'Yes.'

The word is there. In the room. Immutable.

*

I make myself think of Petrie, instead of you. It is easier. I am interested in his ideas.

As well as setting up the first degree course in archaeology and establishing it as a recognised professional science, this amazing man is a dedicated believer in eugenics.

Eugenics.

They are calling it a mathematical science that can predict the traits and behaviour of humans. Believers are convinced that we can improve the human species by controlled breeding, like bulls or pumpkins, so that only the best genes would reproduce.

It is a fascinating theory.

The American Eugenics Society was founded in 1923 and is flourishing. They state that 'scientifically' it has been proven that certain racial stock is superior to others. That certain races possess the traits of intelligence, diligence, cleanliness and all the other good qualities. While others are inferior. Can you breed out the bad things like crime, alcoholism, pauperism, epilepsy ... and mental disease?

Mental disease like mine?

I know I am diseased. Dr Churchward has told me so.

In 1924 America passed its Immigration Act. It set strict quotas on immigration from other countries. Even President Coolidge stated: 'America should be kept American. Biological laws show that Nordics deteriorate when mixed with other races.'

By 'other races' eugenicists like Petrie – and Sir Francis Galton, half cousin to Charles Darwin, and Winston Churchill, George Bernard Shaw, John Maynard Keynes, Marie Stopes, H.G. Wells and many many more prominent intelligent people – mean particularly those from countries of Southern Europe, Africa and Asia. That's an awful lot of countries.

Yet I can see it. To pull up the human weeds and cast them aside. To rid us of social ills. To purify hereditary. To remove defects. It is the dream of human advancement.

So what next, Professor Flinders Petrie?

Sterilization?

I know Dr Churchward would sterilize me if he could. The thought of such manipulation fills me with dread. I am never likely to have children, but I am me. To sterilize me makes me fundamentally worthless as a human being. I bang my head against the door of my room to let them know I am not worthless.

Not to me.

And I can disprove all their science. Eugenics does not work. If it did, why would my parents – two intelligent sane people with an intelligent sane daughter – produce me? An aberration. Something flutters behind my eyes. The soft wing of something brushing my mind, an awareness that I am not safe. What if my father stops paying and Dr Churchward stops medicating? What if they grow tired of me and decide to rid themselves of a weed?

What then?

I *must* work harder. To be normal. To fool them all. Even you, Tim. To fool you, I will go to Petrie's lecture.

I shake all day. The whitecoats make me eat but I vomit over the table, a creamy mess of mashed potato and steamed tasteless fish. I run to my room and hide under the bed but at five o'clock you come and find me.

'Ready?'

'No.'

'You promised.'

'I can't do it.'

'Yes, Georgie, you can.'

You drag me out from under the bed where I have counted the number of bedsprings three thousand and sixty times this afternoon. I stand there, limp, while you inspect me. You have brought me a black raincoat with a big collar that you turn up around my neck and a floppy cap, the kind a farmer wears in books, with a peak that you pull down over my eyes and a pair of black gloves. I like the gloves.

'You look like a spy,' you say.

I want to smile but my cheek muscles are rigid.

241

'You have to stop that noise.'

'What noise?' I ask.

'That noise.'

There is a clicking sound. Coming from my tongue. I make it stop.

'Now, I'll go and check that the landing is clear,' you say. You take a look and beckon me over. My feet stick to the floor. You grab my sleeve and pull me out the door.

Downstairs is silent.

Everyone is napping in their room before supper. That's why you chose this time but I know the front door is locked. That's where we got stuck last time. It is only unlocked when a visitor arrives or leaves – which is not often – or when we file outdoors for our exercise in the garden. We will be stuck again. Dr Churchward will take me to the treatment room and strap me in a chair and put the wires on my head that make my brain implode, so that I have no thoughts at all and cannot even say my own name.

My heart is splitting inside my chest, it is beating so hard, and when a whimper escapes from my mouth you scowl at me. I shut my eyes but bump into a wall.

'Shh!'

At the bottom of the stairs, instead of crossing the huge reception hall with its echoing oak floor and its grandiose oil paintings which are meant to impress visitors at the front door, and instead of turning right to the dining hall and day-room, we turn left.

I have never turned left before.

Screams start to build up inside my head, stacked against each other like a pack of cards, but I jam a hand over my mouth.

I have never turned left before.

You lead me through a green baize door into a narrow corridor. The walls are yellow and lean towards me and I can smell cabbage on them, years and years of watery cabbage. My breathing is all over the place. The air is thick in my throat.

You turn to me.

'This is to make it easier,' you say, and before I can push you away you fix a dog's leather collar around my left wrist and I am attached to you by a thin lead.

I blink. I am not a dog. I am a human being. I feel tears sting my eyes.

'Come on, Georgie,' you whisper. 'You're doing really well.'

I am not doing really well.

You tug on the lead and I force my feet to follow you because you ask it of me, but I can feel panic tearing at my guts with claws six inches long. We pass through another door and into an empty kitchen. It has a high ceiling and cream walls but there is more air here and I drag some past the lump of rock in my throat.

'Hush, Georgie! Be quick. We've only got a minute before someone comes.'

I follow my wrist to a back door. You turn the handle but it is locked. Relief comes to me like an angel, bright and warm, because now I can run back to my room. I try to undo the collar with my other hand but you snap at me.

'No, Georgie. Don't.'

You produce a key from your pocket. I stare at it. I am going to die. I know it.

'How?' I ask.

'Don't shout! It doesn't matter how I got a key, the point is that I have it.' You put it in the lock and turn it.

'How?'

I will not move until you tell me and you know it.

You sigh. 'I've been courting one of the kitchen maids here, so that I could make a copy of it.' You shrug. As if it is nothing.

It is too much. Your words crash against the screams in my head and my mouth opens to let out the pain but at that moment you pull the door wide and darkness hurls itself at my face. You drag me outside and the darkness swallows me.

I am going to die.

'It's all right, Georgie, it's all right. Try not to make that noise.'

What noise? The only noise I hear is the darkness tramping up the gravel path to get at me. I have never been outside at night.

Darkness has always existed safely on the other side of a glass window-pane, but now I am breathing it into my lungs and I will never get it out.

'Well done, Georgie.' The lead tugs at my wrist. 'The back gate is at the end of this path and I have a taxi waiting around the corner for us.' Another tug, harder this time. 'Come on.'

I don't move.

'Do you want me to blindfold you?' you whisper.

My mind is splintering. No. No blindfold. No. One thin sliver of my brain can still function. Walk. If I walk, there will be no blindfold.

One foot, second foot. One foot, second foot. I watch them through the black air. I am walking. A gate that I have never seen before materialises in front of us.

'George Kenton, what are you doing out here?'

The voice booms out of the darkness. My wrist is yanked hard. My heart explodes in my chest and something cold and hard and dead takes its place.

'George! What are you doing out here?'

It is Dr Churchward.

'I am taking him out for the evening,' you say. 'He'll be back in a few hours, don't worry.'

You are so calm. So unafraid. I love you so fiercely.

'That is not allowed, as you well know, Mr Kenton.' Dr Churchward's hand is gripping the middle of the lead.

'Come along, George. Back inside.'

His face is white, floating in the blackness, and his voice is smooth. But I have heard that smoothness before. Before the needles. Before the treatment room. It is the smoothness of ice before it breaks and drowns you in the icy water beneath. I step up close to him and slam my right fist into the middle of his chest. He makes an odd sound. His knees buckle and he folds up like a piece of paper. He hits the ground.

You cheer. A big boisterous cheer, and then you drag me through the gate. You make me run. I have never run, not that I can ever remember. But my legs do it beautifully. They astonish me. While I am running and my fist is throbbing, I am happy, but you climb into the back seat of a car and pull me in after you.

I know immediately that this is where I will die. It is small and cramped and crushing me. All the screams stacked up in my head burst out in a great roar of sound. The car shakes with it. I scream louder. My limbs thrash at the stinking seats, at the glass, at you, and I can do nothing to stop them.

'Stop it, Georgie. Hush, hush, you're safe with me.'

You try to pin me down but I am too strong for you. I flail violently and sounds screech from my mouth.

'Bloody 'ell, guv, I'm not taking that thing anywhere, it's crazy,' a man shouts from the driving seat. 'Get it out of my cab.'

I am not an *it*.

The door next to me is opened suddenly from outside and a figure stands there. I am trapped between you inside and him outside. The darkness is winning. I scream at it.

'Now, now, George. Enough of this.' The figure is Dr Churchward. I thought I had killed him. He seizes my wrist and I feel the familiar quick sting in my flesh.

A needle is always the death of me.

The screams vanish. I wait. I know what comes next. The top of my head lifts off and my brain is sucked out, so that my skull is cold and empty. The damp darkness flows into it.

'Would you like to go back to your room now, George?' Dr Churchward asks, each word precise and polite.

I nod.

'Good. Come along.'

'No, Georgie, don't go, stay with ...' But you look at my face and the words stop. You look at the syringe in his hand. 'What have you done to him?'

Dr Churchward takes the collar off my wrist. 'Young man,' he says to you, 'you do not understand his condition if you think you can take him out for an evening without causing major trauma. I expected better of you.'

He guides me out of the cab and back to the gate. You follow behind. There is something I want to say to you but I cannot find my tongue anywhere in my head. I stumble through the gate but he shuts it on you, barring your way. I have lost my cap.

'Mr Kenton,' he says to you, 'if anything like this ever happens again, I will be forced to ban you from visiting your brother. And we both know what that would do to him, don't we?'

You say nothing. Your shoulders are hunched and you look smaller, as if the darkness has eaten up parts of you. Your gaze is on me and for a brief instant our eyes meet.

You smile and blow me a kiss.

'Goodnight, Georgie. Sleep well.'

We never talk of it again.

30

Jessie woke. She lay very still on her back in the dark, eyes closed. Warm limbs lay entwined with hers, the scent of Monty rose from her pillow and from her skin, and a solid weight of happiness sat on her chest like a cat.

She moved a foot. Just enough to make certain his long bones were real and not part of her dream. Because she had been dreaming of him. A joyful dream of drifting down the Nile in a small boat, her head on his lap, but the boat was packed with street urchins who scrambled up out of the brown waters of the river. Holding out stick-thin hands and crying, '*Baksheesh*!' Monty had been tossing them back into the river one by one, like unwanted fish, when she woke.

She was smiling. Without even knowing it. She was smiling in her sleep because the memory of last night was still vivid. The touch of his fingers branded on her flesh, the taste of his lips seared on her tongue, the feel of him deep inside her creating a heat so intense that it seemed to melt her bones. Now they lay soft and shapeless on the sheet, with a sense of lethargy that was something totally new to her. In fact, it slowly dawned on her, *she* was new to her. This person who didn't wake up alert and watchful. This person who didn't carry her fear of being hurt around in her pocket the way other people carried their pocket-watch. This person who thought nothing of taking the risk of getting too close. This was a new Jessie. A Jessie who made her smile.

Of course she'd had lovers before. At twenty-seven most of her friends – except Tabitha – were already married and up to their elbows in nappies, much to her mother's chagrin, but it had held no appeal to Jessie. When anyone – like Alistair back in London, still waiting for his visit to Kew Gardens – tried to squeeze under her skin, she would put up her *Closed for Refurbishment* boards and move out. She knew it. Didn't like it. But was powerless to stop it.

Until now.

Until this moment of happiness sitting on her chest. When she believed she had lost him to the bomb last night, she thought she was going to crack open with sorrow and bleed into the marbled floor alongside him. Something had happened to her the minute she set foot in Egypt, as though its hot wind and driving sand had stripped away the husk around her. A pulse vibrated under her ribs each time she thought of him. Her skin pressed tighter against him and her ankle hooked around his, weaving them together.

She opened her eyes. He was watching her in the darkness. She could see the glint of his eyes, but their expression was claimed by the shadows.

'Hello,' she whispered.

'Hello.'

'Can't sleep?'

'I've been thinking.'

She rolled over to face him. 'Sounds serious.'

'It is. I think you should return to England and let me continue the search alone.'

'No.' She wrapped a leg over his hip. 'I'm not leaving Egypt. And I'm not leaving you.'

His fingertips stroked her throat and she could barely swallow.

'It's too dangerous,' he said.

'I don't want you hurt. You need me.'

'To watch my back?'

'Exactly.'

His fingertips were descending. 'I need you far more than that,' he murmured so low that the words scarcely bridged the gap between them. 'But I want you somewhere safe.'

'I'm staying.'

Staying here. In Egypt. In your bed.

His breath trickled onto her lips, but he didn't argue.

'What we have to discover,' he said, 'is what Tim is doing out here.'

'I don't care what he's doing. I just need to find him.'

His hand stroked her breast, tender touches. 'The obvious answer is that he is dealing in antiquities from Ancient Egypt, given his area of expertise,' he said.

'I agree.' His thumb brushed her nipple, a soft nudge that sent ripples of fire direct to her groin. 'Legal or illegal, I don't care. He has left a trail for me to follow. That can only mean that he wants me here, he needs my help. So . . . tomorrow we start at the Cairo museum where the king's crown lies, where Tutankhamen's death-mask is on . . .'

'Hush.' He kissed her eyelids. 'Don't think about tomorrow.'

His hand started to descend further with caressing circles and she felt the slow burn of his determination and desire. She caught herself uttering a moan she had never heard before and it startled her. Her hips bucked against him, as she let her tongue taste the salty skin of his chest. Her whole body was hungry for him, as though she had been starved of it all her life. They made love again, but gave themselves all the time in the world while the darkness stretched out around them. Their hands and their mouths touched and explored, learning the curves and intimate hollows of each other. Discovering the secret places, the ones that created delicious shock and ferocious need.

In the final raging heat of passion when he arched over her and her whole world narrowed to this one fragment of time, she felt the shield she had so carefully constructed around herself being scorched into ash. As she lay quietly in his arms afterwards, their bodies slick with sweat and her heart flinging itself against her ribs, she knew something strong and vital had been forged between them. She wanted to call it love. She wanted to call it trust. But those words were too big. Too solid. They still frightened her. So instead she called it belief. She believed in this man. It would do. For now.

Jessie returned to her room just before dawn and tumbled into her own bed. She stretched her limbs, and smiled up at the ceiling where the mosquito net hung unseen on a metal hoop. For once she allowed her mind to drift, as effortlessly as one of the Nile's feluccas, towards the possibilities that were opening up before her.

She closed her eyes, her hands restless as birds on the sheet. The hugeness of love was something that she had struggled all her life to outrun, but not now. Not this time. She tried to understand what had happened, what was different, but couldn't. Except that Monty made her want to stop running.

What was it about Egypt? Why was it here that the dross and debris had suddenly been sifted from her mind, as though caught in one of Tim's wire-mesh sieves? Did some force of the ancient gods still lie buried here? Or was it that the quality of time changed here? Somehow it took on a different dimension, lifting the veil between then and now, between the past and the present.

With no warning at all, it had shifted the sand beneath Jessie's feet.

The Great Pyramid of Cheops rose up against the fiercely blue sky. Jessie stepped back from her window, stunned. The Great Pyramid, the oldest of the seven wonders of the world, seemed almost within touching distance of her balcony. It was immense. Disconcerting and incomprehensible. For thousands of years it was the tallest man-made object in the world, until the Eiffel Tower was erected in 1889.

It consisted of an almost solid mass of limestone that covered thirteen acres, and it loomed up on the Giza plateau, just a short walk away from the hotel up a ramp of scree. It was a vast bleached construction that defied belief and belittled all else. At this hour while the air was cool, human beings crawled over it like ants scaling Everest. Tiny insignificant creatures. Only the desert itself, with its endless wastes of sun-scorched sand and rock stretching to the horizon and beyond, could dwarf the great monolith.

Yet it was the scent of the desert, rather than the sight of the pyramid, that captivated Jessie. It was a scent that would haunt her dreams and whisper ancient secrets close in her ear. The air on the plateau tasted clear and sparkling as it swept into her lungs and she paused to watch the fingers of the morning sun slap what looked like gold paint all down one side of the pyramid. On the opposite side a massive purple shadow lay hunched at the foot of the slope like a sleeping guard-dog. For a split second it made Jessie shiver.

'Breakfast,' she told herself.

'Well, young madam, decided to come outside and sniff the roses at last, have you?'

It was the London woman, the tall one from the train. The one staying at Shepheard's. But here she was at Mena House break-fasting with Monty.

'What a nice surprise, Mrs Randall.'

'Call me Maisie, love. There's no Mr Randall on the scene any more, God rest his dog-eared soul, but I ain't letting that get in my way.' She chuckled and sipped her coffee, little finger extended like a flagpole in true ladylike fashion. 'Me and your Sir Montague here been chewing on what to see first. It's like a bun-fight up there.' She gestured towards the pyramids.

But Jessie looked at Monty. His eyes didn't move from hers.

'Sleep well?' she asked him quietly.

'Very well. And you?'

'A bit restless.'

'What would you like?'

'Pardon?'

'For breakfast, I mean.'

Colour raced to her cheeks. 'Of course.'

She ordered tea and watermelon with yogurt and honey. They were sitting on the hotel's terrace which was already crowded with other guests. It was a popular watering hole among the thousands of tourists visiting the pyramids each season, ever since Howard Carter had triggered a world-wide passion for all things Egyptian and the Thomas Cook travel agency had commenced regular trips to the Middle East, turning Cairo into a fashionable winter resort.

'Nice place you landed in,' Maisie observed, eyeing the hotel's luxurious gardens and incongruous golf course in the middle of the parched desert. Everywhere they looked, Egyptian men in turbans and striped robes were busy directing garden hoses at acacia bushes and at abundant riots of bougainvillea and mimosa. It was an island of greenery in a harsh sea of brown.

'Yes, it's beautiful,' Jessie agreed. She had to force herself not to stare at Monty as he calmly smoked a cigarette, his hair glinting coppery in the sunlight. She wanted to reach across and unhook his shirt buttons. 'I believe this hotel started life as the Khedive Ismail Pasha's hunting lodge in the nineteenth century and is named after King Menes of Memphis.' The words filled up the crystal clear air that separated her from Monty. 'He was the founding father of the first Egyptian dynasty.' She gestured off to one side, past the towering eucalyptus trees. 'Its swimming pool is the first and the largest ever built in Egypt.'

She stopped, her cheeks warm.

Maisie put down her cup. 'Blow me, if you don't know some weird stuff.'

Jessie shrugged self-consciously. 'My brother is an archaeologist. He tells me things. Some of them stick.'

'He must be bleedin' clever, then.'

'He is.'

'That's nice for you.'

Jessie changed the subject. 'Are you off to see the pyramid this morning?'

'Good grief, I've done that already. An early bird, that's me. Always on the go, that's why I'm thin as a stick-insect.' She laughed good naturedly at herself and glanced over at the pyramid. 'Crikey, it's a monster, isn't it?' Her face grew serious. 'I wouldn't want to be buried in there. Trapped for ever under all that rock.' She shuddered dramatically. 'That Pharaoh Khufu must have been a glutton for the dark.'

'It was intended as a gateway to the afterlife,' Jessie pointed out.

'Huh! The afterlife. Over four thousand years later and we still don't know any better.' She looked back at Jessie. 'We're useless at learning from the past.'

Monty immediately became animated. 'I disagree. Look at my Chamford ancestors. They thought nothing of charging around on horseback, lopping off the heads of their enemies during the crusades or our civil war.'

'So what do you do now?' Maisie grinned. 'To those poor ducks who make an enemy of a Chamford?'

Monty raised an eyebrow. 'I am at least civilised about it.'

'What? You mean you ask their permission first,' Jessie teased, 'before you lop off their heads?'

Monty let his gaze rest on the shadow that sprawled at the base of the pyramid, where even in the heat of the day it would be chill.

'No,' he said, 'I sit down and discuss any disagreement calmly with them first. Only then do I lop off their heads.'

They rattled their way into Cairo on the tram.

A special line had been constructed along the rough seven-mile stretch of Pyramid Road, designed to carry tourists to and from the Giza plateau. At the Giza end a queue of morose camels and brightly bedecked donkeys with long eyelashes waited to transport visitors to the pyramids themselves. The trams ran every forty minutes from outside the Mena House Hotel to the Pont des Anglais in the city, and theirs was packed with a multi-lingual mix of French,

English and Germans, red-faced from their exertions. Many had attempted to scale the zigzag line of ascent to the pyramid summit, but not all succeeded. Egyptian guides – dragomen, as they were called – scampered like mountain goats over the face of the pyramid, making it look easy, the wind billowing out their *galabayas* like sails as they hauled the more adventurous tourists with them up the four-foot limestone blocks that formed each step. The overweight Frenchman sitting behind Jessie was less than enthusiastic about the experience.

'The panorama from her summit is . . . poof!' He flicked his fingers. '*C'est très décevant*. Very disappointing. Just more sand out to the west, and the city to the east.' He shrugged Gallic shoulders.

'Crikey Moses!' Maisie jeered. 'What do you expect in a desert? Roses and honeysuckle?' She prodded his seat with her furled black umbrella. 'You saw the Nile and the minarets, didn't you? Anyway, a bit more climbing and a bit less of your fancy French eating would get rid of some of that . . .'

Jessie stopped listening. She was impatient. Her mind was focused on the Museum of Egyptian Antiquities. In the Conan Doyle story of *The Adventure of the Musgrave Ritual* it was the crown of King Charles I that was found. Well, there was no Charles I here in Cairo, but there were plenty of kings, including their mummified remains.

Somewhere there must be something, some sign from Tim.

She gazed out through the dust-speckled window at the passing landscape. The vivid green cultivation of the irrigated fields along the banks of the Nile was outlined in sharp contrast to the bleak and arid expanse beyond, and it struck Jessie that this was a land of three colours. The sumptuous sapphire blue of the sky that enchanted the eyes. The shimmering emerald green of the patchwork of fields of sugar-cane and of berseem, the Egyptian clover that was grown everywhere for fodder. But overwhelming all else were the soft muted shades of the sand and the rocks, of the dirt and the mudbrick houses, of the men's *galabayas* and their warm sun-baked skin. Even the westerners' clothes tended towards creams and fawns, as well as white or khaki drill shorts, all non-colours that were effortlessly swallowed by the landscape.

She spotted an egret rising from the river and watched it spread its ragged white wings as it swooped up into the branches of a tree. Such timeless motion. It lay at the heart of this country. The turn of a waterwheel, the soft thud of a *shaduf* as it emptied its bucket into an irrigation ditch, the rise and fall of the hoes in the fields or the kneading of the dough for *eesh baladi*. All were unchanged from the days of the pharaohs. No wonder Egypt had cast such a heavy spell on her brother, but Jessie would not let it have him.

She intended to find him. To bring him home, even if she had to wrestle him from the grip of Osiris himself.

The centre of Cairo preened itself on its elegance. Broad tree-lined boulevards boasted graceful mansion blocks in French style with wrought-iron balconies and luscious spills of bougainvillea or flame spikes of canna lilies.

To Jessie it felt European to its core. But no European capital saw donkeys plodding down its main streets, knees buckling, piled to breaking point with gigantic loads of fodder or firewood. Paris was not plagued by *gharries*, the horse-drawn cabs that jostled and shouted at each other for business; London remained free from the ill-temper of camel-trains, and no one paraded in Berlin in a scarlet tarboosh worn with a trim three-piece suit and a dead chicken under one arm.

Cairo made Jessie's heart beat faster. Despite its European pretensions, the city assaulted her senses with its noise and its smells, its streets jammed with pedestrians and vehicles. The traders yelled constantly. The rumble of donkey carts choked the pavements. Men squatted on their heels in the street to be shaved and Jessie could not tear her eyes away from a customer on a stool in a doorway having his teeth ripped out.

Shoeshine boys kicked dust over passersby to boost business and bright-eyed urchins roamed in packs, besieging unwary tourists with disarming smiles and quick greedy paws. But this time Jessie was

255

prepared. Her pockets were stuffed with piastres. And there was no such thing as road safety or regard for rules or order. It was so blatant it made her laugh out loud. It was quickly clear that she took her life in her hands when she crossed the road, yet at the same time, in all this chaos, there was an ebb and flow to the rhythm of the city that was as natural as the rise and fall of the Nile itself.

'Ready?' Monty asked.

'Yes.'

He had drawn her arm through his, holding onto her tightly as though he feared some camel-driver might snatch her away. They were walking up from the Pont des Anglais with Maisie Randall stalking ahead, scything out a path with her umbrella and Jessie wanted to slide a hand under his shirt to touch the warm skin of his chest. To say *Don't worry*. To say *I have faith in you. I have faith in Tim. Together we will find him. I believe – insanely, I know – that this will happen, because we will make it happen.* She said all this instead with just an increase in pressure where her shoulder touched his. She heard him say something under his breath, but she didn't catch the words because at that moment the call to prayer rose in an undulating wail throughout the city.

It launched itself with outspread wings from the needle-thin minarets, a reminder to the arrogant westerners five times a day that this was not their country. And never would be.

The museum was as pink as a peony. It stood in a tree-lined square, Midan Ismailiya, in the heart of Cairo, and Jessie liked it on sight. With its sphinxes and lily pond, it was less forbidding than the British Museum.

'I can imagine Tim here,' she told Monty as they entered through the huge stone archway, 'like a child in a sweetshop. His mouth salivating at the sight of all this.'

She could see him. Blue eyes gleaming. Hands touching. Caressing. Mind storing fact after fact as he examined the exhibits. Here she could conjure him into reality and force him through willpower alone to materialise in front of her.

'Where do you want to start?' It was Maisie, regarding her closely.

Monty scanned the atrium where they were standing under a great cupola in the roof, surrounded by towering statues of ancient pharaohs and the flamboyant gods of Egypt.

'We intend to view the King Tutankhamen exhibits first,' he said.

'Not me. Want to save the best till last,' Maisie smiled, unaware of the striking similarity of her face to a basalt figure just behind her with the head of an ibis. Both long and thin, with a nose like a beak and narrow sharp eyes.

'There's a lot to see,' Jessie told her. 'A hundred and seven halls. The huge statues and sarcophagi are on the ground floor, the smaller treasures upstairs.'

'Why don't we meet you here in an hour?' Monty suggested to Maisie. 'Then we can decide how much longer we'll need.'

'Good idea.'

'We'll see you later,' Jessie confirmed and set off at speed towards the first hall.

'Jessie!'

She stopped and turned. Maisie was still standing in the middle of the vast atrium, her arms folded, sunhat in hand and umbrella hooked over one wrist.

'Jessie, my girl, whatever has got you all fired up this morning, you watch your step. I bet me best titfa that this place is just crawling with snakes.'

Jessie shook her head. But her eyes instantly fell on a stone statue of Ramses II, wielding the crook and flail, symbols of authority. On the front of his headdress sat the *uraeus*, the royal cobra poised ready to strike.

'Slow down.'

Jessie was hurrying through the gallery of the Old Kingdom. Almost running.

'Slow down,' Monty said again. 'You are drawing attention to us.'

257

She slowed. Not much.

'Tutankhamen is going nowhere,' he reminded her. 'There's no rush. Take a look at some of these exhibits, they're so amazing the way they—'

'I'm not interested in them.'

'Jessie!' He gripped her arm, forcing her to slow to a tourist's amble. 'The king in your story might not mean Tutankhamen. Look at them all.' He waved a hand at a towering grey statue of Amenhotep III and the severed head of another wearing the tall slender crown with the rounded top which signified a ruler of Upper Egypt. 'It could be any of them.'

'No. If there's anything here from Tim, it's with King Tutankhamen.'

'Why? How can you be so sure?'

She hesitated. She wanted to tell him. But her mouth went dry at the thought. She could feel the warmth of his fingers through her sleeve and hear the concern in his voice as he asked the question. *How can you be so sure?*

But she couldn't tell him. Couldn't bear to see in his eyes the thought that she was crazy – which is what she *would* see if she told him it came to her in a dream. He may manage not to laugh at her, but he wouldn't manage to keep the pity from his voice.

'I just know,' she replied. She shrugged and started up the wide stairs.

The dream had come immediately her head hit the pillow in her own room. She was in the vaulted crypt of a church – it looked like the flag-stoned one under St Martin-in-the-Fields, but they probably all looked alike. Tim was there in black shorts and black shirt, sitting on top of a gigantic marble sarcophagus, as big as a train carriage, dangling his legs over the edge and swinging them back and forth like a child.

'Look at me,' he called to her, laughing. His blond curls were dirty as if he'd been scrabbling underground. 'Look, Jessie.'

He lifted from behind him a mask and held it over his face. Not any old mask. It was the solid gold death-mask of the Egyptian boy

258

king, Tutankhamen. She could tell it was heavy because his wrists shook with the weight of it.

'Tutankhamen is me,' Tim said in a muffled voice and she ran towards him, crying with relief.

She woke with tears on her face.

Tutankhamen is me.

T.I.M. Even to her it sounded crazy.

31

Georgie

England 1930

'How are you today?' you ask.

'I'm fine, thank you,' I reply, quick as a flash.

Hah! You cannot catch me out. I have learned too well. But you stand silently. I realise you are waiting, and I feel the familiar flutter of failure in my chest.

'And how are you?' I ask in a rush. Too late.

'I'm well,' you say.

I do not understand. We are both lying, so why do we have to say the words? You have explained to me again and again that when someone says 'How are you?' they do not want to hear that each of your heartbeats makes a noise in your head like a balloon popping or that your toes have started to smell like mothballs. Or that you believe that both these occurrences are caused by Dr Churchward and his pocketful of new drugs. But what is the point of lying? If you do not want to know how I am really feeling, why ask?

You say 'I'm well,' but you do not look well. I cannot say why I think that, but I do. I know I am no good at understanding facial expressions but I am better with feet. Today your feet are heavy. I want to take your shoes off to make them lighter for you. They clump across my floor and scuff against my skirting-board while you stare out at the garden. At least that is preferable to your staring at me the way you do sometimes, as though you would turn me inside out, my skin on the inside and my workings on the outside. Or is that how you see me anyway? With all the cogs and bloody bits on view. I don't know and I am too frightened to ask, in case you say *Yes*.

So I stare at your back. It is a perfect triangle. Broad straight shoulders, muscular from the years of sport and the Indian club exercises we do together. I am catching up with you. From the back we could be real brothers, you tell me, and I like that. I like it a lot.

'Georgie.' You are talking to the window-pane. 'I have to go to Egypt. On a dig at Medinet Habu, working with a team from the University of Chicago.'

I start to shake.

'I will be gone three weeks.'

I am moaning.

'It will be over quickly and then I'll come back to visit . . .'

'No, no, no, no, no!'

'Stop it, Georgie.'

'No, no, no, no, no!'

You turn to face me and your mouth is all clenched and strange. I hear you sigh as I hurl myself on my bed and start to howl. You pull up a chair next to the bed and you talk to me in a quiet firm voice that I don't want to listen to but which hammers away at my eardrums. I cry. You give me your handkerchief, a pristine square of whiteness that you always bring especially for me. I clamp it over my nose and mouth, but some of your words slide into my head through the pathways of my tears.

'It's a great opportunity for my career,' you say. 'Imagine it, Georgie, seeing Ramses the Third's great temple and fortress with my own eyes. The carvings of his violent wars against the Libyans and the Sea Peoples . . .

'The colossal statue of Ramses as the god Osiris.

'On the west bank of the Nile at Luxor ...

'I'll bring you pictures of the colonnade of broken osiriform figures with ...'

Your voice is drooling like a starving dog at a banquet. I pull my pillow over my head and howl into it. Time stops. My world stops because you are leaving it.

'All right, you've got that straight?'

I nod. What else can I do?

'I'll be back.'

I nod again. You keep saying that. For the last three Saturdays we have had the same conversation. You are going, no matter how many times I beg you not to. It is important, you say. How can you become an Egyptologist if you don't go to Egypt? I tell you to study Anglo Saxon archaeology instead, so that you never have to leave the country, but you shake your head, your mouth tight. We both are victims of the spell cast by Egypt and we both know there is no choice for you.

'You have my itinerary?'

I nod.

'I have written out for you an advance diary of what I hope to do each day in Luxor.'

I nod.

'You must picture me on my knees with my brushes and trowels in the sand and dirt, folding back time as I excavate the trace of a hand or the curve of a *shabti* at Medinet Habu.'

'Or the crown of a king.'

You smile at me. 'Thank you.'

'To look a god in the face will be huge.'

Especially Osiris, green god of the afterlife with his mummy-wrapped legs and huge distinctive *atef* crown with ostrich feathers. I would like a crown like that, one that demands respect. He is always depicted holding a crook and flail, as though his existence depended on them. Like mine does on you. Osiris had a brother

262

too – Set, the god of storms and the desert – but the rivalry between them was intense. It is said to be symbolic of the eternal war between the fertile green lands of the Nile Valley and the barren desert lands just beyond, but I think it more likely that Set just got sick of his tall brother throwing his weight around. You don't do that to me. I know I must listen to your words and I must let you go. But I cannot.

'Here is the calendar,' you say. 'You know what to do.'

I nod.

'You must tick off the days, Georgie.'

I know.

You let a silence into the room. I am hunched on the floor in my favourite corner, hugging my knees and bouncing my chin on them to make my teeth click like a clock, counting away the seconds of my life. You are leaning against my wardrobe, smoking a cigarette, as if you just happen to have come to rest there. But I know and you know that you are blocking my retreat into the dark.

'Say something, Georgie. Anything.'

Maybe the silence has stretched longer than I know.

'You will read hieroglyphs carved in stone,' I say, 'and see the marks of the masons' chisels. You will touch a Ramses cartouche, the sign of a royal name, that is three thousand years old. It is unbelievable.'

'Jealous?'

I do something for you then. Something big.

I nod. 'Yes.'

But it is not true. I say it for you. I lie. I shoot a quick glance at your face and see that your mouth is still tight, but your eyes are shining. The sun of Egypt is already inside you.

'I'll bring you back something ancient,' you promise.

I remember my manners. 'Thank you.'

'You'll be all right.'

'No, I won't.'

'You won't like it maybe, but you'll survive, Georgie. It's only three weeks and it might even do you good.'

'No, it won't.'

'Let's play a last game of chess.'

'No.'

You come closer. You squat down on your haunches and I can feel the energy billowing off you.

'Be happy for me, Georgie. Please.'

'I am.' Another lie. 'But I am sad for me.'

'So am I.'

'What if I die while you are gone?'

'You won't.'

'I might.' Another thought strikes like a hammer to my brain. 'What if you die in Egypt? There are poisonous snakes – cobras and horned vipers. There are scorpions. Suffocating sandstorms and mosquitoes carrying malaria. What if you go out there and your plane crashes on landing or you fall out of a boat into the Nile and drown? What if … ?'

'Georgie, stop shouting!'

For the first time I take your hand in mine and hold it tight.

'Don't go,' I plead. 'Don't leave me.'

'Oh, Georgie. I must.'

I hate you at that moment. I am sick with terror and I hate you.

I cannot speak of it. Those three weeks. Nothing you imagine can come close to how bad they are.

In the end I put my hand in the coal fire to lessen the pain, but they bandage it up and so I have no choice but to break a window and use the glass. I cut deep. My stomach, my thigh, my throat. I do not want to die but I have to let out the pain, and it is the only way. There is so much blood, so much seething redness, that what is left of my mind splinters into a thousand pieces. Dr Churchward is screaming like a child.

You come to see me in hospital. I am alone in a private room that is all white which I like, but I am only a breath from death. You come to my bedside and you cry. You bring me an ancient bronze *ankh*, the looped cross that is the Egyptian hieroglyph for *life*. You tie it to my bed-head.

32

'It is awesome.' Monty was studying the exhibits. Before him stood the magnificent throne, gleaming with sheet gold and richly adorned with lions' heads, winged serpents and the king's cartouches. 'Truly awesome. There is no other word.'

Jessie stared fixedly at the great solid gold death mask of Tutankhamen that was decorated with lapis blue. It weighed twenty-four pounds. No wonder it was heavy in her dream. It possessed a pharaoh's long ceremonial false beard and black eyes of obsidian and quartz that gazed back at her with cold indifference.

Speak to me. Make me hear.

Around her a throng of tourists, eager to see the boy king's glorious funerary equipment, jostled against her but she didn't move. She had already examined the delicate Hathor couch with its golden horns and sun-disk, and admired the beauty of the statuettes and rings, especially the elaborate scarab pectoral necklace. But nothing prepared her for the canopic shrine which stood almost as tall as a man and was fashioned from solid gold. The ornate decorations and carvings of gods and goddesses on it touched a nerve inside her, that someone could care so much for the dead that they created a work of art so sublime. One that would beguile the gods themselves.

But it was in the canopic jars sitting in their alabaster canopic chest that the objects of unparalleled importance lay: the viscera of the king. Carved images of the sons of Horus watched over each jar – Imesti guarded the royal liver, Qebehsenuef protected the intestines, Duamutef the stomach, and the all-important lungs were kept safe by Hapi, with his ape's head. Breathtaking works of art. Fit for a king.

His guardians.

Jessie had felt the power of them. As fresh and strong as when they left their maker's hands. They pulled her in, obliterating her thoughts. Instead of the chatter of the voices in the museum, she heard the sigh of sand whipped over the tomb by the wind, the howl of the desert jackals at night, the cry of the red-tailed kite high in the blinding blue sky watching over the hidden entrance. She closed her eyes and the murmurs grew louder in her head, spiralling inside her skull, spinning in ever tighter twists and turns. She felt dizzy . . . put out a hand . . . Warm firm flesh grasped it.

'Jessie, are you all right?' It was Monty's voice. Close and concerned.

She'd forced open her eyes. The room felt dim and oppressive. She could smell something, some strange unfamiliar incense that teased her nostrils . . .

'I'm fine.'

But she waited for her heart to slow its drumbeat. Gently he led her away from the display of objects destined for the pharaoh's use in the afterlife, and the strange smell faded, the noises in her head fluttered and died.

'I think you are too anxious,' he'd murmured, 'for your brother. And for those hurt in the explosion last night. You need to sit down and rest a moment.'

'No, but thank you.' He still held her arm. 'I need to examine the mask.'

So she was now standing in front of King Tutankhamen, and Monty was studying the golden throne fit for a god.

'It is awesome,' she agreed. 'There is no other word.'

Speak to me. Make me hear.

When she heard the hiss, her heart slammed into her throat. A king cobra rose out of the darkness with its hood flared, ready to strike with a speed beyond mortal eye. It swayed its head, numbing her mind, and though she wanted to run, to shout a warning to Monty, she couldn't move. Couldn't speak. Couldn't breathe.

'You've had enough,' Monty said casually at her side. 'If you can see nothing out of the ordinary,' he slid an arm around her waist, 'I think we should move on, don't you?'

Jessie blinked and let her hand touch his. The hissing slid into silence and the cobra became once again the symbol of royalty standing proud on the front of the golden mask. The *uraeus*. The protector.

Timothy told me that you are his uraeus. That's what Anippe Kalim had told her in the British Museum.

His protector.

So why wasn't she protecting him?

They moved quickly through the rest of the halls. Jessie was unwilling to linger.

'It's an astonishing collection,' Monty commented as they passed a slab of ancient hieroglyphics. 'Very impressive. Who set it up, do you know?'

'It was the Egyptian Antiquities Service. The collection was started by Auguste Mariette, the French archaeologist. Ismail Pasha was determined to stop the looting of his country's priceless artefacts, and quite right too. So he retained Mariette to create a home for them and introduced laws to punish thieves of antiquities.'

'So this place was built specially for the collection, I assume.' They were heading back downstairs towards the entrance to meet with Maisie once more. 'They made a good job of it.'

'Yes.' She had herself back under control now and had organised a smile on her face. 'Though it's a bit of a maze, isn't it?'

There were so many gigantic statues, carefully transported and preserved from the ruins of temples and fortresses in the Nile Valley that it was like walking through a gloomy forest of stone. The scale of everything was so vast, yet the detail of workmanship was immensely skilled and imaginative. Jessie stopped for a moment to inspect more closely a relief of the head of Amun-Ra, depicted with his tall feathered crown cut deep into the stone and a mystifying array of hieroglyphs behind him.

Out of the corner of her eye she saw a flicker of movement. Not the general slow milling around of the tourist crowd, nor the rhythmic whisk of the feather-dusters wielded by the cleaning women shrouded head to toe in black, but a quick flash of bright blue. There one moment, then gone. Quick as a kingfisher. A bright blue and gold headscarf. The last time she had seen a blue and gold scarf was in the British Museum, around the neck of Anippe Kalim.

Jessie darted quickly off to the side where the movement had come from, dodging between exhibits. Squeezing between visitors and checking around corners. The halls flowed confusingly one into another and it was when she was finally standing cursing herself for being too slow, too blind, too plain crazy to believe she would bump into Tim's girlfriend in a museum in Cairo, that Jessie caught another sighting of the elusive blue.

But this time it paused. It was over in a far corner, about to vanish through a half-open door. This time the scarf turned, as if its owner could not resist one final look behind her. Their eyes met. It *was* Anippe Kalim. The same proud face and dark round eyes, but this time the face was marred by a deep scowl.

'Anippe!' Jessie shouted. 'Wait, I need to . . .'

The headscarf vanished. The door slammed. Anippe Kalim was gone.

Jessie ran. Like a dog runs. A bloodhound on a trail. Without thought, without distraction. Blind, deaf and dumb to all else except the scent. She burst through the door marked PRIVATE. STAFF ONLY, behind which Anippe had disappeared, and into a warren of corridors. She didn't even see the people who accosted her or hear the members of staff who questioned her right to be there. She just ran.

The blue scarf bobbed and wove, disappearing and reappearing, coming closer, moving further away. It changed direction. Struck out first one way, then another. Jessie gained ground.

It vanished.

For no more than half a second did Jessie feel disgust at her failure before she smelt the warm gust of air from outside with its scent of ripe fruit and animal dung. A back door hung open. She threw herself through it, blinded for a moment by the fierce glare of the sun, and she squinted. At the far end of the street Anippe was running, hampered by her long brown gown and her innate courtesy to others on the pavement. Jessie had no such compunction.

She raced after her. But Anippe knew these streets. Just when Jessie was gaining ground, Anippe would dodge down a scarcely visible side-alley and Jessie would overshoot, forced to backtrack to find the entrance. Time and again she lost Anippe completely. But at one point she drew so close that she saw the look of shock on the Egyptian woman's face when she glanced over her shoulder. Jessie had no idea how far she ran. Or how long. But slowly she became conscious of the streets growing narrower, of the buildings becoming short, squat, and flat-roofed, the roads turning to dust-paths under her feet. White faces vanished. Instead women in black dress, carrying water jugs on their heads and children on their hips, stopped to stare at her from suspicious eyes as she shot past.

'Anippe!' she called out, gasping for breath.

This time the young woman paused at a corner. She glanced back at her pursuer and slowly shook her head from side to side. In rebuke or in astonishment, Jessie had no idea, but she could see Anippe's chest heaving with effort and knew neither could keep this up much longer. So she stopped running. She stood where she was and beckoned to Anippe, thirty yards away. Why she thought the woman would come towards her when she had just spent the last age running away from her, Jessie had no idea. But it suddenly seemed a good alternative, like tempting a nervous young horse to you instead of flailing around after it.

'Anippe,' she called again, along the length of the small street, 'is Tim in Cairo?'

Did she hear? Was her shake of her head a refusal to answer? Or was it the answer itself?

Jessie realised she would never know, because Anippe ducked around the corner and by the time Jessie reached it, she had vanished from the face of the earth. Only then did Jessie sag exhausted against a wall, dragging woodsmoke into her lungs, and come to her senses.

She was lost. Somewhere deep in the old part of Cairo. Her hat had gone and her hair was plastered to her neck with sweat, attracting the fat glossy flies that pestered unbearably. Blood dripped from her palm onto her shoe and she had a recollection of tearing it while squeezing past a fruit stall during the chase. Her mouth was parched as desert sand and her throat felt raw.

She thought of Monty and knew he would be frantic. *Monty, I'm sorry. But . . .*

But what? How to explain what she'd done? She felt a cold rush of shame. What had possessed her? She ran her undamaged hand over her forehead and felt the burning heat of it. It was as though she had gone mad in there, the exhibits in the museum taking over, invading her mind with their war-chariots and their scarab beetles, driving all reason out before them.

She was lost.

Like Tim.

She closed her eyes and it was as though out here in the heat and the dust, with the normal props of her life removed, everything was unravelling. Everything was changing. She steadied herself with a hand on the warm mud bricks of the wall behind her and let out a deep breath. If everything was changing then it was time to change with them. She breathed in, breathed out, and looked around her. The street was narrow and therefore shady. That was something. Scruffy two-storey houses that opened straight onto the dirt road, shutters keeping the heat from the rooms. Front doors propped open, interiors dark. Further along, two women in black robes were squatting like dark stains in a doorway shelling peas.

Jessie thought of enquiring about Anippe Kalim, but knew it would be a dead end. She was a foreigner, an infidel, who didn't speak their language. Even if Anippe was sitting breathing hard behind one of the nearby shutters, why would anyone betray one of their own to Jessie?

She emptied the grit from her shoes, straightened her dress and ran her fingers through her hair before moving off down the street. The two women watched her without pausing in their work, but it was as though word had spread. In the next street, even meaner, she sensed eyes behind the shutters and heard voices calling from one upstairs room to another across the bruised patch of shade between them. She could smell onions frying somewhere and woodsmoke lingered lazily in the air. Corn husks lay dried and shrivelled in a pile that she carefully skirted, but she tried not to hurry, not to intrude or unbalance the slow pace of life here. She was desperate for a drink of water, but she didn't stop to request one, just kept heading quietly in one direction, hoping it would lead eventually to a main thoroughfare where she could pick up a horse-drawn gharry.

It was the children who alerted her. Grubby little urchins in ragged tunics and bare feet who followed behind like a string of ducklings, chuckling and squawking, rolling their big round eyes at her and flashing their small white teeth. She threw them a handful of piastres which they pounced on with squeals, pecking and pushing each other, but instead of drawing nearer to her, so that she could ask for directions, they turned and fled. Only then did she see the group of four swarthy young men ahead of her.

She didn't fuss. Just nodded politely to them and kept walking. *Don't run. Please, don't do anything stupid, Jessie.* It was when she drew alongside them that their stares turned unwelcoming and she was acutely aware of being a foreign woman, an intruder in their street, with head uncovered and a skirt reaching no further than her knees.

Keep walking.

271

But then she saw it. Tucked between the voluminous folds of the men's *galabayas*, a small dark head and the frightened eyes of a child. A boy with dirty cheeks and big wide mouth; a smear of blood oozed from his nose.

Jessie stopped.

The men said something to her, harsh and hostile. She didn't understand their words but she had no trouble interpreting their meaning: *Go away. You are not wanted here.* The street seemed to grow suddenly smaller.

'Good morning,' she said courteously to the men who had closed tight around the boy. She smiled. 'Is there a problem?'

'No.' The one who replied had a deep voice and a thick beard though he could not be more than twenty. 'You go.' He flapped a hand at her as though shooing away a mangy dog.

'The boy looks upset.'

'You go!'

One of the other men took two steps towards her. Sweat slid down her back. She could smell strong tobacco on him, he was so close. Her mouth was dry.

'I want to speak to the boy,' she said.

A young voice reached her from behind the man, followed by the sound of a slap and a squeal of pain.

'Excuse me, please,' she said briskly and tried to step around the man but he straddled her path, his lean body made bulky by his robe.

For a moment their eyes held, his so angry that she almost backed down, but then, very deliberately, she did the unforgivable. She touched him. Put her unclean hand on his arm and pushed. He leapt back as if she had the plague, and uttered a string of guttural curses, but Jessie now had a clear view of the boy. He was rigid with terror. She reached for him, seized the filthy sleeve of his tunic and yanked him out of the grip of the one who had spoken in English. The boy rocketed forward, relief on his young face, and entwined his dirty fingers deep into the material of her full skirt.

'Good morning, lovely lady,' he beamed up at her and tugged at her skirt. 'I take you home right now this moment. Come please now come, yes.'

'Yes,' she said, her eyes on the pack of young men.

One of the group growled something in Arabic at the boy, but the child didn't even glance in his direction.

'Come come come,' he chattered. 'Lovely lady.'

Together they started walking away and the small hand pulling on her skirt tried to urge her to a faster pace but she refused to run. She knew what wolves did when their prey showed fear. But when they reached the corner of the street she risked a glance behind and saw that the four figures were leaning against the dusty wall.

'Hurry hurry,' the boy hissed.

She obliged once she was out of sight, but she still refused to break into a run.

'What's your name?' she asked.

'Malak.'

'Are you all right?'

'I very all right.'

'Well, Malak, I need to get back to the Museum of Egyptian Antiquities.'

'Yes yes, I take. I good dragoman. Come now here yes.'

He was steering her through a bewildering maze of back streets and alleyways. The stench of rotting vegetation and human filth was strong, but at the same time lines of spotlessly clean washing hung limply across the alleys, so that she had to duck her head, and she passed a girl perched on a three-legged stool diligently washing dishes in a bucket of water. The girl smiled shyly at the boy but he ignored her.

'Malak, what was going on back there with those men?'

He turned his bright young face to her. His eyes were huge and round with soft long lashes, shining with expectation – not just of her, but of life. As though they knew life had an abundance of good things to offer, just waiting to be dug out of the sand. His cheeks were thin and the colour of palest coffee, silky smooth and as touchable as an apricot. His hair was black and dense, in need of

273

a wash. Jessie's heart went out to this child and instinctively she took his hand in hers. He didn't pull away and the gleam in his eyes brightened.

'The men bad. Very bad.' But he shrugged and wiped the blood from his nose, cheerfully. 'They want sell me.'

'Sell you?'

'Oh yes yes. I make much good price.' He puffed out his thin chest.

'Sell you?' she whispered. 'No.'

'Oh yes yes. Men come from you country, jolly good England.'

'For boys?'

'Oh yes yes. Plenty boys.'

'Malak, I'm sorry.'

He twisted his head to look at her. 'Not sorry you. You kind. Thank you, lovely lady.'

'How old are you?'

'Twelve.'

She smiled at him. *Twelve?* He was lying. More like eight, maybe nine at most.

'You speak excellent English, Malak. Where did you learn it? At school?'

They were turning into yet another dingy street where the dust lay thick and a man was skinning the carcase of a goat on a spike. For the first time a flicker of sorrow darkened the boy's face, as brief as the beat of a crow's wing. 'No, no school. I must work. I polish. Lots of polish yes.'

'Polish what?'

'Pots. Brass pots. Tourist want shiny. Many pots and snakes and bowls and many many polish.' He mimicked the act of polishing with his free hand. His other still clung to her.

'So where did you learn English?'

He hesitated. 'From Englishman.'

Jessie tightened her grip. Her heart sickened.

'He good, very lovely good.' He grinned up at her. 'He kind, like you. He say I smart.' He tapped the side of his head. 'Up here. I be

274

lawyer one day. He love me plenty but . . .' he sighed with the weariness of an old man, 'he leave. Must go. Too bad.'

Jessie wanted to cry.

'So where do you live?' she asked.

He released her hand and jumped into the open doorway of a house even more ramshackle than the others.

'Here home! My mother and plenty sisters.'

He said it proudly and she loved him for it. He salaamed formally and invited her in.

One room. Six people lived in it. Malak, his parents and three younger sisters. His father worked on a boat on the Nile, loading and unloading sacks of grain or boxes of machinery or whatever else it happened to be carrying that day. Long hard hours of brutal labour. And yet they lived like this.

It wasn't right.

'Hello. Salaam.'

She greeted his mother, a fine-boned woman with her son's smile, who was seated cross-legged on a square of rush matting, spinning cotton on a spindle that dangled from her hand. Opposite her, three exquisite little girls under five years old sat watching, transfixed by their mother's nimble fingers. Jessie was impatient to return to the museum and Monty, but she was obliged to sit and eat a few mouthfuls of flatbread with her new friends. As she talked to the mother and asked questions, she had a feeling that the answers Malak translated for her bore no relation to the words expressed by the woman. It made them all laugh, but as soon as Jessie finished her mint tea, she rose to leave. She bowed her thanks and gave each of the little girls a note of five Egyptian pounds. The mother kissed the hem of Jessie's skirt which embarrassed her hideously.

'What you do tomorrow?' Malak asked, as he walked her up towards the main road. His mother had gently bathed her hand with herbs and bound it with muslin. 'I good dragoman. Much cheap. I show you big-big pyramid, yes please.'

'I'm sorry, Malak. I will be travelling south to Luxor tomorrow. By train.'

'Ayee!' he squealed, 'I know Luxor much good too. My uncle rich man in Luxor. Big-big house. Water tap *inside* house! I go many days in Luxor. I show you good Luxor cheap guide, yes please, lovely lady.'

Jessie laughed. It hurt to disappoint the hopeful young boy. 'I have work to do there, but thank you for the offer. Next time, perhaps.'

He flashed his wide beguiling grin at her. 'Many next times, yes please.'

'Yes, please.'

She slipped twenty Egyptian pounds into his hand and he lowered his head over it for a moment, cupped his hands. '*Allah akbar*,' he murmured, 'God is great.' And when he looked up, his chin was quivering. Tears glistened in his eyes. '*Shukran*, lovely lady. I thank you. I save for education of my sisters. I not wish them ignorant, *inshallah*.'

They stood together on the side of the road in the hot sun and Jessie was touched by the love of this loyal young boy for his sisters. He would never let one of them be snatched away from under his nose. He would die first. Why had she not slit her own throat the moment they took Georgie away from her?

As a gharry drew up alongside them, she bent and kissed his dirty black hair. 'You are a fine young man, Malak. Thank you for your help. I am sure we will meet again in this life.' She touched his cheek. 'May the peace and blessings of Allah be upon you, always.'

When you are waiting for someone you love, a part of you ceases to exist. You are not a whole person. Jessie could feel the crush of that knowledge with every turn of the wheels of the gharry.

Monty. Wait for me.

There were holes in her. She was aware of them now. Empty holes into which the waited-for-person – the loved one – fits perfectly. She had waited for Georgie most of her life, and the hole had widened when Tim disappeared, tearing open new parts of her. Now she was waiting to see Monty but the teeming traffic, the clogged streets, the agonisingly slow carts, they all blocked the wheels of the gharry.

Will he be there? Will he wait?

She saw him the moment she drew near, prowling relentlessly back and forth in the full sun along the top step of the museum with quick angry strides. His face was set hard. His hat had gone, his jacket abandoned. When he turned she could see the sweat on the back of his shirt. Before she had paid the driver, before she had dismounted from the vehicle, his quick eyes had picked her out of the crowd and he was pushing through the busy courtyard towards her. She stepped into his open arms, feeling the heat of his lips and the thud in his chest, but neither of them spoke.

It was enough. That they had waited for each other.

33

Georgie

England 1931

You are staring at my nose. I touch it self-consciously.

'Georgie, spill the beans. Don't lie to me. You're a wet rag at lying.'

I don't understand you. What have beans and rags to do with our conversation? But despite what you think, I am learning to be good at pretending. I pretend to understand.

'We walk in the garden for exercise,' I say.

'That's true.'

'It was hot yesterday.'

'That's true.'

'I got sunburnt while we were out there.'

'That's not true.'

How do you know? What am I doing wrong? It maddens me that I do not know.

'Don't sulk, Georgie. It's not nice. You stick out your bottom lip and screw up your eyes like a two-year-old.'

I rearrange my face.

'It's not important,' I say.

My foot starts to twitch. We both look at it. It is performing its own private dance. You rise from your chair and pace around the room in silence for a while and I dare to hope you have moved onto some other line of thought, but I should know better.

'Let us, my dear Watson,' you begin, 'examine the facts. Because facts cannot lie. Only people lie.'

I experience a thrill. The excitement of the chase. Even though I am the quarry.

'Fact number one. Your forehead and nose are sunburnt. Correct?'

'Correct,' I say.

'Burnt badly enough for the skin on them to be peeling.'

'Correct.'

'Skin does not peel so quickly. So soon after burning.'

'It has been sunny all week. We go in the garden every day.'

'Ah, but only for an hour. And never when the sun is at its height.'

I pass no comment. You light a cigarette but do not offer one to me.

'Fact number two.'

You pause.

I wait.

'Fact number two is that the skin of your throat in the V of your shirt is brown. Browner than your face. Which means only one thing – that you have been in the sun regularly but have been covering your face. I ask myself why?'

You pace in silence. I remember to breathe and I press on my knee to stop the foot-twitch. Abruptly you come to a halt and stare at me.

'Your hair is paler,' you comment.

My hair?

'Bleached by the sun,' you add. 'This leads me to suspect that if I removed your shirt, I would find that your chest is also tanned.'

I stare at the backs of my hands and notice for the first time how they have become the colour of honey. I am embarrassed and hide them surreptitiously between my legs.

'As the front and back doors are always locked,' you continue, 'I can only conclude that you are removing yourself from here some other way. Let me consider.'

You draw hard on your cigarette and exhale two perfect smoke rings.

I glare at my foot. It is still twitching. Betraying me. I stamp on it with my other foot.

'The obvious choice would be a window. But downstairs the windows are all nailed shut, as I found when I once asked to have one opened for fresh air. Damned unpleasant. But I can see why Dr Churchward insists on it.'

For a long while you return to your pacing, wreathed in tobacco and thought.

'Not this first storey,' you mutter to yourself rather than to me. 'You could descend using sheets and blankets, but how would you ascend again? There is no fire escape. That leaves only the top floor.'

A wail of despair leaps up to my throat and I have to swallow hard to thrust it back down. I watch your fingers, as restless as an insect's antennae on your cigarette. You have me cornered. When finally you stub out your cigarette, I know I am done for.

You place your fingertips together and release a sigh of resignation. 'The roof.'

'Holmes,' I say, 'you are a man of iron.'

The wind is brisk and tugs at our clothes.

'This,' you announce, 'is one of the dramatic moments of fate, when you hear a step upon the stair which is walking into your life, and you know not whether for good or ill.'

It is a quotation. From the beginning of *The Hound of the Baskervilles*. I do not think it appropriate because there is neither a step nor a stair in sight up here, and I know without doubt that it is a moment for ill, not for good.

We have climbed onto the roof. I brought you up the tiny spiral stairs at the far end of this large house, the ones that used to be the servants' staircase, poor disregarded creatures. On the upper floor there is a disused washroom under the eaves, stacked high with empty suitcases now. I have examined them over the years, searching for signs of my name on any of them, but there is nothing. I try hard to remember anything I brought with me from home, but I can't. There is just a blank. Maybe that is why there is no suitcase, because I came just in what I stood up in. Or maybe in my fury I destroyed everything that meant home. I don't know. But I refuse to ask Dr Churchward.

We squeeze into the washroom and I remove the four cases in front of the small window. One is a nice wicker suitcase in which I hide things I do not want anyone to find, like my previous makeshift diaries which I do not read any more because they make me cry. And a table-tennis ball I once found in the garden. I know the whitecoats would take it from me in case I tried to suffocate myself by swallowing it. Don't think I haven't thought of it.

The window is nailed shut. But I show you that the two nails are rusty and the wood rotten. I loosened them long ago and can easily slot them in and out of their holes, so that the window will open. This is the tricky bit. We have to climb out onto the narrow window ledge one at a time. I show you how and you are aghast when I flatten myself against the outside wall, perched forty feet above a concrete yard, and throw myself sideways. I hear your gasp. It amuses me.

I cling to a sturdy iron drainpipe of good Victorian construction. A scrabble of my feet and I slither up to the roof edge which has a low stone parapet all around it. I hook a hand between the ornamentation work and drag myself up and over. Easy.

Now you.

I turn to look at you down on the window sill and my chest locks solid. You look so small. The drop so massive. You will die if you miss the pipe. I vomit. The wind blows dregs of it over you as you jump and I know I have killed you. I crouch behind the parapet and shut my eyes. I start to think of swallowing the table-tennis ball. Then you are there beside me.

'That was bloody exciting, Georgie!' You slap me on the back. 'I'm impressed. I didn't think you had it in you.'

Had what in me? I don't know and don't care. You are alive. I swear to the sky that I will never bring you up on the roof again ... assuming that I get you safely back down again. Going down is harder. I lean back against the slope of the roof slates and try to stop my heart plunging and kicking like a crazy horse in my chest.

'Come on. Show me around.' You drag me to my feet. 'You can see for miles.'

I do not want to see for miles. I want to sit quietly like I always do in the V-shaped centre of the two parallel sections of the roof. There no one can see me and I can see no one. Just the sky and the birds. But you go bounding all over the roof. It scares me. On the inside of the parapet is a narrow walkway used for maintenance which you trot around as if it is a garden path instead of a tightrope up in the clouds.

I beg you to sit with me. Reluctantly you do.

'This is wonderful,' you say. 'No wonder you get sunburnt. Why did you keep it a secret from me?'

'Because I thought you would tell Dr Churchward.'

'Why would I do that?'

'To stop me coming up here. Because it's dangerous.'

'Georgie boy, I would never begrudge you a little danger in your life. How often do you come up here?'

'Only when I am feeling well.'

You nod. 'Good. That makes sense. The fresh air will blow the cobwebs away.'

'I do not have cobwebs.'

'Just a saying, Georgie.' You stretch out on the warm slates and I do the same.

We stay like that for a long time, longer than I would normally risk being away from my room, but the whitecoats don't usually

282

interrupt when they know you are with me. Anyway, on a Saturday afternoon there are fewer staff. We stay there even when the sun leaves and clouds thicken above us, we stay there because it is the first time we have ever been like this together, outdoors and relaxed. We don't talk much but we both smile a lot.

When the rain comes, I panic. I did not notice the clouds turn purple. I have never been up here in the rain. In seconds the roof slates become wet and slippery, and the wind tries to buffet us off our feet.

'Don't worry,' you say.

But I do worry.

'We must be very careful,' you say. The rain is smacking you in the face, making you squint. Your hair sticks to your head.

A sound screeches out of me and makes you jump.

'Shut up, Georgie. For God's sake, stop that racket.'

I clamp a hand over my mouth but I cannot climb like that, so I have to let it go. We scramble out of the V-section of the roof.

'I'll go first,' you say.

'No!'

If we are going to fall, I want to fall first.

I slither down to the parapet and hear your feet skidding behind me. I don't wait, in case you push in front of me. I swing over to the outside of the parapet and start to lower myself to the drainpipe. But a strange gurgling noise is roaring out of it and I do not want to touch it.

'Georgie, let me . . .'

I let go and grasp the drainpipe. It is so wet and feels so vile under my hands that I instantly drop six feet down. Above me you shout my name. I steady myself by jamming my feet against the wall, sticking my bottom over the void. Hand over hand I crawl back up till I am on a level with the window ledge, which is several feet to my left.

This is the danger.

Usually I hold on with my hands and swing my body in an arc sideways, so that my feet just reach the ledge. I have to release my hands at that precise moment or I will be stuck with my feet on one side and my hands still on the pipe, with my body suspended over the chasm below. I have done it so often, my heart normally doesn't miss a beat. But never in the rain. Never with your face peering down at me, fear in your stunned eyes.

Fear kills people. Fear brings failure.

I am shaking. But my mouth is shut hard, my teeth locked on my lip, and I make no sound as I hurl myself to the side. Feet touch, hands release, smooth as silk. I am on the window ledge, safe, unhurt, alive and exhilarated. I even open my mouth to the rain.

'My turn,' you shout.

Everything drains out of me except fear. My knees buckle and I clamber down, so that my legs are in the washroom, my bottom on the sill. I look up and the rain slaps me hard in the face. Through a blur I watch you slide down the drainpipe until you are on a level with me. I stretch out my hand but I cannot reach you.

'Don't die!' I shout. 'You might die.'

'Thank you, Georgie, for that comforting thought.'

'Stay there. I'll fetch Dr Churchward.'

'Don't be ridiculous.' You're spitting out raindrops. 'It's only a short jump. I'll make it.'

You brace yourself. Both hands on the wet drainpipe, feet against the wall, bottom sticking out, as you saw me do. I can't breathe. I feel myself wet my pants.

'I love you,' I shout against the wind.

'Not now, Georgie.'

You jump. Your feet touch easily, a toe, then a heel firmly on the ledge, but you release your hands a fraction too late. For a heart-wrenching second you almost make it, but your top half is off balance and you start to tilt backwards away from the window, arms cart-wheeling in mid-air.

I scream and seize your legs. I wrap my arms around your knees with the grip of an octopus and I know I will never let go, even if it means you drag us both to our death in a bloody heap far below. I bury my face in your thighs, clenching your trousers between my teeth, squeezing you to me, feeling my own feet lift off the floor of the washroom.

For a lifetime we hang there like that. I feel an odd rush of peace pass through me and I can breathe again, smell the tobacco stink of your trousers. Because we are going to die together. Clutching each other. Locked together in our last breath. Your hand seizes my hair and pulls so hard that I scream, but with that one handhold and with me attached to your legs, you haul yourself upright and get a hand on the window frame. With no hurry, you sit down and duck back inside with the cases.

'Well,' you say with a grin, 'that was quite an adventure, wasn't it?'

We are drenched to the skin. Your knuckles are skinned and I am shuddering in my skin so badly that I am frightened it will split and spill my flesh onto the faded lino of the floor. My breath is now coming in great whoops of sound and my trousers are stuck shamefully to my legs.

'That was fun, Georgie!'

'Fun,' I echo through chattering teeth.

'Let's get you to your room and changed into dry clothes.'

As you push the nails back into the wood of the window frame, you chuckle to yourself. 'I think I'll bring a short length of rope next time I come, to tie to the drainpipe. Wouldn't want any accidents, would we, Georgie?'

'No. We wouldn't want any accidents.'

'I shall worry about you until I know you have the rope.'

After you leave, I think about what you have said. That night I lie awake in bed and I am smiling. Happy. Because I know you are worrying about me.

34

Dust and cinders from the steam engine flew in their eyes. Jessie was impatient to climb aboard the train but she was touched that Maisie Randall had taken time to come to the station at this early hour to see them off, so she lingered on the platform instead of taking her seat in the first-class compartment.

'I look forward to seeing you again soon,' she smiled at the tall woman. 'You'll be coming down to Luxor?'

'You bet your life I will. In a day or two, I'll be on my way.'

The train uttered a shrill whistle, making them jump.

'Christ Almighty,' Maisie declared, 'does this city never shut up?'

All around them there was noise and bustle. Porters pushing forward with suitcases, hawkers shouting their wares and thrusting cheap copies of scarabs and basalt cats or bracelets of glass beads under the traveller's nose. Boys squirmed through the crush on the platform in an effort to sell dates and figs, while native passengers crammed themselves and their animals onto the heaving train with such determination that Jessie feared the carriages would burst before they even set off.

She hugged Maisie, all bony hips and skinny ribs and smelling of lemon balm. She would miss the woman's ready smile and quick wit, and worried about her travelling alone, but Maisie seemed blithely indifferent to any dangers.

'You take care, my girl,' Maisie said, hoisting her umbrella against the sun. 'I hear it's hot as a baker's oven down there in those tombs of the pharaohs. And be bloomin' careful of the wretched water.'

'I will.'

'And steer clear of any bombs.'

The mention sent a tremor through Jessie's mind. The dull reverberation of that sound had echoed through her head all night, refusing to dissipate. It was still there, a soft relentless booming, like distant thunder in the mountains.

'We should be safe,' she told Maisie. 'The unrest seems to be centred here in Cairo.'

Maisie stared around and shook her head sadly at the sight of the beggars, at the bare feet and gaunt cheeks. 'You can't blame them, can you? Us westerners are too greedy for our own good. We want to suck the world dry of everything worth having.' Her narrow face wrinkled in disgust. 'We leave 'em the desert because it's no bloody good to us.' She paused and looked directly at Jessie. 'I feel for the poor buggers. I remember a time when I had no shoes on my feet or slop in my belly.'

Jessie was startled by the sudden intimacy of the remark. She touched Maisie's arm and realised how her loose jacket disguised the sparseness of flesh on it. 'I'm glad you're here,' she said warmly. 'With shoes on your feet and coffee in your belly.'

The woman smiled. 'Not half as glad as those little beggars in Luxor will be when I get there. They'll fleece me something dreadful,' Maisie chuckled and the moment passed.

The train gave a jolt. Everyone fluttered handkerchiefs and Monty, who was standing on the carriage steps, called Jessie's name.

'Go to him,' Maisie urged. 'You got a good 'un there.'

Jessie hugged her once more. 'I'll see you in Luxor. Don't get into any mischief.'

'Nor you.'

287

As Jessie turned to board the train, she took a good look at Monty. The engine's steam was ruffling strands of his brown hair and he stretched his long arms, looking for all the world as though he belonged there in that exact spot, like a cat in the sun. He had that knack. Of belonging. It made her want to rest her cheek next to his, to breathe the same air, to place her feet where his had been. Maybe then she'd belong too.

Three hundred and twenty miles. Twelve idle hours of shaking and rattling and feeling the hot air being stirred by the fan till it stuck to Jessie's skin. The first-class carriage was well appointed but was packed full of German tourists in shorts above the knee and Egyptian businessmen in sombre suits and ties. The stifling air smelled of garlic and when Monty presented her with a slice of melon to suck on, Jessie almost wept with relief.

The train moved to its own tune. It would speed up or slow down for no obvious reason, creaking and cracking like an old man's joints. Stopping at flimsy stations with names that looked like paintings, so ornate were they in Arabic script, and speeding through the level crossings that had no barriers, so that goats and children wandered onto the line with alarming indifference. Jessie was enraptured by the buff-coloured landscape that nudged its way into distant folds of hills at the far edges of the Nile valley. She'd expected that a journey of twelve hours would be tedious, but oddly, it didn't turn out to be.

First there was the hypnotic quality of the scenery through which the train was travelling. It hardly varied for hundreds of miles. The rail track was laid on a raised embankment running alongside the Ibrahimiya Canal, a stretch of brownish water about forty feet across, one of the longest artificial canals in the world. It was a huge undertaking by Ismail Pasha in the nineteenth century to supply irrigation water from the Nile to the fields between upper and lower Egypt.

The flatness of the Nile valley – except for the graceful minarets announcing each town – would have been dull and repetitive, but reaching out on either side of the canal was a mile or two of cultivation. It ran like a green river on both sides of the train, startlingly vivid against the half-hearted colours of the distant desert and the white milky sky. Dotted throughout the patchwork of fields were the tiny bent backs of the *fellaheen*, the peasants cutting their feathery maize and their tall stalks of sugar-cane, working their ditches and vegetable strips, their brown *galabayas* part of the landscape.

In the sleepy villages and towns Jessie spotted an occasional black and white cow or a handful of knobbly goats. And everywhere small brown donkeys. Donkeys and women were clearly Egypt's beasts of burden, but the sight of a camel was cause for celebration to break the monotony.

As the hours passed, the sky turned a blazing blue that scorched the land and glossed over the rotting piles of rubbish heaped on the banks of the canal outside towns. Jessie was conscious this water was a vital artery of life – men fished on it in long pointed rowboats, women in black garb washed their clothes and their pots in it and packs of wild urchins urinated into it before leaping into its cool murky depths with shrieks of laughter. It proved endlessly fascinating to Jessie.

The only thing she missed were trees. It wasn't that there weren't any; there were, offering shade in ribbons along the edge of the canal. But there was no variety – they were always palm trees, tall graceful date palms whose delicate fans of greenery leaned over the water like women trying to catch a glimpse of their own reflection. Beside them the banana palms fluttered their large succulent leaves in competition, but their trunks were stunted, like ugly sisters to the date palm.

Men gathered in threes or fours on the canal bank or on a wall outside a house, smoking and taking time to put the world to rights while the figures in black laboured on. It was a world that absorbed Jessie totally. And all the time in the far distance an escarpment or an ancient line of low hills would drift out of the haze unexpectedly, soft petal-pink, never allowing anyone to forget that the desert lay out there. Relentless. Implacable. Unforgiving.

The second reason for the lack of tedium was Monty. His hip touching hers. His eloquent eyebrow raised in amusement when two of the Egyptian businessmen goaded each other into argument over a certain horse running in a race at the Gezirah Club the next day. Their voices were deeper than Europeans', their gestures bigger, their eyes fiercer. Jessie pictured Tim in their midst – blond, soft-featured, mild-mannered Tim, and her stomach swooped with fear for him.

Monty must have sensed it, because he said in a low voice, 'Tell me one of your Egyptian stories, one of the myths about their gods.'

So she told him the tale of the war between the brothers, Osiris and Set.

'Osiris was the wise god of the afterlife, ruler of the dead and of fertility, eldest son of the Earth god, Geb, and the sky goddess, Nut. Set was his jealous younger brother, god of the desert and storms.'

'It bodes ill already,' Monty smiled.

'I know how irritating younger brothers can be,' Jessie murmured and he laughed.

'So what did Set get up to?'

'Nothing good. He wanted his brother's throne, so he did what all wicked brothers do in stories – he killed Osiris.'

'Nasty.'

'Sadly, he didn't stop there. He chopped poor Osiris into fourteen pieces and scattered them over Egypt.'

'Painful!'

'Ah, but you are reckoning without the powers of Osiris' devoted wife, Isis. She was also his sister, by the way.'

'Tell all.'

'Well, she and her sister went searching for these pieces, but they could only find thirteen of the fourteen. Fish had swallowed the last piece.'

Monty opened his eyes in horror. 'Don't tell me. I can guess which piece.'

'Exactly!'

'Poor Osiris!'

'But Isis was a resourceful goddess. She created a new ... ' Jessie's voice dropped to a whisper, 'phallus for him of gold, and used a magic spell to put her beloved husband back together for one last marital fling.'

Monty laughed delightedly and one of the Germans gave him a dour frown. 'Don't stop now,' he urged.

'The inevitable happened, I'm afraid. She became pregnant and gave birth to the beautiful Horus, whom she had to protect desperately from the wicked Set who kept trying to kill him off. But he managed to grow up to become the powerful falcon-headed god of the sun and of war.'

'Not surprising, I suppose. But don't keep me waiting on tenterhooks. Did old Set manage to do for Horus too?'

'It was a close run thing, I can tell you. They had many struggles. For eighty long years. One involves,' she put her lips to his ear, 'semen and lettuce, but we will pass over that.'

Monty gave a snort.

'To finish quickly,' Jessie declared, 'there was a bit of old-fashioned cheating by Horus in a boat race, which meant he won the throne of all Egypt. And he ripped off Set's testicles, making him as barren as the desert.'

'Ouch!'

'But Set got his revenge by gouging out one of Horus' eyes – the fabled Eye of Horus.'

'What then?'

'That's it, really.'

'What? They all lived happily ever after?'

'No. But Horus won. Good over evil.'

'Is that what this is about?' Monty's look was abruptly sombre.

She shook her head, a sudden tightness in her chest. 'How do we know who is good and who is evil?'

In the midst of the heat and chatter in the carriage, the question lay unanswered.

'We have to rely on our own judgement,' Monty said eventually. 'It's all we have.'

'Yes. But can we trust it?'

Monty released a long sigh. 'You women!'

'Pardon?'

'You women. You and Isis. Determined to risk everything to save your beloved brothers.'

It hadn't occurred to her. Isis and herself. Scouring Egypt for traces of their brother. Somehow, in some inexplicable way, it made a difference. She rested a hand on Monty's wrist and turned her head to look out of the window at the fleeing desert where Set lived with his curved snout and forked tail, and nothing but scorpions for company.

The solidity of Monty's flesh and bone under her fingers kept her mind away from the thought that Set was also the god of storms.

The third reason that the long journey from Cairo to Luxor proved to be entertaining was more unexpected. Monty was reading the *Egyptian Gazette* while Jessie was working out whether to ask the smart Egyptian gentleman opposite if he knew of a good hotel in Luxor, when the ticket collector in scarlet uniform and gold sash entered the carriage looking apologetic.

'Miss Kenton?' he asked.

'Yes.'

'Do you have a friend travelling on this train?'

'Yes, I do. He's sitting right here.'

'No.' The official bowed politely to Monty. He was the sort of man with kindly eyes who looked as though he lived with too many women in his household. He had the unassuming browbeaten manner of a man used to being in the wrong. 'I'm sorry to disturb you, Miss Kenton, but I am referring to an Egyptian friend.'

She was surprised. 'No, no one I know.'

'Ah, I thought as much. He claims you will pay for his ticket.'

'Who is this person?' she asked.

'A nobody. Don't concern yourself, madam.'

There was a sudden flash of white teeth as a young face pushed in under his arm and bright black eyes peered in at her with a grin.

'It is me, Missie Kenton. Malak.'

35

Georgie

England 1932

You are here. But you are not here. You do not listen to what I say. You barely speak. You run hands through your hair so roughly that threads of gold float down on your shoulders, and you kick my Indian exercise club so that it rolls back and forth across the floor.

'I want you to go,' I say.

'To leave?'

'Yes.'

You upset me when you are like this. It makes me feel bad inside. I get jittery and nervous because you don't want to be here.

'I have a problem,' you say.

I don't look at you. I open the wardrobe door a crack and peek at the darkness inside. Would you notice if I crept in there for a while? Some people are addicted to alcohol, others to chocolate or cocaine. When I am upset, I am addicted to darkness.

I don't know what to do. I don't know what to say.

'Go and look it up,' you mutter.

'Pardon?'

'On the list, the list of answers.'

'I want you to go,' I mumble again.

'Well, hard luck.' You are flicking your lighter on and off, on and off, and it is driving me crazy.

'Look it up,' you shout at me.

I leave the wardrobe door ajar and pull out the list from my bedside cabinet. I read through it slowly, testing out each possibility in my head. I reject the *please* and *thank you* and travel down to the two last ones. *I'm sorry if I have offended you* and the new one: *You seem unhappy. What has happened?* I regard them with distaste. I do not know how I can have offended you. You arrived like this today. It was nothing I did. But I know that doesn't mean I am not at fault in some way. *Blissful ignorance*, you call it. Ignorance, yes. Blissful, no.

The *What has happened?* question is worse.

I don't want to know what has happened, I just want you back the way you were, back to normal. I have tried different topics of conversation like the latest finds at Medinet Habu. Or whether the new construction of Broadcasting House in Portland Place will expand the BBC's horizons in ways that excite you but won't affect me one jot. That kind of question usually gets you all fired up. Today you stare at my shoes and don't even hear what I say.

Whatever has happened is bad. So I don't want to know about it.

'You seem unhappy,' I say miserably. 'What has happened?'

For the first time you look at me. I glance fleetingly at your face and go to stand right next to the door of the wardrobe. Alarm is chewing on my eyeballs and I need to put them in the dark.

'Georgie, come over here.'

I shuffle a pace closer. You start to talk about our father, about the meetings you attend with him to listen to Sir Oswald Mosley speaking about Fascism and what it will do for this country. I watch my fingers tear a button from my shirt because I am so frightened. You have never done this before, telling me things about Pa.

'You and I have talked about Sir Francis Galton before,' you say carefully. 'Remember?'

'Of course I remember.'

'Tell me.'

'He was the cousin of Charles Darwin and invented the science of eugenics. He put forward the idea that it was possible to produce a highly gifted race of men by selective breeding.'

'And?'

'And discourage the reproduction of undesirables in society.' I walk away from you and pick up my heavy Indian club. 'I know that I am an undesirable.'

'Pa knows that too.'

I swing the club. 'I am not going to reproduce.'

You watch the club. 'Pa spoke to me last night about Adolf Hitler's ideas on maintaining racial purity among the Aryans and about the huge following for Galton's ideas in America and here in Britain at the eugenics centre in Lambeth.'

I raise the wooden club and swing it down onto my bed. The springs moan.

'Pa is very much in favour of the idea,' you tell me.

I swing the club again.

'Georgie, listen to me. I am worried.'

'I want you to leave now. Come back when you—'

'Damn you, Georgie, I am not leaving.'

You are shouting. I cover my ear with my left hand to block out the noise but keep the club in my right.

'I am worried,' you say more calmly, 'that he might be planning to . . .'

You stop. You start to make strange sobbing noises at the back of your throat. I back away further.

'I am worried,' you say again, 'that he will not . . .'

'Shut up! Shut up! Shut up!'

'Don't,' you hiss at me. 'The whitecoats will come.'

I lift the Indian club with both my hands and slam it against the wardrobe door, which splinters into a thousand pieces and the noise scrapes on my eardrums.

The whitecoats come and they make you leave.

I have snakes in my head. It has not been a good week for me, not since you came and talked about Pa. The snakes are there, slithering through cracks in my skull. I hear them. All the time. Their hissing and their squirming, the rustle of their dry scales against the moist curls and coils of my brain.

They are so boisterous that at times I dig a finger deep in my ear to try to hook one out. I am so desperate that I ask Dr Churchward to examine my ears with an otoscope to check on what the serpents are doing in there, but he laughs and sticks a needle in my arm instead. I even insist that he must use the brutal electric wires, attach them to my skull because it is the only way to kill the snakes – to shock them to death. But he refuses and forces a tablet into my mouth. I think about what you told me about Pa's championing of eugenics and I quickly sick the tablet up in the secrecy of my doorless wardrobe. When you come, I am sitting in the gloom of the wardrobe staring at the tablet in its puddle of beetroot, redder and more ferocious than blood. I know it is beetroot, but it still scares me.

You pace. Your footsteps sharp and accusing. I pull a shirt off a hanger and drape it over my face.

'Georgie,' you say. 'Get out here.'

I hiss in tune with the snakes, so that I won't hear you. You wait a while, then you sit down on my bed. You never sit on my bed unless I am on it. I hiss louder.

You say, 'I'll do you a deal. You come out of there and I'll give you this.'

You don't say what *this* is.

I am forced to remove the shirt. You are holding up a new record for my gramophone. I scurry out of the wardrobe and snatch it from your hand to see who it is. It is Louis Armstrong . I squeal with delight, remove it from its mouse-brown sleeve and place it on the turntable. I wind the handle and carefully position the needle in the groove, and when the notes of the trumpet pour into the room, they silence the snakes. I stomp triumphantly across the floor, grinding them into dust under my feet.

I am bereft when the music stops. I start to wind the handle again but you say no.

'Sit down and listen to me, Georgie. That was the deal.'

'That wasn't the deal.'

'Sit. Down.'

I sit. Scared. But the snakes have not returned, so I smile.

'Don't,' you say.

'Don't what?'

'Don't pull faces at me.'

I am disappointed. I shrug and let the smile fall off my face.

'Today,' you say, 'big things are going to happen.'

I look at the wardrobe.

'No,' you say. 'Stay where you are.'

I stay.

'You are going to have to trust me, Georgie. Do you trust me?'

I nod.

'Good,' you say.

But I *don't* trust you. You are going to do something bad to me. I know it, but I don't know how I know it.

'Listen hard, Georgie. I am going to get you out of this place today.'

Air drains out of my lungs as I look at your face and see you are completely serious. Not one of your jokes. I throw myself on my knees and slam my forehead on the floor to wake up the snakes again. I want their noise to drown out the sepulchral sound of your voice.

'I don't trust them.' Your words are quiet and you prod me with your foot. 'Get up.'

I stay down.

'Georgie, don't be difficult. We have to leave. I haven't got long. I went to a séance last night and . . . '

'A séance?'

'Yes. That's not the point. Some people want me to go to Egypt immediately.'

I raise my head. 'Egypt?'

'Yes. Secretly.'

'Why?'

'It doesn't matter why.' Your words tumble out in a rush to batter my ears. 'This is the point. I have told them I can't leave you here, as I don't know when I'll be back. Remember what happened to you last time I was in Egypt two years ago?'

I don't want to remember.

'So this time, Georgie boy, you are coming with me.'

My jaw drops. I am too shocked to scream. Slowly I start to crawl across the floor to the wardrobe.

'No!' Your grey-flannelled legs stand in front of me. 'It's that or . . .'

'Or die,' I finish. 'I would rather die.'

You – who know better than to touch me – seize me by the shoulders and yank me to my feet. You shake me till my teeth rattle.

'Well, hard luck, brother. I'm the one making the choices.' You lift your large heavy canvas knapsack from beside the door and pull out a black eye-mask. 'With or without?'

'I'm not going.'

From the knapsack pocket you remove something enclosed in a box. You open the box. It contains a syringe. 'With or without?' you ask again.

I look at you, grief-stricken. You have turned into Dr Churchward. My legs are shaking. A high thin wail comes out of my mouth.

You grab my arm and push up my sleeve. I hold it there obediently like one of Pavlov's dogs. You stick in the needle as if I am a pin cushion.

We are on the roof.

I don't remember how we get here, how we climb the drainpipe, how you stop the ear-splitting wail coming out of my mouth. All I remember is you taking my cheeks between your strong hands, with your nose so close to mine it feels like the sun has dropped from the sky and is blasting heat in my face. Your mouth is all crooked.

'Don't let me down, Georgie,' you say.

I think you mean let you down from the roof, so I shake my head. Now we are on the roof and from your knapsack you drag a rope-ladder. I stare at it without realising what it is for, and when you drag me to the far end of the roof where I have never been, I start to sway from side to side, as though the wind is buffeting me. The snakes are silent. So I close my eyes with relief and find I am falling asleep on my feet like a horse.

'Christ, Georgie. Move!'

I force up my eyelids and prop them open with my fingers. I can't recall why we're up here but it is pleasant, with a faint trickle of autumn sunlight fingering the back of my neck. I try to sit down.

'Here! Georgie!'

You seize my hands and put them on a vent-pipe that is sticking up just behind the low balustrade. You have hooked the rope ladder over it.

'How did you know it was here?' I ask placidly.

'I have prepared for this eventuality.'

You are curt. Rude, I think. But my tongue has settled on the bottom of my mouth and lies there inert. It does dawn on me slowly that you must have been up here without me. I am jealous.

'Now down the ladder,' you order.

'No.'

'Just do it.'

'No.'

'Please, Georgie.'

'No.'

Before I can object, you push the eye-mask on my head and have me over the parapet, my feet clinging to the ladder. It is wobbly. I screech. You push a brown gob-stopper sweet into my mouth that tastes of flavours I have never before encountered. I roll it round my mouth.

'Down,' you hiss. Like one of the snakes.

I descend. Uncertainly. And slowly. Hand under hand, foot under foot. The taste of sweetness on my idle tongue. You follow above me, and when I reach the ground you jump the last part, snatch off my mask and drag me into a run through a part of the garden I have never seen before.

'Well done, Georgie. You'd make a spiffing burglar.'

'But you are the burglar, Tim,' I say, my words thick and lifeless in my mouth. 'You are stealing me.'

'True. Don't slow down. Keep running.'

I can't run. Parts of me are shutting down.

'Over the wall now.'

A wooden ladder stands in front of us, propped up against the high garden wall by two men I've never seen before. It's obvious they know you. They frighten me. Scare my limbs rigid. I can't move.

You look at me closely and I hear you swear under your breath. Gently, as if I am a kitten, you put an arm around my waist and draw me forward, one step at a time. I have to glare at my feet to make them stumble forward. I want to knock your arm away, I want to run back to the house and bang on the front door to beg them to let me in.

'Climb,' you say softly in my ear.

I climb.

36

Thebes.

King of cities.

City of the king of gods, the great and glorious Amun-Ra.
Fabled capital of Ancient Egypt. Clenched fist of military might.

Centre of learning and profound wisdom, pinnacle of political
power twelve hundred years before Christ set foot in this world.

Thebes was all these things.

Waset was its Egyptian name found in ancient texts and meaning
City of the Sceptre. Let all who gaze upon the place bow down in
awe to the great god Amun-Ra. Given the name *Thebai* by the
ancient Greeks, corrupted to Thebes by Egyptians, it is a city that
has stared in the face of Ra, vying with the sun itself for the brightness of its gold and the immensity of its power. But it is a city that
has also swallowed the dust of the desert and crumbled to ruins
because its hubris inflicted humiliation and destruction.

Thebes became nothing. In its place rose two small villages, Luxor
and Karnak, existing like vultures on the tourism of the dead.

Luxor.

Where Jessie had pinned her hopes.

*

The heat of Luxor hit them even at this hour of the evening. Jessie stripped off her gloves and removed her hat, fanning herself with it, in awe of Monty who had the ability of the English upper classes to regard the heat as nothing more than an unwanted guest at a party and ignore it completely. He strode around in the moonlight gathering their luggage, sweeping aside the begging street urchins, summoning a taxi carriage and producing a native fly-whisk for her, all without breaking sweat or losing his smile.

He found them a suitable hotel, the Blue Nile. Small, discreet and clean. He inspected their rooms for cockroaches before signing the register, declared them habitable, but wanted a torn mosquito net stitched and demanded fresh limes and boiled water to make a drink. The hotel staff in white *galabayas* bowed happily and scurried around to do his bidding. The problem, as Jessie saw it, was not the hotel, the problem was Malak.

The young Egyptian boy weighed on her conscience. He had hopped on the train specially to travel to Luxor with her, so now she had no choice but to feel responsible for him. What would his mother say about it? And his wide-eyed little sisters? Train-travel in Egypt turned out to be extravagantly cheap, so the cost of the boy's fare was negligible, but she and Monty were not here to be shown around the ancient sites by a child-guide. They didn't need a puppy at their heels.

'Here, Malak, take this,' she told him outside their hotel. 'Catch the first train home to Cairo in the morning.'

The boy had let his gaze rest on the money she was offering, his mobile young face a mix of emotions. Desire to pocket the Egyptian pounds struggled against his disappointment at being forced to leave her. He wiped his palms on his grubby striped tunic, as though wiping their greed away. He shook his head melodramatically and applied a soulful droop to his eyes.

'Missie Kenton, I help you. I stay.' He nodded so enthusiastically, his head was in danger of bouncing off. 'I stay yes.'

'No,' Monty declared sternly. He flipped at the boy with the fly-whisk. 'Skedaddle! Shoo! Off with you.'

Malak started to do what he was told, but with sagging shoulders and walking backwards, his sad eyes fixed pleadingly on Jessie.

'Oh, all right,' she sighed and he hopped back to her side, grinning broadly. 'But just one day, that's all. You can fetch and carry for us tomorrow, but then,' she wagged a finger at him and pushed the money into his hand, 'back on the train to your family.'

He danced around her. 'I much help. Good boy. You kind and beautiful. You goddess angel from the sun. You lovely lady. You . . .'

'Enough,' Monty roared at the boy. 'Go!'

'I find uncle. I come back.'

'Tomorrow,' Jessie told him.

He vanished into the gloom. Monty gave her a look.

'Yes, yes, I know,' she shrugged. 'I'm stupid.'

'No,' he said with a smile. 'I think the little brat got it right. You goddess angel from the sun.'

'Shut up!'

'Don't blame me,' he laughed, 'when the little blighter robs you blind and parades around Cairo in your new sunhat.'

'You never know, he might come in useful. He knows Luxor.'

Abruptly the laughter drained out of them. Jessie felt it puddle in the dirt road at their feet, as the thought of what tomorrow might hold brought them back to reality.

Reality was Tim.

Monty came to her room that night. His skin wrapped itself around hers, warm and inviting, his hands explored her body bringing forth strange unfamiliar sounds that ripped from her throat. Startling her.

They took their time, lingering over kisses and over the discovery of what pleased, what roused and what drove each to a frenzy of need. He demanded more of her this time, she could feel it, a kind of pulling at her from within. So that she found herself releasing the locks she had put in place for so many years. Opening doors to him. Clinging to the heart of this man. Breathless and consumed by a heat that scorched her. They stretched time. Elongated it. For what felt like hours they luxuriated in each other, and no other moment existed for them. So it sent a ripple of shock through them both when the dawn call of the muezzin drifted through the shutters, calling the faithful of Luxor to prayer.

Jessie lay contentedly with her head nestled on Monty's shoulder, their bodies and limbs locked together. Hearts slowing to a steadier beat, as thin threads of sunlight reached for the bed and started to creep up their naked legs.

Monty's lips touched her forehead. 'Tell me something about you that I don't know.'

It was another step. Another flinging wide of a door. Jessie smiled and opened her mouth to tell him of the day when, as a child, she went scrumping apples in a neighbour's garden very early one morning. While she was perched up in the tree, her mouth full of apple, her feet balanced on a lichen-tufted branch, a mother fox had pranced daintily into the garden. Behind her scampered a shadow of three young cubs. The vixen proceeded to frolic, there was no other word for it. She leapt and gambolled, chased her cubs, bowled them over and nuzzled their pointy little faces. Lovingly she washed their ears and nibbled dirt from their tails. At that moment Jessie wanted more than anything in the world to be one of those cubs.

She opened her mouth to say all this to Monty. To open that door. But those were not the words that came out.

'I had another brother,' she told him. 'Called Georgie. He disappeared.'

She heard his breathing slow.

'When did he disappear?' His voice was quiet. Flat as glass.

'When I was seven. He was five.'

'What happened?'

'I don't know. He was a very difficult child. I think my parents couldn't cope with him any more and they put him in a home of some sort. They would never tell me.'

'You didn't see this Georgie again?'

'No.'

'Is he still alive?'

'I have no idea.'

'Oh, Jessie.'

'I've never told anyone before.'

He wrapped his arms more tightly around her and pulled her against his bare chest, as though he could thrust her behind his ribs to keep her safe. They lay like that for a long while in silence, except for the wailing call to prayer dying away.

'Now,' she said firmly after a while, 'let's talk about where we start today.'

He propped himself up on one elbow and looked down at her face, studying it minutely, as though committing every line of every feature to memory.

'Where do we start?'

'Well,' she said, 'that's not hard to guess.'

'The king's tomb? King Tutankhamen's resting place.'

She stretched up and kissed his strong chin. Felt the early morning stubble against her lips. 'Right first time. Nothing gets past you.' She smiled. To show she was under control once more.

'Promise me one thing,' he said.

'What's that?'

'That you won't leave my side this time.'

She rested her cheek against his chest, listening to the relentless beat of his heart. 'I promise.'

The Valley of the Kings was nothing like Jessie expected. It was a bleached barren rocky hell-on-earth, where life was not welcome and the sun's heat roared off boulders and crashed against any uncovered flesh. The sky was an immense blinding blue, the brightness an assault on the eyes. Nothing lived here. Nothing. Even lizards and scorpions thought twice. But flies came, swarms of them drawn by the sweat of the men and women brazen enough to venture into the valley of death and by the steaming dung of the donkeys and camels that brought them here.

Malak had been waiting outside their hotel, crouched in a sandy patch of shade with a patience that struck Jessie as far beyond the grasp of English children.

305

'Good morning, Malak.' She had brought him flatbread rolled around goat's cheese from the breakfast table.

'*Ahlan*, lovely lady, hello.' He accepted his breakfast with grace, not with greed, and eyed Monty with respect. 'Good sir,' he salaamed politely, 'I have boat for you, best felucca on Nile, yes sir yes.' He waved his bread in the direction of the river. 'My cousin, he sail, cousin Akil, very good sail yes.'

Monty flipped a coin at him. 'Good lad. We intend to visit the tombs on the West Bank, so ... '

'Akil, he sail you to cross river.'

Monty gave a wry smile and flipped a second coin, that Malak snatched out of the air. 'My uncle rich rich man. He own boat and many many horse. Camel? You want camel?'

'No, thank you,' Jessie said. 'Horses will do.'

She saw Monty's eyes brighten at the prospect of a ride and, surprisingly, Malak arranged it all beautifully. The felucca spread its giant triangular sail like a great white swan and Akil steered them across to the opposite bank of the Nile, the wide river brown and turbulent beneath them at this time of year. It was not long since the inundation when the Nile floods and spreads its rich black silt over the land. Waiting for them on the West Bank were two bay mares with black manes and tails, in slightly better condition than many of the gaunt hollow-ribbed creatures that ambled listlessly through the streets, pulling carts and carriages.

Monty fondled their ears and scratched their dusty necks, and from his pockets produced an apple for each of them that he had snaffled from the breakfast table. The animals munched contentedly but Malak pulled a face at the indulgence of wasting a good apple on a horse. They swung into the rough saddles and rode up from the river through green strips of fertile fields of sugarcane and cabbages, then up a dusty track past mud-brick houses into the bleak desert hills. The relentlessly harsh landscape was carved up by dry valleys that cut through the Theban Hills, and it was into the east valley that they turned, the Valley of the Kings – *Wadi Biban el-Muluk* – where the pharaohs' tombs lay hidden.

Jessie was overwhelmed by the place. It seemed to throb with heat and silence. Above it all loomed a great limestone escarpment whose cliffs were painted rose-pink in the morning light.

'Look,' Jessie pointed out, but in the kind of hushed voice she used in church. 'There's the Qurn.'

It was a pyramid, but a naturally formed one on the peak of the escarpment, and dedicated to the goddess Hathor.

'It gives me the creeps,' she muttered. 'Faintly sinister.'

'Don't get carried away,' Monty chided.

But when two kites effortlessly dipped their wings and circled the peak, she noticed that Monty turned his back on their eerie piercing cries. A number of other tourists were already tramping the valley, all pestered for business by dragomen from the local villages, but Monty brushed the guides aside and headed straight for King Tutankhamen's tomb. The tombs of many great pharaohs had been excavated in the valley, their entrances marked by clearly outlined square doorways cut into the face of the limestone cliffs; some open to the public but some with metal gates barring access.

As they approached the small opening of King Tutankhamen's tomb Jessie was disconcerted by a sudden racing of her pulse. She was nervous. But there was no reason to be. It was just a hole in the ground, for heaven's sake, decorated with paintings. It was absurd to be nervous. But there was something about the place, something unreal and something unnervingly powerful.

'Ready?' Monty asked.

'Of course.' She faked a smile.

As she stared into the darkness, she was blinded after the scorching brilliance outside. The entrance was low and immediately descended a flight of steep steps cut into the rock. The tunnel down to the Tomb itself was dimly lit and so close and narrow that Jessie experienced a rush of claustrophobia. It was as though the walls were coming at her, preparing to crush the air out of her lungs under tons of rock, but she fixed her eyes on the figure of Monty in front of her, bent over to avoid the low roof, and kept going. She placed each foot where he had placed his on the sandy path and eventually found herself entering the sunken burial chamber.

She gasped. Every fear and uncertainty that had plagued her since she'd entered this valley of death fell from her like dead leaves. Her heart was pounding. Her mouth was dry. But this time it was with excitement. The interior of the chamber was the most achingly beautiful thing she'd ever seen. Vivid colours and images of life-size figures decorated each wall from floor to ceiling, all painted on a background of vibrant gold. Even in the dim light of the tomb it was breathtaking.

Oddly, the tomb was unexpectedly hot, not like the cool caves of Britain. It felt like the breath of the dead, making the air thick and heavy, but the silence within the tomb was so deep it did strange things to her mind. It penetrated her brain. She realised she was holding her breath, unwilling to ripple the smooth surface of the silence by moving the air. Time seemed to stop in the tomb. It became irrelevant, unwanted and unheeded. The watch on her wrist became an obscenity.

She stood transfixed in front of the western wall where paintings of baboons, twelve of them, were crouched ready to leap out on her. Vaguely she was aware behind her of a guide entering the chamber with a group of chattering tourists whom he started to regale with the story of the baboon wall. Together they represented the twelve hours of the night through which Tutankhamen must pass before reaching the afterlife. But the boy king had fortunately been presented with a boat in the top right hand corner to assist him on his journey.

She thought for a moment about that boat. In it stood a scarab beetle, its big horny body supported on spindly legs, and it occurred to her how much a small boat can carry, even a small boat like a felucca on the Nile. How easy it would be for someone to travel through the baboons at night.

'Excuse me, madam?'

Jessie became aware of a slightly built man standing at her elbow in the dimly lit corner of the tomb, a grey *galabaya* swamping his

308

figure and a white turban wound around his head. The scent of cinnamon hung around him. His dark eyes were serious, his manner deferential. He did not seem like one of the persistent beggars, yet he stood too close the way they did and she had the feeling he wanted something from her.

'Yes?'

'You are interested in tomb?'

'Of course.'

'My brother is a learned man. He knows much about tombs. He would be willing to give you a tour of . . .'

She stepped back from him. 'No, thank you.' She turned to walk away but he held onto the strap of her handbag that hung over her shoulder, preventing her from leaving.

'I am Ahmed,' he said softly. 'I can help you.'

She glanced over at Monty who was listening to a guide pointing out the depiction of Tutankhamen in the form of Osiris with his vizier, Ay, dressed as a priest. The guide was describing in detail the performing of the opening of the mouth ceremony to bring the dead king to life.

'I do not want your help,' she said in a curt tone and removed her bag's strap from his grip.

He said something soft in Arabic. She paused, expecting him to translate, but when he didn't, she moved away to study another section of the tomb wall. As she stood facing the eastern wall, a painted image of the mummified body of the king beneath a canopy floated unseen in front of her eyes. All she could focus on was the man Ahmed's serious eyes and his serious words, *I can help you.*

Could he help her? Could he mean something other than as a tour guide?

On impulse she turned quickly. She would speak to him again. But her eyes sought in vain for the white turban among the shadows of the tomb. He had gone. She hadn't seen or heard him move, yet he was no longer there. Despite the heat of the place, her skin grew cold.

309

She let her hand find the warmth of Monty's broad back and he turned instantly.

'Are you all right?'

She nodded. 'Fresh air, I think.'

His eyes narrowed, then he scanned the people in the tomb. After a moment's consideration, he said, 'Let's go.' He steered her towards the exit.

But it was already too late. She sensed that something had changed in some subtle way that she didn't quite understand. She could feel the air heavy in her lungs, smell the cloying scent of the cinnamon that had marked out Ahmed, and she experienced an odd reluctance to touch her bag because he had touched it.

As she climbed the steep steps hewn into the rock, ducking her head to avoid the sloping roof-line of the tunnel, she knew something had happened inside the golden tomb, but she didn't know what.

'Well?'

'Nothing.' Jessie sipped her glass of lime juice.

'Are you sure?'

'Yes.'

She didn't look at Monty. She didn't know how to explain what had happened in the tomb this morning. It would be like trying to explain the wisps of a dream, too insubstantial to put into words.

They were seated at a bamboo table in the tiny perfumed garden at the back of their hotel in Luxor, where palm trees offered cooling shade and a profusion of oleanders and zinnias tumbled from pots and well-watered beds, providing a riot of pinks and reds in this muted world. It satisfied Jessie's innate desire as an artist for colour and she was delighted when Monty plucked a scarlet blossom and tucked it behind her ear. Malak, after returning the sweating horses to his uncle, was squatting under one of the tables, tucking into falafel and pita bread, licking the grease from his fingers with relish.

Monty drew out two cigarettes, lit them both and handed one to

Jessie. He kept his gaze on the boy as he said casually, 'But something upset you in there. You say you found nothing in the tomb that could give you a clue about Tim, no trace of him, and I understand that must have been distressing for you.' He exhaled a string of smoke at a passing butterfly. 'But there was something else.' He glanced across at her. 'Wasn't there?'

A small silence drifted onto their table. For a few seconds they let it lie there, but when the gut-wrenching groan of a camel somewhere nearby disrupted the moment, Jessie took a mouthful of lime juice and nodded.

'Yes, there *was* something else, you're right. But it was too insignificant to mean anything, and I was stupid to get upset over it.'

'Tell me.'

So she told him. About Ahmed. About his hand on her bag and his murmured *I can help you*. What she didn't mention was the intangible sense of something having happened.

'Did you see him outside the tomb?' Monty asked. 'Touting for business with other tourists, perhaps?'

'No.'

Monty looked from Jessie's face to her handbag that hung on the back of her chair.

'May I?' he asked, indicating the bag.

Without a word Jessie unhooked it from the chair and handed it over to Monty as cautiously as if it contained a hand-grenade. The bag was a good-sized tan leather one in which she carried her sketchpad and pencils, a set of chalks, a pen and a purse, plus the usual female detritus of powder compact, lipstick, handkerchief and hair comb. In addition there was a small penknife and a chiffon scarf to cover her hair if needed. Monty inspected the fastening. The bag had a flap that folded over the top and was secured by a press-stud fixing. He popped it open. He glanced over at Jessie and raised one thick eyebrow in a question.

'Feel free,' she told him.

He upended the bag and, with a shake, deposited the contents

311

onto the table in a rush. The clatter made the boy look up. Alert for treasure, he stuffed the last of the pita in his mouth and sidled over. Monty inspected the heap of goods and looked at Jessie.

She was staring, jaw rigid, at the jumble of items.

'What is it?' he asked instantly. 'What do you see?'

'The watch,' she breathed and jabbed a finger at the timepiece visible under the chiffon scarf. 'That's Tim's watch.'

37

Jessie didn't touch the watch. She didn't need to. She heard its message loud and clear. Time was running out. Time was slipping like sand through their fingers and if she didn't do something quickly, it would be too late.

Too late for what? She didn't dare think.

Monty lifted the watch from under the scarf and examined it, a furrow of concentration between his eyebrows. The watch was beautiful. It was a Dunhill with an elegant rectangular white face and large gold numerals. He fingered its brown leather strap speculatively and asked, 'How can you be sure it's Tim's?'

'Turn it over.'

He did so. She knew what he would see engraved on the back. *1928 Now you are a man, my son. Pa.* Typical Pa. A Rudyard Kipling quotation, packed with Victorian melodrama.

'It was a gift,' she told Monty. 'For Tim's twenty-first birthday. He would never be parted from it willingly.'

His face remained carefully neutral. 'It could be a message from Tim to you. The watch could be the one thing he was certain you would recognise, but if he was using it as a sign to tell you to trust that man, why didn't Ahmed show it to you and deliver the message?'

Jessie didn't speak. Couldn't speak. The answer to Monty's question was too unthinkable to give words to. Above them the sky was clear as glass, and the noises of the street – the rumble of carts and the shouts of deep-voiced men – were winding up for another bustling day. Malak still hovered beside their table.

'Very much nice watch yes,' he murmured.

Monty replaced it next to the pile of her belongings. Jessie's hands wanted to snatch it up, to hold it, to press it to her ear, to run a finger along the inside of the strap and over the inscription where it had touched his flesh. They wanted to find traces of Tim on the watch, of his skin and of his sweat, but she refused to let them. If she picked up the watch, it would be acknowledging that it was hers now, not his.

'The other question,' Monty said, still in his neutral tone, 'is how this Ahmed knows you are Tim's sister.'

It sent a shiver through Jessie and she glanced instinctively around the garden, seeking watchful eyes, even though they were alone.

'I think we should go out there again,' she said. 'To the tomb.'

'Are you sure?'

She didn't want to go back to that place of the dead, but she gave herself no choice. 'Yes.'

'I agree. If they – whoever *they* are – are keeping a close eye on us, there is a good chance that Ahmed may make contact again.' He glanced sideways at the boy. 'This time I think we'll go alone.'

Jessie blinked. 'Malak?'

'We can't be too careful.'

'No,' she said firmly. 'Not Malak.'

The boy heard his name, and his berry-black eyes danced from one to the other, but he could not follow the meaning of their conversation.

'Wait here,' Monty said and rose to his feet.

He swept the heap of her belongings back into her handbag, lingering for a moment over her sketchpad as if tempted to open it. He placed the watch thoughtfully in an inside pocket of the bag and snapped the fastening shut. Both of them seemed to breathe easier now that the watch was out of sight.

'I'm going to pop up to my room to fetch a map. Won't be a tick. Better to know exactly how the land lies.'

'Good idea.'

Neither gave voice to the thoughts crowding their minds. Monty hung the strap of her bag back on her chair, and as he did so, he rested a hand on her shoulder, his thumb pressing lightly on her collar-bone.

'The game is afoot,' he said, 'my fine fellow.'

She tilted her head back to look up at him, outlined against the blue sky. 'Life,' she said, 'as Sherlock told us, is always more daring than any effort of the imagination.'

He gave her a half-smile and his thumb stroked her collar-bone for a fraction of a second, then he was gone. The garden felt cooler without him.

'Miss Kenton?'

'Yes.'

'A lady is here to see you.'

Jessie was still in the garden, holding her handbag close on her lap, picturing the watch inside. She was expecting Monty to return any minute with his map and she looked with surprise at the attendant in his white robe.

'But I don't know any ladies in Luxor, so who . . . ?' Then it dawned on her. 'Maisie Randall.' She must have arrived early.

Jessie jumped to her feet with a smile on her face and hurried through to the hotel's reception area, where Maisie's tall intimidating figure would cause a stir among the staff, but there was no one. It was empty. She turned to the attendant and he waved a hand towards the entrance doors.

'Out there,' he said cheerfully.

Jessie walked out into the hot street and the smile of welcome melted from her face. It wasn't Maisie. In the quiet shadows of an arched doorway stood Anippe Kalim. Swathed in black from head to toe, she stepped forward with a greeting, but Jessie was too angry to bother with it.

'Why did you run?' she demanded. 'Why did you make me chase you all over Cairo?'

'I am sorry,' the young woman said in a low voice, but her face was still proud, her bearing that of Queen Nefertiti. The apology was worthless.

'Why didn't you stop and talk to me?'

Anippe lowered her eyes. 'I did not want to get Timothy's sister into trouble.'

'Trouble?'

Two smart Egyptian men walked past in suits and tarbooshes and spoke disapprovingly at Jessie in Arabic before moving on.

'They don't like a woman to shout in the street,' Anippe told her. 'It is unseemly.'

'So is getting me lost in Cairo's backstreets.'

Anippe nodded. No denial.

'Where is Tim?' Jessie demanded, holding with one hand onto a fold of Anippe's voluminous robe. No escape this time.

The Egyptian woman's striking face was all that was visible of her and Jessie scanned it eagerly for signs of distress but found none. She was tempted to take that as a good sign, a sign that Tim was unhurt.

'Where is Tim?' she asked again.

The black eyes regarded her solemnly. 'Come with me. I have something to show you.'

'Is it Tim?'

'You shall see.' She turned and started walking away, down the dusty street of low buildings.

'Wait! I must first tell my companion that I am . . .'

But the black figure did not wait, did not stop or even glance behind. She lengthened her stride.

'Anippe!'

Anger burned in her chest. What was Anippe doing? Jessie didn't want to leave the hotel without informing Monty – she had promised him – but the attendant had vanished and there was no one else in sight.

Anippe turned a corner.

That decided it. With a curse, Jessie ran. This time she caught up with the Egyptian woman quickly and side by side they hurried through the town. They left behind the fine houses of Luxor with their elegant arches, fountains and columns, and their scrolled latticework, and instead they entered the old town where Europeans did not stray. Men with skin like leather and long tortoise necks above their flowing robes inspected Jessie with hard hostile eyes when she strode as an interloper through their bleak impoverished alleyways. The streets grew narrow enough to create shade for most of the day and desert-coloured dogs dug their way into the heaps of rubbish that littered the corners.

Jessie wished she had brought Malak with her, so that he could run back to Monty with news or at least speak for her to the woman weaving on her doorstep or the one grinding corn while her barefoot child picked fleas off a dog. She wanted these women to remember her. If Monty came looking.

'Anippe!' Jessie came to a halt. 'Anippe, this is far enough. Tell me what it is you want to show me.'

Anippe didn't break her stride but just kept walking fast.

'Anippe! Where is Tim?'

Reluctantly the black-robed woman slowed and glanced behind.

'Where is he? I'm not moving from here until you tell me.'

They were in an alleyway where a man was chopping up furniture with an axe. He swung at it with such a fury that Jessie was convinced the table and cupboards were not his own. Anippe retraced her last steps until she was within touching distance of Jessie, and despite the scorching heat and the fast pace, she showed no signs of discomfort inside her robes. Her face was calm, her breathing steady.

'You want to see Tim?' she asked.

'You know I do.'

'You do not do a good job as his *uraeus*.'

317

Jessie's stomach lurched. Tim's *uraeus*. The cobra that is there to protect him.

'Stop playing these games,' Jessie snapped sharply. 'Tell me right now what has happened and where he is.'

The Egyptian woman's mouth pulled into a silent line but Jessie couldn't tell whether it was annoyance or sorrow. She felt the gulf between them widen.

'Anippe. Tell me.'

The woman nodded. Without her hair or her throat on view, she looked like a different woman from the one in the British museum, a total stranger.

'Come,' Anippe said. 'Timothy is hurt. A gunshot wound.'

Jessie's heart stopped. 'How bad?'

'Bad enough. Come,' she said again, more gently this time.

Another alleyway in the maze, another row of crumbling shutters and dark secretive interiors before Anippe suddenly veered to her right and pushed open a door. Instantly they were in a small square room with nothing in it but a threadbare rug on the floor. The place smelled of charcoal.

'This way.'

Jessie followed.

'He's in here.' The Egyptian woman pointed to a low door at the back of the house. It stood ajar and a flickering light indicated a candle inside.

'Tim!' Jessie called.

She darted through the door to her brother. The room was windowless, with a rough earthen floor. Except for the lit candle embedded in the earth in one corner, it was empty. Stark and bare. She swung round to confront Anippe, just as the solid wooden door swung shut and there was the sound of a metal bar rattling into place across it.

Jessie was totally alone.

38

'Where is she?'

The boy looked nervous. 'Gone, sir *bey*.'

Monty stopped dead in his tracks. He scanned the small garden, as if Jessie might be hiding under one of the bushes.

'Gone? Gone where?'

'I not know, sir *bey*. Missie Kenton rush out. I wait here but no return from her, no. She leave.'

'Don't be foolish, boy.' His voice was raised. She had promised. 'Of course she wouldn't leave. Did she go to her room?'

'No, sir *bey*. She go to front.' He looked thoroughly miserable and plucked at the raw threads of a rip in his tunic. 'I see.'

'If she went to the front of the hotel, which way did she go?'

'I not see.'

'Boy, you are utterly useless to me.'

He was frightened for her and angry at her, all at the same time. He had said it over and over again: *Don't wander off.* What was she thinking? Didn't she realise the importance of keeping together now? He curbed his outburst with an effort and yanked the boy back by the neck of his tunic when he started to slink away. He gave him a shake.

'What happened? Why did Miss Kenton leave?'

The boy rolled his eyes piteously. 'No my blame, sir. I sit. Wait. I good boy.'

Monty relented, releasing his grip. He dusted the boy's shoulders. 'So, good Malak, tell me what happened. I was only gone a few minutes.' He cursed his luck. An Egyptian businessman in the next room had experienced trouble with his key sticking in the lock and had asked Monty for assistance. It had delayed him.

The boy's eyes were wide and dramatic. 'Lady come.'

'What? Talk sense, boy.'

'Yes, yes true yes. Ask Hamdi.'

'Who or what is Hamdi?'

'He work this hotel.'

'Do you mean that one of the men who work here saw a lady come to talk with Miss Kenton?'

'No, *bey*.'

'Malak! Just tell me, for heaven's sake.' The boy looked ready to run, so Monty seized a handful of tunic on his chest. 'What happened to Miss Kenton?'

'Hamdi come. He say lady to see Miss Kenton.' He was squirming to escape but Monty took not a blind bit of notice. 'Missie look big smile. She say "May sandal".' He looked briefly bewildered but covered it with a big grin that would have been convincing if he hadn't been staring hopefully at the exit door from the garden. 'She want more shoes, you think, sir *bey* sir?'

'You donkey, of course she didn't need more . . .' He stopped. Glared at his captive. 'May sandal? Are you sure she didn't say Maisie Randall?'

Fierce nodding. 'That what I say. May sandal.'

Monty let go of the filthy tunic. 'Wait here, boy. Don't move a damn muscle, you hear me?'

More nodding.

Monty narrowed his eyes. 'I'll hunt you down and thrash you if you leave this garden.'

Another terrified grin. 'I stay.'

'Good!' Monty strode off into the hotel. 'Hamdi!' he called. 'Where the hell is Hamdi.'

A mild-mannered man with a quiet serenity about him that Monty immediately envied appeared out of nowhere. He bowed politely.

'Sir, how can I help you?'

'Did someone call to see Miss Kenton just now?'

The man pointed to the steps the other side of the main entrance door. 'Yes, sir. A woman stood out there and asked me to take a message to Miss Kenton to say she would like to speak to her. She didn't give a name.'

At last. Someone who could think with precision. Monty exhaled with relief, but it didn't change the fact that Jessie had vanished. If she was with Maisie, however, she should be safe. He began to calm down, as the anger started to melt into annoyance.

'Did they say where they were going?'

'No, sir.'

Monty nodded his thanks and passed over a tip that disappeared with alacrity into the pocket of the *galabaya*. It was thoughtless of Jessie in a way he didn't expect of her, to go gallivanting with Maisie without a word. He'd put money on it that she had dashed off to the tombs again. Damn it. Something there had really shaken her up this morning. After a moment's thought, he decided he would have to go chasing after the pair of them and with luck he'd overhaul them on the other bank of the river before they ventured too far. He was almost out the door before he remembered Malak. Poor little runt. He started to head in the direction of the garden, when he realised Hamdi was still standing patiently, waiting to be dismissed.

'Thank you,' Monty said courteously. Then added as an afterthought, 'Was the woman tall with a large sunhat and a black umbrella? An Englishwoman?'

Hamdi smiled gently. 'No, sir. She was Egyptian.'

Monty's jaw hit the floor. 'Egyptian?' There was only one

Egyptian woman in this whole damn country who knew Jessie by name. Anippe Kalim.

'Which way did they go?'

'They turned right.'

Monty was out of the door and racing down the street, knocking against carts and weaving through a group of women in black veils, but it was impossible. Too many turnings, too many entrances into a maze of back streets. He zigzagged through them, tripping over a crate of chickens, but in the end, hot and frustrated, he admitted defeat. Lungs heaving, shirt sticky with sweat, a band of iron tightening inside his skull, he sprinted back to the hotel and burst into the garden. The boy was standing on the exact spot in which he'd left him.

'Malak,' Monty said fiercely, 'you are a good boy. Now take me to your uncle.'

Monty walked and talked like a sane man. He spoke with the boy. Asked for his uncle's name. With all the indications of a rational human being. He didn't roar at the Nile or rip the unblinking sun from the sky which is what he raged inside to do.

The only sign of turmoil came when his foot lashed out at a sleepy lizard that was minding its own business on the gritty path down which Malak was leading him. He knew Jessie wouldn't leave him and disappear with no word, no note, not again, not this time. If she was gone, it was because she had no choice, of that he was convinced. A fist clenched his guts every time he thought of the seriousness of the trouble she could be in.

'Anippe Kalim,' he muttered under his breath as he strode behind the boy who was scampering ahead of him. As if saying her name aloud could rouse her from her snake-basket and conjure her up in front of him.

'How much further, Malak?'

'Here, just here.'

'You've been saying that for the last ten minutes, you monkey.'

Malak grinned nervously over his shoulder at Monty and

322

something that the boy saw in his face made his manner change abruptly. The grin slid away.

'We find her, *bey*,' he said. 'You and me. We find her very much soon.' Then he was off again at top speed, the dusty soles of his feet flying up behind, and it brought some relief to Monty to break into a run.

'Sir, please excuse my humble home. You are most welcome. I am honoured indeed to invite such a distinguished gentleman into my house, Allah be praised.'

'Thank you, Yasser. It is my pleasure to meet you. Your nephew here told me you are a man of great abilities and many resources.'

Yasser el Rahim glanced across at his young nephew and awarded him a nod. Monty was sure money would pass into the young boy's hand later. But Yasser himself came as a surprise. For a start, he was far younger than Monty had expected, twenty-five at most. Tall and handsome with a bush of thick black hair, there was a life and energy that radiated from him and lit up the gloomy room they were seated in. His large round eyes gleamed in antici-pation, as if every fresh breath would be the one that would be blessed by Allah and would make his fortune.

The house was small and built of mud-brick with a line of wash-ing flapping on the flat roof, but its window frames and shutters were smartly painted and it appeared to contain three rooms, plus a kitchen where a shadowy figure in black moved quietly. Brass lanterns were visible in abundance throughout the room as though it gave Yasser immense pleasure to shed light, and a low round brass table held a pitcher of fresh lemon juice. When Monty arrived unannounced with the boy, Yasser had been flicking through a colourful magazine about Egyptian film stars and sucking on a brass *hookah* pipe whose heated charcoal and *shisha* tobacco scented the air. He greeted his visitors warmly and his white teeth gleamed against his dark skin when he laughed, which he did often. It was the same infectious laugh as his nephew's.

323

Yasser clapped his hands imperiously and called out, 'Mint tea for my guest, Souad.' He flared out his olive green *galabaya* like a conjuror about to perform a trick and waved Monty to a seat covered in bright materials of red and blue and green in patterns that echoed the curls and swooping lines of Arabic script. 'Sir, please sit and tell me what I can do for you.'

Monty took his place reluctantly. He did not have time for courtesies but knew he would get nowhere in Egyptian business dealings without them.

'Thank you, Yasser. And my thanks for the arrangements this morning with the felucca and the horses.'

'Good. All went well? You enjoyed the tombs?'

'The valley is certainly interesting. My companion Miss Kenton and myself were particularly interested in King Tutankhamen's tomb.'

He laughed. 'You and half the world!'

'That's true. Many people come to Egypt now to admire its antiquities.'

Yasser's eyes brightened. 'Many many people.'

'People who need someone like you to arrange things for them.'

'Yes, indeed. If I can be of humble service, I am always glad to help them.'

I bet you are.

At that moment the black shadow from the kitchen emerged silently into the room carrying a tray which she placed on the table. Monty knew better than to look at her but he had the impression of a lighter-skinned woman with soft beautiful hands. When she had glided once more back to the kitchen, he accepted a glass of mint tea and settled down to business. Malak had been given a short length of sugarcane to chew on and he sat on his heels in a corner, relishing the fibrous sweet white heart of it.

'I am looking for someone,' Monty announced. 'I hoped you might be able to help me.'

'Ah.' Yasser's large black eyes regarded him shrewdly over the steaming rim of his glass. 'I will put all my abilities at your service, sir. Who may this person be who is missing from you?'

'My companion. An Englishwoman, Miss Jessica Kenton.'

'Indeed? The young lady who went to the tombs this morning?'

'The same.'

'So.' He put down his drink and his smile. 'Tell me.'

Monty supplied him with a rapid summary of Jessie's disappearance after they had returned to their hotel this morning.

'I need to find this young Egyptian woman, to discover who and where she is,' Monty told him. 'She must have arrived here yesterday from Cairo and has somehow persuaded Miss Kenton to go with her.'

Monty was no fool. He knew the only bait to tempt Jessie away would be Tim, though it didn't mean that her brother was still here in Luxor. Jessie could already be on her way to any god-forsaken patch of scrubby Egyptian desert in the belief that Tim was waiting for her there.

'Miss Anippe Kalim,' Yasser murmured, picking up his *shisha* pipe and twiddling the mouth-piece between his fingers to give himself time. The water gurgled in the smoke-filled glass jar with each breath. 'I am interested to know *why* she has taken your Miss Kenton.'

'I assure you, so am I.'

'No money demand for her yet?'

'No. Let me worry about that. I want you to find out who this Anippe Kalim is.' Monty lit a cigarette, took out an envelope of Egyptian bank notes from his pocket and placed it on the brass table in front of him. ' Now,' he said, his eyes fixed on Yasser's, 'let us talk business.'

Instantly the young Egyptian abandoned his *shisha* pipe and his smile leapt back in place as he reached out for the envelope, but the flat of Monty's hand clamped down on it first.

'One more thing.'

Yasser's gaze reluctantly moved away from the envelope. 'Yes?'

'There is someone else I am searching for. A man who goes by the name of either Timothy Kenton or Sir Reginald Musgrave.' He flashed a photograph in front of the other's bright black eyes. 'This man.'

The Egyptian considered it. Then nodded solemnly and shrugged. 'I will try.'

'For him I pay double.'

The white teeth gleamed. 'Then I will try harder.'

'We understand each other, I think.'

'Yes, *bey*. I will work fast.'

Monty knocked back his mint tea and rose to his feet. 'Come, Malak, we have work to do.'

They tried every hotel in Luxor. On the off-chance. It was a long shot but Monty couldn't just sit in the Blue Nile doing nothing, tormented by images of what could be happening to Jessie. Fortunately there were not many hotels in Luxor, a couple of larger ones for visiting tourists and dignitaries who expected something grander than the handful of small ones favoured by Egyptians eager to view the tombs. Monty tried them all with no success – no Anippe Kalim, no Jessica Kenton and no Sir Reginald Musgrave or Timothy Kenton. What was it that Jessie's brother was up to? What mess had he used Anippe Kalim to draw Jessie into?

At one point when he emerged on to a wider street of elaborately decorated houses overlooking the broad silvery expanse of the Nile and was just about to return to the Blue Nile Hotel to check whether Jessie had returned, a woman's voice hailed him.

'Sir Montague!'

He looked round, his heart leaping ahead of him. But it wasn't Jessie.

'Blow me down with a Nile catfish if it isn't his lordship himself.'

'Good afternoon, Maisie, I didn't expect to find you in Luxor yet.'

Maisie Randall was ambling along the riverbank under her umbrella, kicking up a wake of sand-dust, her grey muslin blouse making her resemblance to a heron on the prowl for a stray fish even stronger than usual.

'I caught the night train,' she explained cheerfully. 'That was a bloomin' nightmare I wouldn't want to repeat, I can tell you. So much snoring and shaking and screeching, you wouldn't believe it. It stopped at every little goat-hut of a station and I . . . ' she stopped. Abruptly she furled her umbrella and peered at Monty. 'What's wrong?'

39

Jessie stood in the dark. Only the thinnest lick of light around the door made it bearable. Not enough for her to see her prison, but her other senses took over. Beneath her feet the earthen floor felt cold and rough and from somewhere she could hear the throb of a generator. She smelled woodsmoke, something cooking. The ordinariness of it gave her hope. How could the world be spinning out of control when she could smell onions frying?

She wanted to scream and shout, to batter the door down. *Anippe had locked her up.* Why? Why would she lock her up?

But her thoughts jammed. They could get no further. What did Anippe hope to gain by this? It didn't make sense.

She banged on the door. She called out. Angrily at first, but then more calmly, and finally without hope. Silence sat on the other side of the door like a guard with orders to keep her shut in the small dark space. She paced it out, four paces one way, three the other, her fingertips touching the blank mudbrick walls, the emptiness of the room frightening her more than anything else. It meant someone had prepared it as a prison for her, someone had planned this.

Why?

*

The metal bar rattled out of its brackets. Jessie was off the floor and up on her feet before the sliver of light grew into a bright rectangle that momentarily blinded her. She could make out the outline of two figures silhouetted in the doorway, both male.

'Tim?'

She uttered his name but without expectation. If it were Tim he would have rushed in and thrown his arms around her in a hug that would have squeezed the breath out of her. *Sis*, he would say, *what a clever little Watson you are – to have tracked me down like this. Wounded? Of course I'm not wounded. That was Anippe being silly to get . . .*

A guttural voice said something in Arabic, shattering the fleeting fantasy she was building for herself. She blinked hard to sharpen her vision in the gloom and to clear her mind. How long had she been here crouched on the floor in the darkness, alone? She had no idea. One hour? Three hours? Not longer, surely, her thoughts crawling like rats through her head.

The guttural voice spoke again, its tone impatient this time.

'I want to speak to . . . ' she started but a strong hand seized her wrist and twisted it behind her. 'To Anippe Kalim,' she added quickly, 'or to my brother, Timothy Kenton.'

A sack descended over her head.

She screamed and kicked out with her feet, connecting with a shin-bone and bringing forth a grunt of pain. But it was like fighting one of their field oxen, muscles hardened by years of labour, and before she could even consider escape through the open door, her wrists were roped behind her back, the sack was tightened around her neck and she was on her knees in the dark. Panic swelled in her throat, blocking her airways and making a thin high whistle issue somewhere inside her head. She couldn't breathe. A drum was thudding in her chest. The blackness was inside as well as out, spreading like ink in her brain.

The voice again. It meant nothing. Her chin slumped forward but a male hand lifted it and released the bottom of the sack. Air buffeted its way in and she dragged it into her lungs until the whistling ceased. Two pairs of hands jerked her to her feet and

329

marched her through the doorway, hands that were not rough, but not gentle either. She could see a slice of the uneven ground under her feet when she peered downwards through the opening of the sack, and caught a glimpse of the bottom of the black *galabayas* swaying either side of her.

'Wait!' she shouted. She dug her heels in the ground. 'Stop this! I refuse to walk further until you—'

They didn't even break their stride. Between them the two men raised her a few inches off the ground and kept walking. It was as if she had ceased to exist as a person any more and had become just a package to deliver. The enormity hit her. Of how helpless she was. Of how pointless resistance would be. How useless, here in this vast unknown land of the pharaohs, were all her clever clues and secret signs. They dwindled to less than nothing here.

'Monty,' she whispered. 'Take care.'

The stink of diesel. The grinding of gears. The jolting and jarring of the truck as the wheels slipped and slid, fighting for a grip in the sand. The hard edges of packing crates cracked against her back and knocked her head as she was shaken and jerked from one side of the back of the truck to the other. Jessie fought for breath inside her sack. Fear sat in her throat, stolid and steadfast, never leaving her, never yielding to her rational mind. She argued with it, reasoned with it, bullied it and tormented it with all the objections her frantic thoughts could conjure up.

If they intended to kill her, they would have done so by now.

If they meant her harm, they wouldn't bother to drive her miles out into the desert in a truck first.

If they wanted to make her leave Egypt, this was the obvious way to scare her away.

If they were going to hide her somewhere, it meant a ransom and a life at the end of it.

Good reasons. Strong arguments. Clear logic. So why did the fear sit there in her throat?

*

They dragged her out of the truck and tore the sack off her head. The heat of the desert reared up and for a moment paralysed her so that her feet wouldn't move, nor her brain function. One of the black *galabayas*, the one with the dense moustache and the young earnest face, said something she couldn't understand until she realised he was holding out a goat-skin waterbag to her. He poured the warm sour-tasting water down her parched throat and that simple gesture of kindness by her captor reassured her.

'*Shukran*,' she said. 'Thank you.'

Around her the desert stretched in an endless expanse of sand, a world of buff and beige, of brown and yellow, of stony gulleys and dried-up wadis. Her eyes struggled to find focus, as everything merged into everything else. Rocks were there one moment, but gone the next. Purple shadows seemed to move restlessly from one outcrop to another, the air shimmering deceptively in the heat, and Jessie could feel the sun leeching all moisture from her skin.

Her hands were still tethered behind her back, so she could not raise an arm to shield her eyes as she turned to gaze up at the cliff-face of yellow rock that rose in a low ridge behind her. Set into it along perilous rocky tracks was a honeycomb of what looked at first like grey stains but which, when she blinked away the dust, she realised were narrow openings. It dawned on her with a shudder of alarm that what she was looking at was a network of caves.

'Please, Miss Kenton, do not be distressed. We mean you no harm.'

'If you mean me no harm, why am I tied up and carted around the country likes a worthless goat against my will?'

Jessie made the question fierce. She did not want them to sense her fear. Nor to smell the blood in her mouth where her teeth clenched too tight on her tongue to stop the trembling.

'If you mean me no harm, drive me back to Luxor, and there we can discuss whatever it is you wish to discuss over a glass of mint tea like civilised people.'

The man seated on a rug in front of her looked disappointed, as though he'd expected better of her. He was a tall angular figure with sharp edges to his cheekbones, his jaw, his shoulders and elbows. No more than thirty years old or thirty-five at most, with a quiet intensity about him that made Jessie uneasy. He struck her as the kind of man who would walk barefoot through fire without blinking if he believed it to be the right thing to do. She had been bustled into one of the cave mouths, a narrow crevice in the yellow rock, that had opened up into a large chamber with ancient patterned rugs scattered on the limestone floor and old tea-chests stacked along one rough wall. She didn't know what the chests contained but she could make a fair guess. Two oil lamps provided a flickering light.

'Please, sit, Miss Kenton.'

Warily, she sat down cross-legged on the rug in front of the man. He wore a black scarf wound around his head in turban style and a black robe with an unadorned dagger conspicuous at his waist. Beside him, in full view, lay an Enfield revolver and what at first looked to Jessie like a mottled grey duck-egg next to his knee, until with a ripple of shock she recognised it as a hand grenade.

'I am Fareed.' He spoke softly and leaned forward with his dagger, twisting around her to sever her ropes.

'Not your real name, I assume.'

A faint smile. 'It is the name my followers choose to call me. It means Rare One.'

Jessie glanced at the array of black-eyed men seated against the walls, all regarding her with suspicious eyes, and her heart jerked, but she reminded herself that they had brought her to this hideout *alive*. They must want something from her.

'There is a subject I wish to discuss with you, Miss Kenton.'

'You could have come to Luxor to discuss it.'

'My apologies.' Again the half smile that was not a smile. 'I am not welcome in Luxor. Had I invited you to join me here, I do not think you would have come alone.'

'And Anippe? What is her part in this?'

'Ah, Anippe is a committed warrior.'

Warrior? The word brought the smell of death and carnage into the cave.

'Now I'm here,' she said, summoning every scrap of Monty's high-handed manner, 'the sooner we get this *discussion* over, the better.'

'Indeed.'

'So what is it that you want?'

Fareed's thick brow hunched over half-hooded eyes. 'I want to talk to you about your brother, Timothy Kenton.'

Jessie stopped breathing.

'We know,' he continued in his low voice, 'that he is here.'

'That's not a crime.'

'No. But what he is doing is.'

Jessie said nothing.

'We have information that he ... ' a pause while the black eyes watched her intently, ' ... is involved with a group who are smuggling Egyptian antiquities out of the country illegally.' Fareed did not attempt to hide the disgust in his voice. 'It is why we sent Anippe to work alongside him in your British Museum.'

'You sent her?'

'Yes.'

'She is spying on him for you?'

The smallest ripple of amusement softened the hard line of his mouth. 'She is a good Muslim woman. She would never choose to go with an infidel of her own free will, but you westerners believe no one can resist your charm and money. You are the same, are you not? You thought young Anippe was fortunate indeed to have attracted the interest of your blond, blue-eyed brother. Is that not true? You did not question why she would want him.'

Jessie felt her cheeks colour. 'Yes,' she admitted. 'I didn't question it. But there is one thing I need to know. She told me Tim is wounded. Is it true?'

'No.'

He regarded her for a moment, assessing the impact of his

response because she was unable to hide the rush of relief that went through her.

'So where is he?' she asked directly.

'Now, that is the question indeed. I cannot tell you that,' he spread his hands apologetically, 'I am sorry, because if I do, you will have no reason to tell me what it is I want to know.'

If I do. Three words. That meant everything.

If I do. They meant that this Fareed knew exactly where Tim was. She saw her hand on her lap start to clench and she quickly tucked it under the other.

'What is it you want to know?'

Ask me anything. Anything at all. I will tell you my innermost secrets, if that's what it takes.

'It is clear that your brother has revealed to you his plans, or you would not be here. I will tell you where he is hiding, in exchange for knowledge about this group he works with and about the find they have made in the hills.'

Jessie's throat felt as if sand had been poured down it. So close. So close she could almost touch Tim, yet now suddenly he was snatched away as far as the moon. She studied her questioner and made herself think carefully. In silence she considered the men in black robes squatting around the edge of the cave, their hard and dedicated faces. Outside she could hear a wind picking up, sand churning and swirling, and a truck was grinding its gears as it climbed the slope of scree.

'Who are you?' Jessie asked. 'What is it that you and your followers want?'

Fareed issued a command, a rapid burst of Arabic, and the line of men rose soundlessly to their feet. Each one carried a curved dagger in his hand, pointed at his own heart. Jessie had to force herself to remain seated, to fight the urge to leap to her feet and flee. A wave of sound came at her, as the men's voices chanted as one and left Jessie in no doubt that this was some kind of dedication of self to a cause that would brush her aside like a mosquito if she got in their way.

334

'Who are you?' she asked again.

Fareed's face had changed. It had grown hungry. His cheeks seemed to sink into hollows, his eyes withdrew deeper into his head, as though something inside him was consuming him.

He raised his own dagger to his throat and translated for her. 'Allah is our objective. The Prophet is our leader. Qur'an is our law. Jihad is our way. Dying in the way of Allah is our highest hope.' His gaze fixed fiercely on her.

'We are the friends of Hassan al-Banna.'

Hassan al-Banna. Jessie remembered the name. Monty had mentioned him in Cairo. The American ambassador had told him that a schoolteacher named al-Banna had set up an organisation called the Muslim Brotherhood with the aim of returning society to the precepts of the Qur'an. One of their main intentions was to rid the country of the British and to seize back military and political control of Egypt in the hands of the people. The last thought made her acutely aware of her own vulnerability as one of the hated westerners.

They wanted information. But she had nothing to trade.

'So you do not know where their find is in the hills?' She acted surprised. As if it were the least they should know.

He frowned at her. 'No. They cover their tracks well and post sentries in the desert. Two of our men have been killed trying to follow them.'

Killed. Tim is working with men who kill?

She looked around her again to hide her moment of shock, letting her gaze roam over the cave and the silent men.

'What is this place?' she asked.

'You are asking questions,' he said softly, 'not giving answers.'

She nodded and asked again, 'What is this place?'

He took a full minute to consider whether to answer, but eventually waved a hand in the direction of the mouth of the cave. 'Many men come to me, wanting to bring the holy word of most bountiful Allah back into the lives of our people. They are angry at the foreigners here,' he paused and narrowed his sunken eyes, 'especially you British who have robbed us of power in our own country. Hassan al-Banna is working to educate the illiterate and to build hospitals for the poor, but these brave men,' he gestured at the black-clad figures, 'come here for more than words to fight the British with.'

'Is this a training camp? A military centre?'

Fareed did not say yes, but neither did he say no. 'They come here to intensify their personal piety. But it is the nature of Islam to dominate, not to be dominated.'

Jessie could not look at him. She stared down at the rope marks on her wrists because if she looked at this implacable man for one more second she would give up hope, and she couldn't afford to do that.

'Tea?' he asked politely.

She almost laughed. Tea? In a cave? With a man with a gun at his side, ready and willing to kill her, she was certain, with no more thought than he would stamp on a cockroach. Tea?

'Yes, please,' she said.

He uttered something in Arabic and one of the men, scarcely more than a boy, disappeared into a tunnel at the back. For a while no one spoke, giving Jessie time to consider her next response, but she was taken by surprise when Anippe Kalim entered the cave bearing a tray with two glasses of mint tea and a small pot of honey.

The young woman gave no hint of recognition. She inspected Jessie with cold unfriendly eyes for a moment, before she glanced at Fareed. Instantly she lowered her eyes respectfully and served him first. He nodded at her but said nothing, and she withdrew on silent feet.

'Now,' he stirred honey into his tea, 'tell me what you know of this group of thieves your brother is involved with.'

She could confess the truth – that she knew nothing. Or she could lie. The choice was easy.

'I don't know much.' She watched Fareed. Displeasure came easily to him and furrowed his forehead. 'But,' she added quickly, 'I am ready to pass on what information I do have in exchange for learning where Timothy is now.'

'You lie.' Anger overlaid his formal politeness for the first time. 'You lied to Anippe in London, pretending you didn't know where your brother had gone, yet you knew exactly to follow him to Egypt. To Cairo. To the Mena House Hotel. To Luxor. Clearly you know far more than you claim.'

She didn't deny it. If he thought she knew nothing, what use was she to him? He would toss her aside like garbage. It frightened her that they had kept track of her movements so closely while she was blithely unaware of it. Were they the ones who had followed her round the streets of London and broken into her flat? She finished her tea in a silence that seemed to echo through the cave, and only when she placed her empty glass on the brass tray once more did she look at Fareed directly.

'They are stealing antiquities, I believe,' she told him coldly. 'It is an organisation that buys knowledge from local farmers about where new finds are turning up in the desert.'

No reaction. 'Go on.'

She held her breath for a moment to steady herself. 'They use my brother's expert knowledge to select what to take and what to leave behind. He can date the objects for them, choose the most valuable pieces – the older the better, of course.'

'All this we know.'

So her guesses were right.

'They excavate at night,' she added. 'In the caves.'

'What about this new find they've made?'

'I don't know the royal name but it is a queen.'

'Her tomb?'

'Yes.'

His hand clenched into a fist and she could feel his anger, as an extra presence in the cave.

'Who are these people? And how do they transport the treasures?' he demanded. 'What tracks do they take through the desert?'

She opened her mouth, as if to reply, but closed it again and for a moment there was silence. 'Tell me where my brother is living.'

He didn't hesitate this time. 'In a house set back beyond the fields

337

by the curve in the river downstream. We keep watch on them. Four men. Another comes and goes.'

'How will I recognise the house?'

'It is old and painted green. In front is an alabaster factory with a broken tower on one end. You can just see it from the river.'

'If you know that this group is stealing ancient artefacts from Egypt, why don't you inform the police? Isn't it their job to ... ?'

He uttered a harsh sound that was instantly swallowed by the limestone rock encircling them. 'Money passes from hand to hand to make eyes look the other way.'

'Corruption?'

He regarded her with distaste. 'Do you know how little a police-man in Luxor earns?'

She was embarrassed by her ignorance and for the first time looked away. The men in black *galabayas* were alert and watching Fareed closely, as if eager for a signal from him that would allow them to fall on her with their daggers. She had to give him some-thing more, something that would keep their blades in their belts.

'Fareed,' she said quickly through dry lips, 'if I can find my brother, I can tell you more about who is running this illegal activ-ity and ... '

In one swift movement he rose to his feet and was towering over her. 'You know more!' His anger seemed to feed on her words.

Something. She had to give him *something*.

'They transport it all by boat,' she lied. 'Not through the desert but by boat to Cairo at night.'

His black eyes gleamed brighter in the yellow light of the oil lamp and she knew she had surprised him, but she was not prepared for his response.

'I cannot trust you. You lie to me.'

'No!'

'Yes. You already know the leader of these robbers.'

'I don't.'

'Yes, it is true. You have been seen with him.'

'No! It's a lie!'

338

She saw no signal but two of the black *galabayas* advanced on her, and her heart leapt to her throat as she scrambled to her feet.

'Who?' she demanded. 'Who is he?'

Fareed could scarcely bear to look at her. 'You know.'

'Tell me his name.'

As hands twisted her wrists behind her back she heard Fareed's reply.

'The fat man,' he said. 'Their leader is the fat man.'

40

Georgie

Egypt 1932

The heat.

The sand.

The shouting.

The worst of these is the shouting. It hurts my ears and makes me vomit up my fried eggs. I hate that. The taste in my mouth. I stink. I can smell sweat on me and feel sand like mouse-dirts in my hair. I mention it to you and you laugh. You are different here. You are busy, not just your hands but your mind as well, and I am squeezed into a small corner of it. I no longer write down my thoughts, but they are still here in my head, growing bigger and heavier, until they fall out of my mouth at the wrong time.

'Please, Georgie,' you say. 'Please! Try to behave.'

I am trying.

For you.

I am trying for you. And because I am frightened of the Fat Man.

I am in my tent. It is hot. But the light is not so fierce inside and I am unseen by the others. More important to me, I do not see the desert. It sucks out my eyeballs and makes me blind. I have to crush my hands over my eye sockets to protect them and you have given me a white muslin scarf that I can wind around my face but I still see through it just enough. I do not know why you love the empty wasteland so much that you go walking in it each evening. 'It will swallow you,' I warn but you pat my shoulder and laugh.

The desert's face changes. Sometimes it is pink, smiling and soft, but at others it scowls its rocky frown, all browns and greys, and I understand that it is hungry. In my tent I hear it growl. I hate the desert. I hate the dead hills. I hate the sky. There is too much of it to fit in my head. I need my old room. My ceiling with its crack. The dark corners of my wardrobe. My beautiful uncomfortable chairs.

I tell you these things.

'I don't want to hear this, Georgie.'

'Why not?'

'Because we're here now. Try to make the best of it.'

I try. I try. But I am sick and I sweat. I tie the scarf over my mouth and my ears to stop the noises coming out or going in and you pin a black *galabaya* over the canvas of my tent to make it darker inside.

I hate so many things. I shake all the time.

Except . . .

Except . . .

My mind cannot say the word. Instead I cradle a *shabti* carved out of alabaster in my hand and the shaking stops. When I hold these objects that were held in the hands of tomb-makers three thousand years ago, I feel that I am a member of the human race, part of a continuous process of birth and death, not some dirty aberration to be swept under the carpet and forgotten. I am one of the droplets in the Nile, as significant as every other droplet. This thought calms me. No shaking. No sweating.

I tell you this and you say, 'Georgie, your mind is growing.'

I touch my head. 'No, it is the same size.'

You smile, but then the Fat Man shouts and you vanish. I am on my knees on the sand in my tent with thirty-one *shabtis* in a neat row in front of me. Am I watching over them or are they watching over me?

A *shabti* is a human figure. Most are about as tall as my hand but some are as small as my thumb. Others can be much bigger. *Shabtis* are usually carved out of wood or stone, alabaster or quartzite, or made out of faience, which is glazed earthenware. They are workers, male or female, that were placed in the tombs of the Ancient Egyptians to carry out the manual tasks that the dead person will be required to do in the afterlife. It strikes me that Egyptians must have been extremely lazy, if they need such figures to do the work for them.

I study the one in my hand and I feel the same tightening in my chest as I do whenever I look at the chairs you gave me. You say it is a normal response to beauty, but I think you are wrong. It is more than that. It is an awareness of myself. A knowledge that I will never be able to create such beauty. The feeling is one of deep sadness, mixed with admiration. I don't tell you that and I don't know why. Maybe because I want to be like you. Not a substitute person like the six-inch man in my hand.

This one is made of blue-green faience, a beautiful colour that I imagine underwater-sea to be like. His legs are mummified and down the front of them is inscribed in hieroglyphs the Spell 472 of the *Coffin Texts* found in Chapter Six of the *Book of the Dead*. You see, they believed in magic. The spell would animate the *shabti* to work throughout eternity as a substitute labourer in the fields of Osiris.

I want to believe in magic.

I hate so many things. I shake all the time.

Except . . .

I want to believe there is a spell here in Egypt that will cure me.

*

342

'Where is the imbecile?'

'Georgie is not an imbecile. He is my brother and he is highly intelligent, so I expect some respect for him.'

'He's a buffoon, Timothy. Don't fool yourself into thinking he is worth a moment's thought just because he can recite the Encyclopaedia Britannica.'

'He's good at cataloguing what we're bringing out. Extremely thorough. Doing a useful job that is—'

'Give it a rest, Timothy. He's a pain in the bloody neck and we both know it. He's only here because you insisted on bringing him with you. If I had my way I would . . .'

'I know perfectly well what you'd do.'

'He's a damn fool.'

'He knows far more about dating Ancient Egyptian artefacts than you do.'

'For God's sake, Timothy, look what he did yesterday.'

'I admit that it was unfortunate. But he didn't mean to. It wasn't his fault.'

'He didn't mean to kill a donkey? By slamming a rock down on its head? If you think that, you must be as crazy as he is.'

'It was the noise it was making. He was trying to shut it up.'

'Remind me to do the same to the imbecile next time he starts shouting.'

'Don't you dare even joke about—'

'What makes you think I'm joking.'

The voices move away from my tent. But the Fat Man's laugh stays and rolls around the tent pegs, as though it wants to loosen them, so that the canvas will collapse on top of me.

Imbecile.

I put down my notepad in which I am recording each *shabti* with detailed measurements and description of its decoration and hieroglyphs. I roll into a ball, feeling flies gathering on my skin the way they do on the dead, and bury my face in the sand.

Imbecile.

*

The Fat Man comes to me with his needles. They bite my arms, my buttocks, my thigh. Like Dr Churchward, he wants to eradicate the person I am and put a new person inside me instead. He only comes when you are busy in the tomb. I was melting wax today to hold the faience on a wooden canopic chest in place when he came into my work-tent and told me to stop laughing like a bloody hyena.

'Was I laughing?'

'Yes,' he says, 'but you're too stupid to know.'

'I was enjoying my work,' I explain. 'I have never had work to do before.'

He takes off his spectacles and wipes them. When he puts them back on, his eyes have changed as if he has wiped them too. I have a photograph in a book in my room in the clinic of an eagle landing on the back of a lamb, its eyes savage with hunger for blood. That's what the Fat Man's eyes look like. I stare at my sandals.

'I'm sorry, I don't understand. I didn't mean to offend you,' I say quickly, grasping at one of my phrases.

He slaps me. 'I only tolerate you,' he says, 'because I need Timothy.'

I continue to stare at my feet. 'I only tolerate you,' I say, 'because I need Tim.'

He slaps me again. The touch of his hand is vile but I stand quietly, just my arms are shaking.

'I could get rid of Tim,' he growls at me.

'No.'

'Why not?'

'He loves his work in the tomb.'

'Then you must behave.'

'I know.'

Meekly I hold out my arm and the needle bites. When you return at nightfall you are so excited about the discovery of a calcite perfume vase inlaid with gold that you do not even notice that there is nothing in my head except the buzzing of sand flies.

41

The truck didn't stop. It slowed, spitting up sand as the big wheels struggled for grip and jolted over ridges. The rear door hung open. Only a fool would try to escape in this lifeless landscape and they knew Jessie was no fool.

No fool? So what was she doing tied up in the back of a truck, driven by men who clearly had orders to get rid of her? A bullet in the head, a body buried in the sand far from habitation. Fareed had finished with her. In his cave hideout he would fight on to protect his country's heritage from theft and to lift the yoke of British rule from Egypt's neck, and she didn't blame him. He had squeezed what he could from her and when she was no further use to him, fit only to be thrown on the refuse heap along with the city's trash, he had given the order.

She didn't blame him but that didn't mean she had to agree with him. Even more urgently now, she had to find Tim. To warn him.

Dawn had painted the desert floor a vivid blood-red and the sun's warmth was tempting the snakes and scorpions from their holes for another scorching day. There was no wind, nothing but the tracks of the truck biting into the sand and shale.

Jessie edged closer to the rear opening. Dust kicked up in her face. She wished she had the use of her hands but wishing was a pointless waste of effort. She took a deep breath, relaxed her shoulders, chose her spot and jumped.

Alone in a desert was nothing like she imagined.

The emptiness, she expected. The raw barren rocks and the utter loneliness, they were all part of the desert images in her head, the ones she had gleaned from photographs and pictures of camel trains and Lawrence of Arabia stirring up the sands.

What she was not prepared for was the silence. It crushed her. The overwhelming grinding silence that reduced her mind to dust and numbed any attempt at thought. It shocked her that she was so easily stripped of what made her who she was – her rational mind and her ability to think. The silence crept inside her head and spread its tentacles until even the act of blinking became an effort.

And with the silence came fear.

Cold. Irrational. Unrelenting.

Fear of no one and nothing; fear of everyone and everything. It stalked her footsteps, climbed up the bare skin of her legs, stuck spikes in her heart and raked her tongue with its claws. Fear held her hand and wouldn't let go.

She had not expected that.

As the sun slipped loose from the horizon and rose higher, the shadows shortened and the colours of the desert changed. The reds became browns, yellows merged into a bleached soulless beige that nudged the purple and grey into dark crevices under rocks.

She saw the zigzag trail of a snake.

Concentrate, just concentrate on getting out of here. She forced her mind to work out that the tomb valleys were situated west of the Nile, so probably the cave system of Fareed lay even further west than that. Therefore she must walk east. If she kept heading east, she would have to hit the Nile eventually and she knew which direction was east because that's where the sun still hovered.

What she didn't know was how far. Or how long.

She put one foot in front of the other and walked.

*

Sand chafed her feet. It was impossible to keep it out of her shoes, or out of her mind. Her sunhat had vanished in the caves but she still had her handbag strapped across her body from her shoulder to her hip like a bandolier and she took time to winkle out the small penknife it contained and open its blade to saw through the rope at her wrists. It was painstakingly slow and she took a chunk out of the base of her thumb but when finally the rope fell away, it felt like an achievement.

She was in control.

She shook out her sore arms and narrowed her eyes against the glare as she stared ahead of her. Endless ridges of arid rock. Stretching on and on to eternity.

No. Don't even think that.

She shook her head and regretted it immediately. A pounding headache leapt into life and she knew the sun would fry her brain if she didn't do something about it. Her fingers touched the hair on the top of her head and she was startled by the heat of it. She felt her cheeks. They were burning. She removed the chiffon scarf from her bag and tied its flimsy material around her head.

The blazing sun was sucking moisture from her body at an alarming rate, desiccating and dehydrating her vital organs, but her feet kept moving. One step. Another step. Up a gravel ridge. Down a scree slope. Into a dried-up wadi where large rocks had been carried down from up-river and here she crouched for two minutes in a patch of shade from a boulder. She tore off her petticoat and wrapped it around her head as well, across her forehead, looping just above her eyes to cut down the glare.

Her throat was parched.

Her tongue was growing too large for her mouth, as unwieldy as a pillow, and she picked up a small round pebble. She placed it in her mouth and retched for a moment at the sour taste of it, as though a camel had pissed on it, but it was just the taste of the desert, bleak and bitter on her tongue. But sucking the pebble brought a trickle of moisture into her mouth.

Monty.

His name murmured like a wind through her mind. What was he thinking? What was he doing? He would be searching Luxor, ransacking its homes, trying to find her. *Don't wander off*, he'd said.

Monty, I'm sorry. I'm coming back.

The thought of him speeded up her feet. Above her the sky was immense, a vast sheet of intense blue that seemed to take up the whole world, with just a smear of sand at the bottom that she was trudging over. No wonder Fareed had set up his headquarters out here, where only scorpions cared to venture. As she walked, she went over in her head their conversation in the cave, forcing her mind to consider each of his words. They frightened her. It was only a matter of time before he let those black *galabayas* loose on the group in the house they were watching.

She scrambled up a steep bank of slippery sand and could not suppress the hope that from the summit she would see something in the distance. Her heart plummeted when from the top she saw nothing but desert. It had swallowed her and was never going to spit her out.

She stepped over snakes. Squirming masses of them. Yet when she blinked they were just ripples in the sand. Her heart banged noisily in her chest. She was seeing things. Trees waving their branches in the wind, a cool inviting lake floating in the sky. Scarab beetles scuttling around her feet and crawling up her legs. Worst was Tim's head. It kept bobbing up disembodied on ridges and boulders, rolling like a football down into gulleys or lying half-buried in wave after wave of sand. Eyes wide open.

She tried to be rational. How much can dehydration warp the brain?

She didn't know. The landscape seemed to throb with heat and the desert became a blur around her. She lost track of time and spent hours thinking of nothing but placing each foot in front of the other. She felt something start to grow inside her, something hot and hard in her chest and it took her a while to recognise it as hatred. She hated the sun, hammering on her head. She hated the desert that would not relent. She hated each grain of sand and grit that rubbed her skin raw. She hated Fareed. She hated his moral fervour, she hated his passion for his country, she hated him for being right.

She clung to the hatred, cradled it to her, and used its strength to drive her forward. It was when she realised that the sky was starting to grow darker and that for hours she had still been following the sun that she collapsed on to her knees in a rocky wadi and screamed her rage. She lifted a stone to hurl at the laughing face of the sun in the west.

Instantly she felt a needle-sharp pain in her hand. She dropped the stone and watched a dark crab-like creature scuttle away from it. It was a scorpion.

'Montague, stop it. You'll get yourself killed.'

Monty was not going to get himself killed. Nor was he going to stop. He was searching the riverbank, checking the interior of every hut, every mud-brick house and every boat this side of the river. There was a row of houseboats moored along the Nile and he barged his way aboard each one, using every scrap of his English charm to make it work and a good deal of the money in his pocket when it didn't. He had convinced himself that the Nile was the key – so the logical action now was to search the riverbank for her.

'Jessie! Jessie!'

He bellowed her name, but there was no answering call. He headed for a mud hut with a rush mat roof that was isolated from the rest. It looked promising.

'Montague, you daft bugger. I mean it. What you're doing is dangerous. You're asking for trouble.'

'Jessie!' he called.

'Are you listening to me or have you got cloth ears?'

'I'm listening, Maisie.'

'This isn't helping.'

For the first time since he'd heard of Jessie's disappearance,

349

something snapped in Monty and he drew to a halt. Maisie was right. This wasn't helping. All he was doing was blocking out reality, replacing pain with activity, in an attempt to forget that he had left her alone at a moment when she had needed him. This blind search was not the way to find her. Even he knew that.

'Montague,' Maisie said, taking both his lapels in her hands, 'what would you do if you were chasing a fox?'

He frowned at her tall grey figure. 'I'd follow the hounds.'

'Well,' she gave him a shake, 'let's do that.'

Jessie heard the figure beside her as a soft murmur in the sand. Her own shadow stretched far ahead of her, as the sun sighed and sank down on to the horizon behind her, so it struck her as odd that the figure had no shadow.

When she turned her head she realised why. Serket had come to her. It took an effort to decide whether this was good or bad. Her hand was extremely painful, the poison seeping along her arm and burning her flesh. She had tied it with her blouse across her chest, keeping the hand higher than her heart. She kept telling her mind that most scorpion bites were not fatal but her mind kept arguing that what if this was one of the scorpions of Egypt that carry deadly poison? What then? She should not be pumping poison around her body by walking. She should rest.

If she rested, she would die.

Red welts had risen on the skin of her arm like burns. Her vision kept blurring, so that she stumbled over stones and missed her footing on the sand, so that time and again she was on her knees, the broken landscape distorted and swollen around her, a strange hissing sound coming from her parched mouth.

And now Serket was here.

Goddess daughter of Ra. She was beautiful, draped in red garments with raven-black hair and bearing an *ankh* in her hand, the Egyptian key of life. Because Serket can kill or Serket can heal. On her crown she wears an enormous scorpion and her name can be translated as 'she who tightens the throat' or 'she who causes the throat to breathe'. The bringer of life and the bringer of death.

Serket had come for her.

'Sir Montague Chamford, sir, I have fine news for you. I have learned who Anippe Kalim is.'

'Yasser, you are a man of rare ability.'

'Allah is mighty and bountiful in bestowing his blessings,' Yasser beamed, but his eyes were sharp and more nervous than previously.

'So you know where this young woman lives?' Maisie Randall asked. She discarded the mint tea with scorn. 'Come along, cough it up. Where can we find the girl?'

The handsome young Egyptian focused his attention only on Monty. 'It is not all good news, *bey*.'

'I'm waiting!'

'The price has gone up.'

'What?'

'You did not tell me that your Anippe Kalim is running with dangerous dogs.'

'What do you mean by that?'

'She is an archaeology student from Cairo University. When she was there, she became part of a revolutionary group who are known to use violent methods to achieve their aims.'

'And what are their aims?'

'To rid Egypt of the invading forces and give Egypt back to the Egyptians.' He said it in a toneless voice which carried no hint of his own opinion. 'They are not to be crossed, *bey*.'

'Why would they be interested in Jessie Kenton?'

'That I don't know, I'm sorry.'

'So where does this revolutionary organisation have its headquarters?'

'No one knows for sure. But there are rumours.'

Monty sighed elaborately. Yasser was playing a strong hand. He reached into his pocket for his wallet but it was Maisie who folded her arms across her chest and addressed Yasser firmly.

'Listen here, sonny. We are talking about a young woman's

life here. I want you to get that into your head right now. It's not a game played for money, dangling scraps of information in front of us till Sir Montague digs deeper into his pockets again. A young woman's life, Yasser. Remember that! Imagine if it was your daughter.'

The Egyptian was taken aback by her outburst, and for the first time Monty stepped closer than politeness allowed. He stood a good head taller than Yasser and could smell his hair oil.

'What are the rumours?' he demanded.

Yasser glanced quickly from Monty to Maisie Randall and back again. The smile faded. 'There is talk of caves. Somewhere off to the west.' He bowed his head respectfully to Maisie. 'Mrs Randall, I have a daughter, my little Rabiah. She is my treasure, Allah be praised.'

'So help us.'

'I warn you, there are stories of the desert devouring any trucks that dare to enter that area. Even whole camel trains have vanished. People are frightened. Some say that Set, the god of the desert, takes revenge on non-believers who would steal his secrets.'

'That's poppycock, and you know it,' Monty asserted.

Yasser shrugged. 'It is still dangerous, *bey.*'

'If we track down Anippe,' Monty insisted, 'we'll find Jessie.'

'God willing,' Yasser murmured unhappily.

'And if we find Jessie,' Maisie added, 'we'll quickly run her brother to earth.'

Monty had a sense of something unexpected having slipped into the room. He turned to her and the woman's face looked soft and changed in the slanted light from the window blinds, for once more human than heron.

'How do you know about her brother?' he asked.

'She told me about him in Cairo.'

'Really?'

'Yes, the poor kid was all chewed up at losing him. But I told her at the time, we all lose things, honey. That's the way life is. What you've got to do is learn to live without.'

Monty swung back to Yasser. 'Any news on the whereabouts of Timothy Kenton?'

'No, sir. I think you must be mistaken. He is not in Luxor or I would know by now.'

He looked sincere. But Monty didn't believe him for a second. Something had scared him. A chill ran through Monty and for a long moment he stared at the street outside going about its business, a laden donkey chewing on weeds in the dust.

'Yasser,' he said steadily, 'it is the nature of man to want to survive, is it not?'

'Most certainly, yes, sir.' His words were uneasy.

'Then let us assume that Miss Kenton is surviving. You may have written off her chances, but I have not, and I intend to track her down.'

'It is not wise, Sir Montague.' He shook his head dolefully.

Monty lost patience. 'Just find me a damn camel!'

Maisie unfolded her arms. 'And one for me.'

The moon hung over Jessie's head. It was so vast and so bright that Jessie feared it might fall on her. Its light slid in and out of the dips and hollows of the desert, turning them into silvery blanket-folds that invited her to lie down and rest.

She was cold. So cold she couldn't feel her feet properly or push the strange fogginess from her brain, and her ears were filled with the night hum of the desert. The vibration of it ran through her whole body and through the ancient stones under her feet. Sometimes she looked around her, startled, convinced the vibration came from the hooves of horses, but there was never anything but rocks and ridges and the taste of sand between her teeth.

Her arm was on fire. But it was only when she stumbled and fell to her knees that she realised Serket had abandoned her. The goddess had gone. Left her alone. That was when she began to suspect that she might be dead. If Serket had vanished, it was because she had completed her job with her poison and her sting, and now

Jessie was wandering through the blackness of Duat, the ancient underworld peopled by monsters and demons. Waiting to have her soul weighed against Ma'at's feather.

She tipped her head back and howled at the black sky and for answer a shooting star streaked across the heavens, so fast she would have missed it if she'd blinked. It made her force herself to her feet once more and walk. As long as she had breath in her body she would walk, because there were no shooting stars in Duat.

Something touched her infected arm. Jessie drew a quick stunned breath, but she did not dare take her eyes from the shadowy patch of ground in front of her in case she fell again. The falls were happening again and again, jarring and disorientating.

'Jessie.'

She took no notice. *Keep walking.* A thousand times in the last hours she had heard Monty whisper her name in her ear, and she had steeled herself to ignore it.

'Jessie.'

Tears rolled down her cheeks, warm on the icy skin of her face. She could feel his breath, sense his touch on her shoulder, and she became aware of the warmth of his chest as he drew her against him. She knew then that the balance of her mind had gone and reality had become a thing of her own making.

'Monty,' she breathed.

Again it came in a gentle whisper. 'Jessie.'

But it wasn't Monty. She could smell the *galabaya* this person wore and hear the bad-tempered groan of a camel. It couldn't be Monty. When strong arms lifted her, she struck out with her good hand and heard a grunt of pain. She wanted to see another shooting star to prove to herself she wasn't dead, but blackness slithered up from within her and spread as cold as the desert night through her head.

Monty could not take his eyes off her. Her face on the pillow looked wretched. Her creamy skin was burnt by the sun and her lips were parched and cracked, but the doctor had given her something to make her sleep and something for the pain. She was lying quietly now. The terrible moaning had stopped and her head lay still, instead of tossing from side to side

'The doc said it's a bloody scorpion sting but she should recover in a few days. So don't look so grim.' Maisie cuffed his shoulder. 'You got to race through the desert on a bloomin' camel, didn't you? A great Lawrence of Arabia story to tell her when she wakes up.'

'I know. She's strong.' But still he could not take his eyes off her. He softly rubbed ointment onto her lips. 'But her arm is bad.'

'Like a bloody plank. Poor kid.'

'Maisie.'

'What is it?'

'Thank you.'

'Don't be a daft bugger.' She cuffed him again. 'You're the one who did the hunting.'

'I'm sorry they wouldn't let you come with me, but you might have found it tough.'

Maisie grinned. 'Anything you can do, Sir Montague *bey*, I can do just as good, I tell you straight.'

'I believe you.'

'Silly towel-headed camel-drivers! Why did they think I'd be unlucky for them?'

'Just an excuse, Maisie. They didn't want a woman along.'

She huffed and puffed her annoyance, but he knew it was more for show than anything else.

'I still don't know how you found her out there at night.'

'I did what you said, I followed the hounds. I paid Yasser handsomely to find me a local man brave enough to take me out into the area around the caves. He was an expert tracker, even by moonlight.'

'You were lucky that the moon was full.'

'Yes.' He picked up Jessie's bandaged hand in his. 'I was very lucky. The devil looks after his own.'

Maisie laughed. 'You toffs! You've got more brass than sense. You could have got yourself killed.'

He stroked the swollen fingers. 'I was lucky.'

He didn't want to tell the truth. That he had stood in the aching silence of the desert and listened for her heartbeat.

42

Georgie

Egypt 1932

I beg. I plead. You sigh and say yes.

You take me up to the tomb. I am not good at climbing, I slip and slide, and I panic when the gravel under my feet starts to roll down the hillside, taking me with it. So you attach a rope around my waist.

'Take it slowly,' you tell me.

But I am so frightened of the hill that I rush at it and nearly drag us both down to the bottom.

'Teamwork,' you say as you haul me up again.

I have no idea what that means.

I scramble through the narrow slit in the fawn hillside, thankful to escape into the gloom. Outside, everything is too big. There is too much sky and too much desert and far too much air. It crawls inside my lungs and gets stuck there. You tell me to breathe more deeply, but you don't seem to understand the impossibility of breathing deeply if your lungs are filling up with layers of sand. I know that if I stay here long enough, the sand will win. When I look at the hills and the crevices and the eerie desert landscape, I know that the sand will always win.

Inside is different. Inside the rock, the sand cannot win. One step is all it takes and the burning sun is no more, its light denied access as the passageway descends through the rock. The tunnel is so narrow and so low that I have to duck my head and at first I was frightened by it, but now I have been here five times. You promise me that the limestone rock above my head will not collapse on me, and despite my knowledge of roof falls in coal mines like the one in the Easthouses Colliery on 14th January 1930 or in the Deans pit at Bathgate on 15th October 1930, I decide to believe you. If I don't, I will never get to see the tomb.

'Ready?' you call out.

'Yes.'

'Watch where you put your feet.'

I watch.

'Don't hurry,' you tell me.

I always hurry.

The ground slopes down in a frighteningly steep staircase cut inside the rock. But you are not frightened. You are never frightened. I realise here in Egypt how brave you are and it makes me love you even more, because you have enough bravery for both of us. That's why I go down the staircase.

'If you fall,' you say each time, as you descend in front of me and my torch beam bobs on your yellow curls, 'fall on me, not on the rocks. I don't want you breaking anything.'

But what if I break you?

'You have thirty minutes,' you say.

It's not enough. It is never enough.

We have passed through the huge outer chamber with its massive stone pillars in the papyrus bud form. Twenty-two columns, one for each year that Wahankh was an army general under the rule of

King Tuthmosis III during the 15th century BC. He lived at the time of the New Kingdom, the greatest period in Egyptian history, and must have spent most of his life preparing this tomb for his death.

We are in the burial chamber. I could live here. The silence is so intense that it crushes everything and all that is left is a clarity in my head that enables me to think with precision. I want to spend a night here but you won't let me. You say it is bad for my lungs. It may be. But it is good for my brain, and my brain matters more to me than my lungs.

The chamber is so full of colour from floor to ceiling that I am glad we have not lit the lamps this time. I like to study the decorations a piece at a time with my torch; that way my mind does not feel as if Wahankh is laying siege to my head with his army. But I like his life. The wall-paintings show it to me. I see Wahankh as a boy on a farm, sowing grain in the fields where crows peck at what they can steal. I think I might like that life. But he is not satisfied. He makes offerings to the falcon-headed Horus, the god of war, and Horus grants his wish. He becomes a great general with the Eye of Horus, the *Wedjat*, painted on his chariot for protection.

I would like the Eye of Horus painted on you and me.

I sit on the rock floor in the middle of the chamber. My torch beam encircles Wahankh's chariot where he stands with spear raised to strike his enemy. I try to imagine what it would be like to kill someone, but I cannot. Does it hurt you? Or is it like stamping on a beetle? You tell me not to stamp on the beetles in the desert, that it is their territory, not ours, but I don't want them in my tent and anyway I like the popping noise it makes. I start to read the hieroglyphs that tell of the general's great victories.

'Georgie.'

I read on.

'Georgie, listen to me. I want to talk to you.'

'You are talking to me.'

'I mean about something important. I want you to pay attention.'

I don't like it when you say that. It means something bad is coming. I shuffle closer to the dramatic decorations on the wall, further away from where you stand in the shadows.

'Are you listening?'

'Yes.'

I hear you draw in a deep breath.

'You like it here, don't you?' you say.

'Yes.'

'We've made a routine for you.'

'Yes.'

Each morning in the house you fry me two eggs and a piece of millet bread. It is not the same as at the clinic but I like it. It is always on my special plate – used by no one else – and I sit at the table alone to eat it. I sleep in a bare room on my own, which means you have to sleep on the floor in the living room, because the two Egyptians share the other bedroom. They smell different which interests me but they do not talk much. One is an archaeologist, I think, but I don't know what the other one does. I suspect he is a guard because he carries a gun under his jacket. I don't look at him.

Worse is the drive out to the desert. I hide in the back of the van under a blanket; stifling, but safe. It takes a long time and the track is rough, but when it ends the worst is to come. The climb up into the hills. I refuse even to think about it now.

'We are working fast,' you say.

'The Fat Man says not fast enough.'

'I know. We have to speed up.'

'Why?'

'It's complicated.'

I hate that word. It always upsets me. I don't ask anything more.

'The thing is, Georgie . . . '

I stare harder at the painting. At the horse with a spear through its chest. Something bad is coming.

' . . . we might have to leave in a hurry.'

The horse's mouth is open, screaming.

'I don't want to leave,' I say.

'I know. You like it here. You enjoy the work.'

'And I like you. Every day I like you. Not just Saturdays.'

You say nothing. But I hear you suck in a breath.

'Well, I'm sorry, Georgie, but we might have to leave fast.'

'Today?'

'No, not today.'

'Tomorrow?'

'No, not tomorrow.'

'When?'

'I don't know. But I want you to be ready for it. Prepare your mind.'

I want to be the horse, so that I can stay in this tomb forever.

'Please, Georgie, stop it.'

I am wailing. The sound of it is piercing in this place of silence. I put a hand over my mouth but it doesn't stop. You come over and sit cross-legged on the ground next to me, though you do not touch me. You direct your torch on the horse.

'I'm sorry, Georgie. Don't cry. I'm sorry for putting you through all this.'

I refuse to think of the journey back to England. It will put me in hell again. You will give me drugs that make me sleep but which give me living nightmares. You said my behaviour on the plane coming here was embarrassing but I don't care. Better to be embarrassed than to be caught in the torment of hell.

'I want to stay,' I say.

'I know.'

'We could abandon the Fat Man and stay here together. Just you and me.' I turn my head away from the horse and look at you, hopeful.

'Oh, Georgie, life isn't that simple.'

'Why not?'

But before you answer, I know what you will say.

'It's complicated.'

43

It was there. Each time Jessie forced open her eyes, it was there. Beside her bed. Monty's face. Until she didn't know whether it was inside or outside her head. There was something she wanted to ask him, but her jaw wouldn't move and the fog in her brain got in the way. Someone was sawing off her arm.

Stop. Please, stop.

The pain made her eyes water and her blood catch fire in her veins, and far away she heard Monty murmur, 'Don't cry, my love.'

My love.

Time seemed to be broken. It went fast or it went slow, so slow she could hear the creak of its wheels. Then it would stop altogether. At one point it wound backwards and she was in the fierce glare of the desert again. She cried out for water and this time it came, cool and life-giving on her lips, but always there was something wrong, something nagging at her. There was something she had to do but her parched brain could not recall what it was. Except that it had something to do with the sleek and steely surface of the Nile. Purple shadows skated across its image in her mind, clouding it from her view, and she struggled to brush them aside.

'Hush, my sweet, take it easy.'

She heard his voice, felt his hands holding her face, halting its thrashing from side to side. Felt the sweet warmth of his lips on her forehead.

'How is she?' A woman's voice.

'Not good.'

'Not going to turn up her toes, is she?'

'No.'

The *No* sounded so certain. As if Monty would wrest her from the grip of Anubis himself, if he had to. It pleased her. For a split second the person sawing off her arm paused, allowing her to smile at him before the saw dug its teeth in once more.

He told her things. Things about his life.

It was just his voice he was giving her, even in her confused state she understood that. What he said didn't matter but the continuous unbroken sound of his voice did. It held her in place. In the room. In her bed. It didn't let her go.

Her eyes were clamped shut and however hard she tried, she couldn't prise them open, yet he talked to her about Chamford House, about how much he loved it. He told her of his passion for its bricks and mortar, of his love for its grotesque stone finials and his desire to see every cottage on the estate restored to its former glory for his tenants. She learned that he had built a school in the village and employed two local spinsters as teachers, at a time when schools were closing because after the Stock Market crash of 1929 there were no jobs. No jobs meant there was no money in homes, so children were pushed out to work. Monty supplied hot food to tempt the children back into school and when lessons were done, he gave them work to do on the estate, mending fences, digging potatoes or packing apples into boxes for market.

He turned a blind eye to poaching but would have no truck with stealing. He loved a pheasant shoot on a crisp winter's day and hated with bitter enmity the towering army of factory chimneys that were marching ever closer to Chamford Estate's fragile boundaries.

She tried to tell him he was living in the wrong century. That he was a patron of rural life at a time when rural life was in retreat. But the words emerged as mumbled murmurs and he bathed her burning neck, pressed cold compresses on her forehead and cradled the fingers of her damaged hand lightly between his own.

She couldn't stop herself drifting far away to other places and other times – she woke up to find herself playing snowballs with Tim in the woods, and once she was feeding goldfish with Georgie in the park, tossing crumbs to Farintosh, Armitage and Hatherley, all named by Georgie after characters in Conan Doyle's stories. She tried to stay there by the lily pond and started to explain to her little brother how she had fought to extract his address from her parents because she missed him so much but . . .

She woke in the bed. Her eyelids were heavy but her ears caught Monty's voice, soft and regretful.

'I'm sorry,' he said.

For what? she wanted to ask. *Why are you apologising to me?* What had he said? What had she missed?

He lifted her bandaged hand and kissed her swollen fingers.

'Don't hate me,' he said.

'I insist,' Monty said imperiously, 'that you return to your room at once.'

Jessie was drinking morning coffee under a parasol in the hotel garden. She smiled at him. 'Come and join me.'

'You should not be out of bed, young lady.'

'I've played the wilting flower long enough, and now we need to—'

'The only thing you need is rest. You heard the doctor.'

'Don't, Monty.'

'One more day, Jessie. Please stay in bed just one more—'

'Let's concentrate on finding Tim. I've had enough of pillows to last me a lifetime.'

She had been shocked. When she woke at five-thirty this morning and found Monty asleep in the chair next to her bed, his fine-boned face shadowed with exhaustion and in need of a shave, beside him lay yesterday's *Egyptian Gazette* and she had looked at the date. She had lost a day. A whole day. Twenty-four hours gone. With a jerk she threw off the bedsheet and sat up, but she was unprepared for the impact of the movement on her skull. It took a while but now she was dressed, her arm in a sling and sipping coffee with a good resemblance to a normal human being.

'Enough about bed, Monty.'

He studied her intently, narrowing his eyes in the way he did when he was displeased. He drew in a breath and released it sharply.

'Very well, Jessie. What is it you want?'

'We need a boat.'

The river moved beneath them, dark and secretive. The Nile was broad and even at this early hour was filled with boats of all shapes and sizes, plying their business of ferrying or fishing or transporting goods from one bank to the other. A small rowboat, almost sinking under its load, manoeuvred out of the path of their felucca and Monty tightened the tall triangular sail as the wind veered to the west. He was a good sailor, which surprised Jessie. Horse-riding and shooting, yes, probably tennis and polo too. But sailing? She hadn't expected that one.

'I knocked around in boats when I spent time in Alex years go,' he told her as he ran an eye over the rigging. 'A felucca isn't fast but it's remarkably stable.'

Jessie wanted fast. As fast as it would go. Monty perched next to the tiller in the stern, bare foot jammed against the benching, while she sat near the bow in the shade of the sail, her eyes scouring the land beyond on the riverbank.

'Here, use these.' Monty offered her a pair of binoculars that seemed to materialise from nowhere.

She gave him a quick smile of thanks and adjusted them with her good hand. Oddly, talking made her arm hurt more, as if her tongue was connected to the tendons of her wrist in some strange way. Monty seemed to understand her need for silence, he didn't press her for words, but she could feel his gaze on her when it should be on the houses visible from the river. They were searching for the broken tower of an alabaster factory and a green-painted house. Oh yes, and a curve in the river.

Even Jessie had to admit it wasn't much to go on.

She scanned the west bank as they sailed downstream, unable to ignore the looming presence of the desert hills. Today they gleamed as tawny as a lion's pelt, stark and naked against the vivid blue sky. She concentrated on the houses. She'd had enough of the desert and its relentless ability to win. Bright green fields of sugarcane and animal fodder bristled alongside the river, criss-crossed by sunken irrigation channels that were controlled by sluices. *Fellaheen*, the labourers in the fields, jumped up at her in the binocular lenses and women in black trudged the dusty paths with wooden crates of bright yellow melons on their heads.

No green houses. No broken towers. She blinked, impatient to conjure one up.

'Jessie.'

She nodded, but didn't remove her eyes from the binoculars, still skimming over the palm trees.

'Jessie, if this Fareed is watching the house that he claims your brother is in, he is probably watching us as well. Do you realise that?'

She nodded again. 'Unless he thinks I'm not worth bothering about any more.' Her arm throbbed.

'He could have been lying about the green house.'

She lowered the binoculars. 'It's all I have to go on, Monty.'

He eased the tiller over and the wind ruffled his hair. 'I know.'

'There!'

Monty saw it first. The shift in the Nile's course was so slight it was scarcely a curve, more a faint ripple in the bank where the trees hung close to the water.

'There!' he said again, his arm outstretched.

'Where?'

'There, up behind the fields, where the lands starts to rise between those folds. That white building with the stubby tower. See? It's collapsing on one side.'

She saw it. A low scruffy building. It must be the alabaster factory that Fareed mentioned. Quickly she scanned behind it and found a stretch of barren ground that rose up towards the lower slopes of the Theban Hills, but tucked on its own in a slight hollow stood a house with dull greenish paint and around it lay a low dry-stone wall.

'That's it,' she said. 'That's the house.'

'Don't get too excited, Jessie. Tim might not be there.'

'I realise that, of course.'

But he might.

Monty chose to sail further downriver to put some distance between the boat and the alabaster factory before he moored and threw down the length of wood that served as a gangplank to shore. He was worried about Jessie but didn't want to show it. He stretched out a hand to her as she walked along the plank and helped her on to the stony bank, careful of her arm in its sling. A flock of white ibis swept up into the air at their intrusion and drifted inland over the fields like a milky cloud.

'You wait here,' he said casually. 'While I go up to check the house.'

She didn't release his fingers. Her grip was firm, which reassured him, but her step was uneven, her balance not quite steady.

'Monty! Don't mollycoddle me. I'm fine.'

She made the words sound cross but her eyes smiled at him, clear and blue as the wide Egyptian sky, and he kept her hand in his as he walked her along the raised dirt paths, passing between the fields of sugarcane. They were less visible here among the tall stalks, less conspicuous on the landscape until they came to the spot where the irrigation channels stopped and the desert began.

He thought about using her sling to tether her to a tree.

*

The house was an odd mix of colonial and Egyptian styles with a covered verandah along the front, but a flat roof and arched windows. The green paint was peeling and the place looked deserted, shutters closed. Dilapidated and isolated, there was no sense of life to it. Monty hung back in the deep shade of a clump of palm trees about twenty yards from the house and his hand kept a firm hold on Jessie.

'What do you think?' she whispered.

'It feels empty.'

'Let's take a look.'

'Wait.'

He made her remain in the shadows. Ten minutes they stood there, eyes fixed on the house until they knew every cracked and broken shutter but still had heard no sound, nor seen any movement.

'We do this together,' she told him.

He nodded. He couldn't force her to stay under the trees.

'Stay close,' he muttered and moved forward.

He headed for the back of the building first, skirting the low wall and climbing over it at a corner where there were no windows to overlook their trespass. They stole up to the shutters at the back.

'All right?' he mouthed.

'Yes.'

He could see the hope in her, and the way she struggled to swallow because her mouth was so dry, preventing her from crashing into the house and crying out Tim's name. He wanted to say, *Don't Jessie, don't do this to yourself*, but instead he tried one of the shutters. It was rotten and two of the slats gave way easily, allowing him to put his eye to the gap and peer inside.

'What can you see?' she whispered.

'Not much. It's dark. Two bedrolls on the floor and a dusty prayer mat in the corner. Not promising.'

She stayed quietly at his side as they moved together around the corner to the next shutter. This side of the house was in shade and a couple of scrawny chickens fluttered up out of the cool dust with a clatter of wings, startling them.

That was when they heard the engine.

Both registered the grinding of gears as the truck struggled up the slope at the front of the house. Monty seized Jessie's good wrist and started to run, keeping to the back of the house. Over the wall, crouching low. They skidded down into a narrow gulley that led back round to the front but came out further down the slope. On the track above them they could see a filthy van with the name *Meriot Fishery* painted on the side. It drew to a halt just inside the wall and its door opened, but it was on the far side and Monty couldn't make out the figure who climbed out.

'Can you see?' he whispered.

She shook her head. 'Let's get over to those trees.'

The group of palm trees where they had first sheltered lay about fifteen feet ahead of them, nearer the house. Not far, as long as the driver didn't glance down in their direction when they sprinted across the gap. Monty weighed their chances.

'We could always walk up to the front door and say hello. Like normal tourists,' he suggested.

She swung round to stare at him, eyes wide with surprise. 'Why not? We could just ask the way, as if we're lost.'

'Come on.'

Monty climbed out of the gulley, gently eased Jessie up after him and brushed the worst of the dust off their clothes before starting to walk towards the Meriot truck. Its engine was still ticking over noisily, vibrating the dust on its bonnet, and they could see the driver, an Egyptian man who was busy lighting a cigarette. Just as they approached the palm trees, the other man walked around to the rear doors of the truck to open them and in doing so, stood full in the blast of bright sunlight. He was a westerner wearing a panama hat and sand-coloured cotton drill trousers with a cream linen jacket. Even in the dust and heat he looked smart. Out of his top pocket protruded the end of a briar pipe and on his chin gleamed a small silvery beard.

369

Monty stepped immediately into the shadows behind the palm trees and pulled Jessie with him. He held her there in the gloom. He recognised her eagerness to rush forward. She opened her mouth to shout out to the man in the linen jacket and he slapped his open hand over it, feeling the moisture of her breath on his palm. She shook her head, trying to dislodge his hand but he frowned urgently and murmured, 'Hush, Jessie. Quiet!'

Her blue eyes questioned him, puzzled, and her hand rose and slowly lifted his fingers from her lips.

'What is it, Monty? It's your friend, Dr Scott.'

Friend? Monty wanted to wipe the word off her tongue.

'We don't know what he's doing here, Jessie. Let's see what he's up to first.'

Again the look of puzzlement swept over her face. 'You don't think he's involved, surely?'

'You'll always find Dr Septon Scott and his ilk wherever there's the smell of money.'

'If he's knows this house, he may have an idea where Tim is.' She tried to start forward but he held her slight frame easily with one arm.

'If he knows you're here and that you are aware of his connection with this house, he may not be altogether happy.'

She looked at the house, at the van, then back to Monty, uncertain how far to trust Scott.

'Jessie,' he said in a low voice, 'he is not a man you want to cross.'

'I thought he was your friend.'

'You thought wrong. I'm sorry if I misinformed you.'

'What on earth could he do to me? This isn't another cave in the desert,' she whispered.

At that moment the driver swung down from his cab and strutted round to the rear door, where he spoke with Scott in a voice too low to hear. But neither Monty nor Jessie could miss the gun in a holster on his chest when he tossed his jacket into the back of the truck. They ducked back behind the trees.

Men who kill. Fareed had warned Jessie. Scott may be a sharp dealer, but a killer? There was a big difference. The thought roused in Monty the anger that had been his constant companion in the trenches of wartime Flanders. He'd seen men there who liked to kill, who possessed the blood-lust that made them intrepid and adventurous soldiers. Of course Monty had killed, but only when he had to. His only aim now was to get Jessie out of there.

He pulled her into a crouch behind the wide bole of the tree but his heart sank when he looked at her profile, at the intent expression on her face as she pushed it forward through the sparse undergrowth. It reminded him of one of his hunting dogs when it had caught the scent of blood in its nostrils. He laid a hand on her shoulder to hold her still, to bring her back into his world. Whatever was going on in her head was unsafe.

She turned to him in the shadows. 'I think I should go and speak to Scott. To ask him to take me to Tim, if he knows where he is.'

'And then what?'

She frowned at him.

He asked again, 'And then what? So you meet up with Tim. Do you really think Scott will just let you walk away, if they are involved in something criminal?' He looked at her sling, aware of how vulnerable she was. 'Of course he won't.'

She shook her head at him, mutely. The two men were heading towards the house, where they unlocked the front door and entered, their movements hurried.

'Now,' Monty said, 'we leave.'

He should have been suspicious when she didn't argue. They rose silently, but just when they were about to step out of the shadows and retreat to the gulley, Jessie darted forward to the truck, keeping its bulk between herself and the house. She was only there a few seconds, just enough for a quick glance in the back and a scribble with her hand in the sand-dust on the truck just above the rear wheel arch. The moment she returned, they ran for the gulley, slithering into it just in time. The two men's voices emerged by the vehicle again and Monty raised his head enough to see them drop an armload of bedding and a cardboard box of equipment into the back of the truck.

'Moving day,' he muttered.

Jessie leaned against him. 'There was nothing in the truck. It was empty.'

'It's probable that they won't risk carting their illegal pickings around in broad daylight.' He looped an arm around her to support her and she kissed his cheek, but he was not to be distracted. 'What did you write on the truck?'

'It was a drawing.'

'You think now is the time for artwork?'

'Don't be angry.'

The sound of doors slamming jolted the silence and the engine rattled its way back down the slope. They waited till the crows had settled back in the palm trees before they breathed freely.

'Now,' Monty said.

The house was empty. The door wasn't even locked. Inside was dim and dusty, the closed shutters keeping out the sun's heat but making the air taste thick and stale. Monty looked around. Scott had certainly done a good job of clearing the place out, leaving nothing but footprints in the dust and a few candle stubs on one of the windowsills. No sign of the bedrolls he'd viewed through the broken shutter or the prayer mat, but interestingly one of the rooms was spotless. Its floor looked freshly scrubbed and the walls had been whitewashed.

'Jessie, look at this.'

She was resting against the door frame, her eyes half closed, barely able even to stand up straight. 'What is it?'

He noticed for the first time that her skirt was filthy and her eau-de-nil blouse was torn at the elbow, but still she looked . . . he sought for the right word . . . she looked unbreakable. As if nothing could stop her. Not the arm. Not the sunburn. Not the doctor's pills. And certainly not Dr Scott.

He went over to her and lightly kissed her mouth. She tasted salty. 'I found this squashed behind the shutters.'

He held out a screwed-up cigarette packet. She took it from him and opened up its blue and white folds.

'Senior Service,' she said quietly. Her eyes lifted to Monty's. 'Tim smokes Senior Service. Tim was here.'

'We're close,' he said. 'Very close.'

44

At the Blue Nile Hotel Malak was waiting and his gigantic smile at their return made them both laugh. It felt good to laugh. Monty carefully sat Jessie down in the cool interior under the whirring ceiling fan and ordered fresh lemonade for her and for the boy and a straight scotch whisky for himself. As an afterthought he added a dish of *kushari* for the boy and a few mezzes for Jessie and himself. She drank the lemonade but didn't touch the food. Instead she took out her drawing pad from her bag and sat in silence for a few minutes sketching something. Malak watched her with amazed eyes, as if she were pulling rabbits from hats.

'Who's the scruffy ragamuffin?' It was Maisie who breezed in brandishing her faithful furled umbrella at the boy. 'Looks like something the cat dragged in.'

'This is Malak,' Monty introduced him. 'He's our dragoman in Luxor, our man on the ground. He is proving very useful.' He nodded at Malak. 'Very efficient.'

Maisie inspected the boy who was regarding her alarming figure warily. 'Does it talk?' she asked eventually.

'Course I talk, good yes, very good. I excellent fine friend to Missie Kenton and sir *bey*, you ask, I get, and I get good with Uncle.

374

Camels you want I get and horses, yes, very strong backs, and I very fine fellow also you know and . . . '

'Does it shut up?'

'If you ask him politely.'

Maisie tapped Malak on top of his thick black hair with her umbrella. 'I don't need a horse, what I need is a chair.'

Instantly Malak pushed a large armchair up behind her and she plopped down in it, folding her long legs out of the way.

'Good. Now,' she looked closely at Jessie's face, taking in the lines of exhaustion, 'what news? Feeling any better?'

Monty shook his head but said nothing.

'I'm a lot better, thank you, Maisie.'

'What is it you're drawing there?'

'Look, Malak,' Jessie said quietly.

She held her drawing out to the boy and he gazed at it in awe, his mouth falling open to reveal lentils and tomatoes.

'How you do that very clever, Miss Kenton, yes?'

She smiled at him fondly. 'I went to art college.'

'In big nice city?'

'Yes, in London.'

'I go to London one day yes please, very nice city.'

'I hope you do, Malak. But Cairo is a very nice city too.'

The boy wrinkled his nose. 'Cairo full of Egyptians.'

'I'd like you to do something for me, Malak.'

'Yes, Missie, I do very good. I very efficient.' His black eyes shone. 'You ask.'

'You see this man?' She tore the drawing out of her pad and turned it to face him. With a shiver of unease, Monty saw that it was an unnervingly accurate sketch of Dr Scott's face, even down to the mole in front of his left ear and the ridge of rough skin above one of his silvery eyebrows. 'I want you to take this and see if you can find him anywhere around Luxor. His name is Dr Scott but – this is important, Malak – he could be dangerous, so I don't want you to go near him. You understand?'

'Yes, Missie.'

'Don't speak to him.'

'No, Missie.'

'Just tell me if you spot him somewhere. I'd like to know where he goes.'

'I do that easy.'

'Don't go near him, remember?'

'I too quick for old man,' he laughed.

Monty saw the way he held the drawing close to his chest, as something precious. He probably owned almost nothing else.

'Here, Malak.' Monty tossed him a couple of coins. 'When you come back, there will be more. But pay attention to what Miss Kenton said. Don't speak to this man. We don't want you hurt.'

Malak gobbled down the last mouthful of his *kushari*. 'I pay attention good,' he said solemnly and slid toward the door. 'You have cigarette for me, sir *bey*?'

'No, Malak.' Maisie shook her head sternly. 'You're far too young a whippersnapper.'

Monty took out a cigarette, lit it for himself and tossed the rest of the packet to the boy who snatched it from the air. 'If he's old enough to work for us, he's old enough to smoke.'

'Thank much to you, sir *bey*. You excellent good man.'

'Get off!'

Malak grinned and scampered away. 'The boy needs new shoes,' Monty remarked. 'In the morning we must buy him some.'

But in the morning shoes would be the last thing on his mind.

Monty put Jessie to bed. He showered the sand off her skin, avoiding water contact with her bandaged arm, and brushed the grit out of her hair. He had half-carried her to her room and peeled her clothes off her body, gently lifting her torn blouse from her shoulder-blades. The bruises on them and the scrapes on her hip and gashes on her knees made him wonder once more how much she went through in the desert. How bad it had been. Standing naked in the bathroom, she leaned against him, her head on his shoulder, and despite the shower he could still smell the lingering scent of the

376

Nile in her hair. With an arm curled around her waist, he guided her towards the bed. Her skin felt hot.

'Monty, I'm sorry I . . .'

'Shh, don't talk. Rest now. What you need is sleep.'

She let her lips touch his neck and he felt his blood leap to the spot. He held her close, aware of the warmth of her breasts, the creamy silk of her skin, the delicate bones of her back, but it was the uncertainty of her steps towards the bed that touched him most. The weakness that she would never show when in good health was what overwhelmed him now, as he eased her on to the bed and folded the sheet over her. Her face on the pillow looked uncertain and damaged, with purple smudges darkening her eye sockets.

He bent down and kissed each of her eyelids. 'Sleep,' he told her and her lips tried to find a smile but failed. Almost immediately she was asleep, her breathing regular but too fast. Even in sleep her good hand held on to him and did not let go, so he gently slid into the bed beside her, wrapped her in his arms, and her body moulded to his. Her fingers found his and laced together, and their neediness pulled at his heart.

He lay there silently, hour after hour, listening to the rhythm of her breathing. She woke once, hot and fretful, clearly in pain, so he gave her a couple of the doctor's pills and held the glass to her lips as she sipped some water. Her drowsy blue eyes looked up at him over the rim, examining his face as if seeking some missing key.

When he settled her back on the pillow, she murmured, 'Tell me about you and Dr Scott.'

Now was not the time. But he didn't argue.

'Nothing much to tell. My father borrowed from him when the estate found itself on the financial skids. Borrowed heavily. Scott holds a mortgage on much of the land, including our village of Chamford, but my father believed he could trust him. He was wrong.'

Jessie's finger soothed the hard muscle in his cheek. 'And now?'

'He is threatening to call in the loans. He wants to break up the estate, turf the villagers out of their houses where they have lived for generations, and intends to build factories.' He said the words calmly, with no hint of the rage inside his chest at the mention of it.

'Factories bring jobs,' she murmured, her eyes already closing once more.

'You're right,' he acknowledged.

But her eyelids lifted and she drew his head closer to hers until her lips could touch his. He remained beside her until the light started to darken as the sun sank below the desert hills. The air in the room grew cooler and he knew he would have to leave her.

'Thank you for coming over,' Monty said in a quiet voice, so as not to disturb Jessie in the bed.

'Oh, I'm happy to sit with her. You know I want to lend a hand,' Maisie said cheerfully. 'Poor little mite, she looks ...' Her words stuttered to a halt.

'What is it, Maisie?'

'She has spirit, that one.'

'Too much, sometimes.'

She nodded and rested her hand on her throat as though to quieten the pulse there. 'She's very pretty.'

It was such an odd thing to say just then. They both studied the face in the bed, its delicate lines unguarded in sleep, her hair a jumble of golden threads on the pillow. Her cheekbones were still burnt from the sun in the desert and the skin on her nose was peeling. It emphasised the vulnerability she took such pains to hide.

'Is that brother of hers worth all this?' Maisie asked. She was frowning, unhappy about something.

'I hope so. I don't know him.'

'If you ask me, he's a ...' The words dried up again. She turned away and shrugged her bony shoulders. 'A blinkin' burden to her,' she finished.

'I don't think she ever sees him like that.'

'Then he's a lucky blighter.'

'Yes,' Monty agreed. 'I think he is.'

45

Georgie

Egypt 1932

'Control him.'

'I try,' you say. 'But he is upset by the move.'

You are discussing me again, you and the Fat Man, and I hate it. The heat is bad today, made worse by the hot wind that whips up the sand and scours the skin. I am working under an awning this morning. It has a canvas roof and three canvas sides but the front is open to the elements and to the desert dwellers. A buff-coloured lizard scuttles in and hides behind one of my crates.

I chop one of Tim's sieves in half and trap the creature in it, so that I can touch it and study its interesting toe-fringes. These are projecting spines, a modification of toe scales on sand lizards to improve their movement on slippery sand and to aid burrowing into it. A fascinating example of Darwin's theory of evolution that I now hold in my hand. Two weeks ago I was hiding in my wardrobe. My mind fizzes at the speed of these changes.

You and the Fat Man are off to one side, so I cannot see you, but I can hear you. There is something about very dry air that allows sound to carry further – it is a phenomenon that I want to explore when I can. *When I can*. But I have no idea when that will be. I have no idea about anything any more, and the thought makes my hands start to shake so badly that I have to put down the bronze statuette I am packing. It is the beautiful goddess Isis, first daughter of Geb, god of the Earth, and Nut, goddess of the sky, and with each piece that I wrap in tissue and cotton wool I am slow because I caress them. My fingers will not leave them alone.

'Hurry, hurry,' I mutter to myself, but my hands are shaking so much that I have to tuck them under my armpits to keep them still. I don't want you to see them.

'The move has upset all of us,' the Fat Man grumbles, 'but we don't go around wailing and beating our heads against the ground.'

'He is adjusting better, now that I've got him working again.'

'Tell him to speed up.'

You say nothing. Not far behind my awning the two Egyptians who shared the house with us are also at work, crating up the heavier stone artefacts, and I hear them laugh.

Are they laughing at me?

I start to feel sick.

'We're leaving tomorrow night,' the Fat Man tells you and I hear you gasp.

'Tomorrow?'

'Yes.'

'So soon? There is so much we still have to extract from the tomb.'

'Just drag the best stuff out and get it down here and into the crates. Tomorrow night we ship out of here.'

'Why so soon?' you ask. I can hear the anger in your voice.

'It's Fareed and his bloody nationalists. Making more trouble last night. We have to move faster and get out of here before he tracks us down.'

'Is the transport arranged?'

'Of course. We're all waiting for you and that brother of yours. Look, I've brought you an extra pair of hands.' He raised his voice. 'Malak, over here, boy.'

'Yes, sir *bey*, I come right now.' The young voice comes closer and I sit down in the sand with my face in my hands to shut out all the people. 'Good morning, excellent fine morning, sir Timothy, sir, I pleased much to help in many many ways, yes.'

You give the grunt you make when you are cross. 'A bit young, I think.'

'No, sir Timothy sir, you see I big strong.'

'Get yourself a shovel from the pile, Malak.'

'Immediately, sir, yes.'

After a pause you ask in a lower voice. 'What good is a boy to me?'

'Just put him to work, for God's sake, Timothy. You and your imbecile are never satisfied. Get the tomb emptied fast and make damn sure you control him.'

I hear a big rush of air, like the winter wind but I know it has come from your mouth.

'Georgie is not a dog. Nor a child. And he is certainly not an imbecile. He is my brother.' You shout the last four words and I wrap tissue-paper around my head.

I watch the boy stride easily up the hills, even up the steep parts, balancing a wooden crate on his shoulders. It is far too big for him to carry, but he does it without effort. It is as much as I can do just to carry myself up the hills and even then I need your hand to get me up the steep parts. I am glad when he is swallowed by the purple shadows.

'Don't look at him like that, Georgie. He's only a kid.' You are under my awning with me.

'Look at him like what?'

'Like you could kill him.'

I turn away and meticulously start to wrap a set of gold and enamel amulets in tissue-paper. 'Where did he come from?'

'The boy? Oh, just someone Scott picked up in Luxor last night. An extra pair of hands and a tongue that doesn't ask questions.'

'Why choose a child?'

'Because he does what he's told.' You glance up at the silhouettes disappearing over a sandy ridge on the barren hill and you smile. 'And because the boy is very engaging.'

I want you to look away from the hill. 'What does that mean?'

'It means that he's easy to like.'

I think about that as I fold a thick layer of cotton wool around the tissue-paper. 'You are engaging.'

'Ah,' you say. That is all.

But you come across the sand until you are standing close and I know you are staring at me, though I don't look up from my work. Against all the rules you place your arm across my shoulders. You know and I know that it makes me nervous and can tip me into an *episode*, but we both let it lie there.

'Thank you, Georgie.'

'You're welcome.'

'Your manners are impeccable today.' You squeeze my shoulder and it takes all my strength not to beg you to stop.

I glance sideways at you. The sun is behind you, turning your hair into a halo, and you are wearing your usual shorts and a short-sleeved shirt. I always dress in full-length trousers and long-sleeved shirts, whatever the heat, because I cannot bear this burning sun on my limbs. It makes them shrivel inside. I want to say something to you. To thank you for telling the Fat Man I am not an imbecile.

'I am proud,' I say, looking down at the silver figure of Anubis with his handsome jackal's head lying on my palm, 'proud that you are my brother.'

You withdraw your arm abruptly. I try not to show my relief. I glance at you again and your eyes have gone small, your mouth is a strange shape and you are shaking your head from side to side. I have no idea what it means and I feel the edge of panic. I squeeze Anubis tight.

382

'Georgie,' you say in an odd voice, 'how is it that you have the power to undo me?'

'I know I am not engaging.'

You start to laugh, great billows of sound that buffet the canvas awning, and I don't know why but I laugh with you.

The truck is filthy. I don't like it. I refuse to climb in. We are meant to be loading more crates on board but I walk away and squat down in the cooler air of its shadow on the sand. I feel sick again.

I know why. It's because the Fat Man won't leave me alone. He goads me. With insults and with kicks every time your back is turned, the way a matador goads a wounded silent stupid bull. I want to trample him in the dirt and rip open his belly with sharp horns. Maybe beautiful Isis will lend me hers.

In front of him I remain silent and stupid.

You stand beside me, smoking a cigarette. You don't offer me one, so I know you are cross with me.

'Not helping us?' you ask.

'No.'

'Why not?'

'I don't want to.'

You don't bother to argue but you exhale heavily. We don't speak. I am thinking of the tent I must sleep in tonight and the insects that will share it with me. I grit my teeth together, so that no noise will crawl out. Suddenly you grip my shoulder and haul me to my feet so roughly that my knees are unsteady.

'Look!' you say.

I look at your hand.

'No.' You point. 'Look at the side of the truck.'

I stare wildly. See nothing but dirt.

'Look there.'

You indicate a patch of dirt that has been disturbed near the rear wheel arch. I squint at it. It is a snake. Someone has drawn a short snake in the filth on the truck. My mouth drops open and a weird whooping noise comes out. You prod me in the ribs and I clamp my jaw shut.

'Hush, Georgie!'

But you are grinning. We are both grinning. Because in ancient Egyptian hieroglyphs a snake is the letter 'J'. and 'J' stands for only one person.

Jessie.

46

Monty stood in a doorway in the dark street. He waited.

Nothing.

He listened for the soft footfalls.

Nothing.

Minutes passed. The night air grew colder. But still there was no sound, not even a match being struck or a smothered cough. Nothing. Whoever it was who was following him, he had the patience of the devil.

Monty had moved through the streets, treading with care because there were few lamps to show the way, just the lacy light of the moon, and you never knew what might be lying underfoot. He'd headed across town to the square in front of Luxor Temple where the ruins of the columns with their papyrus-form carvings rose eerie and unearthly into the darkness. The nearby souk was closed at this hour, but Monty had spotted a bar further down the road, its spill of yellow light picking out the rats that skulked along the wall.

The coffee houses in the streets of Luxor – the ones used by Egyptians, that is, not the smart cafés frequented by westerners – were not unwelcoming, but neither were they exactly welcoming. As soon as he set foot in one he became the focus of attention. Dark faces and darker eyes fixed on him with interest and curiosity, but he sensed little hostility and he took his time drifting from one place to another. Calling for a coffee here, a *shisha* pipe there until his brain was turning cartwheels. He fell into conversations. One with an old man who possessed only one eye and had fought fifty years earlier in the Battle of Tel-El-Keber, when General Sir Garnet Wolseley's British victory had opened up the whole of Egypt to British occupation.

'Some of them fought in skirts,' the old man said, baying with laughter and wiping his good eye on the sleeve of his *galabaya*. 'Soldiers in short skirts. Like girls.'

'They would be Highlanders,' Monty remarked.

'One took my eye on his bayonet as a souvenir.'

Monty bought him a pipe of *shisha*. 'It was war, my friend. Bad things happen.'

Comrades with half their brains blown out. Horses blind and screaming. Men hanging from barbed-wire, dripping blood for the rats to devour. A no-man's land that was everyman's hell. Yes, bad things happen.

With another he discussed the price of cotton and the disease brucellosis which had decimated his flock of goats, while another wanted to enthuse over the films of Mary Pickford and the greatness of King Fuad. Each coffee house brought new understanding to Monty and each bar a fresh perspective on Egyptian life, but no one wanted to talk about the caves in the hills or knew the first thing about a man called Fareed who wore black. Or so they said.

It was when he entered the bar near the souk that he glanced in the large mirror on the opposite wall, pitted and grainy but framing a perfect image of an Egyptian man standing on the opposite pavement. Behind Monty's back he was staring hard at him. Then he was gone. Monty ordered a beer and tried to conjure up the man again – a slight figure in a white *galabaya* and dark jacket, an earnest-looking face and the soft movements of a cat.

This time he didn't linger. He passed his beer to a man receiving a haircut by the door and strode up the street, past the shuttered shops and around the next corner. A tent-maker's tiny establishment was still open, the owner seated on the floor and stitching a sheet of canvas held between his bare feet, but just beyond it was a deep-set doorway that lay in darkness.

Monty stepped into it. Anyone following him would have to pass through the patch of yellow light from the tent-maker's workshop. So now he stood there, thinking and waiting. Listening for the devil on cat's feet. From here he could smell the river odour of the Nile and caught the steady chug of a paddle-steamer manoeuvring to a new berth, preparing for its next day's cargo of tourists. He breathed softly, stilling the clamour in his chest and letting his eyes focus on the shadows in the darkness. He could feel his feet eager to move, his head curious to peek out around the corner of the doorway, but he denied them both. His muscles remained tense and in his hand, flat against his leg, he carried a knife.

Bad things happen.

The white *galabaya* was not hard to spot when it crossed his field of vision in the doorway. It took barely a second to step out and put a blade to the man's throat from behind. Instantly he froze and wisely offered no resistance.

Monty drew him into the doorway.

'Who are you?'

'I am nobody, sir.'

'Why are you following me?'

'I am not following. I am going home. I mean no harm to you, sir.'

Monty hesitated. 'Turn around.'

Slowly the Egyptian turned and Monty stepped back to inspect him. He was small-boned, his skin dark, with calm intelligent black eyes and a quiet inoffensive manner. 'I mean no harm to you, sir,' he said again. He turned his palms out to show he held no weapon.

Monty almost apologised, almost put away the knife with a respectful salaam. But in the split second that the words took to travel from his brain to his tongue, he drew breath, and that was when he smelt the warm and woody scent of cinnamon. It seemed to emanate from the man's clothing, as if he ground up the spicy bark each day and its dust filtered into the material of his *galabaya* or into the creases of his skin. Instantly it brought back a memory. For a moment it hovered tantalisingly out of reach but Monty shook his head to jog it loose and abruptly it came to him.

'The tomb,' he said sharply. 'King Tutankhamen's tomb. You were there. You put a wrist-watch in Miss Kenton's handbag.'

The dark eyes assessed him seriously. 'Yes, I did. The watch was to show that she could trust me, though I didn't risk telling her my name there.'

'So who are you? What are you doing here – with the wrist-watch of Miss Kenton's brother?'

The man nodded, as though debating with himself. 'Come, let us drink tea.'

'I am Ahmed Rashid. I am based in Cairo but I have travelled down to Luxor because I am interested in you and in Miss Kenton.'

The moment they sat down in the small chess café in a side-alley-way where the customers were too absorbed in their own ardent chess games to pay much attention to the newcomers, Monty noticed that Ahmed Rashid had shed his diffident manner. Though still polite, he became much more businesslike, the edges of his face somehow sharper. Monty had a grim sense of the situation slipping from bad to worse, and he kept a close eye on the door.

'What is it,' he asked, 'that you want from us?'

The man smiled courteously and sipped his mint tea, refusing to be hurried.

Monty changed tack. 'Who are you and what is your business?'

More success this time. Ahmed Rashid leaned forward across the small wooden table, so that his voice need be no more than a whisper. Monty could smell the mint on his breath.

'I am an officer with the Egyptian Department of Antiquities.' He paused. 'A police officer.'

388

Monty felt the ground slide under his feet. His hand gripped his tea-glass tighter, but he did not react with anything more than a raised eyebrow. 'Is that a fact, Mr Rashid?'

'Captain Rashid.'

'So why are you here?'

Rashid leaned back in his seat, eyes fixed on Monty's face, watching for any telltale tic or twitch. 'Come now, Mr Chamford.' Monty noted the error with his name. Either this man did not know as much as he implied or it was a deliberate insult. 'We both know why I am here.'

'Enlighten me.'

'I am here because of Timothy Kenton.'

Oh, Christ! Tim was about to be arrested and chucked into prison. Digging up Egyptian treasures without a licence. Stealing valuable antiquities. Exporting them without a licence. Travelling on a false passport. The list was horribly impressive.

Monty smiled engagingly. 'Well, that makes two of us. Do you know where he is to be found?'

Rashid started to shake his head. He opened his mouth to speak, just as the ear-splitting sound of a gunshot crashed through the quiet room, deafening everyone in it and leaving a neat red flower on the white sleeve of Rashid's *galabaya*. Monty dived to the floor, dragging the bleeding Egyptian with him, while others screamed and one man fell to his knees in loud prayer to Allah.

Only then did Monty see the four men looming in the doorway. They wore black robes and the one in front held a gun in his hand. It was a very old Browning semi-automatic but Monty knew it was none the less deadly for all that. He tipped the table on to the floor for protection for Rashid and himself. Not much, but something. His knife was in his hand and he prepared to rush forward. If he was going to die, he would die fighting.

Jessie. It was the only word in his head.

The four men came for him. Him alone. Not Rashid. Nor anyone else in the café. He swung the knife. Cut twice. Saw blood. But they overpowered him with their numbers and hauled him out into the street, threw him on the ground where the one who carried a stick beat his back. The blows were well aimed.

They left him. In the dirt. Alive.

'Open door! Open door, please, Mr Monty sir *bey*. Quick, yes please.'

Monty shuddered. He was standing under the shower taking the full force of the cold water on his back. He flinched as he stooped to pick up a towel and wrap it around his waist. Malak's fist was banging on the door, waking up the whole damn corridor, otherwise Monty might have ignored the boy and stayed in the shower.

'All right! Quiet down.' He swung open the door. Outside in the corridor Malak looked small and frightened. 'Get in here, boy.'

'I did it, sir *bey*, I did it, yes.'

'Did what?'

'Found special dead place, big secret, I did.' His words were tumbling over each other and his eyes were darting all around the room, as if he feared to find someone else there.

Monty stood, stunned. He stared at the boy, disbelieving. 'You found the tomb?'

Malak puffed out his skinny chest. 'Yes sir.'

'How?'

'I find your Dr Scott, so clever I am.'

'You spoke to him?'

A nod for reply.

'We told you not to because he—'

'Oh but I so clever, I help him much loading boat. I know him from Missie's picture and I carry much I strong.' He waved a puny arm at Monty to prove it. 'I say I want much good work. He laugh at me, sir *bey*.' He flashed his disarming smile around the room but was clearly jumpy.

'What is it, Malak? What's the problem?'

The boy's face crumpled unexpectedly and his huge black eyes filled with tears. 'I go with Dr Scott, yes *bey*, to camp and tonight he kill a man I see yes. I see it.'

'Oh, Malak.' He put his arm around the small trembling shoulders. 'You are a brave young man. Very full of courage. To walk right into the lion's den.'

The boy tilted his head back and looked up at him. 'No lions, sir *bey*. Man shot.' He mimicked a gun. 'He enemy man. I not know more how he bad. Dr Scott shoot. In head. I see.' Tears were rolling down his grubby cheeks.

Don't let it be Tim. He hugged Malak to him until the boy stopped shaking and then he walked over to the glass of whisky already standing waiting by his bed. But when he turned his back to pick it up, the boy squealed alarmingly.

'What is . . . ?' Monty started, then stopped. He quickly snatched his shirt from the bed and, with a curse under his breath as he stretched out his arm, slipped it on. 'It's nothing, Malak.'

'That not nothing, sir *bey*. That bad yes, very bad.'

'Forget about it, Malak.' He lowered himself on the edge of the bed and took a decent swig of the whisky. 'Come here.'

Malak shot to his side.

'Let's get this straight, Malak. You went to Scott's camp.'

'Yes sir *bey*.'

'You travelled in his truck? Last night?'

'Yes sir *bey*.'

'With others?'

'Two men. Egyptian donkey-heads, sir *bey*.'

'You spent today working at the camp?'

A nod. 'I carry much. From dead place.'

'The tomb?'

'Yes sir *bey*.'

Monty ruffled the boy's filthy hair. 'You, young man, are impressive. Tell me, was there a blond Englishman there?'

'Oh yes, oh *bey*. He strange.'

Monty smiled. 'Well, what do you expect? He's English. Did you speak to him?'

'No, sir, no.'

'We must go and tell Miss Kenton.'

391

He didn't want to ask the next question but he had no choice. 'Can you lead us back to the camp?'

Monty saw the boy hesitate, saw the battle in his young face between pride and fear. He didn't urge him. Just let him make his own choice in his own time.

'Yes, *bey*.'

Monty pushed himself to his feet, his breathing shallow. He could hardly bear to use his lungs.

'Let's go see Miss Kenton.'

It was one o'clock in the morning.

'You tell her you bad back yes?'

'No, Malak. Definitely not yes.' He mimed a button on the boy's lips. 'No bad back. Just the tomb and the blond Englishman.'

The boy rolled his eyes. 'I show.'

'Thank you, Malak. You're a very brave boy.'

Malak looked up at him. 'You very brave man yes.'

Jessie stared out of her hotel window at the vast night sky and imagined Tim out there somewhere, looking up at the same stars and the same moon. Did he know she was here? Had he seen her drawing on the truck? Was he feeling on his skin the same chill night breeze off the Nile?

She had woken abruptly not long after midnight, feeling much better. Twelve hours' sleep. Monty had been right. Her body had needed total rest to rid itself of toxins. Her hand was still sore but the swelling in her arm was much reduced, so that it looked almost normal and she could move it, no longer so stiff. The drumbeat was still in her head but as soon as she opened her eyes she was aware that Monty had gone. Where her hand touched the sheet, it was cold.

'Back in the land of the living, I see.'

'Maisie!'

She was sitting in the chair beside the bed. Her hair was released from the grip of its tight bun at the back of her head and fell in soft waves around her narrow face, so that she looked much less intrepid. Wrapped in the soft camel-coloured folds of her dressing

392

gown with her umbrella at her side and her eyes drooping with tiredness, she looked worried.

Instantly Jessie sat up. 'Where is he?'

'I don't know. He asked me to watch over you. Said he'd not be long.'

'How long?'

'Over two hours.'

Jessie swung her legs out of bed.

'And where,' Maisie said sternly, 'do you think you're off to, young lady?'

'I have to get dressed.'

'Now? I'm telling you, young madam, that you are going exactly nowhere.'

But Jessie insisted on dressing and drinking glass after glass of water to rehydrate herself. She took two of her tablets and sat by the window. Ready and waiting.

It was Maisie who answered the knock on the door. Jessie could hear words tumbling into the room, words about Tim and the tomb, about Scott and a gun, about Malak tramping through the desert hills on his own for hour after hour, navigating as best he could by the stars to find his way back to Luxor. Talk of police. Words that were important.

Yet all she could see was Monty's face. There was a darkness in his eyes and a tightness around his mouth. When she asked what was wrong, he gave her a laugh that wasn't a laugh and said, 'Everything.'

Something had happened. In those two hours something had hurt him, and whatever it was, it made her sick to her stomach that he wasn't telling her. She saw that his knuckles were skinned, and when he walked to the door to fetch his coat from his room and one of his jackets for Malak, he moved as though his bones were tied together with barbed-wire.

Whatever had happened was bad.

*

They travelled through the middle of the night on camels provided by Yasser, just the three of them – Monty, Malak and herself. Maisie cursed Monty to hell and back because he refused to let her ride with them, but he would not budge.

'The risk is too great,' he said flatly.

'The risk is of my own choosing, you camel-brained toff!' Maisie shouted after him. He did not even look back.

They rode in near silence, except for the hiss of the wind across the sand and the churning rumble of the camel's gut as they moved on cushioned feet over the stony ground. Jessie was wrapped up with a long scarf around her head and neck, as well as an Arab robe against the icy night air, and she took a while to adjust to the odd pitching and rolling gait of her animal, but she urged it on ever faster, discarding her sling. It was when the lights of Luxor vanished behind them and the great sea of darkness that was the desert rose up around them that Jessie shuddered and moved her camel closer to Monty's. The boy was up ahead, chirruping blithely and kicking his heels at his beast as he guided the way by moonlight.

'Monty,' she said softly. 'What happened tonight? With the police.'

She could make out the outline of his head, bulky in its scarf, and saw it lift from his chest on which it had sunk.

'Nothing much. A policeman in plain clothes questioned me about Tim but I told him I knew nothing.'

'What then?'

'I had to leave the police officer for a few minutes and when I came back he had gone. I have no idea how he knew me.'

'Is that all?'

'Yes.'

'You're lying to me.'

She heard him give a throaty chuckle. 'It's better that way.'

They left it at that.

47

The desert shimmered in the first light of dawn and it seemed to sigh as if it were breathing. Silver skeins of mist wound in and out of the wadis, sliding down the smooth waves of sand and writhing through narrow gulleys. Jessie lay flat on her stomach alongside Monty on a low ridge, watching the dunes around them ripple away to where sand and rocks became a dark blur.

'The desert plays tricks on you,' she murmured. She didn't trust it.

They lay immobile, taking in the stillness and waiting for the three tents on the gravel flats below them to emerge from the darkness. The silence was intense. They had left the camels, frothing at the mouth, in the care of Malak about a mile back in the lee of a steep slope that would keep the animals' mumblings out of earshot. It had taken a long ride for the boy to find the exact location of the camp again and at times they had to double back on themselves and retrace their steps in the sand to regain the correct direction. But they were here in time to see the first rays of the sun start to paint the desert blood-red.

They lay close together, shoulder to shoulder, hip to hip, sharing their heat, keeping each other's body warm. She could tell something hurt but he'd tell her when he was ready and until then she linked her hand with his, holding him safe. It occurred to her that he had changed. No longer the amiable English gent. No longer bubbling with charm and disarming smiles. Something darker lay beside her now, someone who possessed his own private torments and troubles that she could only guess at.

But he trusted her. As she trusted him, and she valued that. It was something she had not been capable of before but, stretched out here in the cold desert dawn, she was willing to risk more than just her neck on these rocky slopes with him. But when he turned to look at her and his eyes in the shadows were so intent, so tenacious, she knew exactly what was coming.

'No,' she said before he asked.

'You don't know what I'm going to say.'

'Say it then.'

'Please, Jessie, will you stay here? Let me go down on my own.'

'The answer is still no.'

He made a despairing noise under his breath. 'There is no point us both getting into trouble.'

'I agree, Monty. So why don't I go down on my own? They won't take much notice of a stupid girl, one who has just come chasing after her brother. Let me ...'

'Forget that. I'm not letting you go marching down to those tents on your own, so don't let's waste breath discussing it.' He wrapped an arm around her and pulled her so close against him that she could smell the stale odour of his robe and see the pulse at the angle of his jaw. Tucked against his ribs under the robe the outline of something metallic jarred against her.

'A gun? Monty, no. If they see you with a gun they might ...'

'Hush, it's just for show. Not for use. It was my father's.'

Jessie shivered. For a moment she buried her face in the damp material of his shoulder.

'Very well, we do what we agreed,' he said eventually. 'Don't worry so much.' He gave a soft chuckle that almost sounded real. 'Tim won't let them hurt his big sister.'

The mist was beginning to thin and the ridgepoles of the three tents rose above it, disembodied and ghostly. At that moment the flap of one of the tents flicked open and a large muscular Egyptian emerged, scratching his beard and scanning the horizon. Instantly Jessie recognised him as the driver of the truck and she felt Monty flatten her closer to the rocks. The man was wearing nothing more than a long undershirt and a gun holster. With a yawn that was audible up on the ridge he walked away from the tents, urinated, then squatted to defecate in the sand, and all the time he watched the slopes above him.

The camp was well-placed. On a small flat pan at the foot of a cluster of rock-strewn hills that curved away to the north, barren and desolate, while to the west a sea of sand and gravel stretched to the horizon, rising and falling like sun-scorched waves. Jessie could just make them out in the dim light and her eyes turned away from the sight of them quickly. She found Monty watching her.

'Do you know,' she whispered, pointing at the canopy of stars that hung above them, 'that Ancient Egyptians believed that stars were the souls of the dead?'

He smiled at her and shook his head.

'The souls,' she continued, 'are waiting in the darkness for the return of the sun-god Ra.' She touched his cheek and let her fingers follow the line of his jaw. 'That's what I've been doing. All these years. Waiting in the darkness.'

He kissed her mouth and she tasted the sour tang of the desert on his lips. Two other men suddenly emerged from the tent into the semi-darkness, one with a large belly under his *galabaya*, and all three washed vigorously in a bowl of water, then proceeded to say their dawn prayers. Facing east, the shadowy figures went through the ritual of devotion, of standing and kneeling on their prayer mats, touching their foreheads to the ground and reciting their morning prayers.

Jessie found the process oddly disarming. It was so calm. She wanted to shout to them, to call out, '*Salaam*, look at us, we're part of creation too. Don't shoot us. Just let me talk to my brother. Peace be upon you.'

She even opened her mouth. But she allowed no sound to escape. It wasn't the living that mattered here, it was the dead. And the treasure that was buried with them.

48

Georgie

Egypt 1932

Today is not a good day. It starts badly. You are not concentrating. You break the yolks when you are frying my eggs and they all run together, so that it looks like diarrhoea.

'The eggs taste the same,' you say. 'I haven't time to cook more. Just eat it, Georgie, please.'

I would rather eat cat-sick.

I cannot understand your face but I can hear in your voice that something is wrong.

Usually your movements are slow and calm, as if to counter-balance my jerky ones, but today they are quick and impatient. You hurry in and out of my tent, all rapid words and long legs, and there are more people rushing around outside. I hear their deep voices. I feel small bubbles of panic start to fizz in my blood until they pop in my brain. I struggle hard to breathe quietly. I stay in my tent. I sit in my canvas chair which I like and I count silently in my head. It is the only way I can block out your words. I reach two thousand and eighty-four before you notice.

'Georgie, you're not listening to me.'

You are pacing up and down along the centre of the tent where the roof is highest. Even so, it touches your blond curls. I search for the right words to say to you but none of the sentences I have learned seems to fit, and then I recall what you say to me.

'What is the matter? Why are you upset?' I ask.

You stop pacing and look at me. I recognise your expression. It is surprise. You kneel down in front of me and speak quietly.

'I'm sorry, Georgie. I don't mean to scare you.'

You look at what I'm wearing. A shirt, two sweaters, a jacket and scarf, and a blanket. It's not the cold. I pile on clothes when I am upset. The weight of them comforts me.

'Georgie, we're leaving today. The man I told you about who wants to take our tomb objects from us, Fareed, is too close now. So we're packing everything on camels to carry down to the truck. We have to work fast.'

'Is that why you are upset?'

You clench your hands together. I have never seen you like this.

'Don't, Georgie.'

I realise I am wailing. I wrap the blanket over my mouth.

'I need your help,' you say, but now your voice is calm and steady. 'I have to go up to the tomb one last time . . .'

'Take me with you.'

'No, Georgie, I have to be fast and anyway I need you to work here while I'm gone.'

'I don't want you to be gone.'

'I know. But it won't be for long. There are still the canopic jars and the jewellery for you to pack up. I'll do the gold chair myself when I get back.'

'Is that why you're upset?'

Instead of replying, you thrust your fingers into your hair and jam the heels of your hands hard against your eyes. An odd low grunt comes out of your mouth.

I want to go back. To tiptoe back to before we started this conversation, to before pieces of you seemed to fall apart. I don't know what to say to you. I don't have any words. So I take off my blanket and wrap it around your shoulders. Then I wait. I count in my head to stop myself screaming. When I reach one hundred and sixty-nine you lift your hands away from your face.

'Thank you, Georgie.'

'You're welcome.'

You smile but it is lopsided.

'I'll tell you why I am upset,' you say.

I say nothing. I don't want to know. It is going to be bad.

'I'm upset because . . . ' you draw in a deep breath, 'the gunshot you heard yesterday was Dr Scott killing one of Fareed's men. I saw it, Georgie. It was terrible. A bullet in the head. Cold murder. I had no idea that . . . ' You stop. Your lip is trembling. For a moment you shut your eyes, and when you open them, you are you again.

'Hello,' I say.

You give an odd kind of laugh and rise to your feet. You throw the blanket on to my camp-bed. 'Now, you must go to that awning of yours and get on with your work.'

I nod.

'I will be back soon,' you say and walk over to the tent flap.

As you lift it up, I ask, because I know I get things wrong sometimes, 'Do you hate Dr Scott now?'

You look at the sand and the dirt outside, and you utter that odd low grunt again. Then you leave.

Is that a yes? Or a no?

I particularly don't like the sky today. It is too big and too bright. It has crumbled the desert into dust and I fear it will do the same to me. I work under the awning with my back to it and I wear your corduroy jacket even though it is hot. It gives me unexpected pleasure to wear a piece of your clothing.

Your *episode* this morning has frightened me and I am careful to do exactly as you asked. I work fast. Sorting, wrapping, packing. No

400

one comes near me – no one ever does – despite the fact there are many more men today with camels to carry the wooden packing crates. Only the Fat Man, the one you call Dr Scott, stands just outside the awning and watches me every now and again. His skin is so smooth and shiny, it looks as if he oils and polishes it every morning and trims his horrible little beard with nail-scissors. I don't look at him.

'Has your brother told you?'

I don't answer.

'That we are clearing out of this dust-bowl today,' he continues.

If I say nothing, he will go away. I separate a beautiful heavy gold pendant from its matching bracelet, jot down a description and measurements in my notebook, and fold it in a sheet of wrapping.

'We could leave you behind.'

My hand shakes.

'For Fareed to find.'

I almost drop the pendant.

He laughs.

I turn to face him. 'Dr Scott, why do you hate me?'

'Because you're an imbecile.'

'No, I am not. I am highly intelligent.'

He laughs again and I see spittle come from his mouth, tiny darts of poison. He is wearing a panama hat and a pale linen suit, sweaty under the sun, but he doesn't step forward under the shade of the awning. That would be too close. For him. And for me. Behind him lie the rocky slopes of the hills and I see movement there.

'You are an imbecile,' Scott tells me, and all his laughter has dripped into the sand, leaving an expression I cannot place but which makes me look away quickly. 'That is why you were locked away. Don't look surprised. I know your father. He's a fine chap and deserves a better son than you. And Timothy deserves a better brother.'

I cannot stop the tears. They drip on to the gold bracelet with its engraving of Hathor wearing the sun-disk.

I cannot stop my tongue. 'Is he ashamed of me?' it asks.

'Of course he is. Wouldn't you be?'

I nod.

Satisfied, he walks away.

'Tim!'

The word hisses across the sand.

'Tim! It's me.'

The desert distorts sound. I cannot tell from which direction it comes. I keep my head down as I hold a gold ring forged in the shape of a ram's head. I stroke its exquisite workmanship and it helps calm the juddering in my chest.

'Tim!'

A figure steps out of the bright sun and under my canvas shelter so quickly that I jump back, alarmed. He is wearing a grey Egyptian robe and scarf around the head, but when I turn to face him he freezes, hand half outstretched.

'You're not Tim!'

I look at the face. Not a man's, despite the clothes. It is fine-boned with strong cheekbones and startled blue eyes that I never thought to see again. I know it instantly.

'Jessie.'

Her face unfreezes. She shakes her head back and forth. Her eyes are huge. 'No,' she whispers. 'It can't be you.'

I nod. I smile. I cannot speak.

'Georgie?'

'Yes.'

She yanks the scarf from around her head, as though she cannot breathe, and comes forward to embrace me, but something in my face makes her hold back. Her eyes are brimming with unshed tears.

'How?' she asks. 'How are you here?'

'Tim brought me.'

'Tim?'

I break my rule. I look at her face, at her eyes and her mouth, at her beautiful straight nose and the curl of her golden lashes, at the

402

movement of her thick blonde hair. Something is choking inside me, hurting in the middle of my breastbone. I try to cough it up but it won't budge. She is speaking but I cannot hear her because my blood is pounding against my eardrums, and I cry out her name.

'Jessie!'

She stops speaking. She understands. Her gaze dances all over my face and my hair and my clothes, and back to my eyes. She is smiling so hard I fear her lovely face will split, and I do not hide from her scrutiny. We have twenty years of staring at each other to catch up on.

I touch her. Her hand. It is bandaged.

'Georgie,' she whispers and holds out her fingers tentatively.

I let her touch my face.

A shadow falls across the entrance. 'Well, well, what do we have here?'

It is the Fat Man and I open my mouth to tell Jessie to beware, but he sticks a gun in her face and seizes her arm and drags her out into the harsh light of the sun. I pick up one of the tall ancient canopic jars made of heavy alabaster and swing it at his head. The jar shatters into pieces, but so does his face.

49

Monty heard the crash and the scream. Instantly, he was on the move. He had been standing guard in the shadow of the largest tent, keeping a sharp eye on the sentries – four of them now – who were patrolling the outskirts of the camp, Lee-Enfields at the ready, while Jessie entered the shelter where they had spotted Tim working.

They had shuffled into camp by attaching themselves to the tail-end of one of the camel-trains, unheeded in their enveloping Egyptian garb. Everyone was rushing and shouting, the camp seething with the frantic activity of packing. But Monty was well aware that they had only minutes. That was all. Before they would be spotted. So he tracked each guard's position with sharp eyes while Jessie was speaking with Tim.

Everything depended on what her brother had to say.

When the camp had first come to life at dawn, he and Jessie had been forced by the patrols to retreat deeper into the hills for a few hours, though it was the piles of wooden crates in the centre of the camp that kept drawing the attention of the guards, the way a golden flame draws moths. But now everyone was running to the screams.

Monty yanked his scarf lower over his face as he raced to the front of the shelter but what he saw was not what he expected. Scott was writhing on the ground. His face and hands were a mask of blood. Over him stood Jessie's brother, his face rigid in a rictus grin. In his hand he clutched the shattered base of a jar and Jessie was staring at him in horror.

'You could have killed him,' she gasped.

'Tim,' Monty snapped, 'let's get out of here while we—'

'I'm not Tim. I'm Georgie.'

Monty seized Jessie's arm. 'Out! Now!'

She didn't move. She didn't take her eyes off her brother.

'Jessie, we have to . . .'

But it was too late. A line of Egyptian workmen stood in front of them and Monty knew his options had just shrunk to zero.

He drew his gun.

50

Georgie

Egypt 1932

He's not dead. That's what I tell myself. The Fat Man is not dead.
But his forehead is scoured by deep gashes, his nose is a bloody pulp
and two of his front teeth have gone missing.

He's lucky he's not dead.

But even I know you're not supposed to do that to someone, not
wreck his face. The blood, thick and slimy, is the worst thing. I hate
it even more than the screaming. But he let go of Jessie and the gun.
I fixed that for her. But she's acting oddly. She doesn't walk right,
she doesn't talk right. Not even to the tall man holding the gun and
scaring the life out of the Egyptians. She looks like a sleepwalker we
had back at the clinic, seeing only what's inside her head. Yet she
doesn't shift her gaze off me, not even for a second and I know I'm
shaking. I don't want her to see me shaking.

'Here,' the tall Englishman says sharply.

He yanks off his headscarf and pushes it into the Fat Man's face.

The Fat Man bellows. I don't know if it's pain or rage, I can't tell, but the Tall Man drags him to his feet.

'Tell your men to get back to work, loading up the camels. We don't want to be here when Fareed arrives.'

The Fat Man shouts something. I don't hear it. All I see is you. You come striding down from the hills into the camp and I call out your name. You look at me, your hair covered in limestone dust and your boots the colour of the desert, and then you look at Jessie. When you look at Jessie you smile like the great sun-god Ra and it pierces my throat so I cannot speak.

She runs to you. Not like normal people run. She runs like I imagine a gazelle would run, with long bounding steps, leaping over the distance between you.

'Tim!'

'Jessie! How did you get here? I knew you'd find me, I knew it. You're amazing to find me.'

Brother and sister. You throw your arms around each other, wrapping tight, holding close.

'Oh Tim, thank God you're alive, I was so frightened that . . . '

You hush her, more gently than you hush me when I am upset. You wipe tears from her cheek with your finger. I don't know why she's crying. Is it because the Fat Man is hurt?

'Where did you find him, Tim? Where? Why is he here in Egypt?' she asks quickly.

'I couldn't take the risk of leaving him in England. I didn't know what might happen.'

'He doesn't look good,' she says. Her face twists oddly.

'I know, but give him time. He's damaged.'

Yes, it is the Fat Man they must mean. I damaged him.

'You must make allowance, Jessie,' you say. 'Don't judge him on this. He's very upset at the moment.'

I'd be upset too if my face was knocked in.

'I'll help him, Tim. As much as I can, I'll help him.'

'It would mean a lot to him.'

'Are you sure? Does he want me?'

407

'Yes.'

Why? I want to shout at her. Why should she help the Fat Man?

'What's going on here, Tim?' she asks, indifferent to me. 'Why all this secrecy?'

You lean your head against hers and speak so low that I can't hear your words, but I see your hair and her hair merge into one golden mesh. Despite the heat I suddenly feel cold. I'm shivering. I shut my eyes to block you out. When I open them you are still holding her but over her shoulder you are looking at the group of men, at the Fat Man covered in blood and at the Tall Man with the gun.

'Who are you?' you ask.

'My name's Monty Chamford. A friend of Jessie. I presume you are Timothy Kenton.'

You nod. 'What happened to Scott?'

'Georgie happened to Scott.'

You release Jessie and inspect me. I am standing in the shadows, but I know you will see my hands clutching each other tight in distress. I try to smile at you but it doesn't sit straight on my face and you draw your dusty eyebrows down in a frown.

I glance across at my tent. My blanket is there. I need it. I take a step towards it.

That is when the Fat Man starts screaming at you through his blood. 'You betrayed me, Kenton! You betrayed me! And you betrayed your father!'

Over and over.

My blanket. I need it. To smother the noise.

'Don't bring my father into this,' you shout.

'You know he's involved.' He mops his face with the Tall Man's scarf. 'He knows what we're doing to raise money for the Fascist cause.'

'You may fool him but you don't fool me.' I have never seen your face like this. It frightens me. 'You are stealing these treasures for your own pocket, you and your whole organisation out here.'

'Stop it,' I say. No one even looks at me.

The heat is fierce. But not from the sun. It is their anger that is scorching the air as it enters my lungs, and I put a hand over my mouth to keep it out.

Blood is dripping off the Fat Man's chin, but still he screams at you. 'You betrayed me. You were supposed to tell no one. No one! Yet look at them here.' He points at Jessie and the Tall Man.

It is the Tall Man who pulls Jessie aside, out of the way of the Fat Man's fury. I like him for that. He is the kind of man I would listen to.

He says, 'Don't be a fool, Scott. He has betrayed no one. We're here because of Jessie's guesswork and you are the—'

'Shut up, Chamford! You helped get Kenton here, don't you forget that. At that séance.'

I think the Fat Man has gone mad. He is shaking. Worse than I shake. Did I wreck his brain as well as his face? He charges at one of the guards near him and snatches the rifle from his shoulder. The air changes. I feel it. It turns thin and empty, as if there is no oxygen in it. Faces change. Eyes widen. No one breathes.

'Scott, put it down,' the Tall Man orders and points his own gun at him.

'You won't shoot me, Chamford. You need my loan on that mausoleum of yours.'

'Put that rifle down or I will pull this trigger.'

Before the words are finished, the Fat Man shouts again, 'You betrayed me, Kenton!' The rifle is moving towards you. 'Don't think that I don't know you've got Chamford in the pocket of the police. We've seen him talking with them.'

He is going to kill you.

No one takes notice of me. I snatch from my waistband the revolver that Scott dropped on the sand when I hit him and I pull the trigger immediately. The strength of the explosion in my hands scares the life out of me and I fling the gun away, but I see the Fat Man crumple to his knees. He sways for a moment. There is so much blood on him already that I do not know whether I have hit him or not.

My hands are dancing and my breath is escaping in a thin high noise that sounds like a bird's alarm call. If he stands up, he will kill me. But he doesn't stand up. He falls forward flat on his face and buries his bloody nose in the sand. That's how I know he is dead.

51

Jessie and Tim sat either side of Georgie on the sand in the shade of the truck. They sipped water that was warm and ignored the fact that their brother was swaddled from head to toe in a dark brown blanket.

'It's hard for him, Jessie.'

'I know.'

'He's better when everything is quiet.'

'So why did you bring him out here to Egypt?'

Tim looked away. 'I was worried. I had to come out here, but I couldn't leave him behind in the clinic.'

'Why not?'

'Because of Pa.'

Oh Pa, what have you done to my brothers?

'What did he do?'

'Haven't you noticed how deeply he is now involved not only in Fascism, but in the Eugenics Society as well? He and Captain Pitt-Rivers, the anthropologist, are as thick as thieves with Oswald Mosley. They all feed off each other.' He shook his head in dismay, scattering limestone dust. 'They believe society can be improved through imposed birth control and selective breeding.'

The brown bundle beside them shivered.

'I don't trust Pa.' Tim lowered his voice. 'All it would take is an extra syringe in the hands of Dr Churchward. No questions asked.'

'For heaven's sake, Tim, Pa wouldn't do such a terrible thing.'

'Wouldn't he? How well do you know him now?'

Jessie's stomach churned. 'Not well.' She studied the black leather briefcase at Tim's feet. It had Dr Scott's initials on it in brass lettering. 'You told me how you found the address of the clinic in Pa's safe, but why didn't Dr Churchward tell Pa about your visits?'

Tim laughed without humour and prodded at a sand beetle that bumped into his boot. 'That's easy. The first couple of times I visited Georgie, Churchward was on holiday in Germany, so he had no idea that his staff had let me in. When he returned, he learned how much better Georgie was behaving,' he patted the brown lump between them. 'Whenever Georgie got out of hand, the attendants threatened to stop my visits, and that kept him under control. So Churchward decided to let the visits continue. Unknown to me, I was their secret weapon. It made life easier for Churchward, but he knew Pa would put a stop to it if he was informed, so he kept it secret. Probably he thought I would soon give up anyway.'

'But you didn't.'

'No, I didn't.'

'Why not? It couldn't have been easy for a young boy.'

'It wasn't.'

A camel walked past, kicking up sand in its wake, as men loaded the crates into the truck.

'So why?' Jessie urged gently.

Tim hesitated. He glanced up at the hills and she knew he was thinking of Fareed somewhere out there, searching for them. Beside him lay Scott's revolver and Jessie wanted to hurl it behind the rocks. It had done too much damage for one day.

'I felt responsible. If our parents hadn't found me, they might have kept Georgie.'

Jessie shook her head. 'That would never have happened.'

'But also,' he paused and thought about his choice of words, 'I felt Georgie and I were, in an odd way, the same person. I stepped into his shoes, literally.'

She stared at the blanket. 'And into his pyjamas, I recall.'

'Yes, into everything that was his. We even looked alike. And you loved him so much. I wanted you to love me like that.'

'Oh Tim, I quickly learned to love you too.'

'I couldn't walk away from Georgie. It would have been like walking away from myself.' He nodded at the blanket. 'I love the blasted idiot.'

'It's obvious he loves you.' Jessie felt a huge wrench in her chest. 'I'm so happy he's had you for company all those years that I wasn't there. He wasn't alone. But why didn't you tell me? I could have . . .'

'He wouldn't let me. He didn't want you to see him so . . . damaged.'

'Oh, Georgie!'

For a while neither spoke. A sudden gust of wind swirled sand into their faces and they covered their eyes. It made it easier to say what she had to say.

'Tim, Anippe Kalim is here.'

He swung to face her. 'Anippe? In Luxor? Have you seen her?'

'Yes. I've spoken to her.'

'Here in Egypt. I can't believe she came looking for me too. Did she . . .'

'Tim, she's with Fareed. She's been working for him and his cause all along to get information from you.'

His face looked as if she'd slapped him. It took on a fixed expression, as though something of importance had just been squeezed out of him.

'I see,' he said. Nothing more.

'I'm sorry, Tim. Maybe when she knows you are not really working with Scott, she will . . .'

He shook his head. 'No. It all makes sense now. I was stupid to think there was a chance.'

His gaze swept across the hills, as though he still hoped he might spot Anippe's dark figure in the distance, but then he shook himself

413

and looked away. He lowered his eyelids, almost closing his eyes in the way she recognised. It meant he had something to confess.

'What is it, Tim?'

'There's something else.'

She waited. She could feel an uneasy anger stirring inside her but she didn't know exactly why or at whom.

'I should have told you years ago,' Tim said. 'When I found the papers in the safe about the clinic where Georgie was kept, there were other papers too.'

She sat forward. 'What papers?'

'My adoption papers.'

'Oh, Tim, what did ... ?'

'And Georgie's.'

'What?'

'Georgie is also adopted.'

'No!'

'Yes.' He looked at her intently. 'And yours.'

Jessie leaned back against the truck. Closed her eyes. Her throat was tight, her mouth dry. 'Are you sure?'

'Yes. It looks as if we were all part of an experiment. Blond, blue eyes, good bones and presumably good head measurements to fit the theories of human improvement and eugenics. All from different families, in case there were any mistakes.'

He didn't sound bitter. It amazed her that he didn't sound bitter.

'It explains a lot, Jessie,' he said gently. 'And when you think about it, it shows Pa has been generous in his care of Georgie all these years.'

'Generous?' She jumped to her feet. 'Georgie is his son, adopted or not. You don't put your son in a cage,' she said fiercely.

But he was right. It explained so much. The disappointment in her that she'd always seen on her father's face but never understood. For the first time she realised that he had married the same template of a human being too, and she wondered if her mother felt the same crushing weight of his disappointment, never able to live up to the ideal.

All of them adopted.

It shifted something fundamental inside her and when she looked down at Tim, crouched so protectively next to the brown hump that was Georgie on the sand, she felt the connection between herself and her brothers deepen into something different, into something more binding. As though their roots had locked together. She understood them better, suddenly. She felt their weaknesses were her weaknesses and their strengths were her strengths. She would be much slower to pass judgement in future when . . .

In future? What future?

'Tim,' she said urgently, 'what's the matter with me? I've been asking all the wrong questions. I should be giving you hell about this camp of yours. You, of all people, pillaging Egypt's history.' Her voice was rising in the still air. 'I'd never have believed it of you. That's why I came – to get you out of trouble because I believed in you. But what do I find? You've been organising the whole scheme with Dr Scott.'

'Jessie, I—'

'Tim, you wretch. You are a criminal.'

The blanket flew across the sand as Georgie scrambled to his feet, his limbs jerking in all directions, his mouth alarming in its contortions.

'He is not a criminal,' he shouted.

Tim was gratified by his unexpected champion, Jessie could see it in his face.

'You tell her, Georgie!'

Georgie swung towards her. 'Tim is not a criminal because he is committing no crime.'

'Look at those.' She gestured angrily at the crates.

'No, no, no. He's working with the police.'

'That's right, Georgie boy,' Tim hissed. 'Shout it out loud, why don't you? That way everyone can know.'

52

Georgie

Egypt 1932

I am a murderer.

I watch the Tall Man – the one Jessie calls Monty – bury the dead body under the sand. Big hands on a big shovel. It is dead meat, nothing more. It isn't the Fat Man now. His *Ba* – his soul – has flown to the underworld of Osiris and when I look at the flesh left behind, I feel nothing for it. But I hurt inside. I think his *Ba* has torn mine from my chest. Is that what happens when you kill a person? You kill part of yourself as well and it can never come back to life. I walk around wrapped in my blanket to try to keep my *Ba* inside but I fear it is too late.

You hurry me. You move fast. You talk loud.

You speak with the Egyptians but I try not to listen because I do not want to know that you offer them double money or that one of Fareed's men has been seen. I don't know where and I don't care. But you do. You care so much that you forget who I am. You flap me away with the same impatient hand that you use to flap away a fly that torments you, and it is Jessie who tells me you are the boss now and have much to do.

I hear the truck driver say to the Tall Man, 'Fareed kill Mister Tim quick, if he catch him.'

Suddenly I am in a hurry too. I run around throwing anything I can pick up into the back of the truck until you tell me to stop. You throw my things back in the sand. It is Jessie who stays. She doesn't leave me or shout at me. She is still and quiet and picks up my blanket when it falls off.

'Don't blame Tim,' she says in the low voice that I remember from when we used to hide under the bed. 'He has a lot on his mind.'

He doesn't have me on his mind.

It is Jessie who makes a safe corner for me in the back of the truck when the crates are all roped in and it is Jessie who sits in it with me in the dark when the doors are shut. Just before the doors close completely, I see the desert reduced to a thin beige strip behind the truck and I breathe a sigh of relief. I prefer the desert that way, no wider than my hand, too small to hurt me any more.

'Georgie,' Jessie tells me, 'I didn't want you to leave when you were a child. I tried to find you.'

But I don't want to talk about it because the memory of that night turns my lungs inside out and I can't breathe. Instead I say, 'I liked Hatherley.'

She laughs and says, 'So did I.'

She remembers the fish in the pond. She does not talk much, which I like, and while we wait for the engine to start, my mind drifts in the darkness through a room with green curtains and a proper bookcase and a cricket bat against the wall. You and the Tall Man are going to ride in the front with the driver and the guard and I know you will have guns on your lap, which makes me nervous. Only then does it occur to me that Jessie may be silent in the truck because she thinks I am going to kill her because I am a murderer.

'Jessie,' I say. I don't know what to say next.

Quietly she says, 'Shall we name all the characters in *The Adventure of the Creeping Man*?'

I smile. That's easy.

417

53

Monty was angry. He kept one hand on the gun at his waist while his eyes scoured the rocky ridges ahead of where he stood, away from the truck. The heat and the dust shifted shapes, so that nothing was ever what you thought it was and that did strange things to the mind.

He was angry about Jessie. He didn't want her to ride in the back of the truck and it wasn't just her arm he was worried about. He wasn't happy that she was shut alone in there with that strange brother of hers, but she had insisted. Monty was impatient to be on the move, eager to whisk her out of this place just as fast as he could, but the driver was taking an age to top up the radiator water, and all the time the sun was growing hotter. At Monty's elbow stood Timothy Kenton, his blue eyes narrowed against the glare as he kept alert for signs of movement.

'Tim, is Georgie safe to be with?'

'What do you mean?'

'He is violent.'

Tim glanced at him quickly and considered what Monty was saying. 'Don't worry. He'd never hurt Jessie. He worships her.'

Monty was not sure he believed him but now was not the time to argue the point. The relationship between the three siblings was clearly unusual and complex in a way that he didn't totally understand, but his only aim now was to get Jessie to safety.

'You should never have brought them out here,' he said in a quiet undertone. 'It wasn't right.'

Tim jerked round, eyes wide. 'They're family,' he said fiercely. 'I couldn't abandon Georgie. Of course it wasn't right to bring him here. Don't you think I am well aware of that? It's been hard for both of us but . . .' He stopped and stared down at the desert sand on his boots for a long moment. 'He's with me,' he continued softly, 'and he's alive. It's the best I could give him. I had no other option.'

'And Jessie? Why drag her out here? Why all the clues?'

Tim stepped away from him, stiff-legged, like a dog preparing to defend its territory. 'It was a risk, I know that. I love my sister and brother. To put them in danger is the last thing I would ever want to do, but I ran out of choices. I had to leave the Sherlock clues. I needed Jessie and I knew she wouldn't let me down. We're family – it's that simple.'

But he must have seen Monty's frown and sensed his anger because he continued rapidly, 'When Scott first asked me to take part in this scheme of his, I refused. But when I reported it to the museum's directors they called in the police. It was the police who asked me to go along with it. They wanted to discover the whole network that Scott was using in Egypt for transport and the illegal export of the ancient treasures, not just to arrest Scott himself.'

'So you said yes.'

He nodded. 'I couldn't bear what Scott was doing.'

'I sympathise with you there,' Monty replied grimly.

'So I went along with it, but Scott didn't trust my change of heart. He drugged my drink at a séance to make sure that I complied, and insisted on bundling me out of the country quickly with no contact with anyone at all.'

'Except Georgie.'

'Georgie was my one condition.'

'How did you manage to bring him here?'

'On that Friday night after the séance I was in no fit state to travel, so Scott kept me under close guard, but the next day he had his men drive me to snatch Georgie from the clinic. After that, we set off for Egypt. The journey was a nightmare for poor Georgie.' He shook his head at the memory of it and said again, 'I couldn't abandon him.'

Monty was touched by the intensity of his statement: *We're family – it's that simple.* Part of him began to understand and he recognised in this young man's passion for Egypt the same emotions he felt himself for Chamford.

'So why the clues?' he asked again, more warmly this time.

'I didn't trust Scott and I didn't know how much I could rely on the Egyptian police. So Jessie was my lifeline. There was no one else who would come to get Georgie and myself out of trouble if things turned nasty with Scott. I knew she would come looking.'

My lifeline.

Tim turned to look at Monty, his face tense. 'That's why I told Scott about McPherson, Hatherley, Hosmer and Phelps when I woke and found myself at his place on the Saturday morning. I pretended that I needed to inform them that I was leaving. Made a great fuss about it, so that he wouldn't forget their names in a hurry.'

'Scott told us that it was at the séance that you mentioned them.'

'Well, Scott was lying. He couldn't very well tell you the truth, could he? But I knew that when Jessie tracked him down, he would be eager to know who this foursome was and would ask her. Then she'd work it out.'

'All fictional.'

'Yes, but he didn't know that, and it gave Jessie the clue for the Nile.'

They were clever, this pair.

Monty heard the slam of the truck's bonnet behind them and he said quickly, 'The Egyptian policeman, Ahmed Rashid, contacted me, and asked if I had any idea where you were. He claimed he didn't know.'

Tim shrugged. 'It doesn't surprise me. I've got Scott's briefcase now with all his contacts. I just hope Captain Rashid has put his men in place when I take this lot downriver to—'

A bullet smacked into the windscreen of the truck.

The attack came out of nowhere. Bullets spat into the sand and ricocheted with a high-pitched whine off rocks, sending the workmen racing for cover, but there was none. They cowered behind the camels. Monty dragged Tim under the truck, his heart kicking damn great holes in his ribs, where they lay flat on their stomachs behind the shelter of the wheels. Gun in hand, he sought out the attackers.

A flash of black. He took precise aim. Pulled the trigger and heard a scream. Beside him Tim was firing off shots at random from Scott's gun. Wasting bullets. It occurred to Monty that Tim had never been shot at before. Moving swiftly on his elbows and stomach, Monty shifted towards the back, determined to put a bullet smack in the middle of anyone who attempted to open the rear doors.

'Save your bullets!' he yelled at Tim.

The wild firing ceased. The sudden silence was worse. It felt like the silence in the tombs, a silence that sapped your strength and seeped through your eyes and your ears, deadening your brain. He scanned the bleak horizon, as much of it as he could make out from under the truck, and waited.

A thin eerie sound rose into the silence. It stopped his breath and made his skin crawl. It was as if the desert itself had cracked open and was screaming. But Tim, who had been so panicked by the bullets, showed no surprise at this.

'Georgie!' he roared. 'Georgie, stop that noise!'

Georgie.

That noise was coming from Georgie? It didn't even sound human. Monty glanced at the truck above him and thought of Jessie in the darkness up there with that noise. He banged his fist on the underside of the truck to let her know he was here.

'Timothy Kenton!' The voice echoed bleakly across the sands.

Tim looked at Monty. 'Fareed.'

'Is that you, Fareed?' he shouted out.

'It is.'

Another bullet cracked through the air and Monty caught sight of one of the bearded guards. He was huddled behind a kneeling camel and his rifle was firing at a fall of rocks over to the right of the truck, but at the sound of the sudden shot, the unearthly wailing grew louder and more piercing.

'Timothy Kenton,' Fareed's voice had to fight against Georgie's, 'you and Scott and the treasures of Egypt are all I want. The rest can leave unharmed. I do not wish to harm my own people.'

Monty heard Tim draw in a sharp breath.

'No, Tim, wait!'

But Tim was starting to wriggle forward.

'Fareed,' Monty shouted, 'Scott is dead.'

'How?'

'Shot. By one of us.'

For a long moment there was nothing but the sound of Georgie's scream and of the wind flinging hot air and a layer of dust over them.

'Timothy Kenton, let me see you.'

'No, Tim.'

Before the words were out of his mouth, Tim was rolling out from under the truck. He stood in the blazing sun, his hair gleaming gold, and Monty took aim at the ragged rocks from which Fareed's voice seemed to come. He breathed out slowly and tightened his finger on the trigger. He waited.

'Tell your friend under the truck to throw out his gun, and the foolish man with the rifle.'

Tim turned, but he could not see Monty's face under the truck. 'Monty,' he said, 'you'll be safe. He only wants me. Please, throw out your gun. It's the only chance the others have got.'

'How good is his word?'

'Monty, we have no choice.'

Monty felt acid burning in his throat. Either way Jessie would lose, because either way Tim was doing to die. He dragged the dusty air into his lungs and with a curse, tossed out his gun. It hit the sand ten feet away with a soft thud and immediately the guard did the same with his rifle. Only then did Fareed stand up, followed by ten figures in black robes who all carried rifles.

Tim walked forward, his back straight and his head held ridiculously high, and only Monty could see the tremor in his hands at his sides. For a long moment Monty closed his eyes, the eerie cry still hammering in his ears, then he slid out from under the truck and went to stand in front of its rear doors. He folded his arms across his chest and watched Fareed in his black robe approach Tim. The Egyptian spat on the ground in front of Tim's feet.

'You pillage my country's treasures,' he said.

His black eyes burned with a passion that robbed Monty of any last hope that he could be reasoned with. Or bribed. Or bargained with. This was a man who knew what he wanted and only an act of God would deter him from getting it. And what he wanted was Tim's head on a platter.

'I am not stealing from your country, Fareed,' Tim said solemnly. 'I am working with your police to ensnare people like Scott and his organisation of accomplices, so that—'

Fareed barked an order in Arabic and repeated it in English. 'Kneel!'

Tim knelt on the stony sand.

'You lie,' Fareed said. 'Your mouth is full of lies that you expect me to believe because you think you are the educated Englishman and I am the ignorant Egyptian.'

'No, Fareed,' Monty said and moved closer, until Fareed raised his rifle.

'Near enough.'

'Mr Kenton is telling you the truth. He is working with the police. Don't jeopardise this. There are hundreds of tombs out in these hills, waiting to be found, and you need the co-operation of—'

Fareed fired a shot into the sand. 'I need no Englishman's co-operation.' His voice was bitter and angry.

The shot caused Georgie's cry to rise higher. Without a glance at Fareed, Monty walked over and opened the back of the truck. The noise and the heat billowed out of it with such force that for a moment he jerked back, but when he saw Jessie's expression and the way she was sitting rigid on the truck floor with Georgie's head wrapped in a blanket and howling on her lap, he reached in and lifted Georgie down. Then he wrapped his arms around her and brought her to his side. He could smell the sweat on her and feel the tension in her muscles.

'Stay calm,' he warned, as she blinked in the sudden dazzling sunlight.

Immediately she caught sight of Tim on his knees. She saw the rifle. But she didn't move. Just the faintest of moans passed her lips. Georgie had crouched in the dust, wailing more softly now and rocking back and forth. Gently Jessie adjusted the blanket to cover his head and face.

'What is that?' Fareed demanded.

'He is my brother,' Tim answered. Tears had started down his cheeks.

'It is a monster.'

Fareed lifted his rifle and at that exact moment a cheerful voice called out loudly behind him.

'Hello, gents! I hope you're not thinking of shooting that poor boy.'

Fareed swung around. Monty's jaw fell open and Georgie threw off his blanket.

It was Maisie. She was striding out of the hills with her umbrella aloft and Malak's small figure trailing uncertainly behind with a camel. She was wearing her sunhat with the bright red peony and looked for all the world as if she were taking a stroll along the Corniche-el-Nil. Except that her stride was long and her energy high, and she covered the distance between the scree slope and the black figures at a speed no one expected.

'Well, what the heck is going on here?' she asked with an unflustered smile, but the sight of the rifle so ready for use in Fareed's

424

hand made her lower her umbrella and glance from Tim on his knees to Monty ten paces away.

'Maisie,' Jessie called in a tight voice, 'stay out of this.'

Maisie nodded but remained exactly where she was. 'Do you intend to kill him?' she asked in a cold tone.

'Yes.'

54

Georgie

Egypt 1932

Do you intend to kill him? she asks.

Yes, he says.

You turn your head to look over your shoulder at me. At me. Your eyes are huge blue seas of emotion in which I am drowning because for once I know what your expression is. It is sorrow. You are sorry.

I am sorry.

'Tim!' I scream your name and hurtle towards you.

Snick. Snap. Smack.

Bullets whine past me and kick at the sand, shooting up tiny tornadoes at my feet, but I do not stop. My limbs jerk and jump, pulling me in frantic directions because I cannot control them, the way a fly buzzes on a windowpane, but I reach out for you.

Don't die. Don't die. Don't die.

I scream.

But the rifle sweeps up and its black fetid eye points at your head and I know I must die with you.

I scream your name.

The finger closes on the trigger. But the Man in Black gives a faint cough and from the middle of his chest protrudes the tip of a long thin blade and I scream again because how can a man grow metal out of his chest?

He coughs once more and there is blood in the air. He stumbles and falls to the ground, breath escaping from him in a soft hiss that I know now is the voice of death. Behind him stands the Tall Woman with the greyhound's face and in her hand she holds the handle of a long thin sword. It is sticking in the man's back. She steps away and vomits something brown and repulsive on to the sand. I grasp the sword-handle and pull at it but it clings to the body, unwilling to leave it, until I yank hard and it comes out in a rush with a wet slurping sound. I wipe it on the man's robe until it is clean and then I offer it to the woman. That's when I see that everyone is watching me. I start to shake.

'Thank you, young man,' the woman says and slides the blade back inside the cane of her umbrella.

I am impressed by the weapon.

Only then do I look at you.

They leave. They take their dead leader and leave, the fluttering men in the black robes go, and the desert feels empty when they have gone, though it is still full of sand. I don't understand why they go. They do not touch us and they do not touch the treasure in the truck.

I ask you.

You say they didn't want to touch us because they think this place is cursed. That the treasure is cursed and that we are cursed.

Why?

You smile at me and say it is because of me. They think I am the curse.

Why me?

427

You touch my shoulder and say it is because I am different, because I am special. You thank me. There are things I want to say to you, about the pain in my heart when I saw you on your knees in the sand, about how you looked like the great god Ra in the sunlight, about the fact that if you were going to die I wanted to die with you. But there are no words on my tongue, just an ugly moan like oxen in the fields make because they are too stupid to know better.

'I know, Georgie,' you say. 'I know.'

You kiss my cheek. And then you go over and kiss Jessie's. Proper brothers and sister.

I have a family.

55

'Wait, you can't just rush off.'

'Yes, I can, Tim.'

'Maisie, I owe you my life.'

'You said thank you. That's enough.'

Maisie straightened her hat, unfurled her black umbrella and with a little hitch of her shoulders set off back towards Malak who was still patiently holding the camel. Jessie could not let her leave. She fell into step beside her and slid an arm around the woman's bony waist. 'It's not fair on him, Maisie.'

'Who said life was ever fair?'

'You owe him that much anyway.'

Maisie halted abruptly and looked sharply from under her umbrella at Jessie. 'What do you mean?'

'Maisie,' Jessie said gently, 'I'm not stupid.'

Maisie uttered a harsh little sob and shook her head. She glanced back at the truck and at the small group gathered in the shade, and halfway between her and the truck the figure of Tim was standing immobile and hatless in the burning sun, watching her.

'Look at him,' Maisie murmured, 'look at what he has achieved. He doesn't need me poking my big nose in.'

'Too late for that.'

Jessie guided her back down the slope, aware of her friend's footsteps slowing as they crossed the sand. 'Tell them, Maisie. Tell them the truth,' Jessie urged.

They stood in the shade, leaning against the side of the truck and sipping water that was warm. Only Georgie had seated himself on the ground.

Maisie lit herself one of her foul-smelling cigars and looked awkwardly at Tim. 'Your sister's a sharp one. She's guessed my secret and won't let me keep it.'

Tim smiled, but was obviously bemused and waiting for more.

'So here it is, smack in your face. I'm your mother, Tim. Your natural mother, that is.' Her cheeks turned crimson. 'Well, that's it, I've said my piece and I'll be off now to . . .'

'My mother?'

'That's right, Tim.'

'My *mother*?'

Jessie saw her brother struggle with the startling news and so she said softly, 'That's why she's here.'

Tim stared at the tall rangy woman who stood in front of him with no obvious similarities to himself except perhaps her height, and he suddenly stepped forward and wrapped his arms around her.

'Timothy,' Maisie murmured and let her hand stroke his curls.

'I didn't chase your tails all over Egypt just for the good of my health, you know. I had Tim when I was sixteen. An ignorant little tea-leaf I was, a thief. Living on me wits in the East End of London, the youngest of ten kids.'

She looked at Tim with what was meant to be casual interest but failed to come close.

'I expect you want to know who your pa was. Well, he was a no-good travelling salesman with enough charm to sink a battleship and the eyes of an angel.' She chuckled at the memory. 'Anyways, it was the old story. Up the duff before I knew it and forced to give the kid away to an orphanage when it came. But I named you.' She tapped her son's strong chest. 'Timothy, that's what I called you. I visited you regular as clockwork at the start but then they stopped me. It was bad for you, they said. Bleedin' fool I was, to believe them.'

She released a sigh and looked at each of the faces. 'Has no one got a drink around here?'

To everyone's surprise it was Georgie who mumbled without looking up from the ground, 'There's a bottle of scotch whisky in the back of the truck.'

They all had a shot. Maisie kept the bottle in her hand when she continued, 'Later I met my Alf and we got hitched. He was a brickie – a bricklayer – a good kind man, and he straightened me out. Made me go back to the orphanage for you but you'd gone to a family in Kent.' She shrugged forlornly. 'We went down to see you but the house was so bloody posh. They could give you everything we couldn't.'

Tim held her hand in his. 'You should have come in to see me.'

'Oh, don't be daft. Your new ma would have liked that, I'm sure! But except for Saturday afternoons when me and Alf went dancing down the Palais, I followed you everywhere – got the photographs on my old Brownie to prove it. Saw you grow from a scruffy little nipper into a right smart gentleman, I did. I'm real proud of you.'

Jessie could feel the tears but she shook her head and asked, 'How did you know he was in Egypt?'

Maisie brightened up, grateful to talk of something else. 'That was easy as pie. When he went missing I got all worked up, so I broke into your flat a number of times, love, and found the travel tickets to Egypt. Tim is an archaeologist. So I just put two and two together ...'

Jessie grinned. 'Clever.'

'I didn't have no smart house or anything but I always had it up here.' Maisie tapped the side of her head. 'After my Alf died, I took over the business and now I own the second biggest brickworks in England. Not bad for a little tea-leaf, eh?'

She took a swig from the neck of the whisky bottle. 'Now, how about me and my son riding up front together and we get this wagon on the road?'

Georgie stood up suddenly, stumbling over his feet, and looked Maisie straight in the eye.

'Does that make you my mother too?'

While the workmen were checked for injuries and Tim paid them off from Scott's briefcase at double-rate, Jessie took another swig of the whisky and handed it over to Monty. On the warm wind she caught the scent of his skin and it stirred something in her, so that she stepped forward and rested a hand on his chest.

'Tell me,' she said quietly.

'Tell you what?'

'Tell me what will happen now that Scott is dead.'

'To Tim?'

She nipped his chin between her thumb and forefinger. 'You know I mean to Chamford Estate.'

'Ah.'

'Exactly.'

She could feel the heavy beat of his heart and knew that her own had matched itself to his. Softly he kissed her hair.

'You taste of sand,' he murmured.

'Don't change the subject.'

'Which was?'

'Chamford Estate. What will happen?'

He sighed, his breath smelling of whisky. 'To be honest, I don't know. Scott's solicitors might call in the loan.'

'Which means?'

'I would lose Chamford. No, don't look like that, because they might extend the loan or I might find a new investor or ...'

'Or what?'

'I might after all sell off some of the estate and try to make it pay for its own upkeep more efficiently. Even if Grandpa Mountjoy Chamford does turn in his very expensive grave.'

Jessie tipped her head back to stare at him. 'Is this Sir Montague I'm talking to or an imposter?'

He laughed. 'You've got me thinking, that's all. Time to shuffle into the twentieth century, perhaps.'

'Well, it is 1932.'

'Mmm, we could come up with some ideas for it.'

'We?'

'Yes, you and me.'

'All right, we can give it a try.'

But Jessie knew they were not talking about Chamford Estate any more. She rested her cheek against his. 'One thing,' she said quietly.

She felt his hands clasp behind her back as if he thought she might run away.

'The séance,' he said.

She waited.

'I didn't realise what was going on,' he said in a low voice. 'I didn't know that Scott had drugged Tim's wine before Madame Anastasia arrived. Yes, I helped carry him to the car, but only because I thought he was ill and needed medical attention, and Scott told me that he had received treatment at a hospital and had recovered.'

'You believed him?'

There was a long pause before he spoke again, and she noticed the shadows of the rocks had started to lengthen.

'Not really.'

'So why did you lie to me?'

'Because I was unwise. Because I was greedy for Chamford Estate. Because Scott promised me that if I did, he'd give me three months extra to repay the latest instalment on my loan.' He pulled back his head to look at her. 'Because I was a fool, Jessie, I'm sorry.'

'I know,' she whispered and kissed the pulse that was fluttering in his throat.

56

Georgie

Egypt 1932

I hear things. People think that because I do not speak, I do not hear. But they are wrong.

I have learned in Egypt the value of money.

I hear Malak's happiness when he is paid by Monty and by the woman who is your mother. He squeals like a pig. I think he is in pain but you tell me it is happiness because now he can buy himself an education. You tell me this and I squeal like a pig to show you I am happy.

I am in the dark. In the truck. My sister sits near me but not touching. I hear her breathing.

I want to thank you.

I want to thank your mother.

There is a giant ball of warmth in my chest, like when I use my Indian clubs too much, but this time it does not go away. I wrap my arms around myself to hold it in. Is this happiness? Is this what Malak has in his chest too?

I am going to live with your mother.

Tears run down my cheeks when I say the words in my head. You will live there too and Jessie will visit often. I stuff my blanket in my mouth to stop my squeals.

I hear other things. I hear Jessie and the Tall Man talking about money. I don't want money, I want happiness. I slide my hand into my pocket under the blanket and my fingers touch the Ancient Egyptian general's gold pendant necklace and his ram's head gold ring. Even in the dark I can feel their beauty and that is why I stole them.

But I am not an imbecile. I know they have great value. I won't give them to Jessie now. Not yet. But when I do, maybe she will love me again.

Reading Group Questions for *Shadows on the Nile*

1. Who was your favourite character and why?

2. Who was your least favourite character and why?

3. Were you interested in Egyptology before you read this book, and/or has it piqued your interest in the subject?

4. Can you imagine yourself in Jessie's situation, having to adapt to a new brother? How would you react?

5. Do you think it was right of Tim to take Georgie to Egypt?

6. Does this book make you want to read the Sherlock Holmes stories or find out more about Conan Doyle, or were you a fan anyway?

7. Were you resistant to the romance unfolding between Jessie and Monty when he was still potentially untrustworthy?

8. Where do you stand on the issue of ancient artefacts being in a museum or left as they are?

9. What were you most relieved about when it was resolved?

10. Did all the plot twists take you by surprise, or did you see any of them coming?

KATE FURNIVALL on her RESEARCH PROCESS

Research. It is a word that gets my heart thumping with excitement. From the moment that I set off on the long and winding road that is signposted RESEARCH, anything and everything is possible. I have no idea who or what I will meet along the way or, more importantly, whether I will discover the kind of details that will make my story jump off the page.

For *Shadows On The Nile* I started with books, with photographs and film footage, to get the feel of the 1930s. Only when I had assembled a good body of material together did I pursue the further details on the internet. I watched on YouTube a political speech by Prime Minister Ramsay MacDonald and the horrific clashes in Trafalgar Square in 1932 between the police and the union marchers against the imposed Means Test. Such moments are invaluable to me to gain a feel for the mood of Britain at the time.

But primarily it was Egypt that I needed to explore, with all its historical glories. I knew exactly where I wanted to start – with Howard Carter and his discovery of King Tutankhamen's tomb in 1922. That was my way in. Wherever possible I like to use primary source material for research, and fortunately Howard Carter left an abundance of it, detailing his work in Egypt in the 1920s and 1930s around the time my story takes place. I am in awe of men like Mariette, Petrie, Pitt Rivers, Carter and now Hawass, who have done so much over the years to excavate and protect its heritage. Each has a fascinating story to tell.

Then came Egypt's history. I studied the long line of pharaohs and learned who were the peaceful ones and who the warriors. I read about the wars they waged against the Hyksos and the Hittites, vividly depicted in their temples and tombs, and about the schism between Upper Egypt and Lower Egypt. Particularly fascinating was the breathtakingly bold decision of King Akhenaten in the 14th century BC to uproot his court and worship only the god Aten, forcing monotheism onto a society that had previously worshipped many gods.

Years ago I was entranced by Norman Mailer's gigantic opus on Egypt, *Ancient Evenings*, so it was with immense pleasure that I delved once more into the mass of stories and myths that surround their ancient gods. I learned again of Kheper, the dung beetle pushing the sun across the sky, of Osiris and Isis, of birth and rebirth, and of the long and tortuous journey to the afterlife. They are magical tales, and it was hard to limit myself to no more than snatches of them here and there in my book.

In order to discover what life was like in early 20th century Egypt, I sought out autobiographies and accounts written by people who lived there at that time. Often it is just a small detail that can trigger an idea that I can run with or even spark a whole scene in my mind. I have always loved history, so it was with great interest that I turned my attention to the political situation of the period, pursuing the tug-of-war that had existed for hundreds of years between varying foreign powers, as they jostled for ownership of Egypt.

It was an odd coincidence that when I undertook my own research trip to Egypt in November 2011, the country chose that moment to erupt in Tahrir Square in Cairo, where I was staying. So I saw at firsthand their anger. I spoke to people there and was impressed by their courage and determination to have free elections, especially after all I'd discovered about their recent history during my research.

There is nothing like seeing a place with your own eyes, registering its sights and smells with your own senses. Books and films cannot compare. So I followed the same trail my characters would take – the long bumpy train journey from Cairo to Luxor, riding on a camel and sailing a felucca down the Nile. Breathing in the same crisp dry air and feeling the constant presence of the desert just a heartbeat away. Nothing had prepared me – however many pictures I had seen – for the impact of the interior of the royal tombs in the Valley of the Kings. I hope I have conveyed a sense of this in *Shadows On The Nile*.

And Georgie?

What research did I do for my dear Georgie? I talked to people who deal with these problems on a daily basis, and I read in depth about autism. I used the internet to open up this world to me. I admit that I did take some liberties when portraying Georgie, and I never use the word autism – it wasn't around in those days. There are different levels of severity, but in the 1930s there seemed to be no option but to hide those affected away in institutions. Let's be grateful that society is better informed and more broad-minded in that respect now and let us remain vigilant that it expands ever further towards acceptance.

What I love about research is that time and again it takes me places that I didn't know I wanted to go. Always there are surprises for me. And for you too, I hope.

WHY SHERLOCK HOLMES?

The decision to include references to Sherlock Holmes in *Shadows On The Nile* was an easy one. Once I had constructed my plot, I knew I needed one character to lay a trail of clues for his sister to follow. So I had to find a subject for these clues that would resonate with the reader.

Instantly the inimitable Sherlock Holmes leapt to mind. He is the supreme master of spotting clues and interpreting each stain on a sleeve or scuff on a shoe. Who else could conjure up such realities out of flimsy hints and fragile threads? I decided that the sleuth of 221B Baker Street was the perfect subject on which to base my own clues.

I have always loved his adventures, so the chance to make use of Sir Arthur Conan Doyle's stories in my own book was irresistible. I first fell in love with Sherlock (I feel I know him well enough to presume to use his first name) when I was about nine years old. I was at school and my teacher was off sick that day, so a spare student-teacher was dragged in to keep us quiet, and she did so by perching on the front of the table that acted as the teacher's desk, crossing her knees nervously and reading to the class the story of *The Adventure of the Speckled Band*. I was spellbound. Never had I encountered such rational thinking or such intensity of purpose in a character. Exactly the qualities I now want in my heroine, Jessie Kenton.

Over the years I devoured the rest of the exploits of Sherlock Holmes and his faithful companion, Dr Watson, which during

Conan Doyle's lifetime were published in *The Strand Magazine* – illustrated by the beautiful line drawings of Sidney Paget.

It comes as no surprise that films, television and radio all jumped onto the lucrative bandwagon to immortalise his name for each new generation. I have loved so many of them, but my two favourite portrayals came from the great Basil Rathbone – he shared with Sherlock a perfect profile and a penchant for disguise which served him well when he worked as an intelligence officer in World War I – and from Benedict Cumberbatch, with his quick intelligence and high cheekbones. For the purists among you out there, you might like to know that seventy-four different actors have so far played the part of Sherlock Holmes on film and stage.

My decision to use pointers from some of the stories meant that I had the perfect excuse to dust off my set of Sherlock Holmes books (four novels and fifty-six short stories) on the shelf and once again relish crossing swords with the indomitable Irene Adler et al. Once I got started, it was tempting to scatter clues like confetti – it became a game that gave me pleasure – but I restrained myself and most of them ended up on my study floor. But I do believe that it is important for an author to entertain herself/himself while writing, as much as to entertain the reader. That way, we both enjoy the book!

Conan Doyle's stories were so popular at the beginning of the 20th century that it is perfectly feasible that Jessie and her two brothers would be very familiar with them. There is no doubt in my mind that the logical reasoning of Sherlock Holmes would particularly appeal to Georgie's orderly mind. It all slotted into place in a way that I feel Sherlock would have been satisfied with, and I hope you will enjoy this added layer of intrigue as much as I did.

Elementary!